THE STILL POINT

ACKNOWLEDGEMENTS

I would like to thank David Roberts, who trusted me.
Allegra Huston, who guided me.
My parents, who encouraged me.
Anthony and Patricia Doyle, who calmed me.
Pat Gavin, who understood me.
And Roisin, who was with me all the time.

The
Still Point

SUBNIV BABUTA

WEIDENFELD AND NICOLSON
LONDON

Copyright © Subniv Babuta 1991
First published in Great Britain in 1991 by
George Weidenfeld and Nicolson
91 Clapham High Street
London SW4 7TA

Epigraph from *Burnt Norton* is quoted
from T.S. Eliot, *Four Quartets*,
reproduced by kind permission of
Faber and Faber Ltd

Proust 'quotations' in Part 2 are
adapted from *Remembrance of Things
Past* by Marcel Proust in an English
translation by Terence Kilmartin,
by kind permission of Chatto &
Windus Ltd

British Cataloguing in Publication Data
applied for

ISBN 0 297 84046 0

Typeset by Deltatype Ltd, Ellesmere Port
Printed by Butler & Tanner Ltd
Frome and London

For Roisin, my companion

At the still point of the turning world. Neither flesh nor fleshless;
Neither from nor towards; at the still point, there the dance is,
But neither arrest nor movement. And do not call it fixity,
Where past and future are gathered. Neither movement from nor towards,
Neither ascent nor decline. Except for the point, the still point,
There would be no dance, and there is only the dance.

T. S. Eliot, *Burnt Norton*

Arrival

A giant's heartbeat resounded through every part of the circular cathedral. It filled every nook with its vibrant pounding, the only sound in this golden monument. Elsewhere, silently, polished slaves with oily skin travelled the same circular routes they had trodden for generations. Back and forth they ran, tireless in their perfect rhythms. As one set strode forward, another stepped back, a dance in perpetual harmony, harnessing the energies of each member for one ultimate goal.

High above their heads, a huge wheel stood motionless, its jagged edge glistening with the oil dripping from the slaves. As thousands of tiny bodies moved in unison, their energies came to a climax. The wheel turned. A dull, golden pulse resounded through the edifice. In this way, the intricate universe had functioned for years, its myriad servants ignorant of its purpose, yet mindful of the need to complete their allotted tasks. But now, deep in a shadowy chasm, one tiny slave, overcome by exhaustion, lay down to rest. In time, his neighbour also gave up his efforts, and in turn, his neighbour too. Gradually, the apathy spread, as more and more labourers came to a halt. Like plague rushing through a city, the tiredness affected everyone, from the highest to the lowest. Finally, sapped of its vital accumulation of energy, the giant wheel stopped. And the cathedral was filled for the first time with a ghostly silence.

A quarter past one. Max was surprised that his watch had stopped. It had been given to him by his grandmother, who in turn had been given it by her father as a wedding gift. Its tick had kept time to the pulse of three generations. Now, in the slippery heat of the Indian desert, it had finally come to a standstill. A quarter past one. The strange thing was that Max was sure he had actually seen the very moment it stopped. He had glanced at his wrist, but felt an overpowering compulsion to hold his eyes there longer than normal. As the hand counted off the final seconds, he could feel the spinning of the cogs, the turning of the wheels. Then, all of a sudden, it stopped. Max shook his wrist, tapping the watch in irritation. He had already come to depend on the reliability of his Western props in this country where nothing really worked properly. Perhaps it was the heat, or the dusty sand, or the ash that covered everything in mournful grey. Max would have it seen to when he got back to England.

'This way, mister, this way to the city,' said the little Indian boy who had, of his own accord, become Max's guide. 'Ancient city of Fatehpur Sikri, very famous for emperor Akbar . . .'

The guide's unbroken voice trailed away into the distance. Imogen had already told Max all about the deserted capital of Fatehpur Sikri, and it was her voice that he now heard. It had been built in the sixteenth century by the emperor Akbar, whose wise men, after studying the stars, had told him that it must be done as a gift for the birth of a son. For years, thousands of workmen chiselled its towers, and moulded its pillars, deep in the plains of Uttar Pradesh, on the edge of the Rajasthani wilderness. As the vultures circled silently above their heads, the workers toiled, obedient to each decree of their architects and their emperor. Soon after their work was completed, Akbar felt he had kept his pledge. The court architect was particularly pleased: for sixteen years he had been grappling with the problem of supplying the royal city with fresh water, a problem he feared would be insurmountable. The emperor's decision resolved his dilemma. The workers were paid off and returned to their villages in the Punjab and in Rajasthan. Akbar moved to Lahore, and the new city was left unused, and perfect, for the vultures.

Years later, the city, long deserted, long forgotten, came back to life. Gradually, the workmen who had fashioned its towers and turrets drifted back to the red stone walls. It drew them back like a possessive, discarded mistress, first one, then another, until a whole new village grew up outside the walls of the city. The workers built themselves small houses from the stones left over from the construction, and at night their fires brought the dark, forbidding desert to life. A few deep wells, their treasure reluctantly given, sufficed for the needs of the remote community. Some of the younger men wondered why they could not live inside the splendid city, since it was there for the taking. But the older workers, the craftsmen of Fatehpur Sikri, knew they had built the city for their emperor.

Max wondered if the people he saw around him were the descendants of those early workmen. The village still looked ancient, and its inhabitants continued to treat the city like a venerated relic. The street leading up to the massive doorway into the city was lined with beggars, the most outlandish array of human deformity and mutation that Max had ever seen. 'Of this too I am capable,' whispered Nature in his ear. One old man had claws instead of fingernails, another shifted his torso heavily on a board with wheels. A lame woman picked desperately at a pomegranate that had, long ago, given up its fruits. A blind boy held a bear on a string. The young Indian guide picked his way nonchalantly through the inferno, clearing the way for his client.

'Come this way, please, mister. Give no money to beggars. Government say begging is bad, so give no money please.'

Max tried to ignore the clutching hands, the moans and the pleas. One young girl caught his eye, sitting quietly under the shadow of a pillar: she was remarkably attractive, despite her poverty. Her eyes moved with the penetrating intelligence and alertness of any teenage beauty, for she knew her true wealth. Max held her gaze, then fumbled in his pockets for a few coins, but as he searched, the girl left the pillar and disappeared into the crowd. He scanned the mass of bodies for her. It was then that Max first noticed the Englishman.

There was no doubt in Max's mind that the stranger was English. He knew it instinctively. Everything about him, his clothes, his demeanour, his facility with the Indian crowds thronging around him, announced the traveller's nationality.

At the bottom of the hill, some two hundred yards away, Max saw the elegant form, quivering in the heat, glimpsed in fragments as if through a thin veil of falling water. Even at this distance, he could make out the Englishman's pale complexion, untouched as yet by the Indian sun. Straining his eyes, Max took in the well-tailored cotton suit, the stylish panama hat, the shining black brogues. Amid the mass of pilgrims, the Englishman stood motionless, staring directly back at Max.

'Who's that man?' Max asked his Indian guide.

'Which man, sir?'

'Over there – the Englishman in the light suit.'

'Oh, yes, mister. He a tourist, like you. But he not so lucky. He not have Raju as guide.'

Max looked down at the boy, who was smiling through rotting teeth.

'Of course, Raju. But have you seen him here before?'

'No mister.'

Max lifted his eyes to find the stranger again. But he was gone. And the place he had occupied, like an island, was now submerged by frail, brown bodies.

Raju had been a guide at Fatehpur Sikri for some seven years. His mother was most proud of Raju, for he was her only son. Three times she had borne girls. Three times, as was the custom amongst Rajasthani women, she had retreated behind the veils of her parents' home to wail and bemoan her destiny. She had a loving husband, but she knew she had failed him. So, she had made a special pilgrimage to the temple of Vaishno Devi in Kulu, a ten-day journey, on foot. A year later, Raju had arrived, a gift from heaven. He was eleven now, and at first had accompanied his father, who too was a guide at the ancient city. His sisters were also guides, but girls always earned less, and anyway, they would soon be married off. They would then look to their new families, leaving Raju to carry on the tradition. Raju hoped they would not get married too soon. He loved his sisters, and between them they had built up a deep and accurate understanding of all the different nationalities that passed through the ghost city. Many years ago, Raju's father had given them all a valuable piece of advice about Englishmen. 'Remember,' his father had said, 'remember that they were our masters. Never argue with an Englishman. He does not like argument. Please him, and he will please you.' In all his years, Raju had never argued with an Englishman. And the money he had made for his family was testimony to his father's good advice. Perhaps it was for this reason, or perhaps because Raju himself had learnt that foreigners were on the whole quite peculiar, that he chose not to contradict Max. The young Indian had seen no Englishman at the bottom of the hill.

The sight of the Englishman haunted Max for days. Who was he? What was he doing here? Max refused to believe he had been just another tourist – somehow, he did not have that idle look about him. Why was he wandering about on his own? He had no camera. No little children were buzzing around him, offering to be his guide. No beggars pestered him. They would never let a tourist like him pass by unapproached. No, the Englishman seemed resolute, as if he were searching for something. His gaze had been purposeful. Why was he staring so fixedly, only then to disappear? Did he know Max?

'So, what are you going to have?'

'Sorry?'

'Do wake up, Max. What are you going to eat?'

'Oh, you order, darling. You're much better at this than I am. Nothing too strong though – I'm still not over the food on the flight.'

Imogen was disappointed that Max had fallen at the first hurdle, but she hoped that the novelty of eating in this small dhabba on the outskirts of Agra would rekindle his appetite. She had an iron stomach, unlike her husband of six days. She had eaten everything on the flight out; he had simply dabbled. Even so, he was suffering, whilst she was well into the most fiery of local concoctions. She had mastered enough of the local language during previous visits to order with confidence. Max had no idea what she was asking for.

'Mutter paneer, and make sure the paneer is not too hard.'

The owner of the dhabba knew at once: these were no simple tourists to be fobbed off with yesterday's food.

'Kabli channa – and puri, but not too greasy.'

He was obviously well off, the Englishman. His clothes looked as if they had come from one of those expensive tailors at whose displays Max used to gaze as he wandered around Oxford.

'And onion raitha. Max, I'm sure you'll enjoy this. Just take a little bit of everything.'

Somewhere at the back of the dhabba, a television was trying to decide whether or not to accept the local signal. As the picture floated up and down the screen, the image occasionally came to rest for a few minutes, and the set threw out an indigestible mixture of static and electronic Hindi movie music. Max was tired. Everything around him was beginning to take on a threatening quality. And he was becoming obsessive about the man he had seen. He had learnt long ago to recognize he symptoms of exhaustion in himself: an inability to let trivial things pass was one of the first.

It had been a frantic few weeks. First the tension of waiting for their finals results. Max need not have fretted. Both Imogen and he got the firsts they deserved. After that, the wedding in the chapel at Merton, with all their university friends there to celebrate the maturing of the undergraduate romance. Finally, the flight to India. It was the first time Max had been to the subcontinent.

'The paneer's good, and the channas. Oh, Max, do try . . .'

Imogen's voice brought him back from his reverie. He took a few spoonfuls of the cheese curry, and some nan, to please her. It was good, very different from the tastes he had become accustomed to in the Indian restaurants around Oxford. He looked at Imogen as she tucked into her food. She seemed so young, so vulnerable, so much in need of protection. He knew it was all in his mind: she had travelled far more extensively and in more rigorous conditions than he had ever done, and she was very much in charge of this trip. But Max relished his fond imaginings. Amid the urgent clattering of steel pans and thalis, the earnest appeals of the cook and the insistent screaming efforts of some Hindi movie singer on the television, he could hear Imogen's voice chattering on.

'The marvellous thing about this place, as you'll see tomorrow on the bus, is that anything goes. There's no point in being British about things that way, you'll get nowhere. You've got to muck in, be like the locals . . .'

'Oh Imogen, just eat your food and give your poor voice a rest.'

Imogen opened her mouth to speak, but changed her mind, and took a spoonful of raitha instead.

Max immediately felt guilty. Imogen was so compliant. He could hardly believe she was his wife now – wife, even the word sounded grown-up and awkward. No, she would never be his wife. She would always be his lover, his friend, his confidante, his little companion. That was odd. Everyone called Imogen little, yet she was almost as tall as Max. She was slim – even thin – but not little. He had a theory why everyone called her little. It was her soul that was young, just starting out on its long and laborious journey through time. And Max had been told by more than one person that he had an old soul.

As Imogen's voice trailed away, Max began to make sense of the static crackle that had now replaced the screeching on the television. The set had revived, following a few good thumps by the proprietor, but now the news report was submerged by a more immediate fracas. The café cook had decided the time had come to discipline his assistant. Unconcerned by the violence in his kitchen, the dhabba owner relaxed into his front-of-house seat, ready to watch the evening bulletin. Max also tried to ignore the shouts in Hindi, and concentrated instead on the newscaster's precise English.

7

'In a carefully worded statement to the Lok Sabha, the Prime Minister, Mr V. P. Singh, announced the main proposal of his reform package. He was determined, he said, to keep his election pledges. After close consultation with his cabinet, Mr Singh has decided to accept the recommendations of the Mandal Commission report shelved by his predecessor, the Congress (I) leader, Rajiv Gandhi. From next year, a quota of twenty-seven per cent of all government positions and all civil-service positions will be specially set aside for those "of backward caste". This will include university jobs, jobs in the police force and the army, and also places on training schemes or in educational establishments. The Prime Minister was clear about his intentions: "My aim is to destroy once and for all this iniquity and inequality that is ingrained in our social system. We can no longer tolerate such discrimination as part of our institutions or our society. This is only the first step." Mr Singh's statement received a mixed response. Some members of the Lok Sabha warned that the Prime Minister's reforms could lead to unrest and unhappiness amongst those of high caste, but . . .'

Suddenly, the picture lost its bearing again. The dhabba owner eased himself reluctantly out of his chair, banged the set a few times, and brought it back to life.

' . . . the police and the army are in a state of readiness, and are confident that they can meet any threat to law and order . . .'

This time, the television gave up the ghost once and for all. The proprietor groaned, and turned off the set. He turned to his English clients and smiled apologetically. 'Much trouble,' he mumbled, under his breath, 'much much trouble.'

Shaking his head in exasperation, the dhabba owner disappeared into his kitchen to sort out the iniquity in his own little kingdom.

Raindrops splattered across the windscreen like the droppings of some huge, predatory bird. The car's wipers were struggling to clear the view. Max looked across to Imogen, seated next to him. She looked angry, seemed almost not to recognize him. He looked back to the road, straining to see the way through the deluge. It was cold outside, but Max was almost naked. Why was he not ashamed? He looked at the passengers in the back of the car. There, his mother and father wore the same angered look as Imogen. But this was a happy day. He wiped some condensation from the inside of the side window, making his hand wet. Forgetting the road, Max licked the fluid off his hand greedily. The viscous juice filled his head with its pungent aroma. As the vapour spread within his head, he relaxed and allowed his eyes to defocus. The waterdrops on the windscreen merged into one grey mass. For a moment, Max drifted into a half-sleep, then returned step by step to consciousness as the vapours cleared from his brain. He was no longer in the car. Instead, he found himself staring straight down at Imogen's face as she lay beneath him. His fingers were still at his mouth, but the nectar was finished. His lips still glistening, Max thrust his hand down and Imogen groaned. He looked at her face, warm and damp in his bed, her red hair scattered across the crisp white cotton of the pillowcase. Her eyes waited expectantly, her lips slightly parted, gasping for breath. Max pressed his mouth onto hers, and sucked her breath deeply. Each part of him filled each part of her, but not deep enough. As he began to thrust, Max became aware that he was being watched. He stopped, and turned slowly. His college room was inexplicably empty, unfurnished except for the bed he occupied with his lover, the walls stripped of their paintings and posters. The floor was uncovered, the bare boards deprived of their carpeting. Max shivered, and saw his breath form into a thick steam as it left his mouth. As he turned, he saw his father standing silently in the corner, observing him with tragic eyes. Max felt the passion flow out of him. He was overcome with guilt. He turned back to look to Imogen for comfort, but the bed was empty. There, where her head had been, on the pillow, Max saw the charred remains of the white cotton, light flakes of black ash now drifting off, lifted by a gentle breeze. Max felt a sudden, frantic desire to scoop the ashes up in his hands, to save them from blowing away. But it was too late. Once more, he closed his eyes, wishing away the horrid image. It was gone instantly. Opening his eyes, Max found himself in the Examination Schools, seated at a small trestle table, scattered with the bewildering print of exam papers and blank sheets. To his right, rows and rows of similar tables, in parallel formation, stretching out as far as he could see, all piled high with completed scripts, their chairs long since abandoned by the candidates. A light breeze blew some papers onto the floor. To his left, more tables, and to his front and behind him. A strong smell of woodsmoke filled the marble hall, but not a soul in sight. Max looked at the papers on his table. The letters on the page formed no recognizable language. As he scanned the sheets, searching for a question he could understand, he heard a single pair of footsteps climbing the stone stairwell leading to the great hall. Max looked up from the sea of incomprehensible ciphers.

'Can you help me to understand this?' he asked desperately.

'Of course I can, Max. Look at the questions carefully. They all make sense.' He saw the look of affection in his mother's eyes, and his panic abated. He looked back at the exam papers before him. The black scrawl had formed itself into English.

> How can you see and not recognize?
> Did you think this happiness would be endless?
> Why did you only listen to the language of the living?

Max looked back to his mother, but she was gone. Gradually, a distant sound of revelry began to grow louder, until it filled the whole building. As he gazed across the expanse of the hall, Max was pleased to see his closest friends enjoying a wedding feast in the college banqueting room. Vast joints of meat, some of them almost raw, adorned the oak tables, decorated with silver jugs of wine. The revellers seemed already bloated with their excesses. But one part of the hall had an impenetrable darkness about it. Try as he might, Max could not make out the figure sitting all alone at the far end of the hall. He tried to ignore him, turning his attention back to the family table. For a few moments, Max lost himself in the celebrations. Then his mother spoke:

'Max,' she said, gently, 'Max.'

Chastened, he excused himself from the table, and walked over to the stranger in the shadow. As he got closer, the sounds of the revelry receded with an echo into the timber frames of the hall. The air became still with the silence. A few seconds later, Max heard his own voice break the stillness.

'Please, my friend. Please be happy with us.'

The stranger turned towards him. As his face emerged from the darkness, Max recognized him at once and smiled, reassured. But, almost immediately, Max was overcome by a deep concern. The guest's face seemed disfigured. Where had that scar come from? What had caused the wound, freshly cut into his cheek? Max put out his hand to touch the injury. Slowly, his index finger reached for the man's face, taking an eternity to attain its destination. As Max saw his fingertip make contact with the scar, the wound disappeared, and he found himself brushing Imogen's face. She smiled, taking his fingers with hers and pressing them softly to her lips. The feel of her warm tongue on his hand transported Max, and he forgot all about the unhappy guest. He shut his eyes, soothed by his lover.

The Deluxe bus standing at the bus station was obviously the figment of some very optimistic imagination. Max could not believe his eyes, or his ears: the scene looked as if a film director had gathered together a crowd of brown actors, hired a dozen buses from the local breaker's yard, dumped the whole lot into a dusty clearing, and cried 'Action'. Young boys clambered like monkeys over the roofs of the buses, twisting and turning the luggage until it all fitted into the racks. The owners of the bags screamed orders from the ground:

'No no, not there bahai. I won't be able to see it there.'

'Be careful, you idiot. I paid good money for that bag.'

'Hey, you, who do you think that bag belongs to, your father?'

Mingled with these instructions were the sing-song chants of the bus conductors, announcing the time and destination of their buses:

'Chandigarh, Chandigarh, Chandigarh, eight, eight, eight.'

'Simla, Simla, Simla, eight five, eight five, eight five.'

'Jaipur, Jaipur, Jaipur, eight twenty, eight twenty, eight twenty.'

'Delhi, Delhi, Delhi, eight, eight, eight.'

'Come on, Max, that's us. Quick now, you give the boy the bags, I'll keep this small one, and I'll get our seats. Mind he puts them in the middle, not on the edges. We don't want our clothes scattered all over the road.'

Max nudged his way to the front of the crowd that had already begun to teem around the Delhi bus, a half hour before its departure. He caught the eye of one of the agile monkeys on the roof of the bus, and passed him his bags.

'Not at side – you put the bags in the middle!' shouted Max.

'Sure, sir, I put the bags safe. Very safe up here. Look, you can come up here to look.'

Max jumped onto the metal ladder along the side of the bus, and clambered up. True to his word, the boy had wedged their bags safely between other, cheaper-looking, native bags.

'Good, that's good.' Max took a five-rupee note from his pocket, and thrust it into the boy's hand. 'Now, you keep an eye on those bags for us, and there'll be another five rupees when we get to Delhi.'

'Oh, sure, mister English. I keep special eye on these bags. You not worry.'

'Delhi, Delhi, Delhi, eight, eight, eight!'

'Are they okay?' asked Imogen, as Max fell back into his seat.

'Yes, the boy says he'll keep an eye on them.'

He opened the English-language paper he had picked up at the hotel as they checked out that morning. The front page was full of reports summarizing the Prime Minister's aims to turn the nation into a casteless society by the year 2000. Other earnest statesmen warned that 'it is too much, too soon.' Caste, they claimed, gave Indian people their sense of purpose, their role; take it away and you remove people's very identities.

'Eight, eight, eight. You bloody fool, give me that bag at once. No, this is not the bus to Hardwar. There is no bus to Hardwar from here. Ask him when I will get the money back. Chandigarh, Chandigarh, Chandigarh.' Suddenly, a thin man rushed into the bus, jumped into the driver's seat, and started up the machine. The bus shook itself awake, excreted some black soot from its exhaust, and started off.

'Wait, wait, my son's still getting his tea. Hurry up, boy, get on, we're leaving.'

'Jump onto the bus, husband, we're off.'

A stream of young men hurtled onto the bus as it moved off, the driver not slowing down at all. But they were obviously expert in the Indian art of mounting buses and trains at the last minute.

The rickety old bus wound its way through narrow streets barely wide enough to accommodate it. The brake and accelerator seemed directly connected to the horn, which, even by Indian standards, was loud. As Max would learn to his cost when he later tried to sleep, the driver was proud of his 'siren' and used every opportunity to show it off to the people he passed. Like a large corpuscle, the bus eased its way through the arteries and veins of Agra. Rickshaw-wallahs trembled at its approach;

taxi drivers moved judiciously into side streets; tonga drivers pulled up their horses, keeping a tight hold on the reins. Slowly, the city began to peter out. As the driver found the open road, he moved up to fourth gear, put his foot down, and the bus, with its fifty passengers, hurtled towards Delhi.

Villages rushed by. Cyclists idled backwards with great ease. Horses cantered comfortably, pulled backwards by their makeshift carriages. A deserted mosque flashed past, its discoloured and dilapidated minarets testimony to centuries of exposure to the Indian climate and to innumerable local wars and conflicts. Even the landscape looked hungry in this insatiable country. Trees yearned skywards, frail and mal-nourished. In the fields, families idled away yet another day, uncon-cerned at the passing of time.

Imogen had fallen asleep. Max looked at her damp, shiny forehead. The combination of the speed of the bus and the heat, and the proximity of so many bodies, made him feel strangely libidinous. Imogen was bathed in perspiration. Max's eyes followed a tiny drop as it slowly descended her face. It passed her perfectly arched eyebrows, down into the chasm of her left eye, traced her aquiline nose, and trickled past her pale, appetizing lips, to her neck. The bead finally disappeared into the depths of Imogen's crisp cotton blouse. The top three buttons were undone, and Max could see the sensuous rhythm of her breasts as they rose and fell with her breathing. He felt guilty scrutinizing her in this way, but he could not take his eyes away. She shifted in her seat, as if conscious of being watched. Max hastily averted his gaze. But he was drawn back. Over a year of intimacy had not diminished their passion for each other, and Max wondered if it would ever really abate. People – older people – told him it would, but he could not believe it. The mixture of the salty smell, of Chanel perfume and the spearmint of the mouthwash Imogen always carried with her made Max stir. He took in a deep breath, closed his eyes, and let the aroma fill his head.

'That's quite a perfume you're wearing,' said Max to the striking girl who had sat down next to him. 'It's Chanel, isn't it?' He had been wondering how to open up the conversation with her as soon as he saw her approach the empty chair by his side. He knew he had made the wrong choice as she replied, turning to face him with the most magnetic smile.

'Thank you. A friend of mine gave it to me this evening, in congratulation actually. He insisted I wear it to the dinner.'

Max's heart sank. The adrenalin pumping around his body played havoc with his reason. He tried to keep his voice steady. 'Can I ask you what he was congratulating you on, your friend?' Max wondered whether he had succeeded in keeping his curiosity out of the final word. She looked at him in surprise, turning to embarrassment at the enquiry.

'Well,' she began, 'I got the Julius Peacock.'

So, this was the unknown competitor whose success Max had been envying for the past ten days. He had coveted the Julius Peacock Prize ever since his tutor first mentioned it to him. It was supposed to be a friendly competition, a diversion after Mods, but Max had taken it very seriously, coming up a fortnight early after the summer vac to revise for the exam. He had been convinced he would succeed and so much wanted the first edition of Keats's *Odes*, which was to be this year's trophy. When the results were pinned up in Schools, Max refused at first to believe the notice, then spent the rest of the morning at the Queen's Lane Coffee House with his friend Nigel, trawling through all the possible reasons for his failure. In the end, on the verge of caffeine poisoning, Nigel had made some excuse about a lecture and sloped off. A week later, Max was still going over the paper in his mind, searching for flaws. Where had he gone wrong? It had been a monumental effort for him to come to this celebration dinner.

'You must be Imogen Fielding, from Balliol?' Max had imagined someone small, dark and intense, someone who spent all her time working, someone who would wear no perfume. Imogen smiled again. 'I'm Max . . . Max Burton.'

Imogen was having trouble with her gown, Max noticed. It kept slipping down, the heavy fabric pulling on her pastel summer dress. Just as it threatened to expose her shoulder completely, Imogen would tug the black gown over her flawless white skin. She shook her hair, pushing it back with long, elegant fingers. In the glowing Oxford sunset, streaming in through the windows of Univ SCR, the golden red strands seemed to be aflame. Imogen fanned her face with the menu.

'I only just made it, you know,' she said, 'I cycled all the way from Charlbury Road.' Max assumed that must be where her 'friend' lived. He breathed in the wafts of warm perfumed air that floated towards him. As her gown slipped again, he noticed a thin streak of perspiration where the cleft of her breasts began. Clearing his throat, Max asked, 'What did you write on for the Julius Peacock?'

'Yeats. And you?'

'Chaucer. *Troilus and Criseyde.*'

Imogen leaned towards Max confidentially, as if she had known him for a long time. 'You see that chap in the glasses, near the decanter?' she whispered. 'He's been staring at my breasts ever since I sat down.' She looked at Max mischievously. He was glad she had won the Julius Peacock.

Max shifted in his seat on the bus, still staring compulsively at Imogen's sleeping face. He had, after all, got the edition of Keats he wanted. Imogen had given him her prize as a wedding gift. He was determined to love everything in India. This too was her gift to him.

'So, when did you first visit India?' asked Max as the waiter discreetly refilled Imogen's glass. It was a fortnight after the Julius Peacock dinner and Max had seen her twice, for tea at the Wykeham. But this was the first time Imogen had agreed to come out to dinner with him. She was methodical, Max had observed with pleasure, as he was, working most mornings in the Radcliffe Camera, scheduling her time carefully to take in the host of societies and friends she had to fit in each week. So it was with excitement and triumph that he now looked at her as they sat at a quiet table in Les Quat' Saisons. It was the first time Max had been there: his bank balance would not have survived regular visits, but Imogen was clearly well known by the staff. Christine, the petite French greeter, welcomed her by her first name, chatted like an old friend and, realizing now who Mr Burton's reservation was for, moved the couple from a mediocre placing to their best table. Christine seemed to like Max. That was a good sign.

'It was just after I left school,' replied Imogen. 'I went out on a special UN project which took a group of us all over India. They were helping remote villages to set up satellite dishes for receiving broadcasts. I saw India the way it really is, not just the tourist track.'

'It obviously made an impact.'

'Changed my life. If I ever get the chance, I'd love to live out there.'

Max's heart sank. How could he compete with the maharajah who would sweep Imogen off to the country she loved? Noticing his crestfallen expression, Imogen asked, 'Have you ever been?'

'No,' replied Max, apologetically, 'no, I haven't. What did you most love about it?'

'Its sense of time,' said Imogen instantly. 'It makes you reassess everything you always thought and believed. There's none of the frantic rush to achieve you get in the West. The days seem longer. Things don't change so rapidly. You can think properly, reflect without feeling guilty. It took me ages to relearn how to live back here in England.' She paused, picking at her food, and looking up at Max. 'Time does strange things in India.'

'What sort of things?' asked Max, inevitably. Imogen opened her mouth, then thought better of it, sighed, and the half-formed syllables turned into an impenetrable smile. She returned to her food, eating with a gusto that excited Max. Did she do everything with such enthusiasm and vigour? The thought made his throat contract and he found it impossible to swallow. He made an excuse about not being hungry, but was sure Imogen probably knew the real reason for his lack of appetite.

When Max said goodbye to Imogen at Balliol porter's lodge, he had already spent the past half-hour composing his next invitation to her. But as she pecked him on each cheek, chastely, Imogen said, 'My turn next.' He was delighted, wondering how long it would be before she could fit him in. 'How about tomorrow night, Max?'

Max looked out of the window of the bus, his attention drawn by the sound of an impatient car horn. A cool black Mercedes slid past, elegant in the filthy heat. The bus veered aside in deference. Max peered at the wealthy Indian family jammed awkwardly into the limousine. A young boy, his cheeks swollen with excess, stared contemptuously out of the back. Blaring its horn once more in a final assertion of superiority, the limousine sped away, shrouded by a cloud of dust.

The Merton scouts, exhausted by their efforts, took a well-deserved break. Max and his guests were now busy with the cake, their glasses fresh with champagne, ready for the toast his father was proposing. It was an appropriate end, thought Max, to Michaelmas term, which had begun with the loss of the Julius Peacock Prize but which had put another, far more desirable, prize within his grasp. He stood by his grandmother's wheelchair, holding her wrinkled hand firmly within his own. He knew this would be the last birthday party of his that she would attend. It was fitting. His twenty- first, the beginning of adulthood she said, though Max had never felt less like an adult. Suddenly Max realized that people were raising their glasses to him. He thanked them, being sure to search out Imogen with his gaze. His grandmother fidgeted, bringing out of her silk bag a slim leather case, carefully decorated with a festive ribbon. Max crouched down.

'This is for you, Max. I know you'll look after it.'

He slid the ribbon off, undid the tiny brass clasp on the side of the case and opened it carefully. 'Oh, Gran. But I can't . . . you mustn't . . .'

'I won't be needing it much longer. I'd like you to have it.' Max took the exquisite antique watch out of the protective folds of creamy satin inside the case. 'It's the original box, Max, and I thought my strap might also fit you. Try it on.'

Max placed the watch delicately on his wrist, pulled the leather strap round and buckled it up. He felt the firm ticking fall into harmony with his pulse at once. 'It's perfect,' he said, stretching across his grand-mother's knees to kiss her.

'It's rather unusual,' said the old woman, holding Max's wrist up to her face. 'You see those dials inside the main one? Well, the one on the left, that counts off the seconds. Next to it is the one that shows the days of the week. But this is my favourite, Max.' His grandmother twisted his wrist gently towards him. 'This little dial is a decade counter. See? It's marked one to ten. Each year, the pointer moves on one.'

Max looked closely at the miniature dial contained within the main face. The gold numerals and hands sparkled against the cream background.

'And there's something else very special about the watch,' continued Max's grandmother. She paused, searching her memory. Max could see the effort as if it had been a physical exertion. 'I know there's something else . . . very special.' Just then, the nurse in charge of the old woman came up, champagne glass in hand, to check all was well. 'I know there's something very special, Max, I know there is . . .'

'Don't worry, Gran. I'll find out. Thank you for a lovely gift. I'll think of you every time I look at it.' Max gazed at his grandmother's pale, dry lips. The skin was drawn so tightly across the bones of her face that he could see the blood coursing through her veins. He put his hand gently on her back and they both watched the crowd of guests, in silence. Every now and then, he felt his grandmother's hand twitch and tighten. Max saw her eyes, milky blue, still alert, follow with interest the slender figure of a young woman as she detached herself from her group and approached.

'Hello. I'm Imogen Fielding. I've been looking forward to meeting you, Mrs Burton. Max has told me so much about you.' Max jumped up and pulled across a chair for Imogen. As she settled down, she saw the grandmother looking closely at her. Then, silently, the old woman put up a hand and stroked Imogen's soft, glossy hair.

'Lovely,' she murmured. She touched Imogen's face thoughtfully. Imogen stayed very still, looking back at Max's grandmother as the skeletal hand slid along her cheek. For a moment, the brittle fingers came to rest on Imogen's lips, then the hand fell away.

Max's grandmother smiled, satisfied. 'Go off and dance, you two. Stop wasting your time with me.'

Lost in his recollections, Max imagined he could feel the ticking of the watch even now. He looked to his wrist. A quarter past one.

It was very late when Max finally saw off the last of his guests at Merton lodge. The birthday party had been a great success. Imogen was still with him. 'I'll just come back and get my things from your room,' she said.

'Yes, do.'

It was the first time that day they were alone, and they climbed the wooden stairs to Max's room in silence, each step echoing through the winding staircase. They would be going home that weekend and Max knew it would be weeks before he could see Imogen again, like this. He pushed open the door to his room.

'Go in.'

She walked over to the window, and gazed out across the Fellows' Garden with Christ Church meadow beyond. The moon was high in the night sky, and flooded the room with its pale blue light. Max saw the silhouette of Imogen's elegant figure, dark beneath the delicate silk of her long dress.

'Come here,' he heard her say softly. 'Look, you can see the astrolabe. The moon's just catching it.'

Max looked out across the lawn, his eyes adjusting to the half-light.

'It's wonderful, isn't it? You know, Chaucer wrote a marvellous treatise . . .' He trailed off, having caught Imogen staring at him, her eyes serious and intense. He could feel the Chanel and the spearmint of her mouthwash rising to his head.

'Hello Max,' she said.

Suddenly, the bus pulled off the road and into a dusty layby. Max noticed a small shack there, and a number of makeshift food stalls waiting in readiness for their daily package of customers. As soon as the bus stopped, small boys boarded, carrying metal pitchers of cool water, and brandishing steel glasses. 'Nimbo-pani! Nimbo-pani!' they all shouted, moving down the bus. Passengers greedily grabbed the glasses from the boys, glasses that were just as quickly filled with ice-cold water, a spoonful of black salt and a hard squeeze of lime.

'Nimbo-pani! Nimbo-pani!'

Imogen had woken up. She loved this great Indian ritual, the comfort stop.

'Would you like a drink?' asked Max.

'I'll have some of the mineral water in our bag.'

Keeping pace with the tiny boys on the bus were older boys outside, walking up and down the length of the vehicle, selling a selection of fruit. Arms dangled from the open windows, holding one-rupee notes, which were dextrously exchanged for a bunch of lychees or a few mangoes.

'Hey, miss, you want fruit? Please to buy fruit.'

Imogen looked at the little urchin holding up his pathetic display of scrawny mangoes for her. Max saw her eyes soften with compassion, their blue deepening with emotion.

'No,' she said reluctantly, 'no fruit, thank you.'

'Hey, mister, you want Limca?'

'No, no.'

The sun lengthens the shadows over the desert sands. Slowly the Earth turns. Another day prepares for heat and silence.

Guru had been selling samosas in this quiet refreshment stop for over three decades. He had started when he was ten, helping his mother carry the iron utensils and oil from their village home some three miles away. It was from her that Guru had learnt to knead the dough, then shape it into triangles and fill it with potatoes and peas. In her declining years, his mother would still come with Guru to the stall, keeping an eye on him, making sure he maintained the standards she had set. As soon as the buses pulled in, Guru would start his culinary origami, knowing that he had only ten minutes to catch his custom. He had fond memories of those early days helping his mother, and he missed her businesslike efficiency. At that time, most of their trade came from Indian travellers. Very few foreign visitors ever used the buses, and those that did were apprehensive of the local food. Now, it was a very different matter: the roads had been considerably improved, the Deluxe buses were much favoured by Westerners, and they had all become accustomed to foods such as samosas. Guru had become rich.

He watched the bus pull off the road and sway like a boat as its tyres left the tarmac surface and hit the dirt of the layby. Even before it had come to a standstill, the little boys mounted the vehicle, screeching like excited birds, mindful too of the ten-minute deadline. Guru dropped his blanched triangles into the boiling oil. As soon as the first few were brown and ready to be taken out, his clients were shoving and pushing to get their share. Guru must have got through a hundred servings that day. As the final few passengers left his stall, Guru paused for breath. He was disappointed. His alert eye had noticed a few Western tourists aboard the bus, but they seemed reluctant to come over to him. Perhaps it was the crowd which deterred them.

So it was with renewed enthusiasm that Guru watched the foreigner approach. He was sure he recognized his Western client. Yes, of course he did.

'What are they all buying over there?' asked Max, sure that Imogen would know.

'Over . . . ? I don't know . . . it looks very popular. Oh, they're buying samosas. Look, that boy's frying them fresh, Max. Let's get some.'

'Are you sure they'll be all right? I mean, you know what the book says about local stuff.'

'I'm sure they'll be fine. Just check that the oil's fresh – it certainly doesn't seem to be doing the others any harm.'

Max's eyes tightened as he descended the bus, and he felt the full glare of the sun on his head. He really was not happy about buying these samosas. Still, as he wandered slowly over to the stall, the crowd began to dissipate. At least he would not have to fight for them. Max stood behind a man who was trying to pay for his snacks and balance a baby in his arms at the same time. As the Indian juggled his precious bundles from hand to hand, Max noticed the old woman sitting behind the stall, on an empty can of oil. It was clear from the tone of her occasional remarks to the young man serving that she was his mother. At times, unasked, she would pass more oil, or a plate of uncooked samosas to her teenage son who was busily cooking and selling. He in turn would pass the money he collected back to her. As Max came to the front of the stall, the young cook, without looking up, asked with his usual abruptness: 'Kitna chai hai?'

'I'm sorry?'

The mother mumbled something to her son.

'What want?' said the boy.

'Three samosas please,' said Max, making it easier for the boy by holding up three fingers and pointing to the boiling cauldron.

The boy fished out three sizzling samosas, dipped them back in the oil to give them a final crispiness, and shook them out onto a piece of torn newspaper. As the oil began to make the ink run, the boy brought across a bowl of chutney, brown and red, and gestured at the greasy pyramids.

'No, no. No thank you,' said Max, and the samosas were handed over. 'How much?'

The boy turned to his mother. 'Three rupees,' she said, holding up three fingers in imitation of Max's earlier gesture.

He knew that he was being overcharged excessively, but Max did not have Imogen's desire – or ability – to bargain out local prices. He took three crumbling notes from his pocket. The boy took them in his slippery hand, and gave them to his mother. She examined them, first one side, then the other, and acknowledged acceptance. Absurdly, Max felt relieved and grateful. He thanked them both. The boy smiled, impressed by the simple honesty of his client. Max nodded, turned and made his way back to the bus. Seeing him return the Indian passengers laughed indulgently, and passed flippant remarks to each other, clearing the way. As Max settled back into his seat, Imogen took the packet delicately from him. Taking a bite, she closed her eyes in mock ecstasy, and encouraged Max to have his share. He took the plunge, saying an inward prayer. They did taste good. He looked over to his left, where a tiny girl was watching him with all the serious scrutiny of a scientist examining a rare specimen.

'Max,' said Imogen, finishing off her second samosa, 'I think I'll go and check on the luggage.'

'No, no, I'll do it,' he replied, wiping his greasy fingers and rising from his seat. The crowd by the doorway cleared a path, someone slapping Max on the back as he walked through. Once outside, he found the metal ladder on the side of the bus, and clambered up again. He peered over the roof and saw, sitting protectively next to their bags, the boy porter to whom he had given five rupees. He smiled reassuringly.

'No need to worry, sahib. Bags very safe.'

From the roof of the bus, the water- and fruit-sellers looked like enormous ants, their dark bodies shining in the midday heat. Beyond them, Max could see the road, now abnormally quiet. Next to it was a line of men using the roadside as an improvised pissoir. Max carefully backed down the ladder. As his feet touched the ground, he was aware he had stepped back into someone. He turned suddenly. It was the young Indian samosa-seller.

'Oh, hello my friend,' said Max. 'Those samosas were excellent.'

The boy clearly did not understand the words, but picked up the warmth in the voice. He looked at Max with the same curiosity he had displayed earlier at the stall. Then, without warning, he thrust something into Max's hand and ran off, disappearing into the crowd.

'Hey, wait, wait,' shouted Max, but the boy was gone. Max looked down at his hand. Crushed into it were two crumpled one-rupee notes. He looked up quickly, scanning the crowd for any sign of the boy. He looked over to the stall, but it was now unmanned, just the mother counting her takings.

Max made his way to his seat, perplexed by the incident.

'The bags are fine,' he said, settling back next to Imogen, 'no problems.'

The driver rushed back on, and turned the ignition. As soon as the engine fired, the small boys on board scarpered, and passengers ran back to find their seats. The bus lurched ahead, mounted the road again, and once more sprinted towards Delhi.

The flight to Varanasi was full. This came as quite a shock to Max since they had confirmed reservations. But so did two hundred other people, on a plane with only a hundred and fifty seats. The mistake Max had made was to queue: had he pushed his way to the front, like everyone else, they might have got on the plane. He was fast learning that only the quick- witted actually got anywhere in this country. It was like an obstacle course, and you earned your place on buses or trains or planes by showing verve and initiative. Imogen already knew this. As Max returned to her, sitting on her suitcase, he seemed crestfallen. She was engrossed in watching the television set fixed to the wall of the departure lounge.

'. . . demonstrations took place all over India as outrage over the Government's proposals spread like wildfire. Students in Delhi, Bombay, Madras and Chandigarh took to the streets to protest at what they consider to be a new form of prejudice against those of high caste, this time by the Government itself . . .' The newscaster's voice trailed over scenes of marching youngsters, waving banners and hockey sticks above their heads, chanting in unison: 'Smash quotas! Smash quotas!' In one sequence, police were charging with lathis at a group of young men, seated in rows on a lawn in front of an official-looking building. The camera panned over to one policeman beating a crouched figure hunched up like a ball on the ground, his arms wrapped around his head to ward off the baton. Then, without warning, the screen was full of brown faces, all shining and desperate, dripping with perspiration or tears, or blood, close up to the lens, struggling to get in front of camera to make their point. Their passion was clear, whether they spoke in their own language, or in English: 'We were only marching peacefully when the police charged on us'; 'They are like animals – we are here to protest, not to fight'; 'My sister was beaten by a police lathi'.

'This is terrible, isn't it?' said Imogen, looking over to Max, also now engrossed in the report on screen. 'I hope it's sorted out soon. Passions run very high in India, particularly over religious issues.'

'Is it a religious issue?' asked Max.

'Oh yes, darling. Caste is central to Hinduism. You're born into a high or a low caste according to your merits or demerits in past lives. And you have to accept your lot as coming from God – whether you are a Brahmin or a Harijan. It really is a very significant thing the Government is trying to do . . . Anyway, what's going on about our flight?'

'They say it's full. We'll have to wait for the next one.'

'Damn,' said Imogen, not relishing the prospect of spending the night in the departure lounge of Delhi airport. 'I suppose there aren't any seats at all?'

'No.'

'They always say that,' she continued, rising stiffly to her feet. 'Let's see if it's really that full.' Max handed Imogen the tickets as she headed for the check-in desk.

'What are you going to do, Imogen?'

'Oh, nothing,' she replied, with that mischievous smile on her face that Max knew well and which still made his heart race. He watched her walk towards the counter, all the desire of the afternoon returning in a rush.

The check-in clerk noticed the attractive English girl approaching. He was sure she was going to try to talk her way on to the plane, but he was determined not to succumb to foreign charms or threats.

'Hello,' said Imogen, flashing her smile momentarily, 'are you Mr Rajan Prasad?'

'Yes madam, yes I am.' So used had Rajan become to wearing his Indian Airlines uniform that he had totally forgotten about the name tag pinned to his breast pocket. Perhaps he had made a mistake. Perhaps this girl was a VIP. But then why was she travelling economy? These foreigners were very strange – somebody had told Rajan that on one occasion a royal princess in England had travelled on a train, second-class, with ordinary people. He would never understand them. You had to be very careful with foreigners. They had no sense of the order of things.

'Well, Mr Prasad, I wonder if *you* can help me. My husband tells me that your flight to Varanasi is full. But it cannot be completely full, I said to him, because we have confirmed bookings on this flight, and Indian Airlines would never let us down like this.'

'Well, madam . . .'

'I am sure he is wrong. You see, it is his first time in India, and he came expecting to find this sort of what he calls "haphazard native organiza-tion". And when people come with prejudice, they are bound to find it, don't you think, Mr Prasad?'

'Oh yes, madam. Some people have terrible prejudices.' She was right, thought Rajan, people have so many preconceptions about India, and they are always looking for bad things.

'I am hoping,' continued Imogen, 'that he will leave India with many less prejudices than he came with. Now, if it is possible to check in our tickets, I am sure he will take back his criticism.'

'Of course, madam, no problem. No problem at all. A pleasure to be of service.' Rajan called up the seat plan on the computer screen. He tapped the cursor along the outline of the Boeing, taking it along the full length of the plane to the tail section. Then, enthused by the opportunity to enhance the reputation of his motherland, Rajan had a thought. He reversed the direction of the cursor, and took it all the way along to the nose of the plane. 'In fact, madam, I see that we have two spare seats in first. Perhaps you and your husband would like . . .'

'Oh, Mr Prasad, we could not possibly take advantage of your kindness.'

'Madam, I insist. I would consider it a personal favour to myself if I can do this for your husband and yourself.'

Before she could argue further, he was tearing off the counterpart on their tickets. 'Oh, and madam,' Rajan continued, made courageous by his own magnanimity, 'when you are in Varanasi, please go to this address. It is my brother. He has a small business. If you need any help, anything at all, or even just to have tea, please go to visit him.' He wrote out the details carefully on an Indian Airlines pad, tore off the top sheet, and handed it to Imogen with her tickets.

'Mr Prasad, you are very kind. We will certainly pay him a visit. Is there any message I can take for you?'

'Just tell him "namaste".'

As Imogen moved away from the counter, the space she vacated was immediately invaded by a dozen impatient bodies. Walking back to Max, Imogen heard a fiery argument break out.

'I am telling you, you scoundrel, that I am a VIP. I must get on that flight.'

'And I am a CIP. I also must get on that flight.'

'My brother is a government minister. I must be on the plane.'

But Rajan Prasad had heard it all before. He was resolute. None of them got on to the plane.

Varanasi, the holy city of the Hindus. At first, it reminded Max more of a medieval vision of Hell, a painting by Hieronymus Bosch, with brown not pale bodies. The city was crawling with people. People coming. People going. People laughing. People crying. People screaming. People whispering. People singing. People sleeping. People eating. People defecating. People begging. People giving. Everywhere you turned, people. Sick people. Healthy people. Young people. Old people. Happy people. Sad people. Kind people. Cruel people. The city was a refuge for all. Thieves, priests, murderers, holy men. Here, all were equal. Women praying for children. Women praying not to have any more children. Girls praying for husbands. Wives praying for an end to their misery. Boys praying for wealth. Wealthy men praying for wisdom.

People were only part of the population of Varanasi. Alongside them, jostling for position, were the animals. Stately cows moved majestically through the muddy streets, bringing traffic to a standstill. One ivory creature had stopped outside a shop selling nuts and grains. As it nosed at the overflowing sacks full of food, the shopkeeper hurried to his wares. Dogs ran about, their tails curled like expensive feathers, speeding through alleyways, avoiding cycles with practised ease and grabbing whatever happened to fall from the supplies being transported a few feet above their heads. One was asleep at the bottom of a flight of steps descending from a particularly popular shrine, yet nobody disturbed him. One by one, with great care, the thousands of pilgrims stepped over the creature, lost in his own dreams. A tiny goat sipped water from a puddle beneath a communal tap, wearing around its waist a sackcloth coat tied by some diligent child who had long ago returned to his home town. Monkeys showed off their gymnastic skills on the roofs of temples, making sweeping raids on any pilgrim foolish enough to be carrying food. Munching through peanuts, they dropped the empty shells onto the heads of passing visitors. And even smaller creatures prospered: a dynasty of rats had established an estate right under the marble altar of the god Hanuman. Their supply of food was guaranteed. Almond burfi was commonplace, as was pistachio cake and rich cashew nuts. Five generations of little rodents had thrived on the best sweetmeats and freshest milk in Varanasi. Of course the altar attendant knew they lived there, but he turned a blind eye. Perhaps they had been princes in a past incarnation – perhaps they would be once again.

And so this strange collection of lives, crushed together, was carried along in its allocated space on the small globe that revolved slowly and deliberately around a dying star.

It had been a very long day, and Max was beginning to drag his feet. Imogen's friend, Charles, must have taken them to every temple in Varanasi, from the most famous to the most obscure. In Max's exhausted imagination, they were all beginning to merge into one, an amorphous mixture of gaudy statues, pungent incense, searing bells, chanting pilgrims and cool, slippery marble floors. They had not bothered to eat properly all day, yet Max was full with the accumulated offerings of prashad from the various shrines.

Imogen had known Charles at Oxford. He was a couple of years older than her, and had been a Finalist when she first went up. Imogen had often talked about him, and, coming out to India, Max had been curious to meet the man who had made such a profound impact upon his wife. There had never been anything romantic between Charles and Imogen: Max was sure of that, even though all Imogen's friends at college had refused to believe that anyone could resist such an attractive young man. At first, Max had also doubted it, teasing his new girlfriend mercilessly. But he soon realized that what held Imogen and Charles together was not sexual attraction to each other, but rather a shared attraction to India. Charles too was a seasoned traveller of the subcontinent: by the time he was finishing off at Balliol, he had been to all the places, seen all the exotic sights Imogen still dreamed of. More than that, he had decided to go out to India, perhaps permanently, once his Finals were over, an idea which Imogen too was already considering.

Meeting Charles for the first time in Varanasi, Max understood the bond at once. He also took to Charles, fascinated by his quiet devotion to a people and a culture so unlike his own. The party of visitors had formed a crocodile, to avoid being swept away by the tides of pilgrims. Charles, now a native of the Varanasi side streets, led the way, followed by Imogen, then finally Max. Night was falling and none of them relished the prospect of being lost in the labyrinth of dark alleys and muddy walkways that led to and from the temples. They clung onto each other's T-shirts, their eyes firmly fixed on the one in front. As they struggled out of the Birla temple, Imogen noticed that a large group up ahead had gathered in the square outside the temple. Curious to know what had caught their attention, she insisted on joining the throng. The human train swerved from its carefully plotted route, and broke up into its individual pieces as it reached the growing mass of spectators. Max kept close to Imogen, not an easy task as she pushed and meandered her way to the front of the crowd. Still, he was too tired to complain and he had already consented privately to allow himself to be carried along by the unrelenting flow of the day. And so it was in this way that Max, much against his will, became part of an audience to events that would haunt him for the rest of his life.

The dissent against the Government's proposed review of quotas of jobs for backward castes had gained momentum at an alarming rate. People all over India had mobilized to protest for or against the policy. A number had already been killed, and were being held up by their supporters as martyrs to the cause. But events had now begun to take a sinister turn. Frustrated by the Government's refusal to listen to their protests and enthused by the vehemence of their beliefs, upper-caste Hindus, in particular students, had taken to dramatic public displays of loyalty to the anti-reservationist cause. In Lucknow, capital of Uttar Pradesh, hundreds of students had just staged a hunger strike; in Chandigarh, a thousand people marched on the State Assembly, bringing proceedings to a halt by their occupation of the building; in Delhi itself, effigies of V. P. Singh had been stoned to shreds outside the Parliament buildings. In Varanasi, a city with a ready audience of millions of Indians, of all castes and from all parts of the nation, students had been at their most vociferous. They hoped to exploit the devout Hindu's belief that caste was a matter of divine ordination, and any man who tried to tinker with the system was committing an act of hubris. Street demonstrations had been organized outside popular temples, petitions were collected, even temple services were being given a political colouring by the Brahmin priests. Pilgrims were encouraged to put their faith not in an ephemeral Prime Minister but rather in that higher destiny that had bestowed upon them a particular role this time around and which might well treat them more or less favourably the next time. As the protests grew, so did the passion, and the need for more dramatic displays of daring.

Now, as dusk descended upon the marble temples, the fading sun colouring the white stone a blood red, Sanjay Veswammy, a twenty-year-old medical student at the university, was about to set in motion a series of events that would eventually engulf the whole country.

Sanjay had thought the whole thing up as a rather elaborate stunt, and his friends had invited along all the local newspaper photographers and journalists to report the drama outside the Birla temple. His plan was to douse his legs in kerosene, and set fire to them. The cameras would begin to click the moment this happened. After thirty seconds, the requisite photographs having been taken, Sanjay's friends would rush forward, extinguish the flames and, apparently against their companion's wishes, save him from total self-immolation. They had calculated that Levi's 501 jeans take at least one minute to burn through. If his colleagues acted as they had rehearsed, Sanjay would escape without even a minor burn.

The boy displayed the can of kerosene to the gathered crowd. Swinging the can around as he surveyed the circle of eager spectators, he declared his sorrow and suffering at the planned reforms aimed at giving privileges to the backward castes. 'So who will clean our streets, when the Harijans are all politicians and businessmen! Who will make our shoes, when the Chamals become officers and diplomats! I cannot tolerate this injustice. I will not live in this world if everything I have worked for is to be turned upside down! Only one thing I ask of you, my friends: when I am gone, somebody take my eyes and give them to V. P. Singh. Perhaps then he will begin to see just what he has done!'

The crowd became impatient, eager for the spectacle they all knew was coming. The photographers held up their cameras and brought the image of the boy into focus, everything behind him melting into an uneven haze. Sensing the spectators' expectancy, Sanjay began to pour the liquid over his trousers, privately careful not to let the kerosene wet his shirt. A silence descended over the audience. The kerosene can was half-empty as Sanjay finished dousing his jeans; he put it down gently on the ground, reminding himself not to forget it later when they all went home. The crowd was restless, as more and more people struggled to get to the front. Taking a large box of matches from his pocket, Sanjay held it up in the air, revolving slowly to let his gathered witnesses take in the horror.

'For God's sake,' exclaimed Max, 'he's really going to do it. Someone's got to stop him.'

He pushed through the row of people in front of him, only to find himself firmly held back by some photographers.

'No, no mister. Not spoil photograph.'

'You must be mad,' shouted Max, 'the boy's going to set fire to himself! Let me go!'

'No mister. No let go.'

The press photographers were experts, and kept Max out of their shot, pushing him back with their elbows. Max looked round to Imogen, harbouring some vain hope that she might be able to help, but she was nowhere to be seen, lost in the mass of eagerly craning necks. He turned back just in time to see the boy strike the match, and throw it onto his trousers.

'Stop!' screamed Max. 'Someone stop him!'

His pleas were lost in the general gasp that went up as the match fell onto Sanjay's jeans. Momentarily, the whole square was lit up as the flashbulbs on a dozen cameras exploded simultaneously, dazzling the spectators. As Max's eyes focused back onto the darkness after the burst of light, he noticed that the kerosene had not ignited. The boy struck another match, and threw it onto his trousers once more. Again, the square lit up with the flashes; again the kerosene failed to ignite. The crowd sighed, seemingly disappointed; somewhere at the back of the mass, some youths laughed in a derisory way, mocking the idiocy of the would-be martyr.

Sanjay was already feeling a fool; when he heard the laughter, he became incensed. Picking up the half-empty can of kerosene, he poured the rest of the contents over his trousers, this time not bothering to check that his shirt remained dry. He was no longer in the mood for showmanship. In one movement, he cast aside the can, struck a match, and dropped it onto his legs. Max tried once again to break through the ranks of journalists, but failed. Imogen had managed to find her way back to the front, and was standing beside him. He looked at her and saw his own panic-stricken face reflected in hers.

The kerosene on Sanjay's trousers had begun to dry, and the vapours were hanging heavily about him. This time, as the flashbulbs exploded, their white light was made orange by the explosion at the centre of the square. In a violent burst, a fireball enveloped Sanjay.

The intense heat prevented anyone from rushing to the boy. As his companions ran to him, so they hit an invisible wall some four feet from the human bonfire. Max also rushed to the furnace; he too hit the wall of heat, the flames singeing his eyebrows. In the centre of the inferno, the boy, still alive, still on his feet, writhed in agony, his arms flailing like the wings of a stricken bird trying to take off. His clothes were already charred, and fragments of ash floated up into the night sky. A solemn silence had descended upon the onlookers, the stillness emphasizing the crackling and snapping of the fire. A thick grey smoke began to stream from the figure as the flames reached flesh, and the stink of roasting meat filled the air. Sanjay's body had begun to convulse; moments later, it collapsed onto the ground, still struggling like some macabre firework. The flames settled into a tiny heap, continuing to flicker erratically.

'Come on, Max, let's get out of here.' Max felt a pair of hands grab him by the shoulders, pulling him away from the crumpled pyre. It was Charles. 'The police will be here any minute, and they'll round up everyone for questioning. We don't want to spend the night in a police station. Let's go.' Max nodded automatically and moved away, following Charles, his head still turned towards the smoking remains on the ground. The flashbulbs were still firing. Suddenly Max pulled away from Charles, and lashed out at one of the cameras. The photographer, more agile than Max, turned the apparatus away, protecting it with his back and pouring out a stream of expletives in Hindi.

Charles steered Max away gently but firmly, cutting a path through the crowd. Standing away from the mass, an Indian woman was comforting Imogen. As Charles and Max emerged from the throng, Imogen turned towards them: the sight of her familiar figure and her kind, resolute face soothed Max, recalling him from the hell into which he had been drawn. She put her arms around him, pulling his drenched, sooty body close to hers.

The next day the front pages were covered with photos of the human inferno. One newspaper even printed a sequence of shots, charting the course of the pyrotechnic display frame by frame. Headlines such as 'Human Fireball', 'Flames of Dissent', 'Quit Quotas', 'Son of India', prefaced articles that tried to squeeze as much political capital as possible from the tragedy. All the reports seemed unaware, or unwilling to acknowledge, that the whole pathetic episode had been intended as a wild publicity stunt. As one of Sanjay's friends would reveal later, the young student had simply wanted to get his photo into the newspapers. Fate had conspired to fulfil his wishes in a most dramatic way. For the journalists, Sanjay Veswammy was a godsend: they had been looking for a suitable candidate to cast as the angry young man. Now that they had found him, he must play his part to the end.

Over the following month, taking their cue from the brave medic of Varanasi, six more students re-enacted the same tragic role. The fires were burning all over India.

Max had not slept. The nightmare image of the burning boy, his frantic convulsions, the smell of the flesh, had recurred all night, lingering in the darkness. In the early hours, to escape the smell, Max took a chair onto the balcony, and there managed for a time to fall into a fretful, erratic slumber. As a new day broke over the Ganges, he saw the shafts of dawn light up the distant ghats. The river was already teeming as devout pilgrims rowed out into the swift currents of the centre, and, standing precariously in the rocking boats, poured out their libations to the goddess in the water. The sight of the devotions, the freshness of the air and the gradual lightening of the sun raised Max's spirits. Time heals the troubled spirit, and time's therapeutic powers were more potent and immediate here. The drama of the previous day was now another small part of the mosaic that formed this hectic, relentless continent. Imogen drifted out onto the balcony, her eyes heavy with sleep. She leaned over

Max and he held her strong living body close to him, breathing in the warm aroma of the night she carried on her skin.

By the time Charles arrived to pick them up, Max had recovered much of his optimism and energy. Imogen, with her deep store of strength and stoicism, had already absorbed the tragedy, slotting it into the intricate network of experiences that formed her inner mechanism for dealing with the world.

'Do you still fancy going out onto the river this morning?' asked Charles, leaning out of the driver's window of his twenty-year-old Ambassador, its engine throbbing. His face was gaunt and hollow, still jaded by the horror of the inferno.

'Of course, Charles,' answered Imogen. 'It'll do us good. Anyway, it's our only chance this time. We're off first thing in the morning.'

Max climbed into the back of the car, and sank into the deep leather seats, now torn and faded, testimony to decades of being overloaded with families and children. The car still retained some of its former grandeur, its heavy bodywork and suspension cushioning the passengers against the ruts and potholes in the muddy road. Imogen sat in the front, the air vent blowing a gentle breeze through her hair, her cheerful voice serving to alleviate the heavy atmosphere inside the car. Charles drove with native expertise, using the car as an assault vehicle to negotiate the mile or so down to the water's edge. There, at the bottom of a long, wide stairway of wet stone steps, full of bodies washing themselves in the holy water, a ferryman waited. He had furnished his boat specially for his foreign guests, pinning new sackcloth onto the wooden planks that formed the seats. He carefully helped each of them, steadying the boat with his legs as they all found their seats. As soon as Charles was on board, the ferryman pushed off with his bamboo pole, avoiding the other boats transporting flowers and pilgrims to the centre of the river. Max looked back at the hundreds of bathers pouring water over themselves with small brass or silver urns. Behind them, the distinctive brown and red curved towers of Hindu temples reached for the sky, majestic and motionless, witnesses to thousands of years of ritual devotion to the Ganges. Steps descended from the temples, plunging deep into the waters, continuing their route all the way to the river bed. On them devotees gathered, thin saffron cloth clinging closely to their sunburnt bodies. Others were completely naked, dark skins shining in the morning sun. Max gazed at one wrinkled pilgrim as he got ready to submerge himself in the murky waters: rubbing himself vigorously with his hands, the old man took a deep breath, held his nose tightly, and disappeared beneath the surface. It was a good half minute before the body surfaced again, the water running off his back and head in a cascade. Tiny boats made of flowers floated along the river, bobbing up and down as people ducked and rose in the water, creating wave upon wave.

Gently the ferryman manoeuvred the boat to the middle of the river. This was the ideal vantage point to see the morning worship, as boatloads of pilgrims swirled and eddied in the fast currents. The shore was now a quarter of a mile away, the bathers like tiny insects, glistening in the light. On the opposite side, Max noticed a row of funeral pyres smoking silently, their fires extinguished, their burdens long ago transformed into ash. In contrast to the other bank, full of noise and teeming with people, the approaching shore was deserted. Here, there were no devotions, no libations, no pilgrims bowing to the new day. A pack of scrawny dogs grappled with each other in the dust and ashes, growling and howling. Some crows had found a safe platform atop one of the smouldering pyres and were screeching their lamentations for the departed souls. Only one solitary figure, an old woman clad in white, moved like a phantasm amidst the charred altars, desperately searching for something, clinging perhaps to the memory of a loved husband or son, given up to the fires by the shore of the holy river. Max watched closely as she meandered between the smoking blocks. Was she the young student's mother, he wondered, unable to believe the newspaper reports, drawn by some unseen force to search for her son amongst the embers and the ashes of the dead?

The boat floated down the river, some twenty feet from the shore, carried along by the currents. Soon the funeral pyres gave way to a straggle of huts and houses on the edge of fertile fields. The river was now flowing freely, the bathers and other ferries left far behind. Only the more expensive flower-boats made it this far down, their banana-leaf hulls standing up well to the battering of the waves. Up ahead, a jetty stuck out into the water, flowers swirling around the base of the rotting wooden pillars. It was to this makeshift landing stage that the ferryman directed his vessel, trailing his bamboo pole in the water as a rudder.

Charles had said that the walk from the landing stage to Sarnath would be about an hour. In fact, in their present desultory mood, it took Max and Imogen almost two hours to reach the holy temple and gardens. It was here amid the shady banyans, a few miles out of the ancient city, that the Buddha had preached his message of enlightenment. Surveying the faded landscape, Max wondered what numinous power had compelled the young prince to come here, away from the praying and chanting that filled the holy city. Perhaps it was precisely that ritual that had driven the wanderer to seek the solitude of the groves. For Max, too, the stillness and silence of Sarnath was a welcome relief from the turmoil of the river. As Charles and Imogen strolled along the grove leading to the holy mound, the resting-place where Lord Buddha sat in communion with his inner spirit, Max held back, relishing the rare moment of privacy and personal space he found here. The avenue leading to the hill was bounded on each side by an embankment lined with palm trees, dry and dusty beneath the scorching sun. Here, in the shade of one of the trees, Max saw a holy man sitting in the lotus position, naked but for a tiny waistcloth, his saffron robes spread around him like a discarded skin. The sadhu's head was shaved except for a tiny rope of hair falling from his crown; his dark forehead was covered in a lattice pattern drawn with ash, a red spot marking the centre point, the much sought-for third eye. The serenity epitomized by the holy man was enthralling. He envied his liberty and self-sufficiency, his freedom from the straits and constraints of the world to which Max was inextricably bound by his personal ambitions, the world to which he would soon be forced to return. He felt a frisson in the deepest recess of his soul: for a moment, he felt totally alone, rooted to this spot of earth, its primeval power surging through him as if he too were but a vertical extension of the dust and the ash and the dried grass. Just like the trees and the holy man. For a few minutes, Max's ears were full of an intolerable burden of noise: crashing waves mingled with the sound of boulders smashing into each other, bursting open as stone exploded upon stone. In the distance, an enormous sheet flapped rhythmically in the breeze, but there was no wind blowing. Giant tree trunks creaked and crunched, the bark prising itself with gargantuan effort out of the solid baked earth. But no tree fell. Max heard the tearing and rustling of undergrowth as if some intrepid explorer were fighting his way through solid walls of vegetation. Somewhere, high in the sky, a circling bird urgently screeched Max's name. He looked up, shading his eyes from the glare of the sun: the eagle soared in its regular path, nonchalantly watching its prey far below. This was the flapping he had heard: no gigantic sheet, but the gossamer beat of a bird's wings. Max looked back at the holy man as the orchestra of noise diminished by degrees. The crashing boulders were no more than tiny balls of dust and sand rolling down the embankment, the ebb and flow of waves became the gentle trickle of sap as it oozed from a gash in the bark of a nearby gum tree. Max saw tiny songbirds playing in the branches, their frolicking causing small twigs to fall to the ground. At the foot of the tree, ants rushed fretfully, gathering their cargoes, trampling with minute legs through the dried grass. Still the eagle circled, calling Max's name.

Imogen and Charles had by now reached the holy mound at Sarnath. Drawn by the lure of the more lavish marble temple, tourists usually left the hill in splendid isolation, its seclusion preserved by its comparative insignificance. Imogen knew that Max had fallen behind, but had decided to leave him to his private reflections. They all needed time to take in the events of the past day, and it was obvious that Max was finding the effort of making social conversation just too much. She looked back at him, standing motionless, staring at the crouched sadhu.

'Shall I run back and get him?' said Charles.

'No. No, let's just leave him for a bit,' answered Imogen. 'He'll catch up with us.' And the two of them continued along their chosen route, turning a corner in the dried avenue, heading up to the mound.

Max was returning slowly to reality. He could feel the perspiration running off his forehead onto his eyebrows. A few drops fell into his eyes, and the burning blurred his vision for a moment. Instinctively, Max put his fingers to his face, but then remembered that he was not in his own sanitized country. Here, hands and fingernails quickly became filthy, and had to be washed every few hours. The land left its mark on you.

Carefully, Max got out his handkerchief, shook out its neatly ironed folds, and dried his brow. His eyes focused again, and he looked back to the holy man across the way. But the spell was now broken, and Max felt an overwhelming impatience to rejoin the others. He searched the horizon for sight of Charles and Imogen. The heat rose in clouds, making everything uncertain of its shape. In the distance, the white marble of the temple formed a second sun, making Max flinch his head away. There was no sign of Imogen or Charles, but Max knew the direction they had taken. He set off, the dried undergrowth breaking beneath his feet.

Max had travelled no more than a hundred yards when he was overcome by a strong sensation that someone was following him. He turned but saw no one, nothing except the grass avenue lined with trees, stretching back like a parched river. Max looked over to the tree where the holy man had sat, but there was no one there either. The air was heavy with the smell of scorching vegetation. He walked on, the twigs and grass crunching louder with each step. There was still no sign of the others: perhaps he should give a shout. He did not want to break the natural silence of the meadow, particularly now that, for some inexplicable reason, even the birds had stopped singing. The crack and crunch of the undergrowth was getting louder, and more frequent. Max realized that, unwittingly, he was almost jogging. He resumed his relaxed walk. His shirt was soaked by now, and the perspiration continued to flow off his forehead. The salt water reactivated the pungent Indian soap Max had used that morning, the smell filling his nostrils with its antiseptic sharpness. He was nearly at the bend that would finally lead him to the holy mound, but the feeling that he was being followed had not really left him. He looked back once more and surveyed the landscape. Nothing. Just as he was about to go on, Max noticed a familiar figure on the opposite side of the avenue. He could not see him properly amongst the shadows, but his brain had registered recognition. The holy man, having completed his meditations for the afternoon, was walking out of the meadow in the same direction as Max. But something was not quite right. Max was just about to turn away when he realized his mistake. This new visitor to the meadow was not dressed in saffron – and in any case, he was not walking. Max stopped to look at him properly. He realized now where he had seen the stranger before. There, motionless, his face hidden by the streaks of darkness cast by the trees, was the Englishman. Max knew him instantly, now that he had woken from his stupor. The cream suit was unmistakable, as was the penetrating gaze, the fixed stance, the imperturbable demeanour. A bead of sweat dropped into Max's eye. He wiped it away instantly, fearful of losing sight of the visitor.

'Hello there!' shouted Max, his voice sounding like an explosion inside his own head.

The Englishman remained silent. Perhaps he had not heard.

'Hello there!'

Max wondered why the stranger showed no acknowledgement. He seemed preoccupied with some deep, private contemplation. In which case, thought Max, he probably doesn't want to be disturbed. But he was loath to give up so easily. He felt a desire to get to know this fellow traveller. After all, they seemed to share the same taste in places to visit in India, and Max was particularly curious to know why the Englishman was travelling alone, so unencumbered, not even a camera over his shoulder. What was bringing him to these locations? Obviously he too liked the seclusion of the meadow. For a moment Max felt scrutinized by the Englishman, in the same way he himself had stared at the holy man a little earlier. It was the eyes that held Max, blue, just like his own, but gaunt, melancholy eyes, telling of a life that had once been full of joy. He decided that calling out was not going to elicit any response. Maybe if he were closer, perhaps then the stranger might react. Max moved towards the embankment, lifting his feet carefully over the undergrowth. The traveller remained fixed. Taking cautious steps, Max neared the side of the avenue. A few metres from the edge, a creeper wrapped itself around Max's shin. He felt for it, refusing to take his eyes off the stranger. But his fingers missed the mark. He searched up and down beneath his knee, but still his hand failed to find it. In frustration, Max glanced down to his foot, grabbed the creeper and tore it off. He looked back to the Englishman. But he was gone, leaving behind him nothing but the chequered shadows of the banyan branches.

Max looked up and down the row of trees impatiently. The traveller must have gone back, away from the avenue, into the thicket of trees.

'Hello!' shouted Max. 'Hello!'

'Over here, Max!'

Max whipped around, delighted to have broken the Englishman's reserve. But his face dropped as he saw that it was Charles who had answered.

'Charles. Did you see an English tourist pass you down the meadow? A man, middle-aged, dressed in a summer suit?'

'No. Why?'

'Oh, no reason. I just thought it was someone I knew.'

'Max. Are you all right? You sounded a bit frantic just then, when you shouted.'

'I'm okay, Charles. Thanks. Just a bit tired after yesterday.'

Max noticed Charles's eyes drop slowly from looking at him directly, down to his feet.

'Max. You're hurt . . .'

'What?'

'Your shin – look.'

Max glanced at his legs. His beige chinos were filthy, covered with the dirt and dye that had come off the drying, crumbling vegetation along the avenue of undergrowth. But near the ankle, a different colour was seeping through the light material. Large patches of crimson were beginning to appear, spreading through the cotton like ink on blotting paper. Max pulled up his trouser leg, only to discover that his hands too were streaked with blood. The creepers that had wrapped themselves around his leg had been lined with enormous thorns. In his excitement and preoccupation with the Englishman, Max had not noticed the sharp spikes tearing his hands and lacerating his shin through the cotton. The long cuts looked like the scratches of some wild creature that had attacked him in a frenzy.

'Oh no,' sighed Max, 'I'd better clean this up, I suppose.'

'I think you need to get back to the hotel. If dirt gets inside those cuts, you'll be well and truly laid up.'

Little drops of blood were beginning to appear along the cuts on Max's right hand. He wrapped his handkerchief round his palm as he and Charles set off down the avenue, towards the mound where Imogen was waiting.

Charles persuaded the guide of a tourist coach to let them all hitch a ride back to town. Max looked around him at their fellow passengers, trying to keep his mind off the pain shooting up his leg. Most of them had their heads buried in guidebooks of one sort or another, whilst others examined their souvenir purchases with perceptible suspicion. 'It's not like *A Passage to India*,' he heard one overweight Texan say to her equally overweight companion.

As they came closer to the centre of Varanasi, the traffic of pilgrims, cows, bullock-carts and cyclists began to build up, until it became almost impossible for the bus to make any progress. Charles leaned across to the guide. She smiled, tapped the driver on the shoulder, and spoke a few words to him in Hindi. He stopped the bus by the side of the road and the door slid open, the air-conditioning hissing as the cold air hit the warmth of the outside world.

The nurse at the hotel was most understanding. Splashing on the Dettol, she interrogated Max closely about where he had got the scratches, what animals had been around, whether he had touched the grazes with his fingers, and so on. The deeper cuts were still seeping, but the shin did not seem so lacerated now that the dirt had been cleaned up. Finally, the nurse covered the cuts in a cooling balm, then wrapped a bright white bandage around the leg.

'There you are, young man,' she said, finishing off the job with a neat little safety pin. 'Now don't go playing in the bushes again, will you?'

As darkness fell, Charles returned to the hotel to pick up Max and Imogen for the evening. He had retrieved his car from the ghats, and everyone had showered and changed for the night. Max was pleased to settle back once again into the soft leather of the Ambassador, and from the comfort of the car he watched the pilgrims rushing past, eager to make the evening services in the temples.

'How are you feeling now?' asked Charles, his eyes fixed on the road.

'Fine,' said Max. 'Listen, Charles. Thank you for looking after us. I'm glad you're around.'

'There's a real treat in store for you tonight,' continued Charles. Then, pulling up by the kerb, he stopped the car and opened the door. 'We'll leave the car here, and walk the rest of the way. It gets too crowded to drive. But first let's grab a bite to eat. There's a great place, right up this little street.'

In the deepening darkness of the evening, the travellers finally took respite, drinking hot milky tea at an overcrowded café. It was a makeshift affair, yet apparently it had been here for decades, one of the final staging posts before pilgrims dived into the warren of alleyways and gutter-like streets that formed the inner sanctum of Varanasi. They served the most appalling tea. The frothy liquid, in conjunction with the heavy intake of sugar from the burfi and sweetmeats, made Max heady. The day was just catching up with him. His energy had crashed, and he was feeling nauseous from the tastes, the smells, the noise, and the constant proximity of people. Thankfully, there was just this one more temple to see – and Imogen assured him it would be the most splendid of the tour. She had never been inside, but had read all about it. The Vishwanath temple, with its solid gold roof, was reputed to be the oldest and holiest of the temples in Varanasi. All pilgrims paid at least one visit to the Vishwanath: lepers were cured, barren women made fertile, old men invigorated, young men made wise. There was a problem getting into the Vishwanath temple, but Max had only caught the gist of the conversation earlier. Some Hindus got very upset by tourists wandering around their holiest shrine in T-shirts and shorts, so the temple authorities had decided to tighten up. But Charles had a friend, a Mr Chatterjee, who could sort it out.

As the sunlight began to fade, the street-stall owners started reluctantly to light their paraffin lamps. The café was full of Western youngsters, vague and untidily attractive, still searching for the enlightenment that had eluded their parents two decades earlier. In the meantime, they were happy to trade their francs, or marks, or dollars, or whatever it was they had of value, for a more mundane form of nirvana.

'Ah, Mr Chatterjee,' said Charles, as if greeting an old schoolmaster.

'Hello, Charley sahib. And this must be your charming friends from England. So very charmed to meet you.' Mr Chatterjee took Imogen's hand in his and held it up to his lips. He had obviously learnt etiquette from some old Hollywood film. He reminded Max of a weasel – the same thin limbs, the shiny eyes full of mischief, the alert reflexes.

'But first,' said the old man, 'I must do some business.'

They all knew what he meant, for the waiting Westerners in the café had already got out their multi-coloured currencies. Max closed his eyes. He felt his limbs relax, and his whole body float slowly away from its surroundings, sinking gently into itself. Sounds around him began to merge into each other, the shuffling of eager pilgrims, the metallic clatter of steel tumblers in the café, the screaming of a child adrift in the sea of supplicants, the hypnotic music of temple bells somewhere in a distant alley.

One by one the sounds faded into the distance. Suddenly, a huge, red-faced monkey reared up in front of Max and stared aggressively at him. He flinched back, startled at the apparition, but the monkey grabbed him by the neck and pulled him down, clawing his scalp with its razor-sharp claws. Max, his face bent towards the dirty floor of the café, saw drops of blood begin to rain down onto the muddy cobbles. Why didn't the others pull the animal off? As the blood began to colour the dingy stones, the deep red spots slowly coalesced into shiny beetles that crawled away into the gutter running alongside the café. Max had to get the creature off: he steeled himself, and pushed his head up with all his strength. The café was gone. Instead, Max found himself all alone in the Rajasthani desert, the fading evening light bringing in a gentle chill. A light wind made the sand swirl and eddy like pools of amber water. He felt the perspiration drying on his skin, cooling him down, and his clothes, which had clung to him all day, began to flap in the breeze. In the distance, a ghost city stood silently, inert and surreal, sand blowing in and out of its regal turrets. Max felt someone close to him.

'Raju? What are you doing here? You've got to take other people around Fatehpur Sikri, now that you've finished with me.'

'Oh no, mister. Oh no, my good friend. There is no one else I have to show around. My duty is only to you. No one else ever comes to this city. Only you. I have been here even before the city was built, when there was nothing but barren sand, the wind and the silence. No vultures circled the air then, no wolves cried in the night. And even then, only you came. And I was always here to be with you. For thousands of years, you came. For thousands more, you will come to me.'

Max looked at the little guide, with his broad smile and rotten teeth. Who was this young boy? His face was very familiar. Max knew they had been together at some important point in his life. He searched his memory desperately, but it was gone. The boy smiled defiantly, then turned half away from Max and pointed up at the distant walls of the ghost city. High up, a classical Indian turret was silhouetted against the enormous fiery ball of a dying sun. Inside the marble pillars, two monkeys fought ferociously, their long arms reaching out at each other, while their heads tilted back for protection. Their screams echoed in the night air. Max strained to see the macabre choreography as the monkeys danced away from each other, then rushed together at great speed. Even at this distance, he could see their claws glistening with blood. The dance went on, still accompanied by the agonized shrieks. As they collided in a final cataclysm, the smaller of the two animals was momentarily lifted off his feet and swept over the side of the turret. His dying scream resounded for some seconds, then the winds engulfed the darkness once again. Max flinched. He looked back to the small companion at his side, but there was no one there, nothing except the sands, swirling gently. Max searched the barren landscape for any sign of the guide, his guide, but he was alone. He turned back to the city walls, in time to see the monkey falling again, as if the image had been momentarily frozen. Max began to run towards the distant metropolis, overcome by concern for the little animal. No sooner had he felt his concern than he was there, at the foot of the high wall, staring impotently at the tiny crumpled body lying awkwardly in the sand. A stream of blood seeped into the dry dust. Max looked up at the wall, towards the turret at its top, and saw high up in the amber gloom a simian face staring down at him in triumph. He bent down over the dead monkey. He touched its fur, still warm and damp from its exertions, and pulled the animal onto its back. As he straightened its limbs, he looked closely at the dead monkey's face, frozen in a grimace of anger and fear, its teeth red with the blood of its opponent. He bent his head closer to the monkey's face and saw his two reflections rise up in the dead animal's fixed eyes. As Max regarded his own image in the dark lenses, the dead creature shrieked and grabbed him by the hair. Stunned by the pain, Max fell back. As he did so, the animal swung round its arm and sliced Max's cheek with its claws. He raised his hand to the side of his head where he could feel torn shreds of his own skin, peeling off the side of his face. The monkey now had a firm hold of Max's head. He struggled up in agony, shaking his assailant from side to side. The monkey's screams filled the air, rising in a deadly crescendo – then silence. The monkey was gone. Max was alone, grasping his own head, fending off a non-existent enemy. He looked up cautiously. He was now inside one of the ghostly citadels, high above the amber city, its empty courtyards and palaces stretching out beneath him. The gash on his cheek had begun to coagulate. As he relaxed and began to breathe normally again, Max felt a small hand put itself gently inside his own. He looked down at his side to see a boy he recognized staring affectionately at him. He felt safe with this new companion. He wanted to ask the boy a question. It formed in his mind: 'Why did you give me back the money?' The young samosa-seller smiled and looked away, into the distance. Max followed his gaze. Far away, in the middle of an exquisite petrified garden, Max saw a lone figure, a man, motionless and attentive, staring directly towards the turret. As his eyes focused to the distance, Max saw that it was the Englishman.

'Hello there!' shouted Max, fearful that the traveller would disappear, 'hello!' But the Englishman was oblivious to his vehement pleas. Then, in a deliberate, melancholy gesture, the stranger looked down at his feet, and Max noticed the form on the ground. A beautiful naked figure slept peacefully, in embryonic posture.

'Imogen,' whispered Max.

The Englishman crouched down, and looked back up, straight towards Max, his eyes full of reproach.

'Imogen.'

Even as Max formed the name with his lips, the Englishman picked up the limp body and rose carefully to his feet. Keeping his eyes fixed on his pitiful burden, he turned and walked away, disappearing into the amber sands. Max felt his face had become wet. He put his hand up to his cheeks, and touched the tears running uncontrollably from his eyes.

He was still crying when he woke up. As Max opened his eyes, he saw the familiar overcrowded café all around him. For a moment, everything was silent, as it had been in the desert. The owner of the café still shouted his orders, but Max heard no voice; people chattered at each table, but their conversation was without sound. Even the pilgrims in the alleyway outside, whose shuffling had been so fretful, were now marching past without a noise. Max looked at the tables in the café. Imogen was there, talking with her usual animation to Charles. Max was glad to see her again, even though her conversation was soundless. He moved to touch her, but failed to notice the steel tumbler perched shakily on the edge of their table. As it fell, Max noticed it hang in the air as if in slow motion. Performing its deliberate revolutions, the tumbler somersaulted, letting go of its contents, which formed themselves into huge droplets. Slowly it fell. Finally it hit the stone cobbles, an immense crash of metal on stone resounding through the air. As the reverberations hit his eardrums, Max felt a detonation inside his head. He put his hands up to his ears, hoping to lessen the pain. Everything became silent once again. Tentatively, Max took his hands away, to hear the normal sounds of the café.

'Oh dear, Max, do be careful. That tea's hot – did you get burnt?'

'No. No I didn't. Imogen, what's going on? Why . . .'

'You've been asleep, Max.'

'How long?'

'Oh, not long. Only a few minutes.'

What could the dream images mean? The fighting monkeys, the Indian boy, the silent desert? Where was the amber city? Who was the Englishman? Why was he angry with Max? Max felt himself beginning to float back into the phantasmagoria. Just then, Mr Chatterjee, his business finished, came back to their table. He was clearly pleased with the day's takings, and now felt that he could afford to be altruistic.

'So, Charley sahib, you want to visit the Vishwanath temple?'

Charles finished off his tea, and wiped his mouth. 'Can you arrange it for us?'

'Anything can be arranged, Charley sahib. I have already spoken with the temple guard.' Mr Chatterjee cast a lascivious look towards Imogen. 'He will let you and your beautiful friends into the temple. Just look after him when you are finished.'

Charles thanked him, then whispered something in his ear and handed him a hundred-rupee note beneath the table.

The alleyways of the old city in Varanasi formed an intricate labyrinth. Even in the daytime, kerosene lamps burned outside the shops that lined the narrow streets. Their green light and warm hiss brought some comfort to the damp and permanent darkness of the alleys. All along the gangways, buildings four storeys high rose up, closing in the walkways like some man-made rainforest. Many of these homes had been here for hundreds of years. And for hundreds of years, without respite, pilgrims had negotiated this penitential maze. No more than two people could walk comfortably along the tight pathways between the shops, yet people were crushed five abreast. Shadowy streets led off to the right and left, brought to life by young children playing in the sodden dirt. But no pilgrim left the main pathway to explore the side streets. Their purpose was set, their aim unfaltering, or almost unfaltering. For as they passed by the myriad shops selling brass and gold, saris and jewellery, plaster statues of gods and demons, even the most devout were tempted by these material distractions. This was the last thing the supplicant expected at the climax of his pilgrimage, coming as he did in a spirit of renunciation – streets full of shops bursting with silks and precious metals. But these were practised businessmen. Their policy of ambushing people at the last moment obviously worked: as the devotees emerged from their visits to the old city and the temple, they were weighed down with carvings, statuettes, brass utensils, all sorts of paraphernalia whose connection with the divine was tenuous, even by Hindu standards.

One by one, Charles, Imogen and Max plunged into the train of pilgrims as it passed by the café. Swept along by the crush, Max tried desperately to keep Imogen in his sights. This was no place to get lost, and he feared his tiredness could lead to trouble. The shops along the passageways floated past like ornate stations. Max looked down at the ground, but could not see it – ahead, behind, to the left and right were pilgrims, pushing and heaving. There was no hope for you if you stumbled. The train thundered on. As the temple bells came closer, Max knew this ordeal was almost at an end. Up ahead, its outline picked out by small oil-lamps, was the Vishwanath temple. The roof glistened in the moonlight and the accumulated sheen of the lamps. At the door, what seemed like a million people struggled to kick off their shoes, or to put on their shoes. As the mass of people carrying them along wound its way to the door, Max and the others also stopped, took off their shoes, and handed them to the old priest seated inside the main door. The keeper of the shoes gave no ticket or receipt for the footwear, preferring to rely instead on his prodigious memory, refined over the many years he had been performing this same function. By his side, an armed soldier stood guard. As Imogen and Max entered, the soldier stepped out, blocking their path.

'No. No enter.'

Max stopped, and felt the mass of people behind him come to a reluctant standstill. A silence fell among the pilgrims, as they sensed a drama about to unfold.

'We made arrangements,' offered Max pathetically.

The soldier was not impressed. Just then, Charles appeared from behind them, and spoke in the guard's ear. The crowd seemed to be getting restless, and Max was fearful that they would give up waiting and try to push through. But the soldier listened attentively. This was a moment of decision for him, a chance to exercise his authority or his clemency. A few seconds later, the whole crowd on tenterhooks, the soldier smiled and stepped aside. Charles beckoned the others to follow him as he walked through.

The Vishwanath temple was a warren of rooms and chambers, each housing an effigy or image that had to be honoured. The scent of flowers was overwhelming: so many garlands were thrown over the statues that it was often impossible to see the figure beneath its array of red, pink and white carnations. Orange bouquets floated in the pools of the temple, the sound of tiny hand-bells and the chanting of pilgrims filled every corner. The mystic word 'Om' reverberated from stone to stone. As the line of pilgrims passed through the first chamber, Max and Imogen observed the Hindus and gave a few coins to the priest crouched by the statue of Lord Shiva. He in turn sprinkled their heads with water, and put some nuts and fruit into their hands. Then, pressing his thumb firmly to their foreheads, the priest marked them with crimson spots. Imogen took the blessed food and put it to her forehead, like the Indians. Max did the same. The Hindu pilgrims were all watching the Western intruders, pleased to see them performing the ritual correctly. Then onto the next room, where another priest was ready to honour Lord Vishnu: another offering of coins, more fruit and nuts in return. Here, Imogen stood aside from the stream of people. She wanted to stay awhile, watching the spectacle, not just be swept along with the others. Max observed her covertly from a distance. The lurid light from the oil-lamps made her hair glow a vibrant red, while her skin showed pale in the mass of dark bodies. He smiled at the incongruity. Charles caught his eye and smiled back, appreciatively.

The third chamber was reserved for Lord Krishna. The priest was busy lighting scented sticks for his effigies, so people just threw their coins into the pool by the statue, and took their own share of prashad. Once again, Imogen found an empty space, and took time to observe the supplicants.

'Isn't it amazing, Max? Just think – so few people from outside India have ever seen this.'

Max was overwhelmed by the sight of so many devotees, all engaged in a single act of worship. There was nothing in his experience to prepare him for this, and he began to understand one of the sources of the power of Hinduism. Max looked over to Imogen, lost in her profound fascination. He smiled, and she kissed him on the forehead. There was a certain quality to the kiss that Max had not felt before, something very permanent. Here, amid the chanting Indians, the scent of flowers, the burning joss sticks, the temple bells and the crush of pilgrims, Max felt his love for Imogen change shape. Freed from the turbulence of pursuit, Max was beginning to know his wife. The expression in the wide blue eyes that met his in the warm light was new to him. He no longer wondered if Imogen loved him. He knew.

Through the dim light, the shadows flit past, made beautiful by their devotions. Slowly, the Earth turns. In a warm haze, the sultry light is absorbed.

Pundit Sharma had been the shoe attendant at the Vishwanath temple since he was a boy. He could chart the political and economic changes of the past five decades through the changing quality of the footwear he guarded. Each day, thousands of people passed through the temple, each of them trusting Pundit Sharma to look after their shoes. You could tell a lot about people from their shoes: you could tell the happy from the unhappy, the faithful from the faithless, the good from the evil. Over the years, Pundit Sharma had become an expert at pairing off people with shoes. He never needed any chit or receipt to remember which shoes belonged to whom: to him, shoes were as individual and as distinctive as a face. Reputedly, the pundit had never made a mistake, always returning the right shoes to the right person. His uncanny memory and abilities had become the talk of Varanasi, and it was said that half the people who came to the Vishwanath came there because of his fame. Mischievous children would often tease Pundit Sharma by trying to claim others' shoes, but they could never catch him out. Some sages can see a person's past or future in the palm of a hand: Pundit Sharma could map out a life from a pair of shoes. It was for this reason that the events of that evening so troubled the pundit. And he would have to wait many years before he found the solution to the enigma.

Very few Western visitors came any more to the Vishwanath temple. In the past, Pundit Sharma had loved to handle the heavy brogues of the British officers and their ladies' elegant court shoes. Now, for the few foreigners who got permission, Pundit Sharma had a special place set aside. Of course, the days of hand-made brogues and stitched loafers were gone. Now, much to his disappointment, the foreigners who came usually handed him strange space-age sports shoes.

A creature of habit, Pundit Sharma had put the young foreigners' shoes in his special place. So it was easier than usual for him to find the footwear when the visitors returned from their tour of the temple. As he saw them approach, Pundit Sharma bent down to the corner of the shelves behind him. Charles took his trainers and passed by. Imogen followed, and after a brief struggle in the crowd, managed finally to prise on her walking shoes. Max, having got caught up in the crush, was last.

As he picked up his brogues, a thought crossed his mind. But the pilgrims were pushing through as ever, and the others were already outside, waiting in the narrow passageway. There was no time to think. Max dropped the shoes to the ground, and pushed his feet into the leather. As his feet moulded themselves back into the shoes, he realized what was troubling him. It was dark at the shoe stall, and in the half-light Max felt sure that these were not his shoes. They were the same size, and very similar, uncannily so, but they felt heavier, more expensive than the pair he had handed in. He was still staring down at his feet when Imogen pushed her head round the corner of the great temple door.

'Are you all right, Max?'

'Just hang on a minute. I've got a problem. Can you wait for me?'

'Sure. We'll be right here.'

Max bent down and took off the brogues. They were certainly like his own shoes: the same colour, the same shape, even the same wear on the heels. But he knew they were not his. He could see how easily the mistake had been made. After a few failed attempts, Max succeeded in attracting the attention of Pundit Sharma.

'Excuse me. Excuse me, sir. I think you have made a mistake.'

'Sahib?'

'These are not my shoes. They are very similar to mine, but they are not mine.'

Pundit Sharma was confident he had not made a mistake. He had a very clear recollection of receiving the shoes. The Westerner must be tired, or confused. 'Well, sahib, I will check the shelf.'

The pundit took the shoes from Max's hand, and turned to his special corner once more. 'You say, sahib, that your shoes are similar?'

'Almost the same. But not so new, or expensive.'

The shelf that Pundit Sharma set aside exclusively for the foreign guests was empty – as he had known it would be. He turned back, bringing the brogues with him.

'Will you please look carefully at the shoes, sahib. I think they *are* yours.' Max took another look at the brogues. These were his shoes, but they certainly were not the ones the pundit had taken away with him. Perhaps the old man was trying to cover up his mistake. Max apologized, and took the offered pair. This was no place to argue. After all, he had got his shoes back. Pundit Sharma looked closely at the young man as he struggled to put on the brogues, and smiled. He had not made a mistake.

Max tried to develop some of Imogen's travelling habits, particularly her ability to take advantage of long journeys to catch up on sleep. Unfortunately, he had not quite mastered the art, and spent most of the bus journey to Khajuraho struggling with himself, his eyes tightly shut, floating in and out of a half sleep. The heat was overwhelming, and the diesel fumes from the bus engine made the air thick with oil. By the time they got to Khajuraho, Max was exhausted, filthy, and in no mood to traipse round the town looking for a hotel. So when the bus-driver offered to take them to a hotel run by his uncle, Max was delighted. He no longer cared what sort of hotel it was. He just wanted to clean up, eat some decent food, and go to sleep. As soon as the last passenger had departed from the bus, and the luggage had been cleared from the roof, the driver came back on board, carrying two Campa-Cola bottles. Max offered to pay, but Narinder Singh would have none of it. 'You are now my honoured guests,' he said firmly. 'If I come to England, you will not ask me to pay, will you?'

Max laughed. There was something very innocent and faultless about such Indian logic. As they sipped the warm, sugary liquid that bore a passing resemblance to Coca-Cola, the Indian carefully placed their luggage on the two seats next to them. Settling into the driving seat he had occupied for the last ten hours, Narinder Singh started up the bus once again, and the almost empty vehicle rattled and trundled through the back streets of Khajuraho. The town was full of Indian tourists, wandering about in their best summer suits, eating savoury snacks and Indian sweets as they meandered through the narrow lanes. Almost as soon as the bus left the main street behind, it pulled into a clearing in front of a small hotel, which someone had proudly named The Tempel Garden. A cheap neon sign flashed from the upper balcony, its garish red lighting up the ground every few seconds. Imogen looked doubtfully at the building: it seemed all right in the dark, but the real test would be when they got inside.

'Come in, come in, my very good friends,' said Narinder Singh's uncle, Santa Singh, overflowing with enthusiasm as the young couple entered the lobby, 'so very pleased to see you at our humble hotel.' Max eyed the ebullient proprietor uneasily as a scrawny-looking boy hastily disappeared upstairs with their bags.

'Hang on a minute,' began Max, but it was too late.

'No need to worry, sir,' continued Santa Singh, 'we have the very best room in the hotel for you. The boy will get it ready straight away.'

'How much will it cost us, for two nights?' asked Imogen, ignoring Santa Singh's practised welcome.

'Anything you like to pay will be welcome to us, your humble servants, madam. Anything at all.'

Max hated this refusal to give a straight answer, but Imogen knew exactly how to handle it.

'Okay, we'll pay you 250 rupees for the room.'

'Plus ten per cent tax,' retorted Santa Singh immediately, replacing his servile tone with a businesslike manner but holding his smile.

'Of course,' replied Imogen, having already taken the extra into account.

The negotiations settled, the boy porter reappeared and showed the young English couple to their room. There seemed to be no other guests at the hotel. The stairway leading to the room was covered in dust, the bulbs that lit the dingy passageway hanging on dangerously exposed live wires. Imogen gave a knowing look to Max. The boy reached the designated room, its door still open. A fan hummed briskly from the ceiling, throwing moving shadow-pictures on the walls. The luggage had been placed carefully next to a teak and mirror wardrobe, and the bed had been made up with new sheets. It was not as horrendous as Max had anticipated. There was even a small television, perched precariously on top of the wardrobe, and a telephone, which had once been cream, next to the bed. Most importantly, however, the bathroom seemed clean: a tap dripped periodically into a metal bucket full of water and a plastic mug floated idly on the water line, banging the side of the pail. There was running water then, and a flush. Max pushed down the handle. A reassuring flood poured into the pan, then gurgled to an ominous silence.

'That's fine,' said Imogen, sending away the boy, 'we'll look after ourselves now.' As he disappeared, she shut the heavy wooden door and collapsed onto the bed. Max sat down beside her, and began to take off his soaking, filthy clothes. The bucket of water looked most inviting.

Breakfast at The Tempel Garden was a splendid affair, the hot parathas with omelettes helping to defuse Max's anger. The flush had refused to work after that initial trial, for which it had been specially filled, by hand. The cool, comforting gush of water from the tap the previous evening had given way to a boiling trickle this morning – it had taken them both an hour to have a shower, but they had persisted. Neither the television nor the telephone worked, each appliance being purely cosmetic and not even connected up: the wires just trailed into nothing behind the wardrobe and the bed. Imogen had been far more stoic than Max. After all, they had managed to get a good night's sleep, and breakfast was beginning to revive their flagging bodies and spirits. The cook, yet another wiry boy, brought out fresh parathas as soon as Max and Imogen finished the ones on their plates. As they were polishing off their third omelette, Santa Singh came over to join the couple. Max's heart sank.

'Well, well. I do hope you both had a very enjoyable night,' he began with a perceptible leer. 'If there is any service we can do for you, sir and madam, we are all humbly at your disposal.'

'That's very kind,' replied Max, 'but we are just about to go off to the temples . . .'

'Ah yes, the temples. You know, I can tell you are both a very highly educated and cultured couple. Were you educated in England?'

'Yes,' said Imogen, 'we were both at university there.'

'What a remarkable coincidence,' exclaimed Santa Singh, 'I too was at university in England. I went to Oxford.'

'Oh really?' inquired Max sceptically. 'Which college were you at?'

'I was at Cambridge College,' replied the hotel-keeper, with proud assurance. 'Do you know it?'

'Of course we know it,' said Max, with perfect composure. 'We love Cambridge College, don't we darling?'

Imogen nodded silently, knowing that if she spoke, she would choke.

'You know,' continued Santa Singh, emboldened by the success of his credibility, 'I have had such an exciting life. And I have never been in need of money, because I am a great devotee of the goddess Laxmi. I used to be a manager with the Hilton company. I managed the Hilton in London, and in Paris. Perhaps you have been there?'

'No,' said Max, 'I'm afraid we're not that rich.'

'I know, I know,' laughed Santa Singh, obviously not having heard what Max had said, 'I used to look after royalty at the Hilton. And I was their favourite manager – they would always demand to be looked after by Santa Singh. Then the owner of the Hilton company, he personally asked me to be his manager in Beirut. For some time, it was the best Hilton in the world. But then the war broke out, and I was there, you know, when the hotel was bombed. I met all the famous TV people – your Cindy Gall was there, so was the American Don Rudder. They were all my friends. Some of them come here to see me, you know.'

'We really must get going now,' said Max. 'It'll start getting really hot soon, and we want to make a start on the temples.'

'Yes yes, my friends, you must use your time well in Khajuraho.'

It was quite a task to throw off the tour groups and the day visitors. The temples near the town sported the usual array of hawkers and entrepreneurs. But Imogen had been here before, and knew that the best idea was to hire bikes. As she and Max cycled a few miles out of town, the tour groups died away, only a few enterprising individuals making it out as far as here. Their clothes were drenched once more because of their exertions. Max watched Imogen as she cycled along, her light blue blouse clinging to her breasts, her white cotton skirt rising up with the breeze. Through the light material, he could see her tanned, athletic thighs pumping up and down. As her body shifted left and right on her saddle, Max was reminded of those other times when both their bodies had joined in a shared rhythm. As then, Imogen's face was flushed with the heat, her hair drenched with her efforts, sticking damply to her neck and forehead. The Indian sun had bleached its normal red colour to a strawberry blonde. As it shone in the sun, throwing golden streaks across her face, Max was overpowered by desire for her.

Soon, Max and Imogen had the ancient monuments and sculptures all to themselves. The sun was high in the sky by now, and the sculptures cast strange, intertwining shadows on the ground. Firm, bulbous breasts mingled with luscious thighs, sinuous arms with elegant necks, legs twisting round heads in impossible acrobatic displays. Gymnasts performed sexual antics upside down, their bodies supported by pairs of compliant courtesans. In one, four stocky courtiers and their mates experimented, twisting their bodies into hitherto untried contortions. It was challenging to try to work out which piece belonged to which person, not that these ardent lovers cared, lost as they were in their orgiastic writhings. Another sculpture showed a princess at the moment of orgasm, her face forever frozen in a grimace of pleasure and agony. Her successful lover stared nervously from beneath her, disbelieving his own triumph. Next to them, two slim bodies formed one perfect, petrified union. Like most people, Max had seen photographs of the erotic statues, but nothing could have prepared him for the reality. Two dimensions reduced the passion to a mere frisson; as he looked at the sculpted figures, with their interplay of light and shadow, depth and height, pain and pleasure, Max began to feel the passion trapped within the stones. Already aroused by his own desire for Imogen, he began to breathe erratically, and the base of his stomach contracted in a gentle paroxysm.

Max and Imogen had by now travelled deep into the deserted temples, miles from the town. They were completely alone, lost in the labyrinth of lovers. It was the hottest part of the afternoon. The fire of the sun, the effort of cycling, and for Max the self-control needed to restrain his passion, made them both feel heavy and tired.

'Let's find some shade and have a bite to eat,' said Imogen. 'We could even take a short nap.'

Max smiled and looked around for a shady corner. The temple they stood in must be the last one. Beyond it, nothing but hundreds of miles of dry, baked soil and sand. A burnt tree stood bravely, alone, a few hundred yards away from the ruins, exposed to the full glare of the sun. Huge flies buzzed limply in and out of the stones, settling occasionally on dry-as- dust faeces roasting in the sun. A lost bird flapped nervously on its perch above a statue of Lord Shiva; as Max looked up, the creature gathered its strength and took off. But it did not have the energy to keep airborne: it swooped, and almost crashed into the ground. Only at the last minute did it manage to heave itself a few feet into the air, avoiding disaster. Somewhere nearby, unseen, a pair of dogs barked and squealed with unconvincing savagery, playing or fighting with each other. Heat wafted up from the powdery ground. As he surveyed the landscape, Max noticed a small garden, the grass a mixture of yellow and brown, shaded by the outer wall of the temple. Above the tiny lawn, an alcove in the wall housed a pair of lovers, their bodies twisted round each other, their faces gripped by their ecstasy. It seemed to be the only likely place amongst the ruins to sit down and rest, and it looked out towards the wilderness.

Max was not sure how long they had slept. The sun seemed to be a lot lower and the sting was gone from the heat. A light breeze had come up, forming tiny eddies in the dust. He noticed that Imogen was already awake. She seemed to have been watching him attentively for some time.

'Are you all right?' asked Max, searching for something to say, embarrassed by the thought of someone, even Imogen, watching him sleep.

'Fine.'

The dogs Max had heard earlier were tussling in the dusty soil, beneath the solitary tree. They were fighting earnestly now, rising onto their hind legs, jumping at each other's throats. Their mouths foamed as they tried to get a grip.

'Shall we make a move?' inquired Max, rhetorically.

'Let's stay here awhile, Max.' Imogen stretched out her hand, and placed it firmly round the back of Max's head. Pulling his face gently towards hers, she kissed him, tentatively at first, but then with an increasing assurance.

That night, exhausted by his labours, Srivastava, the court architect, had a strange dream.

He was a long way from his hometown of Alleppey by the sea in Kerala, and, lying awake in his secluded chamber, high in the newly-built fort, Srivastava felt as if he had been away for many months. In fact, it had only been six weeks since the Prince had asked for the master mason to journey to his palace in the hot plains of Madhya Pradesh. The commission had come as a complete surprise to the craftsman, now in his sixtieth year. He had thought that his days as the darling of the Royals had come to an end, but clearly the Prince of Madhya Pradesh had remembered the old man's fame and past glory. Seventy temples had been built at the behest of the new Prince, a remarkable burst of creative energy, making the royal patron of such an enterprise the talk of all the courts from Persia to the kingdom of Siam. Thousands of masons had worked, day and night, ignoring the searing heat of the plains, determined to fulfil the wish of their master. Pillars, some a hundred feet tall, had risen from the sands; fountains and pools of fresh water bubbled through channels baked dry by thousands of years of unrelenting sun; fruit trees flowered where no desert grass had ever dared take root. After three years of application and effort, the chaos had been harnessed.

But the work was not yet complete. Throughout the myriad temples and their outhouses, alcoves had been built, ready to house a pantheon of sculpted gods and goddesses. Design after design had been submitted to the Prince, but none had found his favour. Day in, day out, sculptors from all over India journeyed to the palace to tempt the royal patron with all manner of magical shapes carved from the finest sandalwood, the most translucent marble, the clearest granite. Like a fairy-tale heir rejecting all aspirants for his hand, the Prince turned away the artists. So, in time, the search spread further afield: Persia, China, Siam, even Rome and the great kingdoms of Arabia sent their finest craftsmen, but still the

Prince was not tempted. It was then, when all hope of finding a suitable executor for the commission seemed to be at an end, that one old courtier mentioned the name of Srivastava. Few had ever heard of him, but all had seen his remarkable sculptures adorning the temples and palaces of the great kings. The Prince's own father had often spoken privately of the sculptor, regretting until his dying day that he had not been able to persuade Srivastava to stay on to be the royal artisan of Madhya Pradesh. And so a delegation had made its way to Alleppey, to ask the venerable sculptor to come back with them to the court of his old friend's son.

Srivastava agreed to take on the commission, but refused to submit any designs to the Prince or his courtiers. He would have to spend time amongst the temples, commune with the stones, let them commune with him before he drew up any proposals. For weeks, from dawn till dusk, Srivastava would wander round the new temples, touching their majestic pillars, sitting beneath the shady alcoves, letting the golden sands that covered the floors run through his wrinkled fingers. He waited for the stones to speak to him, utter the secrets of time past and time to come. No one dared to disturb his meditation, yet eager eyes regarded him as he returned to his chamber at sunset. Deep into the night, a tiny oil-lamp would burn in his room. And regularly, each morning, the servants who kept vigil outside his chamber would rush eagerly to their masters at court and report that the old man was, indeed, drawing up intricate plans for the sculptures. In fact, had they bothered to look into his dimly-lit chamber, the guards would have seen the old sculptor sitting motionless at his spartan desk, staring with fixed eyes into nothingness. The inspirations of his youth had gone.

And so it was that this windswept night, his oil-lamp struggling to keep alight, Srivastava decided to accept his destiny, and slept.

All alone in the afternoon heat, with only the fighting dogs for company, Max and Imogen caressed each other with passionate hands. They were soaked in perspiration. The salty taste as they kissed heightened their appetites and as their desire increased, so they became oblivious of their surroundings. As Max unfastened the buttons down the front of Imogen's blouse, she breathed deeply, pressing herself against him. His lips still fastened to hers, Max pulled the shirt off her back, feeling her firm breasts press gently against his chest. He could feel her damp nipples rubbing against his own skin. Holding her face with his hands, Max followed the contours of her chin and neck with his lips, descending slowly, finally taking her hardened nipple into his mouth. Imogen groaned, raising her face upwards to the sky, her eyes firmly closed, feeling the passion surge through her arteries.

Srivastava had never dreamt such visions, even when he was a virile young man. He was back amongst the temples, but the painful heat and sunlight of the desert had given way to a cool amber haze, covering everything with its deep sunset hues. As the craftsman wandered in and out of the sacred halls and courtyards, the stones began to speak. But theirs was not a language of words. Srivastava turned; behind him, a young girl had sighed, yearning with impatience for her lover. As his eyes focused in the soft light, he saw in a distant courtyard two lovers, locked in embrace. The girl's golden hair was swept lightly by the evening breeze as her face, held softly by her partner's hands, stared at the crimson sky, lost in its own passion. Her lover, with an ardent thirst, pressed his lips firmly to her breast, caressing her with an eager tongue. Srivastava stared, transfixed by the image. Who were these lovers, transported by irresistible passions? As he gazed at the couple, a cloud of mist blew through the courtyard, enveloping the young man and his partner. Slowly, it cleared, and the court was empty once more.

Max urged Imogen backwards, pushing her gently with his lips, until she lay back. He stretched out alongside her slim body, his hand caressing her waist, moving softly across her stomach, and up into the cleft between her breasts. Imogen stared willingly into Max's eyes, silenced by the strength of her own desires. As his hand continued its hypnotic massage, his face moved closer to hers, and once more their lips sealed together. Imogen dug her sharp fingernails into Max's neck, pulling his mouth tighter into her own. Max widened the circle of his massage, and his hand began to reach the boundary formed by the waistband of her white cotton skirt. Impatiently, Imogen turned onto her side. Max stroked the small of her back, and pushed his hand further down. The crinkled waistband was tightly fastened, too tight for him to slip his hand beneath it. Dextrously he undid the buttons running down the side of the skirt, one by one, relishing the ritual. As each button gave way, Imogen's breathing quickened in anticipation; the skirt loosened, open at the side down to her thigh. Max ran his hand along her leg, slowing teasingly just beneath her waist, but choosing to continue its upward motion, coming to rest on her breast. He saw Imogen's nostrils widen perceptibly and felt her body shift uneasily from the waist down. A warm, fishy aroma rose into Max's head, making his eyes close in a narcotic trance. He yearned for the taste on his lips.

In his dream, Srivastava walked on, venturing ever further into the outer chambers of the temple. Not a soul stirred. High above his head, a million tiny eyes, forever fixed in the saffron firmament, kept watch as the old sculptor wandered alone amongst the desert sands. He had now reached one of the most ornate halls, desolate and cold without the life that filled it during the waking hours. As Srivastava stepped over the threshold, he heard the impatient touch of a young man's hand caressing his lover. The sculptor stopped and gazed into the deep, orange shadows. There, once more, were the lovers he had seen earlier, now in a new pose, the youth lying alongside his beloved. His hand gently touched her thigh, nervous and hesitant. The mixture of trepidation and impatience and yearning drawn across the young man's face hypnotized Srivastava. Would he ever be able to recapture it in stone? He drank in the frozen image, relishing its every savour, committing each nuance to memory. A moment later, a veil of fine sand swept across the hall, its tiny motes flashing in the shafts of light. And once more, the phantom lovers were gone.

Like Max, Imogen too responded to the smell, and to the sticky dampness between her legs. As she felt Max stir, she moved her body closer to his, letting her skirt slip further, pressing and caressing his erection with her thigh. Imogen moved her hands down to Max's belt, and unfastened it. As the waist eased, she felt for the buttons down the front. One by one she worked her way down, slowly, letting her hand press firmly and deliberately against Max's white cotton shorts. As she loosened the last button, she put her hand inside the opening she had made, found the cut in the boxer shorts, and released him, throbbing with a mixture of pain and ecstasy. She ran her delicate fingers along the ridges and contours, excited by her power to enrage, then soothe. As she felt along the full length, Imogen tightened her grip a little, and grasped Max firmly within her hand, watching his eyes close. She felt a single drop ooze onto her fingers. Instinctively, she rubbed the juice between her finger and thumb, then lifted her hand to her lips. The bitter taste made her body tighten.

As he wandered about the halls on the periphery of the temple, Srivastava thought of his own youth, far away in his hometown by the sea. He too had been a passionate lover in his time, had made women lose themselves in mazes of delight. The sculptor smiled to himself as he recalled the hot lusty days spent in secret caves high above the waters of the Indian Ocean. In his dream, he could almost feel the roar of the incoming waves, smell the froth of the surf, hear the hiss as the water died, and receded. Still contemplating these images, Srivastava walked through an archway, and turned. He had come through six similar arches, each smaller than the one before it. Now, as he looked back along the length of the avenue, he saw at its far end, bathed in light, the young lovers wrapped around each other, their limbs intertwined, so that Srivastava could not ascertain which belonged to the young man, and which to the girl. As they held each other, the dreamer studied the perfect features of the young woman's face. Surely, this was some goddess: only divinity could possess such fair skin, such faultless eyes, such a delicate brow. And only in the imaginations of ancient artists had such magnificent breasts ever taken shape. The girl held her face up to the light, letting her hair fall freely towards the ground. It seemed aflame as the cool sunlight bathed its silken strands. Only the amber granite of the Kashmir caves could possibly capture this fiery crown, thought the sculptor. As he continued to watch, the light grew brighter, until the glare, white hot, blinded the old man. Then it abated, returning once more to its gentle orange, lighting up the shafts of dust in the empty archways.

Max stopped kissing Imogen, and laid his head on her chest, his lips resting open on her breast, his eyes fixed on the gap between her skin and the top of her skirt. He let his hand run slowly down Imogen's body, over her stomach, underneath the open waistband, down the gentle undulation, and onto the small ridge of hair. He lingered there, massaging the soft follicles, running his finger along the boundaries of the v-shaped clump. At the lower end, he could feel that the hair was soaked, and the individual strands clung together in damp knots. The feel of the moisture between his fingers fascinated Max, and he continued to trace the outline of the hair. He could hear Imogen's heart pumping frantically. Its pace quickened as Max allowed his hand to explore further down. The clumps of hair gave way to warm, damp flesh, which retracted with a reflex action upon touch. But the contraction was only momentary. The more Max stroked, the more Imogen relaxed, and the more the juices flowed. His hand was soon bathed in dampness. He looked up, intrigued by the blush rising in Imogen's breasts, the crimson flooding through the pale skin. Imogen put her own hand down beneath her skirt, and gently pushed aside Max's inquisitive fingers. Then, she plunged her fingers into the crevice, covering them with the moisture. Carefully lifting her shining hand out from underneath the white cotton, she rubbed the cream onto Max's erection. Unable to wait any longer, Max moved onto Imogen. He stared for a moment at her usually gentle face, distorted by the force of her passion. Imogen pulled Max into her. He felt the base of his stomach contract deeply, and he let out a deep sigh.

There was no mistaking it that time: Srivastava had not imagined the gasps of the stones. His wanderings had brought him now to the inner courtyards, where the glimmering light of the outer rooms had gradually been replaced by a deeper hue. It was as he entered one of the innermost chambers of the temple that the old sculptor had heard the sigh. He looked about him, searching the shadows for another sight of his playful lovers. The perfect corners of the room cast long, tenebrous streaks across the marble floor, forming a new mosaic unimagined by the craftsmen who had laboured day and night to decorate the halls. Srivastava looked up at the open sky, trying to locate the position of the sun which was giving out such magnificent light. But there was no sun, only a warm glow, spread deeply, casting its reflections upon the temple beneath. Yet the shadows must have a source. Unable to accept the logic of dreams, Srivastava looked down at the floor, calculating the direction of the shafts of lights. Each alcove, each window, seemed to have its own private source, a dozen suns, casting a multitude of shapes onto the holy ground. As he stared at the intricate shadows, Srivastava saw two of the dark outlines merge, and form one. The pattern rotated, and there, before his eyes, Srivastava saw the silhouette of the amorous pair whose presence filled the temple. The virile youth now straddled his partner, their bodies joined beneath the waist, forming one thick tail. At the other end, two chests and two heads blossomed out, two buds from one branch. The old artist beheld the display, all the time imagining the long, slim boulder inside which he would find the image of this union. The shadows merged, and became once more the central pillar of the latticework that criss-crossed the ground.

Max held his whole weight on his outstretched arms, one each side of Imogen's face. Slowly, he found the pulsating entrance, streams of honey running down the passageway. Max pushed himself in, feeling Imogen's muscles tighten, then expand to accommodate him. She pulled him in, closing her eyes with a sharp intake of breath as she felt the dull pain of collision inside her.

The two bodies tumbled together on the dry grass, striving to push ever deeper into each other. Imogen's white skirt was now completely gathered at her waist, her long, tanned legs winding themselves high around Max's back. As he thrust deep and hard, Imogen's legs moved up and down the small of his back. For ten, fifteen minutes, the eager pounding continued, the lovers' breathing keeping pace with the increasing rhythm, perspiration running off their limbs and faces, making it difficult to retain a firm grip. The bodies slithered and slipped on each other: Max could feel Imogen's breasts undulating beneath his chest, her nipples hardening as his torso rubbed them up and down. His legs were burning from the thighs down, his waist caught up in its own automatic gyrations. He could never get deep enough. Imogen felt the body on her quicken in its movements. She closed her eyes and concentrated on the dramatic surge of feelings taking place within her. It was as if a tiny firefly had found its way into her womb, and was now flying rapidly to all the different, most sensitive parts of her body, setting them aflame. The fiery whirlwind was gathering force, scorching its way through Imogen's arteries, into the network of capillaries, into each and every individual cell. She could hear nothing except the frantic sound of their own breathing, and the ebb and flow of blood rushing in waves past her eardrum.

She felt a rising urgency in Max's thrusting. With a soft but determined push from her waist, Imogen eased Max onto his side, their bodies still joined. For a moment they rested, side by side, staring hungrily at each other. Then, in one smooth movement, Imogen pushed Max underneath her, rising to a crouching position above him. From his new vantage point, lying flat on his back, Max could see Imogen's face dripping, almost a silhouette with the sun behind her. He let his eyes wander down, to rest on her flushed breasts, and his hands came up to fondle them, cupping them, then softly massaging the nipples. The gentle movement of his hands brought Imogen back from her reverie. She threw her head back, holding her face up to the sky, and began to rise and fall rhythmically above her lover. Holding her arms tightly by the biceps, Max kept Imogen in position, pushing her up and pulling her down. At one point, she bent her face down to within an inch of him, her eyes staring straight into his. Like a cobra hypnotizing its victim, she held his gaze, her frantic breathing recovering its normal pace, her hair dripping salt water straight onto his forehead and cheeks. Max was deep inside her, as deep as she could possibly pull him in, and he felt her muscles contract around him. He tried to thrust up, but he was already at his limit, so Imogen's whole body shifted upwards. She continued to hold his gaze. Then, without any warning and keeping her upper body as still as possible, Imogen began to thrust from her waist, plunging and pulling long and deep, testing her lover's strength. Max had no choice. Imogen's body pinned him down, her violent undulations preventing any movement on his part. He loved the sensation of being trapped, was excited beyond measure by the strength of Imogen's slender body. Yet he could feel an irresistible stirring inside him. His inability to move heightened the tension, and Max felt totally out of control. At the last minute, as if reading his mind, Imogen stretched back, pulling Max up from the ground, off his back, and falling backwards herself, the two of them forming a wild see-saw. Still they remained joined together. Clutching him towards her, Imogen once more lay back onto the grass, her legs open wide enough to enclose Max within her.

Srivastava had arrived at the deepest chamber of the holy temple, the hall reserved for the most venerated priests, the most enlightened scholars. Here, the amber light of the other chambers had been replaced by a dark blue, the deep cool shade of a summer's day at dusk, just before the monsoon. The room was empty. As the guiding hand of his dream forced the sculptor to enter, a shiver descended his spine, the cold air of the interior enveloping him. Every corner, each crevice, was suffused with the violet rays. The room drew the long-awaited craftsman inside. Almost immediately, Srivastava heard the passion of the couple making love. But where were they? He looked about him for the now familiar sight, but saw nothing, just the perfect, smooth blue walls of the inner sanctum. There was only one alcove in this room, illuminated by a direct pillar of blue light. Instinctively, Srivastava knew that this would be the most challenging of the commissions. The old man was tired, and the pounding he had heard grew louder by degrees, accompanied by occasional gasps and sighs. Perhaps he was already too old for the task. The presage of mortality depressed Srivastava. He sat down on the cold marble floor, glad to rest his weary legs. Leaning back against the wall, the craftsman stared at the alcove, its emptiness accusing him, impatient, mocking the artist's lack of vigour. Although he knew he was dreaming, Srivastava closed his eyes once more, listening to the ever louder pounding. Suddenly, a new noise joined the symphony. Srivastava opened his eyes, and looked over to his left, searching for the dog that had yelped.

The old man was still in the inner chamber, in the midnight desert near the Prince's palace. It was very cold, and the sculptor was beginning to shiver. For a moment, he imagined that the wall he had leaned against was gone and the room he had entered was no more than a derelict shell, the marble of the floor broken into a thousand tiny pieces, grass and sand protruding through the fissures. Was this a tree that had taken root in the corner of the chamber? The old man looked closely at the decrepit trunk, with its geriatric limbs erupting through the ceramic of the floor. His eyes had deceived him – he was beginning to confuse the shadows with reality. Srivastava knew he would have to wake up, knew that he was alone in his bed, knew he was an old man with only imaginings of passion. But he would hold on to his dream a moment longer. And all the time, the sound of two dogs fighting filled his head, mingling with the vehement sighs of the lovers. It was difficult to separate out the frenzied snarling and howling from the orgasmic gasps. Yet, try as he might, Srivastava could not bring the images out of the sounds. He looked about him, scanning each corner of the room, lingering over every shadow, but there appeared neither beast nor lover. The alcove was still there, empty as before. Disappointed, the sculptor let his eyes fall from the arched shelf to the patch of ground at its foot. He must have one more vision, one final image, to furnish that reproachful emptiness. Gradually, as the dreamer fixed his eyes on the empty patch of ground, the pool of light darkened and began to form a shape. The sounds Srivastava heard inside his ears separated: the dogs were now behind him, some ten feet away, in the corner where the imaginary tree had taken root. And the lovers' yearnings? The light had now coalesced into a definite pattern, and there, clearer than ever before, were the lovers Srivastava sought.

Max knew he was being watched. But he often had this feeling when making love to Imogen, and it was never anything more than a figment of his imagination. He was, once again, above her. He could see her perfectly, his own shadow shielding her face from the fierce sun above them. Max bent down and kissed her, searching her mouth with his tongue. Moments later, he pulled away, and let his tongue begin to explore her neck, which Imogen stretched to its full length as she arched her body backwards. She tasted bitter, and the saline savour, coupled with the aroma rising from lower down, quickened Max's desire. As he traced a path with his tongue between her breasts, he slid his whole body down. Over the ridges he continued, sucking the skin until the blood rose to the surface. Imogen held onto Max's shoulders, restraining him. Then she released him, and he worked his way down, pushing his tongue into the crevices formed beneath each breast, then going on to trace intricate invisible patterns on Imogen's stomach. He felt her hands urging him to go lower, but he waited, resting his cheek on her waist. Max closed his eyes, breathing in the juices deeply, feeding on their promise. Then, almost imperceptibly, he began to descend. Max's tongue moved from the smooth surface of Imogen's womb, into a tiny thicket of soft hair. Slowly and deliberately, he licked each strand dry. Eventually, he reached the crevice between his lover's legs and, frantically, Imogen pressed his head into her, twisting strands of his hair in her fingers. With his tongue, Max pushed aside the soft folds of flesh, feeling at last the warm fluid flowing over his lips.

Imogen relaxed. As soon as she relinquished her hold over herself, the tiny disparate fires that the firefly had set alight inside her suddenly gathered force, and exploded. Wave after wave of fire rushed through Imogen's body. She held Max's head down, drawing it in with her thighs. As he sucked deeper and deeper, so Imogen surrendered to the raging within her.

Srivastava felt the dream slipping from him. The image of the lovers was beginning to fade, and he knew that soon he must leave this place and return to the world of his labours. He was satisfied that he now possessed the visions he would sculpt. He turned to leave the hall through the archway he had entered. But something held Srivastava back. On an impulse, the old man turned back again, and keeping his eyes fixed on the empty alcove on the wall, walked over to it. He touched the smooth plaster. It was still soft and supple, and the sculptor's finger left a tiny trench where he had traced it. Srivastava caressed the wet wall softly, as if stroking a delicate animal. As his eyes looked down, he noticed a pebble at its base. Instinctively, he bent down and picked it up. Its sharp point formed a perfect nib with which to inscribe the plaster. Srivastava smoothed the wall with his hand just below the base of the alcove. Here, deliberately, and with a craftsman's practised care, he took the pebble and began to cut the intricate outlines of Sanskrit characters into the stonework. The pebble sliced easily through the smooth skin. One by one the shapes appeared. Srivastava knew that such a liberty with the Prince's temple would be forbidden him in reality, but here, in his sleeping vision, the old man was master. With a steady hand, Srivastava finished off the word that he had been compelled to write. VIDHI. As the sculptor stepped back to examine his handiwork, his lips formed the sound. 'Vidhi,' he whispered silently to himself. Destiny.

Max pushed further and further into the soft flesh. Imogen had begun to convulse gently, pulling him in, then pushing him away in a regular rhythm. Her hands grasped Max firmly, afraid that he might withdraw. He could feel her gasping for breath. But now Imogen pulled him up sharply, guiding his head the full length of her body, forcing him to shift his body awkwardly and rise once more onto her. As he covered her, Max felt Imogen pull his still glistening mouth hungrily onto her own. At the same time, her hand searched lower down, beneath their waists. Gradually, her firm sensitive fingers tightened on Max, guiding him once again inside her. He felt her thighs shuddering against him. Her gasping became desperate, yet she refused to release her lover's mouth. Her heart pounded with a deafening rhythm.

As Max thrust, and thrust again, Imogen rushed to the edge of the precipice, and looked down into the chasms of fire at her feet. Yet she clung for a moment longer. Together, they would plunge into the inferno. Each tiny movement brought Max closer. He felt her waiting for him. Higher and higher he pushed. Still she waited. Finally, Max too could see the edge of the precipice: as he caught sight of the blazing sea beneath the cliff, he rushed forward with a final explosion of energy, grabbed Imogen as she waited on the edge, and leapt into the chasm.

For a moment, the two bodies, fused together on the dusty patch of grass, stopped. All sound ceased. The breeze did not blow, the dust froze. Even the birds, hiding from the sun in shady nooks, arrested their fidgeting. The shadows on the ground, lengthening each second, held their shapes one instant longer. Into the stillness a shot was fired. The noise tore through the silence, and sound rushed back in through the hole in the vacuum. Birds, startled by the explosion, took off, flapping their wings frantically. The sand began its meanderings once more, blown into flurries and eddies by a new wind. The sun continued on its relentless journey, and the shadows lengthened once more.

Imogen felt the surge deep inside her, and screamed silently. Though audible to no human ear, her cry reached every corner of the derelict temple. The carvings, motionless and inert, safe within their alcoves, heard the song, and for a moment their own sculpted passion came to life. As Imogen cried out her satisfaction, an orgiastic ecstasy filled the wilderness of Madhya Pradesh.

Srivastava awoke in his chamber, high above the palace courtyard. For a moment, the screams he had heard in his dream resounded in his ears, and he was unsure whether they had, indeed, been a part of his reveries. The desert winds had died down, and the little oil-lamp now burned strongly, its flame forming a perfect petal. Worried lest he lose the memory of his dreams, Srivastava left his bed, and moved to the table where his parchments lay unmarked, the charcoal unused. Bringing the oil-lamp closer to him, the master craftsman picked up a pristine stick, and began to draw the visions of his sleep.

Max had no recollection of falling asleep. As he awoke, a slight chill made him shiver. The sun was now low in the sky. He pushed himself up onto his elbows, and was relieved to see that he had had the good sense to put his trousers back on after his exertions earlier in the afternoon. He looked over to Imogen. Her mouth was slightly open as she too slumbered deeply. Max straightened her skirt, covering up the streak of thigh that was still exposed, and pulled down the sleeves of her blouse to the wrists. Impulsively, he stroked her damp, untidy hair. The sun had lost its heat, and the breeze carried with it a desert sharpness. Max felt drugged, pacified, deeply tired, but calm. He let his eyes float lazily across the horizon, only taking in a fraction of what he saw. As he surveyed the landscape, Max forgot for a while the stresses of the past few days. For the first time since the self-immolation of the young boy at Varanasi, he felt at peace. Yet something troubled him. Like a half-remembered face, Max knew that something remained unresolved, but could not define the enigma. What was it? Had he forgotten to do something, make some arrangement, say an important thing to Imogen? No, it was more immediate than that. It was to do with the events of the afternoon. He was getting closer, tracking the memory step by step. The recollection of their lovemaking made Max harden once more. No, it was even more recent than that. Something after he had woken up. Something to do with the wilderness. Max's eyes darted at once to the tree beneath which the dogs had fought. So sudden was his glance that his eyes took a few moments to focus on the distance.

There, motionless and pensive, staring directly at Max, was the Englishman.

The elegant figure, still dressed in the familiar cream suit, formed two perfect images inside Max's dark pupils. Max was too shocked to blink. His mind was racing, the blood pounding in his ears. Slowly, keeping his head absolutely still, his eyes fixed on the stranger, Max rose from the ground. The Englishman held his posture. Nothing seemed to disturb him as he contemplated the young couple. Max was not going to lose him this time. He pushed himself up onto his feet, and first crouched, then stood straight. His senses were heightened far beyond their normal capacities. Somewhere behind him, a bird gave a primeval shriek as it took off into the cool air. The rustling of the leaves filled Max's head as if it were a cascading waterfall. But his mind was closed to everything except the sharp image of the figure beneath the tree. Everything else was a murky haze. The light breeze ruffled the Englishman's hair, and made the lapel of his jacket rise for a second. So, thought Max, he is definitely here, he is not a figment of my imagination. The deduction pleased him. He was beginning to get worried that he was seeing things. The stranger persisted with his imperturbable gaze. Max scrutinized the form in the wilderness. On the Englishman's face, unmistakeable now, was a scar Max had only glimpsed before, a gash running the length of the man's face, from ear to chin, along the curve of his jaw. The cheek looked drawn, the wound obviously an old one. Perhaps the Englishman had been in a war? But which one? He was too young to be a Second World War veteran. Max looked straight into the stranger's eyes as he had done before. They were so hypnotic, so familiar. Like a baby, desperately homed in on its mother's eyes, Max held the Englishman's stare. He felt a warm affection flow from the face of the stranger, a recognition, acknowledging a profound emotional affinity.

How on earth the Englishman had managed to arrive at this same remote temple, Max did not even bother to contemplate. His only concern at this moment was to keep the stranger firmly in his sights. Perhaps the solitary traveller was following them? The unsettling thought chastened Max. If that were the case, then he had been totally wrong to try to make contact. That might have encouraged the man – maybe he was dangerous, driven by some perverse desire for Imogen, or even for Max? He must break down the wall of silence. Did this man never speak? The stranger carried with him an intense atmosphere of loss, of tragedy. Was it possible that the tragedy that had saddened his eyes, and driven him to be such a solitary traveller, was preventing him from making new friends? Unaware of his own movement, Max was beginning to draw closer to the Englishman, his feet taking tiny, hesitant steps along the dusty grass leading to the tree. He begged the form not to move, not to leave him once more in the agony of unknowing. He felt that he now knew each line and crevice on the stranger's face, so intently had he stared at it and reflected upon it. Inexplicably, the recognition seemed to come from a deeper source, a more profound recess of Max's memory than simply the apprehensions of the past few weeks. Max edged closer. He wanted to call out to the stranger, but was worried that the sound of his voice might break the spell. The Englishman's presence seemed to be a function of the isolation and silence of this deserted temple. How old was he? It was difficult to tell – he seemed so elegant, so fit, so in command of his person. In his forties, perhaps? Max looked closely at the Englishman's clothes. He loved the colours, the sense of style. This man was clearly a seasoned traveller in the tropics, for he had that enviable ability to remain sharp and clean, even now, towards the end of a hot, dusty afternoon. And even here, standing in the parched wilderness, where everything was covered with a thin film of dust and ash, the Englishman's shoes glistened.

Max was now some twenty feet from the figure, each step bringing him closer. The stranger continued to stare, but now his eyes seemed to bypass Max, fixed as before on the spot the couple had occupied, where Imogen still slept, curled up beneath the erotic statues. Suddenly, and completely unexpectedly, Max felt anger well up within him. What the hell was this stranger doing staring at his wife while she slept? Had he been spying on their lovemaking? It was odd the way he consistently refused to acknowledge Max. Perhaps the stranger would rather that Max were not there at all. He edged a little to his right, trying to come once more into the line of the Englishman's stare, blocking his view of Imogen. The stranger gazed right through him. Stop staring at my wife, thought Max. Just then the breeze blew again, bringing with it a cloud of dust. Max had not blinked for a good minute, and his eyes were stinging unbearably. The dust burned them, but he was determined to keep the Englishman trapped in his gaze. The wind grew stronger, making the branches on the tree creak and bend, like the complaining limbs of some rejected geriatric. Somewhere behind him, Max heard one of the fighting dogs let out a plaintive whine. The dust thickened, ruffling the stranger's hair, and making his jacket flap open. It blew everywhere, spreading its tiny grains of sand into all the alcoves, into each sculpted crevice of the ancient temple. Imogen slept on, seemingly oblivious to the rising whirlwind. Her hair fluttered in the breeze, and the skirt lifted from her thighs. Above her head, the sculptures persisted in their orgiastic display. A small stone crumbled from the alcove, broken off by the wind, and fell with a dull thud a few inches from Imogen's head. As the dust storm gathered pace, Max was having great difficulty keeping the Englishman in his sights. The wafts of sand would diminish the figure momentarily, and then he would emerge once more from the haze, imperturbable as before, his gaze still fixed on Imogen.

'Hello there!' shouted Max, raising his voice above the rush of the desert wind. 'Are you alone?'

A branch broke off the tree, was carried along sideways a few feet, and fell slowly to earth, tumbling through the dirt and the sand. Max tried again.

'I wouldn't stand there too long, if I were you. That tree doesn't look safe to me.'

The stranger still maintained his stony silence. Max sighed. This was impossible.

'Look, I'm only trying to help. What's wrong with you?'

Just then, Max heard a yelp from the direction of the temple, followed by the swift pounding of short legs running along the soft earth. A moment later, out of the corner of his eye, he noticed rapid movement close to the ground. As he turned his head to look properly, Max was terrified to see one of the fighting dogs galloping towards him, scowling and foaming, its eyes rolling wildly, hurtling at unnatural speed. Max froze. His flimsy clothing would offer no protection. Running away was futile. Max's mind was racing, and reality gradually began to assume the mannered movements of slow motion. The dog bounded over the waste ground, step by step. Its staccato barking echoed all around the landscape, reducing the sandstorm to a whisper. The demented creature's mouth left a long streak of foam floating in the air as it flew along, gagging for breath, baring its curved, yellowing teeth. The rush of the wind had slowed. The dust now moved across the landscape in lazy clouds. Imogen was still asleep, as if under some magical spell. Max felt glad the dog had chosen to attack him, not her. But what to do? Perhaps the traveller would help – he must do in this emergency.

Max looked over to the tree, but it was deserted now. Damn, he thought, damn the coward! The dog was only a few seconds away. In desperation, Max rushed to the tree, picked up a branch that had fallen to the foot of the trunk, and turned just in time to see the dog begin its leap towards him. The beast hit Max's shoulder with all its speed, failed to achieve a grip with its jaw, and fell back, dazed. In the same movement, Max swung the branch round, and brought it down as hard as he could onto the dog's head. The creature screamed as its skull cracked, spilling brains onto the dirt and sand. The dog's mangy body continued to convulse and shake for a few moments, then rested motionless. Max was shaking with anger.

The sight of the dead animal pleased him. He had won. Suddenly, and without thinking, Max began to pound the dog's skull with the branch, smashing it again and again, as if to beat it to a pulp. The blood and the cortex oozed out, creating a slimy pool in the sand. In his frenzy of relief, Max failed to notice the appalling stink that emanated from the dog's open head. Again and again he smashed it, until, at last, he felt his arms weaken, and the anger flowed out of his limbs.

Max stood up. He threw the stick as far as he could, then looked over to Imogen. She was watching him. He felt ashamed of his madness, and wondered how much she had witnessed. The last thing he needed now was to have to explain the killing to her. She stood up and walked along the grass path to meet him.

'Was it rabid?' she asked.

'I think so,' answered Max, his disquiet abating as he heard the familiar voice, 'it was really foaming, and looked murderous.'

'Did it bite you at all?'

'No. Luckily it couldn't grab on.' He felt his shoulder, which was turning sore.

'You did it a favour then, putting it out of its misery.'

'I suppose so. Anyway, I expect the vultures will get it now, finish off the job.'

Max put his arm around Imogen's shoulder. She was so sensible, so understanding of one's exact requirements, whether that were words or actions. They both turned back to the tiny plot of land that had been theirs for the afternoon, and picked up their belongings. Imogen remained silent, giving Max time to come down. As he tidied up their possessions, Max ran through in his mind the strange events that had unfolded since he had woken. The Englishman had disappeared pretty quickly, he thought. So much for the caring look Max had imagined he saw in the stranger's eyes. Perhaps he was still around somewhere. He couldn't have gone far in the past ten minutes. Max looked up into the derelict temple. The light was beginning to fade now and the shadows were growing ever longer. The wind swept in and out of the pillars and broken walls, blowing dried grass and leaves into the alcoves. The sculptures continued in their eternal lovemaking, impervious to the declining day. Max looked at the couple just above his head, the sole witnesses, he hoped, to his own passions a few hours earlier. The unfamiliar shapes beneath the alcove mystified him: was this the name of the god or goddess depicted just above? Or a word of worship, perhaps, an ancient incantation? It seemed less well executed than the rest of the artwork, almost as if the sculptor had added it as an afterthought. The weeds had long ago colonized the tiny channels and trenches, obscuring their outlines. Max stepped closer to the wall, and ran his fingers along the carved letters.

He was now only a few inches away from the round, noble face of the courtesan. From here, he could almost feel her orgasmic vigour, hear the frantic gaspings. The apsara's eyes were half closed, transported in a sensual dream as she sucked in her lover's offerings. Max studied her features closely: her razor-sharp nose had been blunted by the elements, but the perfection of her face was still very much in evidence. A heavy necklace of sculpted flowers hung between her spherical breasts, separating the peaks with their intricate petals. Her half-open mouth revealed a set of exquisitely uniform teeth, their shape highlighted by the darkness of the tiny cavern behind them. As Max stared at it, he imagined it opening wider, as the courtesan gave in further to her pleasures. He frowned, momentarily confused. The curve of the lips, the dazed, slanting eyes. The face was shockingly familiar, and exciting. He felt guilty, and glanced back at Imogen, but she was busy tidying her hair and clothes. Max turned to the apsara again, giving himself up to her seductiveness. He saw the lips tremble. They were definitely moving. He edged a little closer. Just then, a large shining centipede emerged from the sculpted mouth, winding its body round the stone teeth and meandering up the left cheek. Max recoiled as the creature eased out, tiny feet scuttling along in unison. It clung onto the courtesan's face, then disappeared round the back of her head, drawn by the scent of food or the inaudible cries of its young in their nest. Max shuddered. Suddenly, he felt it brush his neck. He flinched, and grabbed its head, turning simultaneously. It was Imogen's fingers.

'Hey, relax darling,' she said, softly. 'Come on. Let's get home. We can clean up, and go out for something to eat.'

Max breathed deeply, stepping back from the stone wall, retracing his steps across the undergrowth. 'Imogen,' he said, 'have you any idea what those letters mean?'

'Which letters?'

'There, underneath the statues.'

Imogen stepped closer to the alcove. 'I can't see any letters,' she ventured, after a few seconds.

'Push the creepers aside. They're underneath all those weeds.'

Imogen pulled the tiny plants to one side, curious to find the inscription. As she searched amid the undergrowth, the wall began to come off in a dusty powder in her hand. She could now see the stone beneath the creepers, but still no inscription. 'I really can't find it. What was it?'

'Oh, forget it,' said Max, sensing that Imogen was impatient to get going. 'I suppose it was just a name or something.'

'They often put holy words on these alcoves, as a sign of worship and respect. It was probably that.'

Imogen looked back at the patch of stone she had exposed. The wall was crumbling away, after years of being covered by the foliage. She drew her hand across it once more. There was no inscription there.

The cold evening air made cycling back much easier than the outward journey had been. The breeze began to dry out Max's clothes, and his scalp felt massaged by icy fingers as his hair lost its dampness. The sun had begun to turn a dark orange, hanging low in the sky, like an enormous eye staring out into a crimson landscape. All along the rutted path leading from the ancient temple tiny creatures, drawn out by the balm of the evening, rushed and scuttled. Crickets and cicadas filled the half-light with their electric buzz, passing a billion messages along their private networks of communication. On the horizon, some three miles away, the lights of the town were just beginning to come on.

For all the drama of the afternoon, Max was sorry to be leaving the ancient site. This was the first time he had been alone, really alone, with Imogen for weeks. At least, he thought they had been alone. The Englishman's presence remained a mystery.

'Max, hang on a minute.'

He braked and looked back at Imogen. She had stopped, and was staring at the derelict temple, now a distant tableau, its stone arches and pillars silhouetted against the setting sun. Max pedalled back to join her.

'Isn't it just magnificent?' whispered Imogen.

Max stared at the ruins, still and alone in the vast wilderness. From this distance, the temple looked no more than a decrepit skeleton, like some final outpost before hostile, uncharted territory. Max imagined that he was some intrepid traveller who, having journeyed across the sea of plains, came across the holy relic. Would he ever have guessed that within its crumbling walls and fallen pillars, he would find an orchestra of passion, playing ceaseless symphonies? Max thought of his ecstatic apsara and her proud lover. Who had designed those joyous figures, carved their yearnings, eternalized the all too brief moments of fulfilment? No depressions clouded these lovers' brows. Had the sculptor spied into the private chambers of noblemen with their courtesans, or perhaps they had invited him to witness and immortalize their passion? Where were they now, those royal princes and their playmates? Was it possible that the sand that blew about the ancient ruins, searching out the alcoves and arches, haunting the courtyards, filling every gap and crevice, was made up, grain by grain, of the embers and ashes of those once-vigorous warriors and kings?

Max let his eyes rise up to the sky, to the solitary star that had just begun to shine in the dusk. The goddess of love, he thought, impatient for cover of night.

A gentle whisper broke the silence.

'Max. Promise me something.' Imogen was still gazing at the temple. 'Promise me, Max, that you'll always do something for me.'

'Yes, Imogen.' Strangely, Max felt no curiosity, no impatience to know his lover's demand. It was as if his own inner voice were calling him to a pact.

'Promise me that we'll always come back here, to this temple, to these cities, to India. Promise that we'll always remember the way it was this afternoon.'

'Of course I promise,' said Max. Then, overcome with tenderness, he added, 'If we can afford it, that is. You might have married a penniless artist.'

Imogen smiled, and turned to Max, looking him straight in the eye. 'Whatever happens, Max.'

'What?'

'Promise we'll come back, whatever happens. And if one day we're no longer together, then promise that you'll still come back, alone.'

'What do you mean, if we're no longer together?' Max refused to accept the implication behind Imogen's suggestion. The thought of a life that might not include her made his throat constrict.

'Oh, I don't know,' she said. 'Just . . . if we're no longer together. Promise me.'

'All right, I promise. I don't need promises to make me want to come back here.' He looked at Imogen's trusting eyes, and found it impossible to refuse the pleading. 'I promise,' he said.

Satisfied, Imogen turned back to look one last time at the ruined temple. It was beginning to merge once more into the primeval darkness. Soon it would be gone altogether, and to the casual observer, unaware of its existence, there would be nothing there in the desert, nothing except the chill winds of the wilderness.

The town was buzzing with activity as Max and Imogen arrived back, cycling along the main street, a narrow lane with which the provincial engineering authority was locked in a constant battle. Many times, they had attempted to harden the soft mud with broken stone and concrete, with tarmac, with every conceivable new concoction designed to withstand the elements and the constant traffic of buses, people, animals, carts and bicycles. But whatever they did, however firm the foundations, the desert would devour their new coverings, and the prehistoric mud would reassert its presence, seeping up through the cracks and crevices in the concrete. So now, every few hundred yards, giant cauldrons of pitch-black lava bubbled incessantly, spewing out dense clouds of heavy smoke, filling the whole place with the acrid stench of boiling tar, blinding the workmen and all passers-by, covering everything with a layer of dark, sticky gum. Soon it was impossible to cycle, so Max and Imogen got off their bikes and wheeled them along the street, weaving in and out of the passing crowds. Most of the tourists had left by now, their coaches and planes having departed hours ago, hurtling onwards to the next item on the itinerary. The town was full of native Indians, the only foreign visitors now being a few young backpackers idly lounging in the cafés and dhabbas, smoking bidis, and making strained conversation with the baffled waiters.

The evening passegiata was obviously a thriving tradition in the main thoroughfare of Khajuraho. Young honeymooning couples, wearing the flamboyant new clothes given to them on their wedding day, traipsed up and down the streets, stopping in front of shops selling silver cooking utensils and shining like caves of strange minerals, lit up by flaming kerosene lamps. The businesses were no more than a row of three-sided boxes ranged one next to the other, open at the front, and covered by a flimsy roof made of corrugated plastic running the full length of the street. Yet each shopkeeper had tried to individualize his shack: some had decorated their three walls with colourful pictures of Hindu gods, garlands of saffron flowers hanging down from the top of the frames. Others put up vast photographs of snow-covered vistas in the Himalayas, the expansive landscapes making the tiny units seem less claustrophobic. Inside some, electric fans, driven by car batteries, whirred busily. The more affluent jewellery-sellers even had portable air-conditioning units, the wafts of cold air blowing out into the street and providing a tiny oasis amid the murky atmosphere of tar and heat.

'I think we turn down here,' said Imogen, directing her bicycle towards a narrow opening in the row of shops. Peering into the passageway, Max could see in the distance the flashing neon sign of The Tempel Garden. Just then he heard the strained grinding and whirring of a large bus engine, trying valiantly to heave itself along the sodden mire of the street. Max turned to watch the dilapidated bus, rocking from side to side, struggling like a tired dinosaur along the road. It was almost empty, only a few passengers huddled together near the driver rocking involuntarily, like visitors to a fairground ride. As the bus came closer to them, Max noticed that the driver was their very own Narinder Singh, who had so enthusiastically introduced them to his uncle's hotel. Max waved to him. Catching sight of the young tourist, Narinder Singh brought his vehicle to a halt, the engine revving up in protest. The bus throbbed as its driver opened the door and beckoned to Max and Imogen to get in. He seemed worried, beckoning the visitors into his bus with urgency.

'What about our bikes?' asked Max, shouting over the din of the engine.

'Carry in,' replied Narinder Singh, 'carry in.'

Vaulting off the bus, Narinder Singh stepped over the mud and puddles of water, and grabbed Max's bike. Lifting it easily above his head, he manhandled it onto the bus, returning swiftly to take Imogen's.

'Come, come quickly,' he said to his friends.

'Is everything all right?' asked Imogen as they climbed aboard.

Narinder Singh closed the door, shutting out the din of the engine, climbed into his driver's seat, and the bus began to rock again, making its very slow progress up the street. In their haste, neither Max nor Imogen had bothered to glance at their fellow passengers, so it was with quite a shock that they both heard an Australian man's voice through the darkness.

'Hello,' said the voice, 'are you friends of Narinder Singh and his family?' A tall figure appeared from out of the darkness. 'Sorry to startle you. I'm Stan Dyer. I've been staying out at Suratpur for the past year. Are you just passing through?'

'Yes,' replied Imogen, hesitantly, 'we're only here for a few days. I'm Imogen, and this is my husband, Max. We're from England. We're travelling round India. What's going on? What's all the commotion?'

'Ah, there's been a hell of a fight out at Suratpur. I'm damned glad Narinder was around, I don't mind telling you. This is all the family, you know.' Stan looked at the passengers squashed together on the vinyl seats. 'Anyway, look, I'd better get back to the kids. I'll catch up with you later.'

Struggling to keep his balance inside the moving bus, the Australian wove his way back to where he had been sitting. Around his vacant seat, a batch of young children waited expectantly, giggling excitedly as their handsome friend returned. Narinder Singh turned off into a side road, where the surface was still in some decent state of repair, and the vehicle picked up speed.

'Big trouble,' said Narinder Singh, 'big trouble in villages.'

Max looked at the Indians, crammed into a few seats at the front, despite having all the bus to themselves. They all had their belongings with them, wrapped in bundles of white cloth like enormous cloves of garlic. There were televisions and videos, a large old-fashioned radiogram, a series of tables, paintings, steel cooking utensils, all seemingly salvaged from some terrible disaster. Apart from the children gathered around Stan Dyer, there were other babies, standing or crouched between their mothers' legs. Each one of the passengers gazed at the two new arrivals, their eyes fixed in an expressionless stare.

'This our family,' said Narinder Singh, his arms sweeping the steering-wheel around as he negotiated the intricate labyrinth of streets. 'Their village completely burned, completely burned. Many people killed.'

'But where was this?' asked Imogen.

'Just here, madam, just twenty miles out of city.'

Imogen looked round and caught Max's eye. Before she could say anything more the bus had pulled into the forecourt of The Tempel Garden, and Max saw Santa Singh rush out of the front door. Narinder Singh and his uncle immediately became locked in urgent and extremely loud conversation. Max could make out just a few stray words in the frantic exchange – 'explosion', 'riot', 'madness', 'government', 'police'.

'Come on,' said Imogen, 'let's find out what's going on.'

Squeezing past their bicycles in the aisle, the two of them got off the bus and walked over to the hotel owner and his nephew. For a few moments, the men continued their conversation, ignoring the young visitors. More words emerged from the gush: 'petrol', 'surgery', 'teacher', 'Thank God', 'bomb', 'doctor'. Imogen interrupted the flow.

'Could you please tell us what's wrong,' she said firmly, bringing them both up short.

'Oh yes, my dear miss, yes, yes, yes. So sorry,' said Santa Singh with his characteristic forced civility. Then, turning to his nephew, he delivered a series of orders. Narinder Singh disappeared into the bus and began to lead the passengers off. Imogen noticed how carefully Stan Dyer encouraged the children to move without fuss, joking and laughing with them, keeping their spirits high.

'Terrible tragedy has happened,' continued Santa Singh to Imogen and Max, 'terrible tragedy. Come inside. I will explain.'

The lobby of The Tempel Garden was full of commotion, a stark contrast to the previous evening. The family members were now running up and down the stairs, moving the various bits and pieces into the rooms on the first floor. For a moment, Max thought the whole scene looked like some bizarre package tour, whose managers had not quite mastered the art of organizing large groups. The women were sitting on the rugs on the floor, feeding the babies from their breasts, talking with animation to each other. Narinder Singh and the hotel servers were doing their best to organize the keys to the rooms, giving out complicated directions and rushing to and fro between the reception and the office. Stan was nowhere to be seen.

Santa Singh took Max and Imogen into the dining room, directing them to one of the empty tables. Catching sight of one of the waiters, the owner shouted over to him: 'Two Campa. Jaldi!'

'No, really,' protested Max, 'we don't want . . .'

'Please, I insist,' said Santa Singh, 'you have had a long day. Please, excuse me. I will be back.' Shouting further orders, Santa Singh disappeared into the lobby.

The young waiter brought over two bottles of Campa-Cola, straws bobbing up and down in the frothing brown liquid. The sight of the cold bottles, water condensing on their outsides, revived Max. He thought wistfully of the cool shower and meal that they had promised themselves, but, once more, events seemed to have overtaken them. He saw Imogen look up towards the entrance to the dining room and glanced over his shoulder. Stan Dyer strode into the hall, looking considerably cleaner and fresher than he had done a few minutes previously. He had a rugged handsomeness, the sort of Australian that Englishmen envy and secretly hope their wives and girlfriends will never meet. Hanging loosely on Stan's muscular shoulders was a startlingly white Benetton T-shirt, and around his neck, a leather necklace. Max guessed he must have been in his early thirties.

'He's nice, isn't he?' asked Max, semi-rhetorically.

'Very,' replied Imogen. Then, seeing Max's crestfallen expression, she added, 'A bit too outback for me, though.'

Max looked at Imogen, and they both smiled. Stan had by now reached their table.

'Well,' he said, sitting down, 'I'm sure glad to be here, I don't mind telling you. I thought I was a goner today.' The waiter, having seen the new arrival, brought over another cold Campa. 'Ah, thanks mate,' said Stan, taking out the straw, and lifting the bottle directly to his lips.

'Stan, can you tell us what's going on?' asked Imogen.

'Sure,' said the Australian. 'I'm a teacher – I've been out at Suratpur for about a year now, teaching the local children English. It's a quiet place, Suratpur, no more than a village really. Now, I don't know if you've been in India long enough to know what's been happening here over the past few weeks?'

'You mean this business about the caste quotas?' offered Max.

'Exactly,' said Stan. 'You probably saw the footage of the boy burning himself, oh, just a few days ago?'

Max looked at Imogen, then back to Stan. 'We were actually in Varanasi when it happened.'

So you know how tense the whole thing's become?'

'We do,' said Imogen. 'Was Suratpur to do with the same thing?'

'Afraid so,' continued Stan, 'it's turning into a bloody war.'

Stan had by now finished his bottle of Cola. 'By the way, I don't know about you guys, but I'm absolutely famished. How about we get some food?'

Max was delighted. 'That's a brilliant idea,' he said. 'Why don't we all meet in the lobby about half an hour from now, and we can go to a café in town . . . if that's safe?'

'Ah yeah,' said Stan, 'there'll be no trouble here. Not tonight. They've had their fill. I'll see you in half an hour.'

By the time Stan resumed his story of the events at Suratpur, the three of them had had more than their fill of the bubbling saag and paneer on offer at Kaka's Khajuraho Kafé. The emaciated waiter had cleared away the dirty plates, and had ordered the cook to put tea for three on the boil over his primus stove. Stan took out some bidis tied into a bundle with a piece of string.

'Do you?' he asked.

'No thanks,' said Imogen, looking over to Max as he too shook his head. 'So, Suratpur has been the scene of caste fighting?'

'Sure has,' continued Stan, drawing deeply on the smouldering bidi. 'I suppose they must have come in truckloads. There were about two hundred of them, all high-caste students, from neighbouring villages and towns. It was a massacre, mate, a real massacre. We didn't know what hit us. I was in my room, lying on my bed, when I heard the screaming and crying down in the street. When I looked out, all I could see was hundreds and hundreds of youngsters, running along the alleyways and streets, hitting out at anything and anyone who got in their way. They all had iron bars, and lathis. I saw one young man, no more than twenty, push over an old woman. Her head must have hit the gutter, because when she put her hand to her hair, it was covered in red. But he didn't stop, the bastard. She was a Harijan, of course, the sort that would mean nothing to a high-caste boy like him. They were all chanting: "Kuon chamar hai?" ' Stan paused momentarily, and looked at Max. 'Do you understand Hindi?'

'No, I don't,' answered Max.

'Well, basically all they wanted to know was who was from the lower castes. And anyone who looked low, you know, had a dark skin or wore cheap rags, they would beat the hell out of them, men, women and children. I could see everything from my window, and I got really worried about the school. It's a special place, you see, for underprivileged kids, boys and girls from poor homes. Nobody had been hurt, but I was too late to save the school. The mob had set the whole place on fire, all the tables and chairs, and equipment that the school had built up over years and years. The building was okay, but outside in the playground they'd built a bloody great bonfire. I'd just managed to bring over a TV and video from Sydney for the kids, and they'd shoved that on it. And a French girl who works with us, Béatrice, she had her slide projectors and films all smashed to hell. Some of those kids had sledgehammers – I don't mind telling you, I was bloody terrified. If they'd found out I was helping the lower-caste families, I think they'd have chucked me on the fire as well.'

The waiter came over with the teas. Taking them from the tray, Imogen put the glasses out on the table, one each in front of Stan, Max and herself.

'Ah, thanks,' said Stan, sipping the boiling milky fluid noisily. 'Anyway, I stayed a few minutes, watching the fire. Then I suddenly thought about the local dispensary, run by some Poms who came here years ago. People, mainly Harijans, came from hundreds of miles for the free treatment they offered. I knew they'd be in for it. There were pills and capsules all over the ground, broken bottles, syringes, bandages rolling down the alleyway. They'd pushed over whole shelves full of medicines. God, those things could have saved people's lives. The couple who run the surgery, David and Margot, were trying to salvage whatever they could. This was their whole life's work, torn to bits in a few minutes of madness.'

Imogen's face was pale in the harsh light of the café. 'This has been coming on for years,' she said. 'It's a mess.'

'But why on earth are the high-caste students doing all this?' asked Max. 'I understand they object to quotas and all that, and I suppose I can see why, though I don't agree with them. But what difference does it make to them if you provide education or medical treatment for the Harijans?'

'You'd understand if you were an Indian,' said Stan. Imogen looked over to Max, and nodded in agreement. Stan continued, 'The lower castes, poor buggers, have always been the slaves of the higher castes, serving them, cleaning up after them, tending to their every need, often for nothing more than a small meal a day. They sweep the streets, clean out the lavatories and work in the fields all day for next to nothing. They're not going to do that if they become educated, are they? And medical treatment has always been a privilege in Indian villages. The higher castes resent their inferiors having access to expensive Western drugs and treatments. They have to pay for those benefits, the poor get them free. If we educate the Harijans, make them healthy and strong, who is going to do the dirty jobs? Those high-caste kids hate people like me, or the Poms who run the surgery, because we make their slaves free.'

Stan took another bidi from his bundle and lit up. He stared for a moment at his half-empty glass of tea, then lifted it slowly to his lips, drinking the second half in three or four large gulps.

'Were those kids on the bus from the school?' asked Imogen.

'Yeah, they were. After helping out David and Margot at the dispensary, I went back to the school to see if there was anything I could save. The fire was still burning, but all the mob had cleared off. There was nothing worth keeping. I went into the school building. It was like a bloody bomb had hit the place. I think they'd smashed everything, every last bit of furniture, torn every book, shattered every pane of glass, cracked all the blackboards. As I wandered around the rooms, I was crying inside. It took me a few seconds to realize that there was someone else in the school. I searched the classrooms, and came across Pushpa, one of my second-years, the niece of Narinder Singh. She was hiding in one of the cupboards, crying her heart out. She'd been in the playground when the mob appeared but had the good sense to hide. She was still shaking with fear when I got to her. Anyway, I knew the family well, because they've often invited me to their home to eat. They're one of the richest families in the town, and I admired them for sending their daughter to our school. Also, they had one of the few phones in Suratpur, so whenever I needed to phone home, or people needed to get in touch with me, they'd let me use their telephone. So I took Pushpa home. Her mother had phoned Santa Singh here, at his hotel. She was lucky to get through – a few hours later and they'd have cut down the phone lines. He sent Narinder in his bus. You see, as soon as the students left in their trucks, the Harijans in Suratpur would turn on the higher-caste families in the town. So Pushpa's mother got her servant boy to run round all the family members, asking them to get together at her home by nightfall. By then, Narinder would be there, and they could all make their escape in darkness. And it was she who persuaded me to join them. Béatrice, apparently, was already in Khajuraho. Pushpa's mother thought it would be good for the kids in the family to have their teacher with them. Plus, there was every possibility that I might just get caught in the crossfire. It seemed a sensible thing to do, so here I am.'

The waiter came over of his own accord, and put another three glasses of boiling tea on the table. Looking out at the street in front of Kaka's Khajuraho Kafé, quiet now as the promenaders had returned to their homes, Max could hardly believe the story of rioting and violence barely an hour's drive away.

'What will you do now?' asked Imogen.

'Oh, I'll wait for a few days for the fuss to die down, then I'll go back to Suratpur, and start again. You can't let the bastards grind you down.'

Imogen smiled approvingly. There was a part of her that could imagine herself and Max teaching in a school in some remote Indian village, using their talents where they were really needed.

'Do you think this thing will die down?' asked Max.

'I don't know, mate. Caste's a funny thing. I don't think we'll ever really understand it, not even you Poms with all your class structures. Hindus believe your caste's determined by your actions and thoughts in a previous life. A good life is rewarded by a high caste in your next incarnation, a bad life by untouchability. So, people think the Government's trying to interfere with destiny and they don't like it. Let me give you an example. Suratpur's split into various areas, some for Harijans, others for the higher castes. Most of the high-caste families live in stone houses, with foundations and walls made of brick and plaster. The Harijans live in huts, away from the stone houses. If a Harijan wants even to walk past one of the higher-caste houses, he must take his shoes off. And if a woman from a Harijan family wants to draw water from the local well, a person of high caste must help her. The high-caste person only can touch the bucket, and when the water is poured into the Harijan's container, the well bucket must never come into contact with the poor person's vessel. If it ever does, it would have to be discarded, since to use it would pollute the whole well and the water supply. In most towns, Harijans and higher castes will never eat together. In Suratpur, we only have one tea shop to speak of, so we all have to share it. But the Harijans know what time the high-caste customers will be there, and they're not allowed to come at the same time. The cups and plates they use are kept separately and at a distance from those used by the higher-caste customers. That's what caste really means, in practice, in the towns and villages. And it's been like that for centuries.'

'Just how easy is it to tell someone's caste?' asked Max, appalled by this catalogue of discrimination.

'Oh, to a practised eye, it's like an open book,' continued Stan. 'The colour of men's turbans, the way they're tied, the direction in which you wax your moustache, the special way of tying the dhoti. They're all giveaway signs. Blue is a Brahmin colour. Have you been to Rajasthan?'

'Not this time,' replied Imogen. 'We only got as far as Fatehpur Sikri.'

'Well,' continued Stan, 'when you go to places like Jodhpur, you'll see some of the houses painted blue. Those belong to the Brahmins – only Brahmins are allowed to use blue for their houses. And the same with clothes. Brahmins usually wear saffron; the middle classes, the Bishnoi or the Jats, businessmen and property holders, usually wear white, or red, green, yellow and mustard. Darker colours, coarser cloth and ankle jewellery made of silver always mark out people as low caste. You see, caste is part of the cosmic cycle, the world is only a reflection of a universal order. And anyone who tries to upset it has to be fought, whether it's government or whether it's us foreigners, bringing education and privileges to the Harijans. Of course, most of the time, they leave us alone. The upper castes let us get on with our work, on the basis that, even if the Harijans were to become educated and healthy, they still couldn't rise up out of their lowly positions.'

'Can they rise up at all?' asked Max.

'Oh yes,' continued Stan, 'India's made great strides over the past forty years, since Independence. Not all Harijans are road-sweepers, not all Brahmins are priests or teachers. With modern mobility, many Harijans have made big money in business, and live very well.'

'But their caste remains unchanged . . .' added Imogen. Stan took a last, lingering drag of his bidi and extinguished the stub on the side of the old wooden table. He looked at Max. He knew from experience that people not accustomed to India found the inconsistencies terribly difficult to resolve. But India was full of contradictions. That's how one could love it and hate it at the same time.

Stan's eyes were full of understanding, and affection – just like the Englishman's, thought Max. He wiped aside the errant thought from his mind, and looked down at his glass of tea, then over to Imogen. The waiters were getting impatient at the back of the café.

'I'll settle up here,' said Max, 'I think we should . . .'

'Oh, sure. I hope I haven't bored you.' Stan looked guilty.

'Not at all, Stan,' answered Imogen. 'Look, we're here for another couple of days. Why don't we meet up tomorrow?'

Counting out the rupees at the makeshift counter, Max heard Imogen's suggestion, and felt a pang of jealousy. Stan was quite a raconteur, and Max could tell that Imogen had been spellbound by his charm.

'That's a great idea,' said Max, deciding to be magnanimous as he turned from the counter.

'Actually,' said Stan, 'I don't think it's a good idea for you to hang around here too long. I think the trouble's died down for a bit, but it might erupt again. What are your plans after Khajuraho?'

'We're going to get the plane back to Delhi, then fly on to Trivandrum,' answered Imogen. 'Will there be trouble down there?'

'Oh no, I wouldn't think so, not in the South. They're a more sedate lot down there. Why don't you try to get on the plane tomorrow afternoon? I'm sure there'll be seats, and if there are any problems, I'd be happy to come down to the airport with you and get you on.'

Despite her disappointment, Imogen had to agree that it made sense to play safe. If things did spill over into Khajuraho itself, it might become extremely difficult to get any form of transport out of the city.

It was late into the night. In the frantic rush of the evening, and the excitement at meeting a new friend, Max and Imogen had forgotten their tiredness after the exertions and drama of the afternoon. As they walked back through the deserted alleyways and side streets, Max thought back on the incredible events of the day. The visit to the deserted temple seemed a very long time ago now, the passions of the afternoon, the Englishman, the rabid dog, the cycle ride back, and now all this. Time seemed to have become negotiable here, contracting and expanding to accommodate the experiences of the day.

In the distance, small fires burned in the darkness, precarious assertions of life. The streetlights had gone off now, and the absence of artificial light made the moon stand out like an ivory globe, checkered with veins. Max looked up at the stars. He had never seen such a sky, speckled with silver. He marvelled at the constellations, familiar friends, reposing in unfamiliar positions in this foreign sky. The town and all its intricate temples, the turbulent villages round about, all seemed insignificant under the vastness of the night. Max thought of the thousands of workmen who must have toiled to erect the erotic monuments: were these the same stars, he wondered, these the same eloquent shapes they had seen as they looked up, released at the day's end from their excruciating labours? Max searched for the brightest star in the sky, and eventually found it, low down in the West. That's where their temple would be, he thought, shrouded by the darkness. He could see nothing except a vast blackness, punctuated by the distant blaze of an isolated fire. Perhaps some local people had taken shelter in the temple, away from the noise and turmoil of this tiny metropolis. Max hoped that the temple's new visitors had found the corpse of the dog, and had put it on their bonfire. That would be a decent send-off.

As Max and Imogen undressed beneath the hum of the ceiling fan that night, the lights all over Khajuraho went off simultaneously. There was a momentary burst of exasperation from the late-night cafés, and a shout of frustration from the room next door. In the darkness, the fan slowed, its wings becoming weary, giving in to a sudden attack of exhaustion. A power cut. A fitting end, thought Max, to this highly-charged day.

He went over to the window, pushing open the shutters even further. Outside, deprived of its artificial illuminations, the landscape had rapidly regressed into a pristine stillness and silence. Watching the ancient town with the plains beyond, Max thought how superficial was the veneer of civilization that had been imposed upon the rugged terrain. He imagined once more the carved lovers, safe in their alcove, forever rapt in ecstasy, the passion without motion, the climax without sound. Gradually, as Max gazed out, he saw the darkness punctured by pinpricks of yellow fire as the few remaining dhabba-wallahs brought out their candles and kerosene lamps, reasserting their presence.

Max turned from the window. The light from the moon and stars gave the room an unearthly violet glow. Silently, Imogen had crept into bed, and was stretched out on the crisp white sheets. He walked over and sat next to her, breathing in the sweet, damp warmth that rose from her ivory skin, glimmering in the half-light. Max stretched across, touched Imogen's neck, and gently ran his hand the full length of her body, from shoulder to ankle.

'You're tempting the mosquitoes,' he whispered. Imogen turned from him, silently. He continued his caressing, massaging her back, tracing the sharp shoulderblades and the curve of her spine. Max could sense Imogen's yearning. He slid onto the bed alongside her, pressing his body against hers. Imogen turned, wrapping her arms around him protectively, as he buried his head in her hair. She raised her body slightly, and at once, Max hardened, feeling her thighs part and the dampness against him. He did not need to see her now, having still in his mind the vivid recollections of the day. The shadowy figure he embraced was the same as the wild lover of the afternoon, but now Imogen's limbs felt loose and cool, now she offered herself submissively to his command. As he entered her again, he felt the raw skin wince. Max moved slowly, cautiously, as Imogen forgot her discomfort. She sighed deeply, locked her ankles around his calves and moved with him, reading his mood perfectly. This time, Max held his face just above hers as he released himself. He felt Imogen's breath rush out in a relaxed gasp and her hands tighten around him. For a few lingering moments, Max held his position. Then, reluctantly, he slid down beside her.

At first, Max could only hear the distant, deep buzz of the dragonfly's wings. He opened his eyes, and stared into the still darkness, listening to the monotonous drone as it rose and fell in eddies. His eyes adjusted to the violet gloom, and scanning the room for the intruder, Max became alert to the merest movement. Suddenly, he saw it, its wings shining in the moonlight, its long, elegant body, like a string of precious jewels, catching the shimmer. Max resolved to keep the creature in his sight, following with alert eyes its erratic rise and fall, its sudden darting and hovering. Even in the half-light, he could make out the exotic colours of the dragonfly's head and limbs, its turquoise and jade hues transformed by the nighttime rays. He kept absolutely still, for fear of disturbing its shy progress. It flew about the room, rushing between stations, floating effortlessly for a few moments, then speeding on. Max could feel it approaching, making its way methodically towards him on the bed. He held his breath, not wanting to discourage the timid insect by the slightest movement or sound. From the corner of his eye, Max could see the dragonfly a few feet away, lingering over the dusty television. It darted once more, heading towards the bed, then hovered thoughtfully above Imogen's head. It surveyed the exquisite, finely-crafted landscape beneath its wings, arching its body now and then. The creature was only a few inches from Max. Would it come to him?

Max closed his eyes, and heard the dragonfly's buzz come closer. For a moment, he felt its delicate wings brush his lips. Then the creature was gone, and the room was silent once more.

Two pairs of enormous wings, each a metre long, were revolving high above Max's head. He stared at the busy insect, marvelling at its speed: the wings beat so rapidly, Max could not see the individual leaves, only the perfect circle they created in harmony. Imogen's hair was blowing gently in the cool air given off by the fan, a few fine wisps falling across Max's face, skimming his lips in the morning light.

Max and Imogen were in luck. The plane out of Khajuraho the next afternoon had plenty of spare seats. Stan had come to the airport, just in case, and the young couple had welcomed his reassuring presence. The sun was high in the sky, burning fiercely, a dry, comfortable heat. Walking out onto the tarmac, heading towards the Indian Airlines plane, Max turned to Stan and said:

'Will we see you in London sometime?'

'I don't think so, sport,' answered the Australian, 'my work's out here, and they keep me mighty busy, you know, these ambitious young boys and girls. Really, there's not much for me to do in a big place like London. I'd rather just stay here, and get on with life. I might go back to my folks in Queensland this Christmas, but London? – no, not for me.'

Imogen looked at him enviously. Max knew exactly how she felt. Once India had hypnotized you, the West seemed so false, so inauthentic. Life back home would feel artificial, two-dimensional, a pale shadow of the experience of the subcontinent.

'That's a shame,' she said. 'We would have liked to have had you to stay, shown you around a bit. If you change your mind, don't forget us.'

Stan smiled. 'Hey, I almost forgot. I have a very good friend who lives in Lincoln. I've written her a letter – would you post it to her when you get back to London?' He unclipped the small Filofax he carried. As he took out the envelope, Max noticed the rich array of souvenirs that the Australian carried with him. The wallet was bursting with pieces of torn paper, on which were scribbled, in a variety of different hands, the personal details of other travellers Stan had met. Amidst the batch of filthy rupee notes, and a thin wad of crisp new Australian dollars, Max saw the gleam of a gold American Express card.

'Do they take Amex in Khajuraho?' teased Max.

'What? Ah, the dreaded card,' said Stan. 'My mother gave it to me before I came out. I think she thought it was like being inoculated.' Then, turning to Imogen, Stan handed her the note. 'Thanks for that.'

'It's nothing,' said Imogen, squeezing the letter into her handbag. 'An old girlfriend, no doubt?'

Stan laughed. 'Yeah, my favourite. Would have got hitched up with Vivienne, but she wouldn't come out here. "It's India or me," she said.'

'What did you say?'

'Ah, not much. I was too busy packing.' Max observed the wistful look in Imogen's eyes as she held Stan's stare for a moment. Then, noticing her husband watching her, Imogen looked down hastily.

'Good to have met you, Stan,' said Max, shaking him by the hand. 'Keep up the good work.'

'And you,' replied the Australian. Then, turning to Imogen, he bent down and kissed her, first on one cheek, then the other. 'Look after yourself.'

The noise of the jet engine rose to a whine and Stan moved away. For a moment, as the Australian began to disappear into the haze and the steam spewing out of the jets, Max imagined a much older man walking away, a man he knew well, a man he had been close to, and with whom there was a long-standing emotional bond. Just then, as if he had sensed Max's disquiet, Stan turned to wave a last farewell. Even at this distance their eyes met, and Max felt a sudden and profound premonition pass through him.

The flight to Delhi was terrifying. There were times in the hour-long journey that Max genuinely believed they were all going to die. It was the monsoon season now, and soon after taking off, the plane had plunged into thick black clouds, full of threatening anger. As Max looked out of his window, he could barely see the flashing light at the tip of the wing, so how on earth could the pilot see anything? These air routes were extremely busy, especially coming into Delhi. Mid-air collisions were not unknown; could the on-board computer be trusted? Was it working? Did this old, third-hand Boeing even have one? And just how experienced was the pilot? Max hoped he had been trained in the West. He trusted British and American instruction. The plane was buffeted and rocked by high winds, at times falling suddenly, the engines only slowly recovering their pitch. The other passengers seemed infuriatingly unconcerned by the dire danger they were in. Max alone knew the full extent of it. The young couple in front were far more interested in getting their second packet of peanuts than in the fact that, at any moment, they might all fall from the sky. Even Imogen was deeply engrossed in the newspaper the hostess had handed to her, though Max could not imagine what was so damned interesting in a newspaper at this critical time. The clouds continued to thicken. Suddenly a piercing whistle filled the cabin, making his heart jump. Looking up, he noticed it was just the 'Fasten Seatbelt' sign. Clicking his belt into place, Max turned to Imogen, affecting a strained nonchalance.

'All right, darling?' he asked.

'Fine . . . you?'

'Oh, fine. This weather's a bit rough.'

'Yes,' continued Imogen, looking back to her newspaper, 'hope the plane doesn't fall out of the sky.'

Max clenched his fists silently. He was superstitious and all his latent fears came to the surface at times like this, making him extremely sensitive to remarks tempting fate. Thinking, and worse still, saying evil things sometimes brought them about. He had mentioned it, jokingly in the past, to Imogen, yet she seemed impervious to his caution. He looked back to Imogen, her attention firmly caught by the article she was reading. Max puffed his lungs out till he could feel his ribs. The plane continued its undulations, rising and falling like some jolly dolphin racing along in the water. Surely Indian Airlines had all their planes inspected by Boeing, didn't they? Max looked at the overhead lockers. The cream fibreglass was badly discoloured, and some of the catches were loose, making the doors swing open and shut. Just how old was this wretched machine? Why had they agreed to take this earlier flight? It was all a terrible mistake, escaping the turmoil on the ground, only to die in some unfortunate heap of a plane. Max avoided looking at the woven net bag attached to the back of the seat in front of him. The emergency instructions it contained reminded him of the danger they were in, and, moreover, he had earlier stuffed their *One World* guidebook in between the air-sickness bags and the months-old magazines the netting still held. And in that guide, there was a whole page on the dangers of flying Indian Airlines. This particular section had been written in a flippant style, and the sarcastic phrases now returned to haunt Max. The harder he tried not to look at the book, the more his eyes were drawn to it. Every time he caught sight of the familiar blue and green cover, another of the warnings would ambush him: 'abysmal safety record'; 'flown by bus-drivers'; 'take a spare parachute'; 'standing room only'.

Surely they must be nearing the end of the flight by now. Max looked at his watch. It still told the time of his afternoon visit to Fatehpur Sikri. He knew they should never have trusted Stan. He had been a demon in disguise, his mission being to get Max and Imogen onto this fateful flight. What a way to die.

Max felt each muscle in his body relax as the plane touched down with a jolt at New Delhi. The ground was soaked from a recent downpour, and he could see the metal body of the plane reflected in the thin film of water that still covered the runway. Imogen folded her paper neatly and tucked it into the bag behind the seat in front.

'Well, we made it,' she said, smiling at Max. He smiled back, now overcome with embarrassment at his earlier fears.

'I hope our connecting flight's not delayed,' he said, making a supreme effort to keep his voice from wavering.

'I expect it will be. The weather doesn't look too good. Anyway, we'll make do, even if it is. I wouldn't mind some more time in Delhi.'

Their connecting flight was delayed. In fact, it had been cancelled altogether. Imogen knew something was wrong the moment they located the check-in desk for Flight AI 707 to Trivandrum. Instead of finding the counter flooded, as usual, with eager passengers, fighting for seats, the corner was ominously quiet. As they drew nearer, Max noticed a stark, handwritten note announcing that Flight AI 707 was 'Cancelled Due To Bad Climate'.

They ended up spending the night at Indian Airlines' expense at the Hyatt Regency. Max was delighted. It would give them a chance to recover from the horrors of the facilities at The Tempel Garden and allow them, at least for one night, to call a truce in the constant battle against dirt and dust and temperamental plumbing and electricity. Max needed a rest from all that struggle, the need for constant vigilance: he needed a respite from India. As the glass doors slid together behind them, closing with a hiss, the heat and the noise of India immediately seemed far, far away. Within minutes of entering the lobby of the Hyatt, Max had forgotten the traumas of the world outside. A few more minutes, and he had adjusted back into the frame of mind that takes for granted such luxuries as hygiene, cleanliness, efficiency, courtesy and, most importantly, space. For the first time in weeks, he was not being jostled. He actually had space about him, free from intrusion by curious strangers. The herd mentality was very much a hallmark of India for Max, and it would remain one of his abiding memories. Even when there was plenty of room on a bus or a train, people crowded together, pressing up against each other's bodies, somehow finding solace in the proximity of human flesh. It was as if the sharing of personal space was an act of hospitality, never to be denied lest the stranger feel unwelcome. And by means of this close bonding, a pact was established, reassuring the individual that he was not alone in his struggle against a hostile universe. But for now, Max was relieved at the veritable acres of space he saw about him. This, surely, was the greatest asset of having money in a place like India – it enabled you to buy personal space.

The marble floor of the lobby shone like a mirror. A young boy in red livery, engaged exclusively to polish its jade surface with an electronic broom, marched back and forth, striding along the full length of the hall in dead straight lines, never once veering to avoid an errant guest. If anyone did get in his way, the cleaner chastened them with a shrill, sharp whistle. Max stopped to allow him to pass, then continued on to the reception desk. Here, he and Imogen found the usual crowd that gathered around anyone in authority in India. These minor bureaucrats and organizers were the essential lubricant that oiled the vast machinery of the nation and were placed strategically at bus stations, airports, railway termini, banks, telegraph offices, and at hotel receptions. They were the guardians of travel, communication and rest. And wherever they were found, a crowd of supplicants was sure to gather. But Max and Imogen had both had enough of the constant struggle, and decided to wait until the frantic rush was over. A deep-cushioned sofa facing the reception desk provided the perfect refuge, and from here they both regarded the frenetic scurryings, like two children enthralled by the secret comings and goings of a termite colony.

A few minutes of watching the buzzing heap and Max was lulled into a semi-consciousness into which shadowy characters floated, remained for a few lingering moments, then disappeared, lost forever in the wilderness that existed outside his awareness. His limbs relaxed, and the noises of the hotel lobby receded into the distance, echoing in the marble chamber. Then, all of a sudden, Max was startled into full consciousness. He looked at Imogen, who was leafing casually through an edition of *Vogue*, three months out of date. He turned towards the crowd, and slowly the awareness dawned on him, like a long-forgotten name returning syllable by syllable.

There, at the back of the crowd, fighting to make his way to the reception desk, was the elusive Englishman. Max was instantly alert, shifting onto the edge of the sofa, eager to go over to the stranger and challenge him face to face. This was the first time the Englishman had appeared in such close proximity to other people, and the first in which he was engaged in such mundane activity as fighting through a crowd. On all other occasions he had had a detached air, an aloof disregard of his surroundings, a sense of not really belonging. And his attention had been exclusively upon Max. But now . . . now he was just like any other impatient tourist. It was Max's turn to observe the stranger.

Max could not see the Englishman's face, but the clothes and the demeanour were instantly familiar. His cream summer suit still looked immaculate, and his black brogues caught the shine of the marble floor, their dark gloss contrasting sharply with the light stone. The stranger clutched a small leather holdall, an antique Gladstone bag Max noticed, which he was at great pains to protect as he fought to clear a path to the receptionist. Max knew his chance might not come again. He was angry that his previous efforts to make contact had been thwarted, and he was determined to find out about the Englishman. Now that the stranger was preoccupied, he would not be able to give Max the slip. Gently and with deliberation, anxious not to draw attention to his movements, Max eased himself off the sofa. His eyes were fixed on the figure of the Englishman whose profile barely, and only intermittently, came into view as he jostled through the throng. Max tried to catch sight of the stranger's face but it eluded him, and he had to remain content with a brief, tantalizing glimpse. Slowly, Max walked over to the crowd. The Englishman was fairly well ensconced in the midst of the group by now, but those on the periphery must have seen Max's determined stride, for they parted automatically to let him through. A few moments later, he was standing a few feet from the Englishman, waiting for a suitable pause in order to catch his attention.

'Excuse me,' ventured Max, quietly. His voice barely left his throat.

'Excuse me,' he repeated, more forcefully. This time, engrossed in his own thoughts, Max had misjudged the tone and volume of voice, and the regimental tone brought the whole crowd to silence. In unison, the eager supplicants turned, all eyes searching for the authoritative speaker. Max stared directly at the Englishman and, as he too turned abruptly, found himself inches from the stranger's face.

'Ja, was ist das?' asked the tourist.

'Oh, gosh,' spluttered Max, 'I am most terribly sorry. I thought . . .'

'Ah, you are English?' asked the German.

'Yes. I am sorry. I thought you were somebody I knew.'

'No problem, my friend. You are lost? Can I be of any assistance?'

'No. No, thank you. I'm sorry I disturbed you. Please . . .' Max felt the ridicule of all eyes fixed upon him. The crowd was beginning to close in once again, and he was finding it difficult to breathe. Max was overcome by a desperate desire to escape, to break out of the pressing throng. As he turned, he felt his elbow jab into someone's chest.

It was the house he had grown up in. Max recognized it at once, and felt reassured by the familiar architecture. He pushed open the garden gate, walked up to the front door, but before he had time to put his key to the lock the door opened, and his father welcomed him with a warm embrace.

'Come in, Max. Your mother's just putting lunch on the table. She's made your favourite . . .'

Max walked into the house, and past the staircase he knew so well. The hallway had shrunk. As he passed through, he caught a glimpse of himself in the mirror above the radiator. It was strange to be seeing this particular scene from the full height of a grown man. In this setting, Max always imagined himself to be a child barely four feet tall, just about able to reach the banister, and always finding the mirror tantalizingly out of reach. He walked on into the dining room at the back of the house. There, his mother had laid the table painstakingly, and was putting the finishing touches to the roast, fresh from the oven. Wiping her hands on a towel, she strode over to him, holding out her arms for him.

'Oh, Max. You look wonderful. Now, come and sit straight down, before the food gets cold.' I must just clean my hands before I eat, thought Max. 'Of course, darling. I've put a new towel out, but don't be long. I'll ask your father to start carving.'

As Max climbed the stairs, he could see his mother settle down near the head of the dining table, and hand a plate to his father. His father was glowing with pride and energy, carving the chicken with relish, and chattering away to his mother. Max's eyes were fixed on his parents as he climbed the stairs, so it was only at the very last moment that he noticed the figure standing at the top of the landing. He stopped in his tracks, and felt his spine freeze. That's impossible. I've just left you downstairs with my mother. Max searched the man's face for some tell-tale sign that this was not his father, was in fact an impostor, a phantasm sent to test him.

'Why weren't you here, Max?' Before Max could form any words with his lips, his father had turned and was walking away into one of the bedrooms. The house was freezing up here, and Max could see his own breath condensing. The cold light of a winter evening came in through the net curtains. All the furniture was covered in dust sheets, the light bulbs hung naked. In desperation, Max glanced down the stairs, towards the dining room where his parents were carving the roast. But the house was empty now. A milky mist was rising from the ground, floating a few inches above the carpets. He followed his father into the bedroom. This too was empty, except for the two of them.

'She couldn't hang on any longer, Max. She was convinced you would come.' But I didn't even know. I didn't even say goodbye to her. And what about you, Dad. His father turned away, silently. Max watched in horror as the billowing mist rose up, engulfing his father and obscuring him from view.

For a few moments, Max was not sure where he was. He stared into the darkness, desperately trying to mobilize his memory. The flight, the bus journey, the hotel lobby . . . and this must be the hotel bedroom. But how did he get here? Imogen slept peacefully by his side. As Max slowly came round, he felt the dampness on his cheeks. He put his hand to his face, and realized that the tears of some disturbed dream had broken through. He frowned and reached over, hovering on the edge of consciousness, and touched Imogen's face. Gradually, he began to piece together the events of the past few hours: the hotel lobby, the Englishman, the crowd near the reception. Imogen stirred.

'Ah,' she whispered, still half-asleep, 'you're awake. Are you okay?'

'Yes, I think so. But what's going on. Where are we?'

Imogen switched on the bedside light, making Max flinch for a second.

'We're in the Hyatt. You passed out in the lobby. Quite a scene really – there were porters running in all directions. I suppose it's one way of jumping the queue.'

'Oh, really?' he said, sitting up slowly.

'Hotel doctor said it was just exhaustion and probably lack of good, solid protein. We haven't had any meat for ages.'

Max felt a little foolish, but within him, the merest spark of fear flickered and subsided at once. 'What time is it?'

Imogen glanced over to the digital display on the bedside table. 'Just coming up to six. Our flight's due to leave at nine, depending on the weather. We might as well get up.'

'Come to think of it,' said Max, 'I do feel quite hungry. Why don't we go down for a real luxury breakfast? Make up for all that lack of protein. I'm sure the meat will be fine here in the hotel.'

Imogen smiled, privately relieved that Max was back to normal. 'By the way,' she said, as Max slipped out of bed and made for the bathroom, 'what were you trying to say to that German chap?'

The breakfast room was already bustling with activity by the time Max and Imogen came down. Waiters in crisp white uniforms, some with extravagant crimson turbans, were rushing to and fro, delivering every variety of Western and Indian delicacies. The sizzle of bacon and egg made Max's mouth water. As he and Imogen meandered among the neatly laid tables, they both saw a familiar face.

'Hey, Max,' whispered Imogen conspiratorially, 'there's Rex Fischer.'

'Do we know him?'

'No, silly. Rex Fischer, you know, *Compass* and all that.'

'Of course.' Max finally placed the face. 'Wonder what he's doing here in India?'

'Let's find out,' said Imogen, plotting a path towards Rex Fischer's table.

'Imogen,' hissed Max, 'he's with a colleague. You can't just go up . . .' But it was too late. Imogen was already at the table, and introducing herself.

'I do hope you don't mind my disturbing you like this, Mr Fischer. My husband and I admire your programme immensely, and I've always wanted to meet you.'

'Not at all, my dear, not at all. We're always pleased to meet fans, aren't we Stephen?' Rex Fischer's companion, a balding man of thirty-five, portly verging on obese, nodded approvingly.

'Of course, of course. Why don't you join us? We're just about to order breakfast.'

'Are you sure?'

'We'd be delighted,' added Rex, 'take our minds off work for a bit.'

Rex Fischer was the face of arts broadcasting on British television. His late-night documentary programme *Compass* was still, after ten years, the flagship arts programme across the networks, and Fischer had also achieved a certain notoriety by continuing to champion seventies fashion long after the rest of the world had moved on. His personal life was peppered with just enough scandal to warrant a couple of paragraphs a week in the gossip columns. He was 'the brain with a face', and had once come second in a competition run by *Cosmopolitan* magazine to see who their readers most wanted to seduce.

Max was excited to meet Rex Fischer, and was even now composing the postcard to his parents.

'Are you here on holiday?' asked Fischer as Imogen finished ordering her breakfast.

'Max and I are on our honeymoon. We've both just finished at Oxford, and got married, and here we are. How about you, Mr Fischer? Are you on a project, or research?'

'Please call me Rex. You make me sound like a teacher or something. Stephen's just finished filming a profile of Robert Kean while the great man's been here directing *A Tiger For Malgudi*. I came out last week to do the interview, and a few links.'

'Where were you filming?' asked Max.

'Mainly in Bangalore, some in Ooti,' said Stephen.

'Well away from the troubles, then,' continued Max.

'Oh yes, well away. There was a bit of bother one day on the set: some of the scene-shifters went on strike in sympathy with their Harijan brothers throughout India, but that was all. That's the closest Rex and I've come to the caste war here.'

A waft of freshly ground coffee presaged the arrival of a trolley full of the most delicious-looking breakfast Max had ever seen. As one waiter poured the cups, another distributed the fare as ordered, piping hot on real china plates. Perhaps because of feeling cool in the air-conditioned environment, perhaps because of the security of knowing the food would be safe, this was the first time Max had felt properly hungry since their arrival in India. Imogen could see it was a great effort for him to restrain his appetite sufficiently to engage in polite conversation, so she took the helm.

'I loved that edition on Lawrence you put out for the centenary. It was superb. We all watched it at college, and thought what a brilliant way of portraying literature, mixing scenes from the author's life with extracts from the novels. It really was very compelling . . . made me think whether one could do a series of documentaries like that, all about great writers. Proust, Kafka, Dostoyevsky, Joyce . . . the list is endless. Make a change from just doing *Compass* every week, wouldn't it?

'You know, Rex,' she continued, having given him just enough time to take in her proposal, 'you've got a great talent for presentation, but it really isn't used nearly enough. I don't know about Stephen here, but it seems most of your producers are always looking for ways to minimize your participation in the films, instead of enhancing it. And all those critics who say *Compass* is too soft. Well, a series on great literary figures would be quite a coup, running in the summer perhaps, when *Compass* is off air.'

Max's heart rose into his throat. He had to admire Imogen's nerve. She knew she had no more than fifteen minutes to make her mark, and she was certainly doing that. Telling Rex Fischer that he had a great talent for presentation! It was all or nothing with Imogen. Then came the masterstroke. Having convinced him of her intellectual credentials, Imogen went for Rex's Achilles' heel.

'You know,' she said, lowering her voice to draw Rex closer and exclude the others, 'you've got quite a following in places like Balliol.'

'Oh, really?' asked Rex, immediately alert to the prospect of yet more female admiration.

'Really,' continued Imogen, deliberately avoiding Max's horrified gaze. 'In fact, some of my friends must be leading members of your fan club.' Rex Fischer was hooked. His eyes had a hunter's alertness, and his whole body had straightened. The breakfast was getting cold. Max looked down at his plate, and devoured another piece of toast. Stephen had seen it all before.

'Tell me, Imogen,' inquired Rex, in an intimate tone signalling a touch of conspiracy, 'tell me, what do you and your husband do back in England?'

'Well, we've only just left university. Max has an offer to teach English at St John's in Chiswick, and I – well, I'll be looking for a job in journalism when we get back.'

'Really? Perhaps you and I should meet for tea, or lunch . . . or something when you get back? Give my secretary a call, and we'll fix it up.'

'I'll certainly do that, Rex.' Then, turning to Max, Imogen looked him straight in the eyes and said, 'Max, I hate to hurry you, but I think the coach for our flight is just about to leave. Please do excuse us, Rex, Stephen. We must rush.'

As the young couple rose to leave, Rex Fischer pushed back his chair and also stood, taking Imogen by the hand in a gallant gesture. 'Now, don't forget,' he said, clasping her hand, 'call me when you're back home.' Reluctantly, Stephen too rose from the table.

'What a charming young woman,' said Rex, continuing to stare at the figures making for the lobby exit.

'I thought she was a bit pushy, actually,' mumbled Stephen, jealous that a complete stranger had commanded more attention from Rex in ten minutes than he, Senior Producer of *Compass*, had had in over three weeks of filming.

It was evening by the time the plane finally arrived in Trivandrum. The sky was blood red, and the humidity hit Max like a warm, wet towel as he descended onto the tarmac. The runway had no electric lights. Instead, a series of oil-lamps edged the concrete path, their flames blowing erratically in the light breeze. In the distance, Max could see a lone figure silhouetted against the evening, patiently extinguishing each lamp now that the last flight of the day had come in. Within minutes, both he and Imogen were soaked, their T-shirts clinging to their backs like sodden rags. Even the terminal building, a single Portakabin set back some two hundred yards from the runway, was lit by a dozen kerosene lamps. All its doors were flung wide open, indicating a disappointing lack of air-conditioning.

The plane had only had a dozen passengers on it by the end, most of the Western tourists having got off at Cochin half an hour earlier. The place seemed deserted, desolate. Max looked out across the wilderness stretching all around the runway. The lights of the town burned faintly in the distance, a remote reminder of life. Walking over to the terminal, they were overtaken by a couple of young boys pulling a two-wheeled rickshaw containing the few suitcases and bags just offloaded from the flight. By the time Max and Imogen reached the Portakabin, their luggage was safely placed on the ground, and there was even a taxi-driver standing guard over it.

'Taxi sir?' he asked, as Max bent down to pick up the cases.

'Yes please. We're staying at the Maya Continental.'

The taxi-driver picked up the cases and carried them outside the terminal. As they came out onto the forecourt, Max noticed that he and Imogen were being carefully observed by a row of men, all wearing long cotton lungis, and all marked with the distinctive Hindu trishul on their foreheads, a three-pronged fork, the sign of Lord Vishnu, etched in grey ash. They were all handsome, young and old, slim, their dark skins shining in the dusk, their hair neatly slicked back. A few carefully held bidis up to their lips, sucking on the tiny cigarettes as they squinted through the smoke at the tourist arrivals. Checking that their luggage was safely in the boot, Max got into the car, edging up alongside Imogen. Their soaking backs made the vinyl of the seats wet. With loving care, the taxi-driver opened the front door, slid into his seat, and shut the fragile metal behind him. He had clearly nursed this cab through thick and thin, and he coaxed it into life with slow, delicate gestures. As he turned the ignition, the taxi came to life, its deep vibrations making the dashboard shake, with its amber beads and portraits of Lords Vishnu and Shiva.

The motion of the car let in a refreshing breeze, and Max felt the perspiration begin to dry on his face and back. He looked over to Imogen, staring out into the darkening wilderness. As they left the clearing of the airport approach behind, they seemed to plunge quite suddenly into thick subtropical forest. The highway was bordered on each side with dense vegetation and exotic trees, their huge leaves glistening in the moonlight. The interior seemed impenetrable and Max imagined for a moment the secrets sleeping undiscovered within the forest. Only the car's headlamps provided any light, and Max noticed sudden flurries of movement as unseen creatures shied away into the safety of the darkness. The road was the usual mixture of pits and bumps, but the driver obviously knew it well, slowing down well in advance of any large holes in the tarmac and easing his vehicle through them. Gradually, the forest began to thin out once more, and Max saw a sprinkling of raised wooden shacks float by, first one, then a couple together, then another one. They were all closed up by this time of night, but the faint glow of a kerosene lamp shone here and there through the cracks of the doors and walls. Outside one or two, old men were sitting motionless, watching the taxi rush by. The surface of the road began to improve and soon a few street lights came into view, shining very faintly through the darkness and heat. There, up ahead, was the consoling sight of a busy little bazaar, its tiny yellow and green lamps fighting a losing battle against the overarching darkness of the south Indian sky. Imogen looked at Max and smiled. She too had been concerned at the isolation of the route they had taken from the airport, and suspicious of the driver's resolute silence. But these worries now seemed childish with the return to civilization. Before they reached the bazaar, the cab veered off onto a small driveway to the right. A multi-coloured fountain adorned the forecourt of the hotel, the water spouting like a string of prisms. On either side grew thick clumps of the same exotic trees they had seen in the forest, except that these were shaped and cultivated, their leaves not so wild. A porter opened the taxi door just as the cab came to a halt.

'Welcome to the Maya Continental, sir, madam,' he said, in an accent that had obviously been perfected through constant repetition of the same phrase.

'Thank you,' replied Max. He looked around at the neatly swept forecourt. The light ended where the trees began. Beyond, the mysterious darkness once more. Max gave a handful of crumpled notes to the driver, who took the rupees, folded them into a tight envelope, kissed them, brushed his forehead with them and finally put them away into an inside pocket. 'Please enter,' continued the porter, practising yet another of his set phrases, 'I will follow with the luggage.' His English accent was so perfect Imogen could not restrain a smile.

'I bet he listens to the World Service,' she whispered to Max. The glass doors of the hotel opened to reveal a luxurious oasis of marble, glass and carved wood. At the centre of the lobby, a massive tree grew out of the ground, towering towards the roof some sixty feet up, its enormous leaves spreading like a canopy over the whole of the reception area. The trunk must have been at least fifteen feet in circumference at the base, and some industrious minion obviously had the task of polishing it up to head level every day. It shone like buffed leather, reflecting the lights of the lobby. The reception desk was at the far end, forcing visitors to move round the tree in order to reach it. As they approached the stately trunk, Max looked up into the crown. Some thirty feet up, the light disappeared.

'Ah, Mr and Mrs Burton,' said another graduate of the World Service, 'we were expecting you yesterday evening. But not to worry. We've kept your room for you.'

'That's very kind of you,' replied Imogen, leaning over the reception desk. 'We can see you're extremely busy.' The irony was lost on the receptionist. He simply shook his head from side to side in the classic south Indian gesture of compliance. It was a combination of a shake and a nod, the result being a circular movement reminiscent of toy dogs in the back of cars.

'Would Mr Burton please be kind enough to sign the register, right here?' continued the receptionist, turning the leatherbound ledger towards Max, pointing to a place on the page, and offering him a pen. 'Thank you, sir. This boy will show you to your suite. Have a nice day.'

'Have a nice day?' thought Max. Obviously the receptionist had mistakenly tuned into the Voice of America on one occasion instead of the World Service.

'By the way,' said Max, 'how far is it to the town centre? Can we walk?'

'You *can* walk, sir, but we have a bus that will take you . . .' The receptionist halted, searching for the word. A younger colleague, busy filing some important documents behind him, looked over, his attention caught by the sudden pause in the conversation. Sifting through his mental lexicon, the receptionist still could not call up the appropriate phrase. Just then, observing his friend's dilemma, the filing clerk whispered the magic word to him. His mental block cleared, the receptionist repeated the sentence: 'You *can* walk, sir, but we have a bus that will take you downtown.' The phrase was a triumph, and the receptionist flashed an exuberant smile towards Imogen.

'Very good,' said Max, 'very good. We'll be sure to take the bus downtown tomorrow evening.'

On their way towards the lift, Max and Imogen passed the tree once more and he felt his gaze drawn up again towards the towering canopy. The serenity of the tree was overwhelming. As he felt the warmth of the trunk, and took in the balmy aroma of the foliage, Max imagined he could hear the rush of sap in the tiny capillaries that criss-crossed their way all over the magnificent bark. Its placidity and strength filled him like an anaesthetic spreading slowly through his body. Trapped and imprisoned within an inert environment, the tree seemed isolated, a stranger in an alien territory. Staring at the lush leaves, Max felt a deep disquiet. The spirit of the tree was uneasy.

He lay awake for hours thinking about the tree in the hotel lobby. How odd that something so apparently uncommunicative as a tree could affect one's mood in that way. As Max stared into the darkness of the room, he began to see the silhouette of the large leaves, the perfect almond shapes of the hanging seedlings.

The honeymoon was almost over. He was not altogether sorry: it had been a frantic few weeks, and much of what had happened on their travels still remained undigested within his consciousness.

The first afternoon at Fatehpur Sikri, accompanied by the diligent guardian Raju; the samosa-seller on the road from Agra to Delhi; the ancient temples of Varanasi, overshadowed by the tragedy of the burning boy; the desolate ghats on the banks of the Ganges; the mistaken pair of shoes at the temple; the afternoon at Khajuraho, and the philanthropic Australian; finally, Rex Fischer, an apparition from a world whose existence and reality Max was seriously beginning to doubt. Like reading through an exciting novel too fast, Max knew these things had happened. But he needed time, and private space, to go over certain passages once again. Most of all, he needed the solace of familiar surroundings to try to make sense of the silent stranger who had been following them all over the subcontinent. Max felt he knew the Englishman well by now: the smartly pressed summer suit, the shining brogues, the suntanned skin and the scar on the cheek, suggestive of some exotic and glamorous escapade in some far-distant land. Perhaps the whole thing was no more than an innocent coincidence: after all, when travelling abroad, one often bumped into fellow travellers again and again, since everyone is inevitably drawn to the same sights in roughly the same sort of schedule. But Max knew deep down that such a mundane explanation was inappropriate. The Englishman had definitely been observing him and Imogen most carefully. Even when they had gone to remote locations, off the tourist track, he had appeared. And there was something else, something about his detachment from his immediate surroundings. The Englishman was always a point of stillness amid the turmoil and frenzy of the subcontinent. His troubled demeanour at once attracted and disconcerted Max. And why had Max felt so disinclined to mention the stranger to Imogen? They discussed almost everything else, so why not this as well? He turned towards Imogen as she slept by his side, just making out her face through the darkness, gentle and peaceful in repose. He knew why he had held back. Since the very first time he saw the Englishman, something had stirred within Max. Deep inside himself, he had felt a frisson of recognition, a sense of kinship with the lone traveller. Max knew that the connection between them, whatever it was, went far beyond the chance sightings in India. One thing was certain. For the time being, Imogen would not understand.

At daybreak, Max was woken by a strange, otherworldly chanting, a lone voice singing some ancient hymn in celebration of the new day. He got out of bed and walked over to the window. Pulling aside the curtain, he flinched at the attack of bright sunlight. Their room was two storeys up and the balcony gave onto a sea of lush palm leaves, spreading out like a soft carpet from the hotel building to the road some three hundred yards beyond. One could almost step onto the canopies of foliage, and stride across the meadow outside the hotel. From above, the leaves glistened with sap and swayed gently in the morning breeze, like a slumbering beast, its body expanding and contracting to a primeval rhythm. The singing became louder, and seemed to be coming from above their balcony; Max twisted his body, and looked up towards the hotel roof. There, a small old man, his blackened torso shimmering with perspiration, held his head up towards the rising sun and greeted the god of light with all the energy his spirit could muster. The melody was hypnotic, spreading through the stillness of the morning like an alluring scent. Every now and then, the devotee would open his mouth fully, catching the sun on a row of symmetrical white teeth. The effort of sounding out the dawn hymn was making the old man shake. Max watched him for a few moments, entranced by the singer's concentration, the perfection of his hymn, and the simplicity of his devotion.

In the distance, rising above the trees, Max could see the tall carved tower of the Padmanabhaswamy temple, the eighteenth-century Dravidian shrine dedicated to Lord Vishnu. Even from here, he could make out the intricate sculptures on its monolithic façade, and the groups of golden-haired monkeys performing daring acrobatics between the carved shelves. Many of the turrets that made up the gopuram seemed to have black plants hanging from them. Max thought they must be overgrown weeds until a bunch of the creepers suddenly took flight, disappearing into the trees. They were fruit bats, as large as eagles. As Max looked towards the temple, rising up out of the seascape of foliage, he realized that between him and the shrine there was not a single shred of the present century – no roads, no power lines, no concrete buildings. So, this must have been much as the original commissioners of the temple had seen it, perhaps listening to a similar dawn hymn as now rang out over the horizon. No doubt many of these same trees had been here even then, covering the earth with their impenetrable darkness, the secret refuge of the temple monkeys and fruit bats.

Climbing the steps of the Padmanabhaswamy temple, Max and Imogen squinted up at the complex façade, astonished by the ferocity of the morning sun. The groups crowding into the temple were from all over India, and Max had now become quite adept at spotting the physiological differences between the various subcontinental cultures. The south Indians, dark-skinned and more refined than their northern compatriots, exuded pride in their heritage as direct descendants of the original Dravidian settlers. It was obvious to Max that the townsfolk had very little time for the Aryans of the north, still regarding them as newcomers, invaders with no claim to the holy soil. What the Aryan, Persian and Greek invaders had failed to do, the pilgrims of modern India were achieving slowly but surely. Imogen turned to the *One World* guidebook and read out loud to Max.

' "Trivandrum derives its name from Thiru-Anantha-Puram, home of the serpent, and is believed to be the lair of the sacred snake Anantha . . . the Padmanabhaswamy temple houses the most magnificent statue of Lord Vishnu, reclining on the holy beast, its full length stretching some thirty feet. Hindus come from all over India to this temple . . ." It's traditional dress only inside the temple, Max. We shouldn't really be going in at all, but that note Charles gave us for his friend ought to help. He works at the Ramakrishna Centre. According to the map, it should be round the back.'

Wandering round the side of the temple, Max and Imogen passed a string of open-fronted houses, each no more than a single room, and containing a handful of sinewy men chopping away at large blocks of wood. Max stopped outside one and peered in: the workroom was full of finely-wrought sandalwood carvings of the Hindu deities. The wood-carvers looked up momentarily from their tasks, not stopping the automatic movement of their hands for a second. As Max gazed at them, he felt the sweet, heavy odour of sandalwood rise to his head.

'Those woodworkers must be high all day,' he mumbled.

'Sir!' The foreman had obviously spotted him. 'Please, sir. Come and buy?'

'No. No thank you. Not just yet. We'll be back.'

Max stepped back out of the front of the shop, taking in a deep breath of warm air. Imogen was up ahead. She had found the place she was looking for.

'So, who is this Prabhu?' asked Max, catching up with her.

'He's in charge of groups and special visitors to the temple. Charles said he could get us in.' Imogen stepped through a wooden door to the final unit in the row that lined the eastern side of the temple. Inside, a young priest, his head shaven, sat at a writing desk, engrossed in paperwork. He was wearing a saffron robe, wrapped like a toga round his wiry body; on his feet, a pair of cheap plastic sandals. Max had often seen similar young men at the Hare Krishna temple close to his parents' home, but there was something more authentic about this fledgling priest, despite the mundane and secular task which seemed to be commanding his attentions.

'Excuse me,' ventured Imogen. 'We're looking for Prabhu Guptara.'

The holy office worker turned and looked up from his ledger. He wore a pair of round Lenin spectacles, giving him an intellectual look that, combined with the simple robe, was magnetic. For a moment, the priest looked curiously at Imogen and Max.

'Perhaps he doesn't understand,' suggested Max quietly. Then, in a louder tone, he addressed the Indian. 'Prabhu Guptara? Yes?'

The priest took off his glasses, folded them carefully, packed them away in a small silk case, and stood up from the desk. His slender body stretched up to its full height as he pushed back his chair and strode over to the couple. 'How do you do?' said the Indian, in impeccable English, his voice deep and gentle. 'I'm Prabhu. How may I help you?'

Imogen smiled and looked at Max, his ears already turning bright red. 'Hello,' she said, 'we're friends of Charles Beckett in Varanasi. He might have written to you?'

'You must be Imogen, and Max Burton. Yes, Charles sent a fax about ten days ago.'

Prabhu beckoned the couple into the office, and moved two chairs towards them. 'Will you have some cold drinks?'

'Thank you,' said Imogen. Prabhu looked over to a small door at the back of the room. Suddenly, he raised his voice: 'Bhittu!' A moment later, a small boy peered round the door, noticed the guests, and hurried off in search of Campa-Cola. 'So, how is Charles?'

Imogen smiled. 'Very well. He seems happy here in India.'

'Good. Charles and I have been close friends ever since our schooldays: the Garrison School in Simla is paired with Wellingborough in England, and we used to have boys come over for a couple of terms in the sixth form as an exchange. That's how I first met Charles. I didn't look like this then, of course.' Prabhu looked at Max and smiled. Just then, the assistant returned, delicately carrying a tray in his hands. On it, three ice-cold bottles.

'Thank you, little boy,' said Imogen affectionately as the child offered her the first choice. He acknowledged the memsahib with a sharp nod of the head: someone had told him that this was the way they did things in England, and these were the first real English people he had met. Max was next to be served, then Prabhu.

'Thank you, Bhittu,' said Prabhu. 'So, how long are you in India for?'

'We've been here for three weeks – it's our honeymoon,' explained Max, 'and Trivandrum is the final place on our itinerary. We're leaving the day after tomorrow.'

'So soon?' Prabhu seemed genuinely disappointed. Max got the impression that he quite liked the company of visitors from England. The combination of his cultured tones and his striking appearance was intriguing.

'What made you take up holy orders?'

'And give up everything for this?' Prabhu smiled. 'It's a long story. I'm sure you don't want to hear it.'

'Oh but we do,' said Imogen, hurt by Prabhu's reluctance. 'Look, I'm sure we've got a lot to talk about – we'd love to know more about you, and Charles did make us promise we'd spend time with you.'

Prabhu looked at his watch. Max noticed that it was an antique wristwatch, rather like his own, but apparently functioning well. 'It's almost twelve. Let *me* take you both to lunch?'

'Well . . .' Imogen hesitated, looking at Max. 'Are you sure that's convenient? I mean, what about the office?'

'Oh, we'll only be across the way, at the temple.' Prabhu had already stood up. The decision had been made.

The priest was obviously well respected at the Padmanabhaswamy temple. He had brought Imogen and Max, still wearing their Western clothes, in through a side entrance, and into what looked like a communal kitchen. The heat was almost intolerable: men and women stood over huge metal cauldrons of boiling water, stirring in handfuls of exotic and colourful ingredients. Elsewhere, a line of four women, their sari veils wrapped around their heads, crouched on the ground, patting out small cakes of dough and flattening them with rolling pins to form perfectly round chappatis. Picking these up delicately, the women slapped them from hand to hand before sticking them down onto a row of hot, smoking griddles. Within seconds, the flattened pancakes of flour had risen to form large footballs, full of hot air. As the women flicked these off the griddles, they landed on an ever-increasing pile, deflating slowly as the air inside them cooled.

'Is there some special lunch party?' asked Max.

'No no,' replied Prabhu, nodding and smiling at the women as he led the way, 'all Hindu temples have a kitchen. The locals come and help out at mealtimes. It's like social work. Those who have the money, but no time, donate the ingredients; those who have the time, but no money, come and make the food. It's prashad. Whoever comes to the temple is given prashad, whatever time, day or night.'

The scent from the food was overpowering. The combination of boiling spices was making Max's mouth and eyes water. Prabhu was leading his guests to a room just beyond the kitchen. Near the door an impossibly thin man, stripped to the waist, was stirring a huge wok. In it, a thick milky substance, glutinous like heavy paste, bubbled and moved reluctantly as the wooden ladle cut through it. Suddenly, with a deft flick of the hand, the old man dropped a handful of whole almonds into the smooth porridge. Noticing the young couple's curiosity, the cook smiled, nodding his head in the direction of the wok, inviting them to share. 'That's halwa,' explained Prabhu. 'We'll have some later, after our lunch.'

The room next to the temple kitchen was full of eager pilgrims, all in their dhotis and saris, tucking in to their prashad. The floor had been covered with a clean white sheet, and the Indians were all sitting crouched on the ground, forming almost a dozen straight parallel lines. In front of each pilgrim, a glossy green leaf, the size of a dinner plate, had been spread. Max looked along the lines of visitors: there were four young boys, their strategy perfectly coordinated, walking along the pathways formed between the crouching guests.

The first boy carried a bucket. As he came back down along the line towards them, Max saw that the bucket contained reams of packed green leaves. The boy would pick out one leaf, shake off the water, and place it in front of the pilgrim. Close behind him, the second assistant carried another bucket. Out of this, he spooned a ladle-full of channas onto one corner of the leaf. A few steps behind him, the third boy handed out two chappatis each. Finally, considerably further behind his companions, the fourth server did his duty. From his basket, he spooned out the halwa: this was obviously the most popular of the offerings on the menu. The fourth assistant was straggling because the pilgrims constantly beckoned for second helpings, forcing him to break his regular progression along the line. The whole process was executed in silence. Not a single voice was heard. Serving prashad was serious business. So was eating it. Even the tiny babies, sitting precariously in their allocated spaces next to their parents, were eating conscientiously. At the far entrance, a neat queue of pilgrims waited patiently, the first orderly queue that Max had seen in all his time in India. As one pilgrim finished eating, he would wrap up his dirty leaf carefully, rise from his position in the ranks and take the rubbish to the bin by the door. Seeing the position vacant, the leading member of the queue would walk delicately to it, crouch down, and wait for the train of serving boys to come round again.

'It's quite a set-up,' commented Max, astounded by the efficiency of the production line.

'We try our best to keep it organized, and running smoothly. I always come here for lunch.' Prabhu looked round the hall, occasionally catching someone's eye and bowing respectfully. 'We could go into a small room by ourselves, if you wish,' he continued, looking expectantly at Imogen. 'We've got a proper table and chairs, and plates.'

'I wouldn't dream of it,' replied Imogen. She looked to Max for support.

'I think that family's just about to leave,' Max said. 'Shall we. . . ?'

Prabhu looked over to the front of the queue by the door. The Indian woman at its head acknowledged his unspoken request, and raised her hands together, in respect and in consent. 'We can wash our hands over here,' he said, turning to a small sink at the back of the hall. The plumbing had broken down, but a young girl stood by the sink, scooping up fresh water from a bucket into a small silver urn, then pouring it over the hands of pilgrims waiting to eat, or who had just eaten. The girl became noticeably nervous as Prabhu approached with his foreign guests, but his smile put her at ease, and she resumed her task. As she poured water over Imogen's hands, the girl kept her eyes fixed upon Imogen's face. She was enthralled by the fair skin, and fascinated by Imogen's blue eyes and the smooth shining sweep of golden red hair. Little Parvathi had never been so close to a white person. She took in a deep breath. Parvathi remembered forever the sweet smell of Imogen's skin, closing her eyes tightly at night, trying ever so hard to recall the alluring aroma.

Soon, Prabhu, Max and Imogen sat with the rest of the pilgrims.

'It's a great feeling eating here,' said Prabhu, taking a small mouthful of channas. 'Gives you a sense of perspective, I suppose. We've got our regulars.' Prabhu looked round. 'That old chap over there, in the far corner. His name's Bodidas. He's been coming here every day as long as I've been here, and, according to the halwa cook, a long time before that as well. It's odd: I see him every day, and we eat together, yet I still know so little about him.' Imogen looked over to the diminutive figure all alone, at the end of the line. Prabhu continued, 'I remember one day he didn't show up. My goodness, you should have seen the people in the kitchen. They were so worried, nobody could work properly. We feared something awful had happened to him. In the end, I had to go to look for him. The halwa cook knew roughly where Bodidas lived. So, we packed his lunch in a leaf, and I took a rickshaw out of town. It was evening by the time I found him. I must have had to ask everyone between here and the village. Anyway, I finally got to his home, a small house made of mud. There were quite a few people crowding round the door, so I knew something was wrong. An oil-lamp was on inside. They saw me, and out of respect for my robes, they let me through. Bodidas was inside, sitting on a stool, holding the hand of an old woman lying on a charpai. It was his wife. I thought she must have been ill.' As Prabhu paused, Imogen looked again at the wizened figure, eating slowly from his leaf. Prabhu's voice broke the silence once more. 'She was dead, had passed away that morning. One of the neighbours told me. They had both lived in the village since they were children. Bodidas had married when he was thirteen, his bride was ten. Fifty years they'd been together. That's the only day he missed his meal here.'

Max had stopped eating, and had been listening attentively to Prabhu's story. For some reason, he was suddenly overcome by an overpowering urge to weep. Something about Bodidas' story touched a nerve, had activated a long-forgotten recollection, perhaps of a dream. Listening to Prabhu's narrative, Max knew exactly how Bodidas must have felt that fateful day. In the silence of his own reflections, Max heard a familiar voice. Why did you only listen to the language of the living?

Imogen noticed Max's disquiet and quickly changed the subject. 'Prabhu. You were beginning to tell us how you came to be a Hindu priest.'

'You really do want to know!' Prabhu laughed. 'All right, but let's get some halwa first, before it all goes.' The fourth assistant came over in response to Prabhu's wave. Seeing the three leaves empty, he filled them all with steaming mounds of hot halwa.

'It wasn't something I planned.' Prabhu's eyes were distracted momentarily as the hall began to empty. The lunchtime crush was ending. 'Papa-ji had sent me to Garrison because it was his old school, and it was a family tradition for the boys to go there. It's a beautiful school, set right into the foothills in Simla. Most days, you get a clear view of the Himalayas, across miles and miles of valleys and mountains. I suppose I did quite well to get in. The school is very traditional, and run like an orthodox English public school: we even used to have an assembly every morning, and sing hymns, though very few of us were actually Christians. And there was the usual emphasis on games. I grew faster than the other boys in my year, so I was quite an asset to the rugby team, and cricket was already a great family tradition. Anyway, as I said, the school is twinned with Wellingborough, and every year a group of their sixth-formers would come over to spend a couple of terms with us. I've got a photo here, somewhere, of Charles when he was over at Garrison.'

Prabhu broke off, and took out an old silk wallet from under his robe. He handed the photograph to Max. Imogen leaned over to see it. It had obviously been taken during the celebrations of a great Garrison victory over rival schools. A group of slim young men, all dark-haired, their olive skins shining with perspiration, posed triumphantly for the camera. Their blue-striped kit hung damply off their shoulders. Some had heavy white sweaters wrapped round their necks. In the middle, carrying a large silver cup, stood Prabhu and Charles, holding one handle each. Imogen peered closely at the picture. Prabhu wore a light blazer over his sports gear, and his hair was slicked back, as if recently combed after a shower. The distinctive smile was evident even here. Charles held himself with his usual coolness, his face in a half-smile.

'You were captain of your eleven, then?' asked Imogen.

'Yes, but still not half as good a batsman as Charles. He was the one who really won the cup for us that year.' One of the young serving boys came over, and took the dirty leaves from the ground in front of them. Prabhu thanked him, then continued. 'Charles has been a real friend from the beginning. When he came to Simla, he must have been about sixteen, just in the second term of the sixth form. Well, as always happened, the Garrison boys were really hostile to the Welburnians at first, testing them out and so on. It was all part of the ritual, and I was as much a part of it as anyone else. The English boys took it really well, and paid us back in kind! Charles was the best of the lot, always game, always on top form. Even then, he was so strong, so composed and self-assured. I took to him straightaway, and we became quite close, very quickly.' Prabhu paused, looked up, and caught Max's eye. The Indian smiled discreetly. 'Some of the older boys, the third-year sixth-formers, used to get at me about it, thought it was unnatural, or disloyal, or something, for a Garrisonite to associate so closely with one of the exchangers. I ignored it at first, but soon it became very clear to me that underneath the superficial fraternity of the two schools, there was a deep-seated and mutual distrust. Charles got it too, you know, from the other Welburnians. It wasn't quite their idea of what the exchange should be, letting the side down and so on. Still, I wasn't going to let it affect my friendship with Charles, and nor was he. And the more we ignored the snide remarks and the sarcastic attacks, the more it got to them. This went on for weeks, then, one day, some of the prefects got together and decided to give me thanda.' Prabhu noticed the look of mystification on the faces of his guests. 'It's another great Garrison tradition. Everyone has it given to them sometime whilst they're there. I'd been lucky to escape it for so long. Thanda: the chill. It's a sort of punishment: you're turfed out of bed first thing, made to take a cold shower, then, still dripping wet, and wearing nothing but a pair of shorts, you have to run round the rugby pitch five times.'

Max felt a chill streak through his spine just at the thought of it. 'And this is what you had to do?' he asked incredulously.

'It does get really cold up there, especially in the winter term,' continued Prabhu. 'The wind blows straight down from the Himalayas. But once you're in for thanda, there's no getting out of it. Anyway, they came up with some pathetic excuse for giving me thanda: I forgot to wear my gown one night to dinner, and apparently, this was the third time I'd committed the same offence, so they sconced me. They fixed on that weekend.

'As luck would have it, it was really cold that Sunday morning. Everyone knew, so all the boys were up at the crack of dawn, wrapped up in woollen scarves and dressing gowns, staring out of the bedroom windows. As I left School House, I looked round, trying to catch a glimpse of Charles, but he wasn't at his window. I was glad. I didn't want him to see me like this. It might have made him think our friendship wasn't worth it after all. The walk to the sports pavilion seemed to take hours. The three prefects in charge were deliberately dawdling, making me even colder. I got doused with freezing water in the shower room, then I walked back out onto the pitch.

'The cold air went through me like a razor. The boys all cheered, waving their scarves out of their windows. Gasping for breath, I set off, as fast as I could, trying desperately to warm up. I made the first turn in record time. I felt the water begin to dry off, like ice all over me. My hair was turning solid. Then the second turn. I'd just passed the front of School House on my first circuit, when I heard another cheer go up. I thought the boys were shouting for me, and I quickened my pace. Just then, I felt someone else edge up by my side, rushing up to catch me, then easing off to match my pace. He too was stripped to the waist. It was Charles.

'He mumbled something to me as we ran together, but I was too moved by his sudden appearance to hear the words. Charles kept pace with me for the rest of the run.'

Prabhu stopped, lost for a few moments in his own recollections. The dining room was almost empty now: even the young boys had disappeared, no doubt having their own share in the kitchen. It was strange how silent the room had become. As Prabhu paused, the distant buzzing of a fly took over, a thin crack in the warm silence. 'What had been a punishment turned into a triumph. Everybody in the school got to hear about it, even people in the other public schools round about.'

Prabhu looked up as a late arrival for lunch nodded respectfully to him. Prabhu smiled back, then resumed his story. 'No one ever criticized us for our friendship again.'

For a moment, silence filled the room once more, broken only by the droning of the persistent bluebottle. The reverie was interrupted by the sudden sound of temple bells wafting in through the open door. Imogen looked at her watch, amazed that almost an hour had gone by.

'I'm glad Charles is here now,' continued Prabhu. 'We get together about once a year, go on a tour of some far-flung state. It's quite an experience for us both. I think there are people all over India still puzzled by the wandering priest and his English friend!'

'So how did you come to take up holy orders?' asked Max.

'Well, I'm only a novice, a sort of freshman priest, I suppose,' answered Prabhu thoughtfully, his gaze held on the distant passing of pilgrims seen through the open doorway. 'I have to admit it's still a bit of a surprise to me. Taking sanayass is not uncommon in India: some people, usually older people, once they've brought up their families, give up everything and become sanayassins. It's a form of renunciation, a sort of preparation for the next life. What *is* unusual is for someone my age to take sanayass. After I finished at Garrison, I went on to the university at Bangalore to study philosophy. In fact, sometimes I still wake up alone at night, and wonder whether all this has been a bizarre dream, and that I'm still back in my digs at Bangalore, waiting to take Finals! Once again, Charles was a major factor in my decision. After he went back to

94

Wellingborough, we kept in touch, and then later, when Charles was at Oxford, I went over to stay with him for a few weeks one Christmas. But mainly, Charles would come over to us, in India, drawn back almost every summer vac by his affection for the country, and for my family. And it was with Charles that I first really saw India, saw it for what it truly is.

'You see, my parents and most of my family are pretty well off. We've got houses all over India, and I suppose I had, technically, seen most of India by the time I was eighteen. But in fact, I had only seen one side of it, the side my parents had allowed me to see. There's a great tendency for Indians, once they've made it, to cut themselves off from the reality of life around them. They work hard for their wealth, and once they've acquired it, the first thing they want to do is to buy themselves barriers against the outside world. Not all wealthy families are like that, but that's what I grew up with: Papa-ji and Mama thought the best they could give me included protecting me from the harsh reality that is India. And I would have gone on quite happily, living in my own cocoon, safe in the knowledge that we had enough wealth to keep us going for the next century. As I say, it was Charles who helped me see the light, so to speak.'

Prabhu looked at Imogen, mindful of her absolute concentration. The dining hall had emptied completely now, and the temple bells had become silent. The stillness of the afternoon siesta had descended like a mist on the Padmanabhaswamy temple.

'It was the summer after Finals. I'd taken mine at Bangalore, and Charles had finished at Oxford. As usual, he'd got on the first flight out to India. But things were different this time. Whereas before, we'd both been happy just to lounge around, having a good time, now Charles yearned for a different kind of experience. So we spent the whole summer travelling around India the cheapest way we could. It was a real revelation. It wasn't so much what I saw that changed me. I wasn't naïve. No, what changed me was the way people treated me. After a few days on the road, Charles and I lost our glossy, clean looks. I learnt to bargain, to shove and push for seats on trains, to argue with officious ticket-sellers, to keep going all day on a single paratha. Most of all, I learnt about myself. That summer Charles and I went round India, when no one we met knew anything about us, that was the happiest I'd ever been. Sure, the poverty was devastating – we were both really shaken sometimes. It was as much as I could do to stop Charles giving away all we had! But I think we must have met more happy people in those weeks than in all my time at Garrison, in England, or in Bangalore.

'When you've got very little in the world, you've also got very little to worry about. I'm not talking about the people who're starving. They've got plenty to worry about, and their plight is a reproach to all of us. But there *is* a certain freedom there, on the streets, a liberty that you or I will never have. You see, those people live in an eternal present. Yesterday holds no great memories, tomorrow promises no great hopes, or fears. Each day is a new beginning, each night another conclusion. And that isn't just an excuse for rich people to ignore the suffering of the poor. For them, each day really is more like a stepping stone, a short resting space on the journey we're all making.

'And the same is true on a larger scale. Reincarnation's a great recipe for stoicism. For most people here, life's a phase, part of a cycle lasting millions and millions of years. The thoughts and actions of this phase will affect the next, might even create the next, but life, like time, is limitless. Each session teaches us valuable lessons, which we carry with us to the next life. And so we go on, from century to century, learning all the time, in preparation for the moment when we'll be one with God. No experience is redundant: so this time, you're a pauper, you pulled the short straw, but we all have to pass through this session, as we all have to learn how to handle wealth, or power. You decide the order of the lessons, and the speed at which you learn.' Prabhu paused, to gather his thoughts.

'You make it sound so simple,' interjected Imogen, 'as if life is some sort of academy to graduate from.'

'That's quite a good way of putting it,' said Prabhu, 'there's no reason why it shouldn't be just as simple as that. After all, our human institutions are but a distant recollection of systems deep in our cosmic memory.'

'So, this cultural experience made you want to give up everything and become a priest?' asked Max.

'Well, I didn't really give up everything. I knew then that my destiny was here, amongst the people, not in some ancient college in Bangalore. So I decided to take sanayass. A close friend of ours was one of the main benefactors of the Ramakrishna centres throughout India. He arranged for me to enter a theological training college in Varanasi, and I did a special six-month course in practical Hinduism. My degree from Bangalore helped me avoid most of the theoretical stuff. I'm here in Trivandrum as my first posting away from base.'

'And are you happy?' asked Imogen. 'Has it turned out to be as you expected?'

'It's very challenging. You see, the movement believes in the practical application of Hindu values. I came to Kerala partly as a priest, but mainly as a teacher. Health care, education, this is what India needs. Religion is nothing without practicality.' The door leading to the kitchen had opened a few inches, just enough to let in Bhittu, Prabhu's assistant. As Max looked up, he saw the little boy treading tentatively towards them.

'I think you might be needed,' said Max to Prabhu.

Prabhu looked towards Bhittu. 'Oh, yes, of course. I am sorry,' said Prabhu, turning to Max and Imogen, 'I became so engaged in our talk. Please excuse me. I have a colleague I must attend to.'

Max, Imogen and Prabhu rose to their feet simultaneously.

'I do hope we haven't detained you too long?' asked Imogen.

'No, no. It's a great pleasure to meet you. But listen, you must want to see inside the temple?'

'That was our hope,' said Imogen.

'Can you come back tomorrow afternoon, say at six? Most of the daytime pilgrims will have gone by then, and I can take you both round the temple myself.'

'Wonderful,' said Imogen, 'thank you. We'll see you then.'

'Excellent, excellent.' Prabhu too seemed enthused by the plan. 'Now, if you'll excuse me, Bhittu will show you the best way out of the grounds.'

Max and Imogen spent the rest of the day at Kovalam beach.

The Ashoka five-star hotel stood at the centre of the resort, dividing the three-mile-long beach in two. On its far side, dozens of thatched bungalows, all air-conditioned, belonging to the hotel and lining a private beach; on the near side, terraces of spartan huts, no electricity, no water, ranged along a beach bursting with sun-worshippers. The hotel building itself acted as a physical barrier between the two sectors and the Ashoka management employed two starched and overdressed Sikhs to protect the exclusivity of the hotel sands. The only traffic between the beaches was the coming and going of dark-skinned boys and pencil-thin girls selling brightly-coloured lungis and kites, fresh pineapples and mangoes. From one end of the beach to the other, along the three miles of sands, the races and classes of Europe stretched out in all their diversity. And the native children had been quick to refine their entrepreneurial skills.

Young Sinappu had been selling lungis along Kovalam beach ever since the foreigners began arriving, a few weeks after the construction of the airport at Trivandrum. At first, he charged three rupees for the skirts, nothing to the Europeans but a fortune to the young boy, for whom it represented a two hundred per cent profit. But now the story was very different.

Sinappu began his sales trek at twelve, by which time most of the sunbathers were out. He started at one end of the beach, the end with the terraced huts. Here, the men and women were pale, and quite overweight. When they first arrived on the beach, Sinappu noticed that they all, invariably, came wearing far too many clothes, as if they were going on an expedition into the jungle. The next morning, however, the men and their women were transformed, appearing on the beach in garishly coloured swimwear: the women in swimsuits, the men in shiny football shorts. A number of them were clearly very proud of their nationality: they had bought shorts in the colours of their national flag. One of the tourists told him it was called the Union Jack. Sinappu marketed his lungis gently here, charging only five rupees: most of the newcomers bought one, and most of them gave him a few rupees extra.

A few hundred yards further along, the sunbathers were of a very different sort: the men and women were usually all blonde, and had much slimmer bodies. They didn't eat or drink as much as the British, but preferred instead to smoke their strange-looking bidis. And they slept more than the others, so Sinappu had to time his sales pitch accurately. He charged the Germans and the Scandinavians seven rupees for each lungi, but asked first for ten, knowing that they had guidebooks that advised them to bargain. He only ever got the exact amount, and they always insisted on their change. Then came the big rocks that Sinappu had been frightened of ever since he was a baby. They formed a small hill on the beach, and were dark and hostile. On one side, in paint that was obviously dripping furiously, someone had written a warning in red: SNAKES! Sinappu took a long route around the rocks, keeping his eyes firmly fixed on the darker hollows. He had never actually seen a snake emerge from the caverns of the tiny mountain, but he knew people who had, and a mere mortal like him would stand no chance.

By the time he had negotiated the rocks, the price of Sinappu's lungis had gone up to ten rupees. The darker-skinned sunbathers along this part of the beach were usually happy to pay this amount, though after considerable negotiations. The customers here spent many minutes and many words deciding on which lungi to buy. Then more words to fix on a price. They took the lungi, showed it to their friends, tried it on, held it up against their other clothes. Only when they were sure, did they hand over the money. Once, one of the men gave Sinappu a magazine. For days, the young boy had stared at the beautiful photographs inside the glossy pages. It was clear that Italians were, indeed, very careful about what they wore and how they spent their money. Before Sinappu entered the grounds of the Ashoka hotel, he invariably broke off his sales routine. He was by now quite close to the road that led up to the bus station some five hundred yards away, so this was a good opportunity to stop for tea, and to hand in the takings of the morning.

Sinappu's aunty ran a small food stall by the bus stands, and she always has his dosas ready. Most importantly, from his vantage point by the bus stop as he ate, the young businessman could check out the afternoon arrivals, and thus fix the prices for the rest of the day.

Today was going to be a very good day, he thought, as he saw the young English couple descend from the bus. A very good day. He would take out his very best lungis, and make sure he held the finest one back.

The starched Sikh guards knew Sinappu well. As the young boy returned from his meal break, he handed them a few samosas each and they waved him conspiratorially into the grounds of the exclusive hotel. Once inside, the boy became transformed. He walked taller, spoke most courteously, refused to bargain, and brought out the little sign he had taken hours to paint one night, pinning it onto the batch of lungis. 'Fine Coton Lungi', it said, 'Only Twenty Rupee'. Then, as an afterthought and written in a more casual hand, a scribbled addendum: 'Fixed Price. No bargain.' The impact this sign made was stupendous. The smart set inside the hotel enclave did not like to negotiate. They liked to know the definite price of things, so Sinappu gave it to them. Once, a guest had tried to argue over money, but Sinappu had seemed so outraged, and had raised his voice so loudly, attracting the attention of the other guests, that the man immediately capitulated, and thrust a fifty-rupee note into the boy's hand, if only to shut him up. Sinappu still remembered the bright checked shorts the man wore, coming down to his knees, and the enormous woman who was his wife, for whom Sinappu had had to search out his largest lungi. To this day, the young boy was intrigued by the woman's T-shirt, as large as a tent, with 'Uncle Sam' emblazoned across the front in red. Its grotesque folds just about enveloped the mounds of her body, but why would anyone want to wear a shirt with a picture of their uncle on it? Still, fifty rupees – who was Sinappu to argue?

These two had been slightly unusual: the normal clientele inside the grounds of the Ashoka was of a different category. Richer than the foreigners on the first part of the beach, but also more sophisticated, more refined. They had slim, elegant bodies, delicate, with shining bronze skin. The women seemed perfect to the young boy, and kind, smiling their affectionate smiles as he wove his way from sunbed to sunbed, trying very hard to keep his eyes off their breasts. He liked this part of his daily routine. The people were nice to him, and spoke softly in a lovely musical language the little Indian boy was just beginning to pick up. He could feel the warmth in their tones and they didn't make him feel like a servant. The men bought lots and lots of lungis for their women. 'Merci, mon petit,' they would say. And Sinappu had learnt the reply: 'Merci beaucoup.' By the end, Sinappu would often be down to his last two or three lungis. If he was very lucky, he might be able to sell these to people on the way home, otherwise he would pack them away, and call it a day.

So, year in, year out, the boy had plied his trade along Kovalam beach, making enough from his daily excursions to pay for their tiny house, and feed his mother and two sisters. By the time he finished, the sun was setting, and Sinappu loved to go into the hotel gardens for a few minutes, to be by himself. There was a small courtyard at the far end of the grounds, overlooking the sea. From here, one had a spectacular view of the sun tumbling into the amber sea. Strangely enough, very few of the hotel guests used this vantage point. By sunset they were mostly back in their rooms, getting ready for dinner. Sinappu often ended the day here, listening to the final, plaintive notes of some solitary bird give way to the warm buzzing of the night crickets and cicadas.

Sinappu was pleased with his business for the day. He had only a few lungis left. One of them, his most special one, he had been holding back all afternoon, keeping it well hidden at the back of the batch. He had been imagining how its vibrant patterns would look against the translucent skin and silky hair of the English lady he had noticed earlier at the bus stand. But perhaps he had been wrong to reserve it. There had been no further sign of the couple. As he strolled into the garden courtyard, he looked at the bright colours on the cotton, changing shades as the sun lost its fire.

Across the dark ocean, the shadows lengthen. Slowly, the Earth turns. A black cloud carries the sun away.

'Hello. Are those lungis still for sale?'

Startled by the interruption to his musings, Sinappu looked up with a sudden twist of the head. He had been sure he was alone. 'Yes sir, yes, yes, still sale,' answered Sinappu. The man who had stopped him was a silhouette against the blood-red sky, but he recognized his shape at once. So where was his companion? The boy looked around the courtyard, searching the shadows.

'The one you're holding is a nice one. How much is it?' continued Max, softly.

'This one, sir. Oh this one very nice, very special.' Sinappu was about to begin on his standard sales pitch, reserved for the beach, but something made him reconsider. He took the special lungi off its wooden handle, unpinning it carefully from the hooks that held it. As he was folding it, the undergrowth rustled nearby, and they were joined by Imogen, emerging from out of the falling darkness.

'Hello, Max,' she said. 'Making a deal?'

'Just about to. But this young man hasn't told me the price yet.'

Sinappu kept his eyes firmly on his task of folding the cotton into a perfect square. As he made the final crease, he handed the cloth to Imogen, staring directly into her eyes. There was a second of absolute silence when even the birds and cicadas and the distant crashing of the waves seemed to disappear.

'But how much is it?' asked Max.

'Five rupee, sahib.'

Max knew this was not nearly enough. He took out two fives from his pocket, and held out the notes to the boy. But Sinappu was adamant. He took one of the notes, smiled, and looked up at Imogen. As their eyes met again in the failing light, Imogen saw the shade of an expression cross Sinappu's face, like the brush of a dark wing. The boy dropped his gaze with a gesture of defeat, then turned away, hurrying off into the darkness. The birds, the cicadas, the crickets, and the sea took up their refrain once more.

'How odd,' said Max, recalling for a moment the samosa-seller and his unexpected generosity.

'Perhaps not,' replied Imogen, continuing for a few moments to look at the shadows into which Sinappu had disappeared. 'Come on, Max, we'll miss the last bus.'

They just made it. The bus was already pulling out of the station by the time Max and Imogen arrived back at the stands. But the driver saw them, and stopped. The bus was virtually empty, save a few dark figures huddled together towards the rear. As they settled into the wooden seats at the front, the driver sped out of the station, leaving behind him a cloud of thick, stinking smoke.

The road between Kovalam and Trivandrum cut its way through deep forest. For a few hundred yards leading out of the station at Kovalam, the road ran parallel to the beach: as the bus sped along, Max looked over to the sands, dotted now with small fires lighting up the darkness. The sun was sinking swiftly, leaving behind it an amber afterglow that hung like the trail of a massive firework over the heaving ocean. Then, suddenly, the scene was blotted out as the route plunged into the thickets of trees and bush. Sitting at the front, Max and Imogen could see the road ahead, lit up by the headlamps of the bus. Occasionally, a lone cyclist or pedestrian would be caught in the light, flashing by in an instant, swallowed up once more by the dark vegetation. The door leading onto the bus had long ago disappeared, and from the opening, wafts of humid vegetation swam in, mingling with the diesel fumes and the smell of spicy perspiration that characterized all public vehicles on the subcontinent. Deeper and deeper they plunged, into the heat of the night jungle, clinging to the road, fearful of the atavistic gloom that pressed on all sides. Soon there were no more cyclists, no more pedestrians to be overtaken. The bus was alone, following its own shaft of light, as it penetrated ever deeper into the tunnel of trees and leaves and dark, unseen foliage.

Max was just beginning to doze off when the bus turned a corner, slowed, and came to a halt outside a tiny shack in a forest clearing. Perhaps someone wanted to get off, he thought, fighting off the seed of a fear that had taken root somewhere deep within him. When the engine was turned off, that fear blossomed instantaneously.

'What's up?' he asked, barely able to keep the panic out of his voice. The shack by which they were parked was lit up by a kerosene lamp, but as before, the light was no match for the darkness of the vast palms surrounding the building. Oblivious to his foreign passenger's plea, the driver turned off the headlamps and the blackness of the night crashed in. Max felt Imogen press his hand. He looked over to the back of the bus: so long as there were other people with them, there would be no problems. There was safety in numbers. But events continued, with the unrelenting certainty of a nightmare. The silhouettes from the back of the bus began to file off. Most worryingly, the driver was now beginning to pack his belongings as if finishing for the night.

'Excuse me,' asked Imogen, going up to the driver's seat. 'Why are we stopping here?' The dark form turned towards her, and remained silent. She could see no features in the face.

'Why are we stopping here?' asked Max, joining Imogen. The faceless silhouette remained silent. The fact was that the driver couldn't understand a word of English, but in the context of the dark isolation of the south Indian forest, his silence took on a sinister aspect.

'How far to the city?' asked Max, almost shouting. Silence. And darkness. Within seconds, the shadows who had left the bus had disappeared into the night, merging once more with the deep darkness from which they had only temporarily broken away. The silence of the forest had become palpable. Every now and then, as the engine of the bus cooled down, a metallic crack would pierce the night, reminding Max and Imogen of their isolation.

'I reckon this bloody bus is just going to stop here,' said Max, finally articulating the thought he had been trying desperately to fight.

'What can we do?' asked Imogen, falling into a natural whisper.

'Well, there's only one thing we can do. We'll have to walk. It can't be that far now – we must be over half way to the city.'

'We can't walk through this,' exclaimed Imogen.

'I really don't think we have much choice,' replied Max.

'Look,' said Imogen loudly, turning once more to the patch of darkness that was the driver, 'this is ridiculous. Now you take us all the way to the city, or else . . .'

'It's no good, Imogen. He can't understand. This might be better.' Max took out his wallet, and removed a clutch of notes from it. He held it up to the silhouette's face, turning the notes slightly in order to catch the light from the kerosene lamp outside. This seemed to be the last straw: the driver shook his head vehemently, opened the door on his side of the bus, and jumped out.

'We're going to have to walk,' said Max sharply to Imogen.

'Okay, but we're going to need some sort of light. Come on.' Imogen grabbed her belongings from the seat, and rushed off the bus. Max followed her, into the wooden shack outside. The driver had gone into the stall, and was busy talking in his own language to another silhouette seated inside. The kerosene lamp threw just enough light to show up the dark, aboriginal features of the two men.

'Give me the notes, Max.' He handed Imogen the money he had taken out, and in one determined movement, she thrust the notes in front of the two men. As they looked down at the money, Imogen took the kerosene lamp off its hook, and left the stall. 'Come on. Let's get going,' she said, walking purposefully down the road, into the darkness.

Max followed unquestioningly. A few strides later, he turned to look at the shack to see what the reaction of its two occupants might be, once they got over the shock of having their light purloined in this way. But the hut was now indistinguishable, enveloped in night, and Max could not even make out where it had been.

The lamp was just strong enough to create a tiny circle around Max and Imogen. As they walked along the road, a thin line through the dense forest, the lantern seemed to create a magic ring around them, protecting them from the primitive darkness that surrounded them. The huge leaves of the palms swayed as Max and Imogen walked past, rustling surreptitiously. For a moment, the arrival of the circle of light would make the cicadas arrest their buzzing, as if the invisible creatures were curious to see the source of the magic; but as soon as it had passed, the electric hum would start up again, an indispensable accompaniment to the heat and the darkness. Max and Imogen walked silently, unwilling to break the spell cast by the trees. This was their territory: Max and Imogen were intruders, and they must abide by the contract of silence that prevailed in this pristine kingdom, one which had been created long before Man had articulated the first word. It seemed almost sacrilegious to speak. Occasionally, as they walked along, there would be a quick rustle from the bush followed by a scampering of agile feet, receding deeper into the security of the foliage. At other times, Max was sure he could see curious eyes, lit up by the lamp, staring out silently from the darkness, watching the two of them pass by. He wondered what mysterious creatures had made their homes amongst the trees, what birds and animals, unseen for centuries, still scurried about in the uncharted, undisturbed undergrowth. A man could easily lose himself in these regions, disappear forever into the deep, warm darkness of the trees. For a moment, the idea of such a communion seemed not unattractive to Max.

Every now and then they would find their way strewn with preter-natural fruits and bloated seedlings that had obviously dropped from one of the overhanging branches. In this way, slowly, each night, the road was being reclaimed by the forest: only the efforts of the day kept the way clear. If no one bothered to pick up the vegetation and throw it back into the bush, then one day the path would be completely covered, and gradually even the tarmac would disintegrate.

The forest was full of life. If you listened hard enough, you could almost hear the vegetation breathing, see the gentle suspiration of the jungle as it took in and let out its life-giving vapours beneath the night sky. Max imagined that they were, in fact, inside a large creature, treading a careful path along one of its vital arteries. The energy of the forest was tangible, entering him through all his senses. Most of all it was the smell that excited Max: the damp, warm, sensuous aroma of earth mingled with vegetation, surrounding him with its promise of satisfaction and security. It was definitely a female smell, and Max was drawn to it like a baby to its mother.

They must have walked for hours. At some point the moon had risen, but the forest devoured any vestige of light it might have cast down. The warmth of the day was receding now and a damp mist was beginning to rise up from the ground, covering the trunks of the trees with a thick, creamy veil. Slowly, the cloud rose, reaching the lower branches with their heavy leaves, then creeping persistently, ever upwards towards the younger buds at the top. Max stared at the writhing vapour as it climbed the towering trees. It was as if the plants were all breathing out a deep sigh of relief, exhaling their vapours into the cool of the night. Looking along the road, two solid curtains of mist were being pushed up, out of the sodden ground, climbing inch by inch to screen off the avenue of trees. Max looked at the ground, where the tarmac of the road finished and the primeval sod began. The mists swirled uneasily at this junction, reluctant to encroach upon the pathway, its stone still hot from the day. On and on they walked. Max's earlier enervation had given way to a profound calm, a sense of peace and serenity, brought on by the proximity of the trees. Their stoic certainty was infectious, and he had felt himself inclined to linger rather than rush back towards the city. So it was with a pang of disappointment that Max heard Imogen's voice break the silence.

'Max.'

'Yes.'

'Look, up ahead. That's the town.' Max gazed into the distance. He could just make out a faint glimmer of lights, possibly some two or three miles away, shining bravely through a blanket of mist.

'Thank God for that,' he said, resigned to the prospect of a return to the world. 'I don't know what we would have done if we'd taken a wrong turning.'

Imogen laughed. 'Come on,' she said, 'let's step on it. We'll be in time for dinner.' The prospect of being back with the visitors of Trivandrum made Max feel sad. He had been happy here, amongst the trees and the night and the mist. As Max and Imogen came closer to the town, the road crossed a bridge and widened, pushing the trees back to a safe distance. The mist still hung in the air, but the lights from the many stalls that served the city's visitors helped to cut through the haze. The natural vapours were supplemented now by wood smoke, filling the sky with its pungent clouds. All along the road, at intervals of a few hundred yards, small bonfires, tended by young boys and girls, lit up the night. The thick, dark features of the children's faces shone in the reflection of the flames as Max and Imogen passed: some of them giggled, amused by the sight of a foreign couple carrying a kerosene lamp. The trees of the forest bordered the clearing, and Max could see that beyond the sides of the road darkness still prevailed. He looked all around him, trying to get his bearings.

'Do you know the way from here?' asked Imogen.

'I think so,' replied Max. 'We're not that far away. Do you want to get a rickshaw?'

'Not really,' said Imogen, 'this is quite interesting. Let's walk on for a bit.' The smell of frying food wafted down the street, making Max's mouth water. As they passed the stand, he looked into the large black metal wok, intrigued by the strange yellow shapes that floated on boats of tiny bubbles. He stopped to see what was frying, and out of the corner of his eye he saw someone else stop, about ten feet away. Max looked over to the man behind them: he was naked from head to toe, except for a small loincloth tied around his waist. Max had never seen such a sight. The stranger was of medium build and must have been quite young, in his twenties perhaps. But his hair had obviously never been cut, for it hung down in long plaits, some extending to his waist. His body was covered in ash, making his natural black colour a shade of grey, and on his forehead was painted, in orange, a large three-pronged trishul.

The thing that disconcerted Max was that the man had obviously been following them for some time. His bare feet had made no sound, so it was only now, when Max happened to turn, that he had become aware of their new companion. Perhaps he had followed them all the way through the forest. He certainly looked like an inhabitant of the woods, not of the city. Max tried not to stare at the wild man, but turned instead, and he and Imogen continued on their way. The stranger followed, keeping ten paces behind.

'We've got a fan,' said Max to Imogen.

'I know, I saw him at the food stall. I don't think he means any trouble. Just curious, I expect.'

'Perhaps he wants his kerosene lamp back,' said Max. He was still behind them. Max saw the turning to the hotel up ahead, and breathed a sigh of relief. He was looking forward now to a shower, and to a large meal, after their long trek. He picked up the pace, gently pushing Imogen along. The wild man too speeded up, still keeping ten feet behind. Suddenly Max stopped and turned. The stranger stopped too, continuing to stare at the young couple. Max waved his hand in a gesture of dismissal. The man of the woods stood his ground, staring unperturbed at the foreigners.

'Come on, Max. He's not doing any harm. Let's just get back to the hotel.'

They continued on towards the Maya Continental. The stranger followed too. They could see the lights of the hotel now, peeping through the trees that surrounded the building. As they turned the final corner into the hotel grounds and walked along the smooth tarmac of the drive up to the reception, Max looked back at their companion. But he was gone.

'And was there no one around with any other means of transport or anything?' asked Prabhu, incredulous.

'This was like deep, deep jungle,' said Imogen. 'We couldn't see anything, and nobody seemed to understand a word we said. Anyway, walking was the only way.'

'Well, you did the right thing. I mean, you couldn't very well just stay there, could you?' Prabhu was privately quite ashamed of his fellow countryman's lack of consideration. 'To be honest,' he continued, 'the road between here and Kovalam is very safe. There's never been any trouble that I know of. The only thing you do have to be careful of is the snakes. They come out onto the tarmac at night, attracted by the heat.'

'You know,' said Max thoughtfully, 'I'm so glad you didn't tell us that yesterday.' The three of them burst into spontaneous laughter. Prabhu took this natural break in the conversation to get up out of his chair and tidy up the paperwork on his desk.

'Shall we go into the temple?' he asked. 'I think it should be fairly empty by now.'

'Is there someone who'll be able to help me with the sari?' asked Imogen.

'The attendants stay around for the evening ceremonies. If we go through the kitchens again, there will be someone able to help both of you put on the required dress.'

When Imogen emerged, at last, from the ladies' dressing room, Max was stunned at the vision. The sari she wore, a deep orange, hung from her like the most elegant long dress, clinging to her slim waist and hips, and tied tightly about her midriff. Imogen's height made even the most humble cotton look like a designer robe. The folds of the material fell in long pleats from her waist to the ground, encircling her body with their modest yet suggestive lines. The blouse that Imogen had been lent was a little too tight for her and pushed her breasts up, enhancing their shape and accentuating the cleft. A single fold of the material covered the area from her midriff to her neck, and Max could see her silky, flawless skin beneath the saffron film. He was not the only one staring at his wife in amazement. The young Indian girls who had helped her to put on the sari were standing around her, gazing longingly at the slender figure of the Englishwoman. Imogen's golden red hair seemed to catch the shine of the saffron, and her face was lit with a gentle glow, softening her features like a muslin gauze. Unnecessarily, the attendants fussed around her, putting the finishing touches to the sari. Finally, one of them pressed a large red spot onto Imogen's forehead, and the image was complete. As Imogen looked up a sudden flash of white light lit up the room, blinding her momentarily.

'You look amazing,' said Max, putting away his camera.

'So do you,' replied Imogen. Max looked down at the dhoti that hung from his waist, covering his legs. The effect was not quite as impressive as Imogen's sari.

'I think you both look wonderful,' said Prabhu, returning from the inner door. 'Shall we?'

Darkness was falling, and the priests of the Padmanabhaswamy temple were lighting the hundreds of tiny oil-lamps that sat precariously along all the edges of the balconies, the sculpture alcoves, the altars and the windows. Gradually, the whole temple would be lit up by these lamps, each one no larger than a small leaf, containing a spoonful of oil and a wick made of cotton wool. Each statue held a lamp, each corner housed a lamp, the doorways were outlined in lamps, even the ground had lamps upon it, marking out the pathways through the myriad courtyards. As Max, Imogen and Prabhu entered through the large wooden door that led from the kitchens, they found themselves at the intersection of two long corridors. The one leading straight ahead seemed to go on for miles, the lamps acting like landing lights on a runway seen from a great height. At a point some two or three hundred yards away, the lights converged, disappearing into the darkness beyond. The corridor that ran to the left and right, at ninety degrees to the first one, also seemed to have no end. As Max looked along the avenues, he noticed that each one was lined with hundreds of magnificent carved sculptures of Indian gods and goddesses. The statues stood some six feet tall and each held a lamp, the flames dancing in the light breeze, animating the carefully carved, and preserved, features on the faces.

In the half-light, the sculptures seemed pristine, brand new, devoid of the ravages of time that Max knew must be there. The yellow flames made everything seem golden. The gods all had blonde hair, their consorts the most glowing skins. Nothing disturbed the serenity of the divine effigies. The priests, young and old, went about their business in silence, hardly making a rustle as they shuffled along the marble floors in their bare feet. Corridor led on to corridor, like a labyrinth. Max looked up at the ceiling, its stonework carved in intricate detail, a homage to the central scenes of the Hindu epics.

'I love coming here at this time of day,' said Prabhu gently, mindful of his visitors' awe. His whisper echoed around the marble, making his sentence sound like a single string of soft syllables. In the distance, temple bells were beginning to sound, sharp metallic strands weaving their way through the maze of avenues.

'I've never seen anything like this,' said Imogen feebly.

'It's one of the finest temples in India,' continued Prabhu. 'Come, let's go on.'

The party moved straight along the central corridor, flanked, like the others, by highly-wrought statues. Each sculpture was an artistic triumph: the quantity had in no way affected the quality of workmanship in the individual pieces. Tall, perfect youths, their features shaped by the finest scalpels, stood side by side with young, voluptuous maidens. Some wore crowns of marble; others held delicate flutes between their finely chiselled fingers. Max and Imogen passed the full Hindu pantheon as they walked along the avenue. Lord Hanuman, the monkey god, defiantly carrying his mountain of herbs; Lord Krishna, the pastoral god, standing side by side with his consort, Radha; Lord Shiva, the god of creation and destruction, dancing his dance of life and death within the circle of flames; the goddess Durga, her hand resting upon a tiger; the elephant god, Ganesh, god of strength and patience, accompanied as ever by his companion, the rat; the sky goddess Aditi, mother of all the gods; Garuda, king of the birds; Lord Prajapati, the god of creatures; the goddess Manasha, protector of snakes; Lord Yama, king of the dead; the celestial deities Indra, Mitra, Rudra, Tvashtar and Varuna; the goddess Laxmi; Kama, the god of desire; Lord Rama, with his brother,

Lakshman, and his consort, Sita; Lord Rudra, master of the beasts; the goddess Jyeshtha, goddess of bad luck.

As Max and Imogen walked along the corridor, the arcane faces of the various deities stared out at them, following their passing with fixed eyes. At times, Max imagined that the sculptures were alive, conscious of the intrusion of the night-time visitors. The furrowed brows of some of the gods seemed to communicate disapproval, but Max took solace in the more welcoming expressions on the faces of the less fierce deities. Some even seemed amused: perhaps they were laughing at the pathetic efforts of this foreigner to keep his dhoti tied properly around his waist. Every few steps it would slip down, forcing Max to pull it up again. Imogen was much more graceful in her sari. Soon Prabhu had led them into another corridor. At the end of this, a large wooden door stood open revealing an inner courtyard, lit up, once again, by countless oil-lamps. Stepping through the doorway, Max noticed that the courtyard must have been almost the size of a tennis lawn, its marble floor glistening with the sparkle of the lamps. At its centre, following the contours of the courtyard, was a huge hangar, some twenty feet high and thirty feet long. The walls of the building were made of the finest marble, a more delicate hue than the marble of the floor, and along one side, at eye-level, there were three windows, evenly spaced along the length of the building.

'We're now at the centre of the temple,' explained Prabhu. 'Look up. We're right underneath the tower.'

Max and Imogen twisted their heads and gazed up into the gopuram. It was like looking into a deep tunnel leading to the centre of the earth. The tower was terraced, each step about six feet above the one below, picked out by ever-decreasing squares of oil-lamps. As the terraces receded, so the aperture became narrower, until the oil-lamps merged together, forming one united source of light.

'How on earth do they light the lamps up there?' asked Imogen.

'Look closely: up there,' replied Prabhu, pointing up into the tunnel. Imogen narrowed her eyes, and just made out a dwarfish figure, walking carefully along one of the terrace walls. He must have been about fifty feet up, yet he was strolling along as if he were firmly on the ground, filling each lamp, and tending to its flame.

'That's Manu. He comes each night just to light the lamps in the tower. He's a woodcutter and an incredible acrobat: just scampers up the walls like a monkey. He'll spend most of the night here, filling the lamps as they go out, making sure that the ledges remain lit.'

Imogen looked back up towards the distant figure: he had obviously spotted them, for this time he took one of the oil-lamps and waved it about in a circular movement as a greeting.

'It must be an amazing view from up there, looking down,' said Max. 'We must look like insects to him.'

'Is this the statue of Vishnu?' asked Imogen.

'It is.'

'How do we get in?' asked Max.

'We don't,' replied Prabhu. Then, after a pause, and sensing his visitors' perplexity, he continued, 'Those latticed windows, they're the only way that pilgrims are allowed to look upon the statue. You see, when the temple was built, the statue of Vishnu was the finest specimen of its kind. It is supposed to be perfect in every detail. There's some story about the sculptor just wasting away after he had completed it, because he had nothing else to live for, but I'm sure that's just superstition. Anyway, the point about the statue is that, being perfect, it is the most exact image of God we have. And to look upon it in one gaze, in all its splendour, would be far too much for human eyes. So, there are those three windows. As you look through one, you see a part of the divine image, just enough for mortal sight. The next window reveals another part, and the third window allows you to complete the picture, but only in your imagination. You can't see the complete statue from any perspective.'

'Does no one ever go inside the building, to clean the statue or anything?' asked Max, intrigued by the logistics of keeping God away from mortal eyes.

'Oh yes, some of the high priests do venture right up to the reclining statue, but they are very disciplined. They keep their eyes fixed firmly on the part they are cleaning, or the area they are dealing with. They never look up or down the full length of the sculpture.'

'And what about our acrobat up there, in the tower?' said Imogen. 'He must have quite a view from his vantage point, looking down.'

'No, no. The roof also has only three openings in it. Manu can't see anything but three sections of the statue, though you are quite right. I suppose his reward for his labours is that he can see all three segments simultaneously.'

Max had edged over to the nearest window and was already peering through. He was by the feet of the god, and through the flickering flames he could make out the translucent marble fashioned into huge toes and nails, one foot resting casually across the other. The pilgrims of the day had strewn the floor with flowers and garlands: some had landed on the feet themselves and lodged between the deep crevices of the ankles or toes. And, with the flowers, the usual array of coins and notes, thrown in for good luck. The stone had clearly been polished innumerable times, for it shone like glass. Max looked along the side of the window, trying to see up the length of the statue, but his ambition was thwarted by the angle at which the god was reclining. The most he could see was the calf muscle, beautifully fashioned, like a huge pear.

'I see there are no windows on the other side,' said Max.

'That's right, this is the only view,' replied Prabhu.

Max moved back from the window, and looked up to the second aperture, half way along the wall. Imogen was standing there on tiptoe, her slim body stretching up to take in the rationed view. He moved along and touched Imogen gently on the waist.

'The feet are fantastic. Go and have a look,' said Max. As Imogen stepped back, he took her place at the latticed opening. The ledge of the window had become smooth through pilgrims' hands rubbing it as they, too, in all eagerness, gazed on the elusive god. From here, Max could see the waist and midriff of the deity. A huge belt had been sculpted, hanging low below an ample, but not obese, belly, and the navel of the god was full of red powder, the ritual colouring used to mark pilgrims and effigies as a sign of blessing. As before, flowers lay all across the marble form. Max tried looking up and down the sculpture once more, but his view was blocked by the sides of the aperture.

'Have you been inside?' he asked, turning to Prabhu.

'Not yet. I don't think I'm ready yet – I'd probably be too tempted to look at the whole thing. But one day, perhaps . . .'

Imogen joined Max, and the two of them walked together to the third window, at the far end of the courtyard. Max looked at her and smiled lovingly. Responding to his warmth, Imogen brought her face up close to his and pecked him on the cheek.

'I'll never forget this day,' she whispered. A little embarrassed, Max cast a furtive glance over towards Prabhu. But the young priest had obviously sensed the privacy of the moment, for he had disappeared, leaving the lovers alone.

'Nor will I,' continued Max. 'It's our last day in India. I wish we could stay on, here, in Trivandrum.'

He looked straight into Imogen's eyes, reflecting upon the impossibility of the suggestion. He knew that once they were back home in England, they would never have the luxury of each other's exclusive attention in the way they had had over the past few weeks. Then, as an afterthought, Max added, 'I will keep my promise, Imogen, whatever happens.'

'I know, Max. I know you will.'

Max pulled Imogen towards him, and kissed her gently on the forehead, carefully avoiding the tiny red dot that had been painted onto her brow in traditional Hindu style. Then, taking her gently by the shoulder, he urged Imogen to the third window. He wanted them to look through the opening together.

Max had never expected the face to be so beautiful, so perfect. Its clean, smooth contours were almost sensuous; the aquiline nose, the almond eyes, the perfectly symmetrical nostrils, the slim lips. There was something unexpectedly modern about the image, something that seemed to accord with the most topical fashion and notions of beauty. It was a familiar face. Yet Max knew he had never seen it before, and that the sculpture had been here for over two centuries. The head was crowned with fresh garlands: red, orange and white carnations, strung together and placed carefully around the forehead. And at the exact centre of the brow was a large red Hindu spot, formed with a thick paste of the ceremonial powder, some six inches in diameter. The colour stood out against the marble, made amber by the oil-lamps. Above the god's head a serpent reared up, like a protective umbrella, forming a resplendent canopy.

'That must be the Anantha,' said Imogen. 'Vishnu is usually seen reclining on a serpent.'

Max looked at the eyes of the god, half-closed in the narcotic serenity so characteristic of Hindu deities. What was it about this face that so held Max? It was more poetic than any Roman or Greek sculpture he had seen. How strange to think that our Western notion of beauty was supposed to relate more closely to those images: the vision of the reclining Vishnu appeared to Max to contain more of the elements that he would consider beautiful in a contemporary face. His eyes followed the lines of the face, inch by inch. The complexion was flawless, polished, like the rest of the marble, to a mirror shine. As he considered the features, Max realized that it was impossible to tell whether the image was that of a man or a woman. It contained elements of both: the gentle, smooth feminine curves of the cheeks, complemented by a more masculine line on the brow and the jaw. And the face was timeless: it would be impossible to tell what age the sculptor imagined his subject. Max looked once more into the eyes, and felt again the surge of tranquillity and comfort that had gone through him the first time he had seen the face. Deep within him, a memory stirred.

High above the heads of the latecomers to the temple, Manu worked ceaselessly at his daily task. He had almost finished filling the oil-lamps on the upper terraces, and the ones below seemed to be burning brightly. They would continue for at least another thirty minutes or so before they needed refilling, just time enough for the patient devotee to rest his feet, here, on one of the wider terraces. Finishing off the last few lamps, Manu stretched out along the full length of the ledge. He was over the front end of the hangar that housed the holy image, and even from this height he could make out the reclining profile of the head through the window in the roof far below. Placing his clay phial of oil carefully by his side, Manu closed his eyes in quiet contemplation. A few minutes passed. He could hear the distant mutterings of the visitors down below. Manu opened his eyes and saw the tiny figures moving excitedly from window to window. He shifted a little, pushing himself further back against the wall of the terrace. Feeling more secure, Manu closed his eyes once again, conjuring in his mind an image of the Vishnu in its entirety.

Unknown to the temple worker, his phial of oil had fallen over and rolled to the side of the ledge. The bulbous body kept it from tumbling right off, but the long neck of the clay bottle had cracked. Slowly, very slowly, and with a relentless, silent effort, the oil began to ooze out of the bottle. It formed at first a thin shiny line, starting at the base of the phial, and extending to the neck. Gradually, the line became thicker, flowing more quickly, and the liquid pushed over the lip of the bottle. Drop by drop it fell onto the dusty ledge, forming a tiny puddle underneath the mouth of the container; then, as the pool became too full, another thin line began to form, out of the puddle, along a fissure that ran from the wall of the terrace to its edge.

Manu was beginning to doze off, captivated by the visions of his imagination. In his dreams he was piecing together the disparate images he had acquired, and was close to assembling the jigsaw.

As more and more oil eased out of the phial, the miniature river that had formed along the crevice began to flood, high above the head of Lord Vishnu. The thin streak of oil reached the edge of the terrace. For a moment, it stopped, arrested by the thick dirt on the lip of the ledge. But then, unable to resist the pressure from behind, a tiny drop plunged over into the void. Slowly, the drop of oil fell, passing on its way the ranged rows of lamps along terrace after terrace. Inside the perfect orb, the reflections of the flames coalesced into a furnace. Ledge after ledge rushed by as the drop travelled along its impeccable straight line. The longer it fell, the more it began to accelerate, and the seamless globe began slowly to elongate. A tail formed behind the fledgling comet as it sped on its way. It passed the final ledge, then headed straight into the roof window above the head of the reclining god. With a preordained accuracy, the viscous missile passed through a hole in the latticework, just clearing the side, and sped onwards along its path, traversing the final twenty feet on its fateful journey.

For a moment, deep within the shining drop, the image of Lord Vishnu was reflected in all its splendour and glory, the sight forever denied to human eyes, a magnificent microcosm of the godhead. But no sooner had the reflection formed than the globe exploded, smashed into a minute crater, as it hit the marble of Lord Vishnu's forehead. A moment later, a second oily missile crashed upon the sculpture, then a third, and a fourth. The force of the impact, and the viscosity of the oil, began to melt the red disc on the brow of the god.

Transported by his visions of divinity, Manu rested from his labours, high above the temple sculpture.

Staring fixedly at the sculpted head, Max began to sink into a profound reflection. His breathing became deeper and slower, as if in a meditative sleep, and his eyes continued to gaze, but saw only an inner vision. Noticing his contemplation, Imogen slipped away from the window, rejoining Prabhu as he returned through the entrance of the courtyard.

'Let's leave him alone for a few minutes,' she said to the young priest. 'I think he needs to be alone.' Prabhu immediately understood, and the two of them went off along one of the temple's labyrinthine corridors, receding quickly into the sparkle of lights.

Max wondered at the strange events that had overtaken his life over the past month. He had expected an assault on his sensibilities, but nothing could have prepared him for the surge of experience that had invaded his perceptions. He would need a long time to digest everything he had seen, heard, felt, tasted, smelt, and dreamt whilst here, on this mystic soil. Lost in his reflections, Max only faintly saw any longer the marble of the sculpture before him.

And what of the Englishman? Max had not seen him again, after Khajuraho. The further away the apparitions floated, the more Max was inclined to believe that the meetings had been pure coincidence at best, petty voyeurism at worst. Perhaps the lone traveller *had* taken a fancy to Imogen? Or to Max? The world was full of lonely people, searching for friendship and solace. Red. Max felt a surge of euphoria as he recalled that he, thankfully, would be free from the possibilities of isolation. He had found his companion, and looked forward to sharing all the happiness, and sorrow no doubt, that life would bring. But what did the future hold for Imogen and him? Blood. He was fixed up with a teaching post, so that, at least, was settled. But what of Imogen? Max had no doubt she would find something exciting and glamorous to do – she always did – but how would he fit into the lifestyle she carved out for herself? And what about children? Gash. Max supposed someday that they would start a family, but at the moment he didn't feel adult enough to have children of his own, and he wasn't ready to share Imogen. Anyway, they had plenty of time. Max knew people who had started families only in their thirties, so he and Imogen could wait even ten years if they wanted to.

Something troubled Max deep within his contemplations. Like a distant noise, half heard in the slumbers of the morning, the interruption was compelling him to forego his meditations and return to the world of waking perception. Reluctantly, Max brought himself up out of his reflections. Gradually, the orange blur in front of his eyes began to form once more into the image of the marble head. The indistinct sparkles of fire, which had coalesced into a single glow, returned to their own individual sources, and became once more the flames of the oil-lamps. It was then that Max realized what had roused him from his contemplation. His eyes widened in horror. This must be some cruel trick. But who would do such a thing? Perhaps he was still trapped within a nightmare? Max willed himself awake, but the vision remained, unchanged.

The perfect complexion of the sculpted face had been destroyed. Where before there had been the smooth contours of alabaster, as delicate and as faultless as the flower petals strewn around, now there was the most horrific defect. Along one side of the god's face, blood gushed forth. Dark, thick blood, shockingly purple against the marble. Max stood motionless, fixed by the horrendous image. It appeared as if the porcelain cheek had been cut from the corner of the left eye to the tiny hollow beneath the lower lip. The blood flowed like a tiny stream, following the contours of the face, starting at the eyebrow, along the curve of the left cheek, down the line of the jaw, into the basin beneath the lip, then, drip, drip, drip, it fell reproachfully onto the shoulder of the deity. And still Lord Vishnu smiled his stoic smile, unaffected by the tragic wound. As Max stared, the gash became wider, the blood rushed more quickly. He clasped the latticework on the window with his fingers, unable to get any closer to the sculpture. In desperation Max turned, searching the shadows for Prabhu, or for any of the other priests. But he was alone. Like a bystander, impotent as death overtakes its victim, Max watched the effigy pour out its blood.

Departure

Jonas Schindler could see that the watch was a masterpiece. Turning it delicately in the palm of his enormous hand, he brought his eyepiece close to the dial. Instantly, the whole field of vision in his left eye was full of sparkling gold numerals and creamy ebonite. Despite his many decades of handling clocks and watches, Schindler was thrilled by the precision of the workmanship: the crafting of the hands, the minuscule pointing of the digits, the perfect symmetry of the dials within the dials. He often thought of himself as a pathologist. First he must examine the body for any outward signs of disease or disorder, then, if that proved unfruitful, he would venture further and carry out a full internal probe.

Max was amused by the watchmaker's archaic gentility. It had been quite an effort to find Schindler & Co.: in and out of tiny alleyways in Whitechapel, along narrow lanes with cobbled stone paths, into arcades where the lights burned all day long, and finally, behind a modest shopfront, the surgery of Jonas Schindler. As Schindler examined the watch, Max looked around at the Aladdin's cave of time he had entered. Clocks of all shapes and sizes were stacked up on the mantelpieces, ticking away in unison, their pendulums swinging enthusiastically. He marvelled at the variety of faces and dials: white, black, oblong, square, metal, ivory, each timepiece meticulously renovated. Grandfather clocks stood to attention along one side of the room, majestic in their polished coats of mahogany and oak; opposite them, a row of smaller grandmother clocks, with higher-pitched tones and more refined bodies. Now and then, a swinging pendulum would catch the light, and throw patterned reflections along the ceiling. Suddenly one of the clocks along the mantelpiece began a series of chimes; another joined in, then a third and a fourth. Soon the whole room was resounding to a cacophony of strikes and chimes. Max swung round, trying to pair off sounds with their owners, but it was impossible. Then, rising above the din, a deep, massive tone struck the hour. As the resonances died away, other chimes struck until, one by one, each timepiece had issued its declaration. It was three o'clock. As the sounds died away, there persisted the lingering, high-pitched song of a tiny clock. Like an insect, the timepiece added its voice to the sounds of the temporal forest. Intrigued to locate the source of the sound, Max tracked the thin sound all over the room only to discover, much to his surprise, that the chiming was coming from his own watch, safe within Jonas Schindler's palm.

'How strange,' said Max, 'I didn't even know it had a chime.'

Schindler kept his eye fixed upon the watch as his fingers played with its various winds. Max could tell he did not want to be disturbed at this juncture. Behind the master horologist there stood four large sideboards made of the finest mahogany, each accommodating hundreds and hundreds of tiny drawers. These held thousands of cogs and wheels, keys, dials, weights, hands, winds, cases, straps, buckles, bars, all manner of spare parts for which Schindler & Co. was unrivalled. Most of these components came from old clocks and watches that had long ago been put to rest. Their bodies had been plundered, the constituent parts catalogued and retained for future repairs. In this way, nothing was ever wasted. Apparently, the boast was that there was no timepiece in existence that Schindler's could not repair, and it was said that if they did not have the required part, they would make it for you. Occasionally, men wearing long white aprons, dirtied with oil and grease, would emerge from the rear of the shop, go automatically to one of the drawers, take the part they required, then disappear once more into the back. They all seemed to be in their sixties and seventies, these workers, except for one young man of twenty or so.

His scrutiny over, Jonas Schindler put the watch down gently onto the chamois mat in front of him. His eyescope was still lodged in his left eye. Putting one of his large, hairy fingers up to his face, Schindler took it out, exercised his eyelid a few times, then looked accusingly at Max, piercing him with an admonishing gaze.

'A watch like this is as delicate as a spider's web, young man. When her creator crafted her, he didn't expect she would be transported to strange parts of the world. No, no, not at all. She was made for temperate climes, not the trials and tribulations of foreign parts.'

'Was it the heat, then, that made it seize up?' asked Max tentatively. No sooner had he spoken than he realized he had said the wrong thing. Schindler's brow contracted into a variety of contours.

' "Made it seize up"? We're dealing here with a masterpiece. Some craftsman put his soul into fashioning this watch – and when he did so, he left a part of himself in it. This is a work of art, my boy. And works of art do not "seize up".' Schindler sighed, frustrated by his efforts to explain. 'This is a living being we're talking about. Treat her properly, she'll go on forever. Abuse her and she'll forsake you.'

'I do understand, Mr Schindler. And I'm sorry not to have been more, er, compassionate.'

Jonas Schindler's face lit up. Perhaps he had been wrong about Max. 'Well,' he said pensively, touching the watch delicately, 'I can't make any promises, you understand, but leave it with me. I'll see what I can do.'

Jonas Schindler was fascinated by the watch. He decided to carry out the repairs himself, which was unusual, since he had so many expert craftsmen working for him. So, late one night, after the rest of the staff had gone home, Schindler got out his own instruments, carefully wrapped in a leather pouch, and proceeded with the utmost care to open up the watch. Crouched over a tiny electric lamp, he exposed the innards of the timepiece, laying each component carefully on the chamois mat by his side. One by one, the cogs and the wheels came out. As the body emptied, Schindler noticed something that made him pull back in horror. Deep within the bowels of the watch, a drop of blood, red and dark, glistened in the half-light, as if freshly spilt. For a moment the horologist could not believe what he had seen. He pulled the light closer to the work surface and bent down again, putting his eyescope right up to the movement. Schindler breathed a sigh of relief. He had been mistaken. It was just a crack, with a build-up of dirt and grease around it.

This was obviously the problem. Filth had gathered around the fissure and the extraneous weight had caused an imbalance within the mechanism. Using the tiniest pliers in his kit, Schindler removed the defunct component and, holding it up to the light-bulb, he blew away the scab around the crack. The cut was irreparable. But did he have a replacement? It was a rare watch and Schindler was determined to save it.

'Taken it to India,' he whispered in disgust to himself, shaking his head. He put down the tools he was holding and pushed back his chair. A watch had recently been plundered by old Mr Isaac which might have had a similar mechanism. Jonas Schindler turned on the dim lamp that hung over the mahogany cemetery of timepieces that had passed away.

'Let me see, now,' he muttered to himself, running his fingers along the drawers. His hand stopped on one of the myriad containers and he pulled it open. Inside, just a single tiny cog, rolling from side to side with the movement of the drawer. He took the cog out of its resting place and held it up to the light. It was not quite right but he could grind it down to size. Schindler returned to his operating table. Taking a miniature file out of his pouch, he began the slow and arduous process of smoothing the cog down to its new size.

'You may remember I came in about four weeks ago . . .' began Max.

'Of course, of course,' interjected Jonas Schindler. He had been looking forward to this moment for weeks. 'You're a very lucky young man,' he said, indulgently.

Max felt a surge of optimism. 'Is the watch all right?'

'Couldn't be better. I've had her under my eye for almost a fortnight now, and she hasn't complained once. Keeping perfect time, chiming on the dot. Marvellous.' Beaming from ear to ear, Schindler turned, bent down to one of the lower drawers on the sideboard, and took out the watch. Max noticed that it had been polished up and, gleaming in the light, it looked almost brand new.

'I put a new leather strap on her for you,' said Schindler. Max nodded, his eyes transfixed by the beauty of the rejuvenated watch. He took it from Schindler's hand and felt the quiet stirrings within the golden body, the vibrations of the movement as it whirred away within the shell. Max held the dial to his ear and listened to the steady, smooth tick. A smile lit up his face and immediately infected Jonas Schindler.

'Mr Schindler, thank you so much. Really, thank you,' said Max.

'It's been a pleasure, my boy. Now, you look after her, won't you? She's an old lady – no more foreign trips, eh?'

Max laughed. 'Mr Schindler, ' he began, 'what was the problem?'

'The cogs that drive the decade counter, here, they were all out of balance. But I've replaced the broken part, and cleaned up the rest. You should have no problems with it now.'

'That's why it's never moved since I had it,' said Max.

'I'm not surprised. The faulty counter was throwing everything else out as well.'

'And how do I set the decade dial?' asked Max.

'You don't. That dial works automatically from the movements of the others. There's no way you can move back or move on the years.' Schindler looked carefully at Max's reaction, scrutinizing him with his penetrating eyes. 'In any case, I wouldn't play around with the watch too much. I set her when I had her open. Just leave it alone. She'll be all right now. The other thing was the chime. That too was out of action. The watch is geared to chime each midday and each midnight. I've set that too, you won't need to do anything. As you wind the watch each day, it loads up the chime as well.'

Max stared at his watch, like an explorer gazing at a new continent he had discovered. 'Mr Schindler, what can I say? Thank you once again, for all your help. Now, how much do I owe you?'

'Just pay me for the strap, young man,' said the horologist warmly. 'It was a pleasure to have such a beautiful watch in my hands, if only for a short time.'

'But Mr Schindler,' protested Max, 'you've worked so hard, I must pay . . .'

Schindler shook his head slowly. 'No, no, no, I absolutely refuse. Take it as a gift from Jonas Schindler. Just one thing: promise that if she needs any more attention, you won't take her anywhere else. Always bring her back here, to me.'

Max reddened with embarrassment. 'I promise, Mr Schindler. Thank you so much. I'll remember this.'

Jonas Schindler undid the new strap of the watch and, beckoning Max for his hand, he wrapped the fresh brown leather around the young man's wrist. Max felt the strap tighten around his skin and the ticking of the watch immediately fall into harmony, once again, with his own pulse.

Silently, the decade counter stole on to its first post.

Midday. As the two golden hands joined together and became one, the watch sounded its harmonious chime.

*

It had been pouring all day, and both Max and Imogen were soaked. The heater inside the car was making their clothes steam and the condensation was beginning to make the air heavy. Fortunately, the rain seemed to be easing as Max turned into a narrow mews, tucked away down a side street in Richmond, and parked outside the last house in a Victorian terrace.

'This is the one,' said Imogen. 'They're expecting us.'

Slamming the car doors shut, Imogen and Max made a dash for the front door which opened as if by magic.

'I saw you arrive,' said Gregory Easton, a distinguished-looking man in his sixties. 'Audrey's put the kettle on. Oh, my goodness, you're soaked. Why don't you both run up to the bathroom and dry off first? Tea will be ready by then.'

'Thank you, Mr Easton,' said Max, entering the hallway, and standing back for Imogen to pass him and lead the way. She knew the house, having spent most of her teenage years here. As they dried off, rubbing their hair with the softest towels he had ever felt, Max heard the Eastons moving about downstairs, putting out the tea.

The house was built on three storeys, two large rooms on each floor. The Eastons had retained the original Victorian layout, furnishing each room in order to show off all the nineteenth-century features: the cast-iron fireplaces, the high ceilings, the beautifully crafted cornices. Walking about the house, Max could tell that Imogen was in love with it: her eyes were full of excitement, despite her efforts to contain herself, for fear of influencing Max's promised 'objective opinion'. But Max could feel the enthusiasm. Imogen carried it with her, from room to room, like a glow.

Imogen had often spoken of the Eastons – they had been close to the family table at the wedding – but strangely enough, this was the first time Max had ever been to the house in Stearns Mews. They were friends of Imogen's parents. Gregory Easton had been head of the civil service department in which Imogen's father had served for the first seven years of his career. The two men had become the closest of friends, and the relationship had survived over thirty years. Imogen used to come to the house as a baby. Then, as a teenager, when her parents were away, usually on a business trip, the Eastons would step in and look after her. They had no children of their own, and they treated Imogen as their own daughter. It was like a second home for her so, when the Eastons finally decided to retire to the Isle of Wight, instead of putting the house on the open market, Gregory Easton contacted the Fieldings and asked them if they knew anyone who wanted to buy. When they heard that Max and Imogen were looking for something larger than their two-bedroomed flat in Fulham, Gregory and Audrey immediately dropped the price by fifteen thousand pounds. So, looking around was somewhat academic. The house was perfect: the location convenient for both Max and Imogen, and the price was a bargain.

'It's the least we can do,' said Audrey, pouring another cup of tea for Max. 'I wished we could have dropped the price even more but we're rather committed to our property on the Isle of Wight you see and we really wouldn't want to lose . . .'

Gregory Easton interrupted, sensing that Audrey was about to embark upon an endless sentence. 'Well, dear boy,' he said, 'the most important thing is, do you like the house?'

'We both love it, Mr Easton,' said Max. 'We'd love to buy it.'

'Oh lovely,' squealed Audrey, clapping her hands together silently. 'I'm so happy. Now the house will stay in the family Greg and you must both come down to visit us in our new home though I'm sure you will be very busy I know how frantic life is in the first few years of being married what with you both having so much to do and then I'm sure you'll be jet-setting away to some exotic locations . . .'

Max bit into his thick fruit cake, and glanced over to Imogen. He could tell she was holding back a smile.

Silently, the decade counter stole on to its second post.

Midday. As the two golden hands joined together and became one, the watch sounded its harmonious chime.

'Hello, *Compass*,' said the bright young thing who was Rex Fischer's secretary.

'Hello, Bridget?'

'Max, hi!'

'Is Imogen there, please?'

'She's in with Rex at the moment. Shall I ask her to ring you back?'

'No, that's okay. Just tell her I rang and I'll see her tonight at home.'

Max could sense that it was good news as Imogen walked up Stearns Mews towards the house. He rushed to the door and opened it just as she stepped onto the doorstep. 'Well?' he said, searching Imogen's eyes.

'Well,' she began, with a deliberate hesitation as she strolled into the hallway, 'I think we should crack the champagne.'

'Oh, Imogen,' exclaimed Max, closing the door behind him, 'that's wonderful.'

'Rex said there was no competition. The other researchers were really nice about it as well. Took me down to the bar for a celebratory drink.'

'You are clever, darling,' sighed Max. 'I suppose I'll be seeing you only in airport lounges and plush hotel lobbies from now on. I know what producers are like. You won't want to associate with a humble teacher like me any more.'

'Oh, don't be ridiculous, Max,' retorted Imogen. 'I'm not going to be getting much more than I used to as a senior researcher.'

'I know,' said Max, 'but you'll be in charge of your own shows now. No more being pushed around by other producers. Just think, now you'll be able to make *your* researcher's life hell! Gosh, when I think of how you managed to talk yourself into that job in the first place.'

Imogen laughed. Max was right. The prospect of being in charge of her own projects filled her with a deep satisfaction. Standing in the darkening hallway, still wearing her overcoat, Imogen threw her arms around Max, pulling his lips tight onto her own.

Silently, the decade counter stole on to its third post.

Midnight. As the two golden hands joined together and became one, the watch sounded its harmonious chime.

Max had never seen so much blood. It was beginning to gush now, like a stream being pumped at regular intervals. He was intrigued by its colour, more a dark brown than purple or red. But what really surprised Max, and made him feel a little nauseous, was not the sight, but rather the smell. Was it safe for a person to lose this much blood? Max looked expectantly at the faces around him. No one else seemed concerned. Imogen's skin had become terribly pale, and the perspiration was beginning to flow off her forehead. She was soaked.

'You'll be fine, you'll be fine,' said Max over and over again, eager to keep Imogen from passing out. But the words came out all muffled, and in any case, Imogen was well past hearing by this time. Max mopped her brow. As he did so, Imogen turned her eyes towards him, and he saw in her face the characteristic pleading, so trusting and so vulnerable, the look of a gentle creature searching its master's face for consolation. The look with which Max had fallen in love, the look that the passing years would never be able to change.

'You'll be fine, you'll be fine . . .'

A shaft of pain shot through Imogen, and she screamed. The noise pierced Max to the core and he felt his eyes begin to fill with tears. He held onto her hand tightly, but felt his grip slip with the moisture. If she lost any more blood, she'd hardly have any left. All around him, the others worked with cold calculation, their movements coordinated for the maximum efficiency. Another lightning streak of pain flashed through Imogen's body, and she gasped, her body tightening with the agony. The nightmare seemed to go on for hours. In fact, it took Imogen only forty minutes to be delivered of a beautiful, seven-pound girl.

Silently, the decade counter stole on to its fifth post.

For a few weeks, the golden hands of the watch were given respite. It was the ideal opportunity to have it serviced.

That Christmas, Max kept his promise to Imogen. And to Jonas Schindler. They left the watch with the horologist and the baby with Max's parents.

India had barely changed in the time Max and Imogen had been away. The caste war, as it had come to be known, had subsided but the issue had never been resolved. The government of V. P. Singh had fallen soon after Max and Imogen's honeymoon and subsequent administrations had tried to woo back the disenfranchised. But the caste struggle became yet another strand in the intricate web of subcontinental strife, lingering on from year to year, dividing the nation against itself. Governments came and went. One more of the Gandhi family was assassinated whilst electioneering in the South; Hindus and Sikhs continued to massacre each other in the Punjab; the Indian army became a permanent part of the Kashmiri landscape; in Sind, communal riots claimed whole towns and villages; Hindu fundamentalism grew. Then a series of natural disasters hit the country. The winds shifted unexpectedly. Twice the monsoon failed to keep its promised times, leaving some states parched, flooding others without warning.

And yet, India survived. For its people, such vagaries of the present were minor hurdles to be crossed along the millennial path.

Max and Imogen plotted new routes through the subcontinent, taking in locations they had missed previously but sure also to revisit favourite haunts and old friends. At Fatehpur Sikri, Max searched out his little guide and introduced him to Imogen. Raju was now somewhat taller but he had never forgotten his kind English client who had promised to return. Guru, the samosa-seller, was still there with his old mother, frying snacks at the resting station on the road from Agra to Delhi. Max tried to pay him twice the price to make up for the unexpected discount last time but Guru dismissed the offer with a broad grin. Charles met them at Varanasi. He had recently started teaching English at a local school and enjoyed showing off his visitors to classes full of awestruck youngsters. At the Vishwanath temple, Pundit Sharma was again in a rush, taking in and giving out shoes to impatient pilgrims. This time, as before, there was no mistake. Then Khajuraho. The deserted temple was as peaceful as Max recalled it, the lovers eternally intertwined, isolated and undisturbed in their sculpted alcove. Stan Dyer had returned to Suratpur and had pieced together the shattered fragments of his school. Along Kovalam beach, the lunghi-sellers continued to ply their trade. Sinappu, suddenly tall and wiry, had adjusted his prices to take account of raging production costs in the local mills. Once more, his best design was reserved for the English lady he remembered so well. Prabhu had become established as a priest and now ran a small institute for the Ramakrishna movement, bringing free education to adults in Kerala.

Max never saw the Englishman again. He knew it was futile, yet despite his better judgement he found himself searching the crowds and the horizons for the well-remembered but elusive figure. Max even lingered a little longer at the locations where he had seen the stranger, harbouring some vain hope that the Englishman also might retrace his steps. Imogen still knew nothing of her husband's private preoccupation.

Silently, the decade counter stole on to its sixth post.

Midnight. As the two golden hands joined together and became one, the watch sounded its harmonious chime.

Max had decided to wait until after Imogen had put Miranda to bed. He was not sure what her reaction would be and he thought it best to break the news over a late-night drink, as they relaxed in front of the fire in the lounge. Imogen had finished her edition of *Compass* the previous Sunday so she had been able for the past few days to unwind and spend some time at home.

'Imogen,' said Max, staring into the flames. Imogen murmured, hypnotized by the flickering. 'I've got some news from school.'

'Oh really?' said Imogen, concerned by Max's less than enthusiastic tone. 'I thought things were going quite well at St John's.'

'Oh, they are, they are. The thing is, Chris has been offered the headship at Challoner, which is marvellous of course. He really deserves it. He asked me what I thought he should do. I told him there was no question. He must take it at once.'

'So, what's the problem? I don't understand,' interjected Imogen.

'Well,' continued Max pensively, still staring fixedly at the flames, 'Chris says he's going to recommend me to take over as head of department when he goes.'

'Oh Max,' exclaimed Imogen, twisting round to face him, 'that's marvellous. You must be so pleased.'

'I suppose I am. The thing is, it will be a lot more work and I don't really want to spend even less time at home, with you and with Miranda.'

'Now come on, Max,' continued Imogen, 'you know you've been wanting this for years. Head of English at St John's. You'll just have to learn to delegate, that's all. And we could do with the extra money. Just think, we could pay for Miranda to go to the Dragon Nursery, and as for time together, well, it'll just have to be more trips away, all on our own.'

Max smiled. He was pleased that Imogen was happy. And she was right. This *was* what he had wanted ever since he began teaching. But, somehow, it worried him. He couldn't quite put his finger on it. The more he thought about it, the more indistinct became the source of his concern, like a faint figure on the horizon which recedes the harder you strain your eyes. The increased pressure on his time was only a small part of his worry. Perhaps it was the sense of time speeding past that unnerved him.

For years, he had held certain visions in his imagination: a vision of his wife-to-be, a vision of his children, a vision of his home, a vision of his profession and his status. As those visions left imagination and became reality, Max felt pangs not of satisfaction but of regret. He realized that the currency for this conversion was time. And what a precious currency that was. When Chris had said to Max that he was going to recommend him for head of department, the first thought that crossed Max's mind was, 'I'm far too young. That's a responsible job for a grown-up.' Only then had he recalled that he was almost thirty and a grown-up himself now. And yet it seemed only a few months ago that Max was taking his entrance exams for Oxford. Strange. How life gives with one hand and takes away with the other.

Another thing also worried Max. It all seemed too smooth. They had both been incredibly lucky, he and Imogen. Rewarding jobs, a splendid home, a beautiful baby, their parents in good health. Not that he would have it any other way. But Max was beginning to feel a little discomfited by all their fortune. He believed in balance in Nature. So far, their credits were substantial. When, he wondered, would they have to start paying back the debt?

Silently, the decade counter stole on to its seventh post.

Midday. As the two golden hands joined together and became one, the watch sounded its harmonious chime.

'That's quite a watch you've got, Max,' said Rex Fischer, interrupting the flow of his exposition to listen to its gentle high-pitched music.

'It's an heirloom. My grandmother gave it to me.'

Rex smiled, giving a sharp nod of the head to indicate that he didn't really want the family history. The interlude was over, and he was wanting to continue his earlier point. 'As I was saying, the reason I asked you to join Imogen and myself for lunch was because I felt it only fair to get your reaction to what I have in mind for your wife. After all, it's always the poor partner stuck at home who has to pay for our gallivanting, isn't it, Imogen?'

Imogen nodded. She was a little disappointed that Rex had decided to play it this way. Earlier in the week, he had asked her out to lunch at Langoustine, which was nothing unusual. They often ate together, Imogen and Rex, usually on some flimsy pretext of work, or 'ideas development'. Rex always developed ideas much better in the company of attractive young women. But, when he invited Max as well, Imogen had thought it rather unusual. Was he salving a guilty conscience perhaps?

'Has Imogen spoken to you about the *Literary Masters* project, Max?'

'She did mention that it was an idea you were developing for Channel

Four. But I thought it was just a gleam in the eye at the moment.'

'Well, it was,' said Rex, leaning back to allow the waitress to serve him his food, 'until last night. I was having dinner with Orlando, their commissioning editor for arts, Max, and well, we've got the go-ahead.'

'That's marvellous,' interjected Max, knowing now what Rex was about to say. He cast a glance towards Imogen, who was pretending to be busy with her food.

'The only thing is, I did rather sell the idea to Orlando on the basis that Imogen would produce the series.'

Max kept staring at Imogen. Sheepishly, she looked up, having made a complete mess of her salade Niçoise, and met his eyes. A faint smile appeared at the corner of her mouth.

'How do you feel about that, darling?' asked Max, wishing she could have warned him privately.

'I'm very flattered. I only heard about it this morning, Max . . .'

'. . . otherwise she would have discussed it with you privately,' said Rex, 'yes, I know, I should have let the two of you talk about it alone. But the fact is that Imogen is indispensable to this project. She's done all the development work and I'm sure Orlando's rather taken with her. It's quite an investment. We're asking for a million. And Riverside desperately needs the commission. The franchises come up for renewal again in two years' time and a prestige series like this is just what we need to put us ahead.'

Max was still looking at Imogen, trying hard to ignore Rex in his right ear. None of them had touched their food.

'Do you want to do it, Imogen?' asked Max.

'Of course I *want* to do it,' she snapped, impatiently. Then, regaining her composure, Imogen said, 'Look, Max, this is a big break for me, my own series and it's a prestige project. I can't pass on this.'

'I'm sure Max wouldn't want you to give up such an opportunity,' interjected Rex, taking a huge mouthful of salad, and munching it with relish, 'would you, Max?'

Something about Rex's gusto made Max feel as if he were being a spoilsport. 'I know how much this means to Imogen . . . and to you, of course, Rex.'

Max looked over to Imogen. She had given up on her salad. It was very uncharacteristic of Imogen to leave her food in this way. He knew she must be very upset. Taking a few mouthfuls from his own plate in order to normalize the atmosphere, Max asked in the most matter-of-fact tone he could muster, 'So, when does it have to be made for?'

The calm normality of Max's voice encouraged Imogen. She looked up, first to Rex, then to Max and smiled. 'We originally put in a production schedule of eighteen months. I don't know what Channel Four has agreed to.'

'I think eighteen months is about right,' said Rex. 'They want delivery by spring two years' time.'

Imogen was slowly beginning to rediscover her appetite. The salmon she had ordered was steaming through its silver foil jacket, gleaming amidst a rainbow of multicoloured sauces around it.

'That looks lovely, Imogen,' said Max affectionately.

While Rex explained more of the *Literary Masters* series to Max, she set to work on her food, making up for the wasted salad. Yet she knew that Max was concerned. And he was as much concerned for her and for Miranda as for himself. Promotion had served to increase the demands on Imogen's time. Somehow, it hadn't turned out quite the way she had expected. The stakes had got higher: the need to stay ahead, to break new ground, to push the programme to its limits. It all meant more time spent on *Compass*, more time away from Max and Miranda.

Not that Max had ever complained. He soldiered on patiently, looking after Miranda, taking her back and forth from the Dragon Nursery each day, easing the way for Imogen, and all the time running the English department at St John's.

Imogen glanced at him, carefully eating his chicken and listening attentively to Rex Fischer holding forth about the series or the company or himself. They had come a long way since those stolen afternoons in Max's college room in Merton Street and he had never once stood in her way. She loved him passionately. But Imogen was baffled by a gradual change in Max's way of looking at the world, which seemed to have come with their increasing success and happiness. At Oxford, he had been ambitious and thrusting, always looking towards the future, making plans, concocting elaborate strategies. Now, he talked constantly of the past and Imogen often felt that he was trying to suspend it in words, cling on to experience with language. Each passing year found him more introspective, less willing to move on. He wanted things to slow down. He wanted a breathing space, time to reflect. He was, she thought, suspicious of their good luck.

Max always paid his debts. Imogen knew, although he had never told her specifically, that he was expecting to be called to account at any time.

Rex obviously had an arrangement at Langoustine, for no bill was offered at the end of their meal. Max was feeling much more optimistic, now that Rex had explained the series to him. In fact, unknown to Imogen, engrossed in her own reflections, Max and Rex Fischer had come to a mutual agreement. *Compass* would find some money in its huge budget to pay for Max to go out to location, school vacations permitting. Max thought it a splendid arrangement and had warmed to Rex when he proposed it. As the three of them descended the stone steps leading out of the restaurant, Rex's driver pulled up in his Mercedes limousine.

'Can I offer either of you a lift anywhere?' asked Rex, glancing up at the dark clouds overhead. 'It looks like rain.'

'No thanks,' answered Imogen, 'I've got to get a few things in town. We'll walk. Thanks anyway. I'll see you tomorrow.'

Rex smiled goodbye, slammed the door shut and the car sped off beneath the flashing red and green neon lights dancing constantly in the Soho shop windows.

'Well,' said Max, watching the car disappear. They looked at each other, Imogen nervous in anticipation at Max's reaction to being ambushed in this way. Max searched her worried eyes for a moment, then smiled and put his arm around her.

'Congratulations, darling,' he said, pulling her head towards him, and kissing her on the brow. 'I'm very proud of you.'

Imogen smiled in relief. She was glad there was going to be no unpleasant post-mortem of the lunch. It was almost four o'clock, but the storm clouds made everything so dark. The street lights had come on, their sensors deceived by the premature arrival of night. Still holding each other, Max and Imogen turned to walk up Erasmus Street.

It was at times like this that Max felt most threatened, most out of control. His happiness for Imogen was genuine. He wanted her to reach for higher and higher goals and he was delighted that she seemed to have found her element in arts broadcasting and with Rex Fischer. The personal cost was one that Max was willing to pay, for the sake of a future when the frantic scramblings of these early years would be past and he, Imogen and Miranda could settle down to a more peaceful and controlled lifestyle. How he had changed. It often amused him to consider the reversal of his and Imogen's aspirations. At Oxford, it was he who had been the ambitious one, constantly worrying about his future and his career, striving ceaselessly to make contacts who might be useful to him. As a student Max had had very specific notions of success, all revolving around the idea of making an intervention, of leaving behind in some way a positive trace of one's all too ephemeral existence. This, combined with a profound sense of urgency, had made him persistently restless, and the mixture of ambition and impatience had not been a healthy one. He had often been accused of being overly competitive by his tutors and his peers, and those who knew him well had warned Max about such an unreasonable drawing up of the lines with mortality. But try as he might, Max simply could not rid himself of the constant need to achieve, the need to push himself to the limits, to win, the need for recognition. It was his defence against his own ever-present fear of a wasted life.

It was Imogen who had helped him to get things into the right perspective. Time spent with Imogen gave Max a satisfaction he had never sensed before. With her, he realized that the emotional and spiritual growth that comes from a sharing of one's soul could be a far more definite barrier against the passing years than any worldly achievement. Max learned to give something of himself, something intensely personal and precious, a gift rather than a sacrifice. What Imogen offered in return was far more substantial, far more permanent than the momentary triumphs of academic or professional success. And if Imogen had helped him to become aware of the value of shared experience and growth, India had asserted to Max the utter futility of investing in worldly advance. Their trip back had underlined for him the messages he had only half-heard the first time he had braved the subcontinent. Half-heard and deliberately only half-acknowledged. The experience had disorientated Max, sent his safe and ordered world view into a flaming spiral. He had thought at first that he would get over it, settle back down to his cosy life in London, absorb the adventures like periodic excursions away from his real world. But Max had been wrong, so wrong. Only now was he beginning to realize that the immediacy, the authenticity of India, its insistent reality, its refusal to allow the individual to cloak himself in worldly success, was, in fact, far more substantial than the life for which he had striven so hard. So now, the more he and Imogen acquired the success to which they had aspired so ardently in the past, the more Max felt its essential futility.

Suddenly, an enormous white crack opened up in the dark clouds and a momentary flash lit up the sky. A moment later, thunder drowned out all the sounds of the street. Max and Imogen looked up simultaneously at the apocalyptic sky. Just then, as they turned, a passer-by crashed into them. Imogen stepped back, startled.

'Oh, sorry guv,' said the youth, dressed in denim. His hair was closely cropped and he wore a tiny gold earring. He had had his head bowed, obviously rushing to avoid the coming downpour. 'Didn't see yer there.'

'That's all right,' replied Max, 'my fault.'

Stepping off the kerb, the young man continued on his way. Imogen put him in his thirties.

Most people did. He had always been big for his age. At school, they used to call him the Hulk. Even the teachers. 'Hoskins!' they would shout, just as the school gates were swinging shut at nine o'clock precisely, 'Hoskins! Get that big hulk of yours in here at once!' That was only a few years ago. Despite his looks, Craig Hoskins was only nineteen.

They lived in Stratford, the Hoskins family, or clan as everyone locally thought of them. Three generations of Hoskinses had been born in the semi. It was a lucky house, that's what Millie always said, and whenever she said it, which was at least twice a day, she would also add: 'Good job we moved from that bloody terrace in Mile End.' Millie was Craig's grandmother, queen bee of the family. She lived with them in the semi, had her own room at the top of the house. Last year, Craig's dad and a couple of his mates had put in a chairlift all the way up the stairs. Made life a lot easier for Millie. No one asked too closely where the lift came from. High Street Ken, or High Street for short, had 'acquired' it in the course of a transaction a few weeks back. Craig had never seen a chairlift made in China before. Still, as High Street had said, 'It swings the old girl up and down a dream.'

Craig had started to get fed up being imprisoned at home all day, listening to his mum shouting: 'So, when ya gonna get yaself a proper job, eh?'

'Oh mum, leave off. You know I'm looking round.'

She was always getting at him, his mum, making him out to be the black sheep. All his brothers had gone into business, wholesale and retail along the Whitechapel, but Craig just wasn't interested in that. He was what you might call more creative. Anyway, he was fed up, so last week he had gone out with a mate of his and got himself a job up town. He told his mum he was a trainee manager for a small hotel in the West End. She was very proud of him, even shed a tear at the thought of her little boy moving up in the world, making a name for himself.

'You stick in there, Craig,' she advised him. 'Before ya know it, they'll be asking ya to be manager.'

Possibly. But it wasn't the sort of hotel his mum would have approved of. They rented rooms by the hour, rather than by the night. And the trainee manager's job was rather loosely defined. At the moment, it meant keeping out the riff-raff. But that was only temporary. Soon Craig would be inside, perhaps taking money, perhaps even answering the phones. For the time being, however, Craig Hoskins was doing the thing he was best at. Using his enormous body to intimidate people.

He was late that day. And he'd have to stand outside all afternoon, getting soaked. He hated it when it rained. There were always more loonies wandering in when it rained. Bloody perverts. Why was it, wondered Craig, that they all wore really strong, Coke-bottle glasses? What the hell did they do to themselves or with themselves that made their eyes so bad? He'd love to ask one of them one day. Mind you, most of them couldn't string a sentence together. Turning the corner into Aristotle Street, Craig put his hands into his trouser pockets. It was pouring now and his denims were changing colour from blue to black. He felt something damp in his hand. Craig pulled out the paper from his pocket and unfolded it. It was a little poster someone had thrust into his hand a few days ago outside Stratford tube station. He hadn't bothered to read it but now, just before he threw it away, curiosity won out. Craig examined the circular carefully.

'OUT OF WORK?' it demanded, in an aggressive red ink. 'NOWHERE TO LIVE? FED UP WITH THE FILTH?' Then, in a more subdued black ink, the poster continued: 'We all know what it's like to be out of work, not have a decent roof over your head, not have enough to eat. So, how does it make you feel when you see Blacks and Asians living it up all around you? You've seen their flashy cars, their expensive houses. Some of these foreign filth have even had the nerve to marry our women. And their mongrel children mix with our brothers, our sisters, our sons and our daughters. This must stop. Now. You can help.'

As Craig cast his eyes down the page, the lettering turned red again: 'KICK OUT THE FILTH. KEEP BRITAIN WHITE. JOIN US TODAY! MEETING, NEWHAM CHURCH HALL, SAT. NIGHT, 10.'

Finally, at the bottom, an address to write to: 'Crusade, PO Box 6,

Guildford.' Craig screwed up the sodden paper and threw it into the gutter. He watched it float off down the street, in a pool of red ink. Craig looked at his hands. They too were red from the cheap print.

By the time they got to their front door, Max and Imogen were drenched. As he ran up the garden path, Max fumbled about in his pocket, found the keys and took them out, ready to attack the front-door lock. The storm was at its height now, lightning flashing across the sky every few minutes, followed closely by resounding claps of thunder. Max entered the hallway and shut the door behind him. He was alone. The house seemed very quiet, unnaturally so, and there was an inexplicable chill he had never felt before. As he strained his ears to listen to the silence, Max heard the distant tapping of a typewriter. He strode down the hall and into the study. The door swung open slowly, to reveal an empty room. On the writing desk, set into the bay window that gave onto the front garden, the typewriter lay, unused and silent. Then another sound entered the silence. It was someone calling.

'Max!' said the voice. 'Max! Max!'

Max gave the study one final look then turned and walked up the stairs, towards the call. The house was really cold now. Someone must have left a window open, he thought, and the heating won't come on till seven. As he reached the first landing, Max brushed the radiator with his hand, a reflex action. With a start, he pulled it away at once. The radiator was boiling. It had scorched Max's hand. The calling became louder and more persistent. 'Max! Max!' it demanded. He reached the lounge. The call was definitely coming from inside the room. The door was shut, and Max hesitated for a moment before opening it.

'Do come in, my dear boy,' said a genial voice. 'We've been expecting you.'

For a few seconds, Max couldn't believe the scene before him. He had broken in upon a tea party. It was in full swing, with much chatter, and laughter, great tinkling of china teacups and the warm gurgle of hot tea being poured from a silver teapot. But who were these people?

'You must be freezing, Max,' said a woman seated on the sofa. Max looked over to her. It was his mother. He relaxed, feeling the tension of his temples and neck slip away. 'Come and have a hot cup of tea.'

Max looked over to the easy chair, where a man was pouring tea from the pot into a cup.

'Dad?' whispered Max, 'Dad. What's going on? Who are all these people? Why are you all here? Where's Imogen?'

The couple on the far end of the sofa burst into laughter. Max's eyes followed the sound. Gregory Easton had obviously told some hilarious joke and Audrey, loyal to the last, was convulsed with laughter.

'Oh, Gregory,' she squealed, 'you must tell that to Jonas.' Then, turning to the man opposite her, Audrey said, 'Mr Schindler you must hear Gregory's story it's the funniest thing I've ever heard . . .' Jonas

Schindler was too busy eating his cucumber sandwich to pay any attention to Mrs Easton. Max watched him eating with the very same precision he had shown when handling the watch. The presence of Jonas Schindler confused Max most of all. What was he doing here?

'But surely you must remember, young man,' said Schindler, finishing off his mouthful and staring straight towards Max. His voice rose above the hubbub in the room, and a sudden silence descended upon the festive company. Outside, a shaft of lightning fell to earth, tearing the heavens, applauded by a burst of thunder. Max saw all faces turn towards him. Jonas Schindler put out his left arm, taking hold of the hand of the woman sitting in the chair by his side.

'You can't have forgotten,' he continued. 'Your grandmother invited me.' As Jonas Schindler patted the hand of the old woman seated next to him, she turned towards Max. Her face was wizened with age, the folds of the skin forming deep trenches across her brow and cheeks. But, for all the ravages of time, Max still recognized her, still saw the beauty of the eyes, the kindness he recalled from his childhood years, the charm of the smile. He felt his lips form words, but heard nothing.

'Don't worry, my dear,' said his grandmother, softly, 'don't worry. She's safe now, safe with us.' Amid his confusion, Max felt a deep solace, a profound relief. He did not know what or who his grandmother was referring to, but he felt happy. It was just then that Max heard the typewriter begin once again its distant tap tap tap. Casting his eyes around the lounge, he saw his grandmother get up out of her chair with slow, careful movements, helped by Jonas Schindler's steadying hand. As she found her feet, the old woman leaned over to her side and picked up her carved walking-stick. The room had become suddenly very quiet, everyone watching the grandmother as she headed cautiously towards the door and Max. He knew instinctively that she meant him to follow her out. As she edged past, Max turned and left the room, taking short, slow steps behind his grandmother as, one by one, she descended the steep staircase. It was still intensely cold and he shivered involuntarily. The typing was coming from the study, as it had done before, but this time the rhythm was far more regular, the sound more furious and determined as if someone were trying desperately to beat a deadline. Step by step, his grandmother continued her descent, Max following close behind. His eyes were fixed on her still dark hair, neatly pulled back and held with a silver hairclip. He noticed that the clasp was engraved with a miniature hunting scene, an exquisitely detailed doe being dragged to the ground by a single hound.

At last, stepping off the final stair onto the ground floor, the old woman steadied herself, then continued down the hallway, past the study and towards the front door. Max kept pace, but hesitated momentarily as he reached the study door. It had swung shut since he was last here. He looked along the hall towards his grandmother, but she was gone. Max pushed the study door open once more. Once more it slid over the thick carpet, gradually revealing the bookshelves and the figure of a woman, sitting at the writing desk, hunched over the typewriter. Max thought he recognized her but was not sure. She was engrossed in her work.

'Hello?' he said, tentatively. The figure remained busy in her task, refusing to turn around. 'Hello?' said Max, more firmly. Still the woman continued typing. Perhaps she can't hear, thought Max. He edged closer to her, careful not to make a sound, for fear of startling the stranger. As he closed in on her, he saw the back of her head become larger and larger, as if she were floating towards him, rather than he treading towards her. Suddenly, the woman sensed someone behind her and stopped typing. As the sound stopped, so Max too came to a halt. For a moment the stranger looked straight ahead of her, out of the bay window that gave onto the front garden. Max could hear his own breathing now, as he waited expectantly for her to turn around.

Slowly, deliberately, taking her time, the woman turned. Semi-profile, profile, then finally, straight towards Max. Lightning cracked across the sky, illuminating the room, followed by thunder. Max flinched. A shock sped down his spine, and he felt his body go numb.

'Imogen,' he whispered to himself, aghast at the apparition. He had failed to recognize her. The woman looked at Max, smiled, then turned back to her work. For a few seconds, she looked out at the garden again, as if lost in a pensive recollection. Then she bowed her head and began to type once more.

Max could still hear the tapping of the typewriter keys in the darkness. Tap, tap, tap. Gradually, the image of the woman hunched over her machine faded into the night, and Max became aware of himself, awake in the small hours of the morning. Imogen's regular breathing next to him lulled him into a half-sleeping, reflective state. Soon, his own breathing began to keep time with hers. He thought about the lunch with Rex, the prospect of Imogen being away for long periods at a stretch, the added pressures that would place upon Miranda and upon him. Perhaps he should ask the Head for his old job back and give up all the extra responsibilities. After all, they didn't really need the money now. Riverside would pay Imogen a fortune now that she was to be a series producer. What Max earned was merely pocket money. He would think about it. He looked over to the electronic clock on the mantelpiece, its red figures burning into the darkness. He stared at the numbers until the final digit changed. Another minute had passed, silently, surreptitiously. Lying in his bed, in the darkness, Max thought back to the first time he and Imogen had travelled in India, on their honeymoon. It seemed such a long time ago, yet the memories of that journey were so vivid, much more alive than the recollections of the subsequent trip. Most vivid of all was still the image of the Englishman, the stranger who seemed to have followed Max and Imogen all over India, yet who had remained impenetrable. Even now, seven years on, Max could see the image of the traveller so clearly, pick out the smallest detail of his clothes, almost feel the pain of the scar on his cheek. Max still looked at people quite closely in the street, expecting one day to bump into the mysterious stranger. On a number of occasions Max was sure he had seen the Englishman, standing on a railway platform, jumping onto a bus, flashing by in a taxi, eating in a restaurant window, but each time he had been mistaken.

And in all these years, Max had not shared his private mystery with Imogen. He thought of her as she had been then, so innocent, so open-minded, so eager for him to love India the way she did. He turned restlessly towards her. Where was that girl now? The face was the same, young and unlined, but Max felt a surge of yearning for the uncynical freshness of the Imogen he had known at Oxford. Watching her still, gentle face, he clenched his fists, resentful of the gruelling practicalities that seemed to be damaging Imogen's spirit. Over the years, the more she spent her life with journalists and media people, the more she lost her sense of the numinous. As all traces of her early mysticism faded from her life, it seemed more than ever impossible that Max should discuss with Imogen his long-treasured obsession with the Englishman.

Max really had not been sure about travelling all the way up to Oxford just to see Anjali dance. He had not complained about having to give up his Saturday, but he had gone into an extended silence, his eyes fixed on the motorway ahead. Still, Imogen had assured him that it would be quite a treat and he was keen to meet the young Indian dancer who seemed to have captivated her. They had met when Anjali had come into studio to perform some Kathak for *Compass*. Imogen had produced the item, and the two women had got on at once. Now, Anjali had invited Imogen and Max to an evening of Indian music and dance in the Holywell Music Rooms. Max knew that Anjali was extremely beautiful: that much he had gleaned instantly as he watched her perform on television, so there was to be some compensation for the long journey. By the time they took up their seats in the packed Music Rooms, Max had overcome his initial reticence and was quite enthusiastic.

The stage was bare but for the three musicians sitting in a semicircle by the right-hand edge. Max looked around the cramped auditorium, which was packed to the brim. A few years ago, he and Imogen would have known at least a dozen people still here from their undergraduate days. But not now. The students were beginning to look young, and they cast fairly deferential looks towards Max as he caught their gaze. He wondered how old he must look to them. The thought filled him with horror. He turned back to the brochure he had bought at the entrance, and read all about Anjali. According to the biography, Anjali, now a second-year postgraduate at Magdalen, was working for a D.Phil. in Oriental Studies. Intrigued, Max read on. 'A dancer from the age of four, Anjali has continued to pursue her study of the classical Indian dance forms, often spending months of her vacations in India, training with the top instructors in the subcontinent. She has won almost every prize for dancing and has appeared in films and on television as an expert in her chosen craft. Anjali's specialities are the Kathak and Bharat Natyam forms . . .'

Max scanned the page, skimming across the explanations of the dance styles. 'Bharat Natyam: one of the most popular classical dance styles, Bharat Natyam originated in the ancient temples of South India. The dances usually tell of events in the life of Lord Krishna . . . Kathak: a dance form more characteristic of the north, at first very similar to Bharat Natyam. Persian and Moslem influence transformed the dance from a temple ritual to courtly entertainment . . .'

He looked up from the pamphlet. The auditorium was still buzzing with noise as people filed in and searched the stacked rows for the few remaining seats. There was a lavish sprinkling of Indian people present, the women in luxurious silk saris, the men in smart Nehru suits. Apparently, Anjali's family were great personal friends of the Indian High Commissioner in London and the whole front row had been reserved for the diplomatic entourage. Gradually, the noise in the Music Rooms began to abate, and then the lights dimmed. A sharp, shrill drumbeat pierced the silence. Then another beat and another, followed by a sequence of guttural sounds. 'Da, da da. Da, da da. Da . . .' The sounds accelerated with the drumming. Soon, the tabla player had struck up a hypnotic rhythm, followed closely by the mellifluous strains of the sitar and then the strangely Western melody of the violin. Max looked at the three musicians, each of them rolling his head in time to the beat. As the music rose in a crescendo, the spotlight flashed over to the opposite corner and Anjali appeared, floating across the stage, taking tiny footsteps, moving sideways as if swimming on air.

The audience was still, enthralled by the vision on the stage. Anjali's costume, a close-fitting silk tunic embroidered with thousands of sequins, glistened in the light, throwing out multicoloured rays in all directions. On her head she wore a crown of fresh carnations and narcissi, and her arms were covered with more of the sequins, leading down to meticulously painted hands. On each wrist and on each ankle she wore bracelets of tiny bells. As she stamped and twisted her arms to the music, the sound of the bells accompanied the beat, completing the quartet. But most striking of all was the makeup. At first, Max did not recognize the Indian dancer, for her face was completely painted in vibrant emerald and gold. Her eyes had been picked out by large almond outlines starting at the bridge of her nose and extending right round to the temples. Her dark irises, made even darker by the liberal application of kajal, shone like hazelnuts lying in the centre of two huge pods. As she danced, Anjali used her eyes for maximum expression, moving them in time to the music, and synchronized perfectly to the movements of her body.

The three musicians, their eyes following the merest movement on the stage, swayed from side to side. Max watched Anjali carefully as she performed her repertoire. It was remarkable to behold the sheer extent of the energy coming from the slight, perfectly proportioned body. Anjali had complete control over each movement, each individual muscle and fibre. At any given moment, dozens of different parts of her body were moving autonomously, in perfect harmony to the music, and all coordinated centrally by pure will. But it was Anjali's face that most captivated Max. Amid all the frenetic activity it remained placid, still, stoic. The more her body twisted and turned, the more her arms and legs cut through the air, accompanied by the shrill music of the bells, the more Anjali's face retained its central peace. It was as if her soul was the eye of the storm, tranquil and unmoved, amidst the frenzy of the body. Round and round she turned, faster and faster, round and round. The ankle chains were flying in circles around her feet, the bells silenced by the speed of movement. The music too had risen to a rhythm so perfect it was almost inaudible, merely a part of the unique aura created by the dance. Round and round, faster and faster, her head remaining absolutely still, Anjali lost herself in the dance, and all motion stopped.

For a moment, Max forgot where he was. And instead of the young Indian dancer, enthused by the perfection of her dance, he saw before him the vision of the young boy burning outside the temple at Varanasi. Max struggled to break free from the crowd of people holding him back. He must help the boy before it was too late. Looking into the heat of the petrol flames, Max caught sight once more of the youthful face, writhing in agony. The boy turned, round and round, causing the flames to swirl about him, like a typhoon or a human Catherine wheel. Then, at once, the pain was gone. Max looked again at the boy's face, amid the flames. Across his lips, a smile had formed, and his brow was smooth and serene.

At the still point of the turning world, thought Max.

He gazed at Anjali in pure admiration. There was not a single note, not a single movement out of place. And all through her performance, Anjali maintained on her lips that same narcotic smile that so characterized the divine statues and effigies Max had seen all over the subcontinent. It was positively mesmeric. At one point, he became so hypnotized by the rhythm and the movement that his eyes lost their focus and all he could see before him was a blur of sparkles and colour and movement.

It was an explosion of applause from the audience that brought Max round from his reverie. Slowly, the distant spangles and kaleidoscope of lights formed themselves into definite shapes, converging into the elegant but exhausted figure on the stage. Anjali bowed her head first to the left, then to the right, finally to the centre of the audience. She noticed Imogen and smiled. Then she looked at Max. As their eyes met, Anjali's smile sobered momentarily. She dropped her gaze, then continued with her warm acknowledgement of other friends. Max continued to stare, his hands coming together in a final, silent clap. He kept his damp palms joined, lost in his own thoughts.

'Isn't she marvellous?' asked Imogen, above the roar of the applause.

Max was still too rapt in the dance to answer, but he managed to mumble an incoherent reply. For some time after the end of the performance, the music and the movement continued to resound within his head. Slowly, as the Music Rooms emptied, Max replayed the visions in his imagination, enthralled once more by the sublimity of the art.

Seventy miles to the east, other lights continued to burn, late into the night, amid the darkness of a bleak and barren housing estate. From a distance, one might have assumed a party was in progress. But there was no music, only the sound of a single voice, a man's voice, occasionally rising in passion. As one got nearer to the church hall, one might have just picked out a few words from the speaker's electronic voice: 'No more space . . . Back home . . . Britain for the British . . . Filth . . .' And nearer still, drawn by curiosity, one might have heard complete sentences.

'We have remained silent for too long. The eighties were a time of class war, when our neighbourhoods, our families, our whole lifestyle was threatened by people who wanted to buy us out. We fought hard, and we fought together. Now we face another war, and the enemy is one we have confronted before . . .'

It was curiosity that had drawn Craig Hoskins to the church hall that Saturday night. Curiosity and boredom. Business at the Naughty Nighties had been slack all week and the management had decided to give Craig the weekend off. So, being at a loose end, Craig and a few of his friends had gone to the Sundial for a few drinks. There, inside the public bar, they had been approached by a youngster handing out more Crusade leaflets, just like the one Craig had had given to him outside the tube station last week. The four friends had almost run out of money for drinks anyway, so it was either coming on here or going home to watch the television. They had come to the church hall, to see what all the fuss was about and because there was just the slim possibility that some attractive girls might turn up.

The two sentries at the door to the church hall saw Craig and his friends approaching and decided that they fitted the bill for membership. By the time Craig and the others reached the entrance, they were welcomed like old friends, comrades in arms. A row of seats was cleared for them and they were each given a glossy folder, its front embossed with the logo of Crusade: a silver knight's helmet, above a cross made up of a burning arrow and a hammer. Inside, Craig found a selection of newspaper cuttings, leaflets and pamphlets explaining the philosophy of Crusade, and photographs of new young recruits 'from all walks of life', all dressed in black. Finally, attached to the back, a membership form.

Craig was surprised and a little shocked by what he found at the hall.

He had expected a group of people like himself, gathered to hear what Crusade had to say, then perhaps a few drinks and a bit of chat. A sort of late-night booze-up, in fact. Instead, he discovered that he and his mates had stumbled upon a pretty heavy political rally. The stage was harsh, all covered in black cloth carefully draped over the walls, floor and ceiling. At the centre, the black was interrupted by a large flag bearing the logo of Crusade: the helmet, arrow and hammer. It rose high above a lectern, placed with meticulous accuracy in the centre of the stage. This too carried the martial symbol. The combination of the black and the silver and the golden flames of the arrow was at once elegant and sinister. When Craig and his friends first arrived, the stage was empty, yet the hall was relatively silent, with only the hiss of hushed whispers. Most of the audience was also dressed in black. The front few rows were exclusively occupied by young men and women, all in their teens or twenties, all wearing the Crusade uniform of black polo-neck sweaters above black trousers and heavy black boots, each pair highly polished. These, as Craig would soon find out, were the new recruits to the organization, the novices, all recently embarked upon their training for the cause. Further back, the audience was a mix of middle-aged men, some women, but mostly labourers, many of whom had obviously wandered over from the local men's clubs. Some had made an attempt to wear black, but it was a mishmash of leather jackets, black jeans, grey shirts, dark T-shirts, nothing as carefully orchestrated as the uniforms of the elite at the front.

It was as Craig was looking at the brochure photographs of young people like himself, on some adventure training weekend and apparently having a marvellous time, that the lights in the hall dimmed, plunging the audience into darkness. Suddenly, from three or four speakers mounted high up in the hall, the opening strains of 'Mars', from the *Planets* suite, started to play, beginning gently, then rising to a deafening climax. As the music rose to a pitch, a spotlight flashed on to the lectern, revealing a tall, hard-featured man dressed in black jumper and black trousers, carefully pressed, his dark hair cut short, almost to the scalp. Even from this distance, at the back of the hall, Craig could make out that the man had merciless eyes, honed by years of street-fighting.

'Told you it was worth coming,' said Ian, sitting to the left of Craig.

'Yeah,' whispered Jack, to Craig's right. 'Wouldn't like to meet 'im on a dark night.'

For a few lingering moments, the man remained motionless, waiting for the music to subside, and holding the audience's attention with his gaze. Then more lights flashed on, illuminating the area either side of the lectern, revealing two rows of young men, six on each side, all wearing the same black uniform and, most unsettling of all, black balaclava hats, completely covering the face except for three openings, one for each eye, one for the mouth. They stood in perfect formation, like two wings, fanning out carefully at an acute angle from the centre. Gradually, as the final strains of the music disappeared, with not a single movement of his head, the speaker began.

'Each one of us here today shares a dream.' He paused, letting his voice reverberate around the hall. The sound fell into each person's consciousness, like drops of blood falling into clear water. 'Each one of us shares a vision. It's a vision of a future. And it's a future we are going to create together.'

On the word 'together', the front few rows suddenly and in perfect unison erupted in one voice: 'TOGETHER!' The hall shook with the sound and startled Craig, shaking him out of his torpor.

'Over the years,' continued the speaker, 'we have all seen our homes, our streets, our country being taken over by outsiders. These people have no right to be here. They are not part of this country. Slowly, secretly, they have invaded our land. Aliens, from places still back in the dark ages. Look around you. Streets where we used to play as children. Homes where our families grew up. Towns and cities we used to be proud of, whose names dominated the world: Manchester, Birmingham, Coventry, Sheffield, London. Places known throughout the world. What are they now? Slums, not good enough even for rats . . .' A fire burned in the speaker's eyes. He scanned the audience, holding each person in turn with his direct, unflinching stare.

'Don't let them tell you the aliens have brought prosperity back to this country. Prosperity? For whom? Do you see the blacks helping anyone not their own colour? Do their shops and factories take on any of us? Do their businesses help us? No. It is money for themselves they want. And they are bleeding us dry. How many people here tonight have been put out of work? It's impossible now to earn a decent wage, even to bring in enough to look after your own family.'

A murmur of assent spread around the hall, ending in a passionate shout from a frustrated labourer: 'Kick 'em out!'

'Whole communities just wiped out. The streets are no longer safe for our children or our women. Our old people live in fear, even inside their homes. Fear of the savages who have invaded our land.' The speaker paused once more, giving time for his words to infect the audience, and allowing the dissent to grow. Agitation had set in and Craig, looking around him, was aware of vehement whispering and vigorous nodding of heads.

'But all is not lost!' boomed the speaker's voice. Another pause, allowing silence to descend once more. 'All is not lost. We can rid our nation of this filth in our midst. We can stand up and fight and reclaim our land, the land for which our fathers and their fathers before them fought so bravely. We can drive the invader from our shores. We can win, if we stand united!'

Once more, on the word 'united', the audience erupted, speaking as one voice: 'UNITED!' This time, even the older people at the back of the hall joined in, as if carried along automatically by the impetus of the group. The speaker looked around the hall slowly, his head moving to the sounds of the chant. As the noise died down, he raised both arms in a gesture of supplication: 'We bring hope to this nation, and to its people. We are the chosen few, ready to die for our cause. We are the guardians of the future. We are the CRUSADE!'

At the precise moment the word 'crusade' reverberated around the hall, the twelve elite guards on the stage shouted 'CRUSADE!', unfolded their arms in one movement and reached round their backs. Each balaclava'ed gladiator pulled out a powerful pair of nunchakas, swinging them round to the front and raising them high above their heads. The weapon was made up of two heavy wooden staves, joined together by a metal chain. Pulling the nunchakas tight, the twelve Crusaders on stage held them high, ready for action. Craig was both startled and excited by their military precision. He had seen nunchakas in martial arts magazines, and in Chinese kung-fu films, where agile little gymnasts used the weapons to show off their dexterity. Used properly, the wooden staves, swinging round, could kill an opponent instantly. The wood and the steel of the nunchakas glistened in the spotlights, and the uniformity of the Crusaders' movements filled all the people in the hall with an excitement and a yearning to be part of the group. At this time, from this distance, the actions on stage looked no more real than events on celluloid, and Craig felt as if he were, for a moment, watching a glamorous movie. But he could, if he wished, take part in this one. Here was one world that would not exclude him.

'CRUSADE!' shouted the recruits on stage. Soon their chanting spread through the assembly: 'CRUSADE! CRUSADE! CRUSADE!' As the flow increased and the whole crowd joined in, the hypnotic syllables began to make the building reverberate with their rhythm. 'CRUSADE! CRUSADE! CRUSADE!' It was a war cry, and the mass of the audience raised it as a call to arms. On stage, the speaker gazed round the hall, maintaining his cold imperturbability. He was not chanting. He was not one of the troops. The more he controlled his passion, the more frenzied his disciples became in their own. 'CRUSADE! CRUSADE! CRUSADE!' The rhythm made Craig sway with its energy. Soon, his own lips began to move, forming the irresistible syllables.

'Crusade,' he whispered, barely audibly. 'Crusade.'

Outside, a few hundred yards from the hall, a police car slid silently into the estate, its engine humming in the still of the night. All the flats were quiet, their lights extinguished long ago. In the distance a cat played with an empty tin can, its hollow metallic song piercing the night like a sharp cut. As the car turned into the avenue leading to the hall, the chanting inside became louder, carried across the concrete wasteland by a light breeze. The patrol car stopped. The hall lights sparkled in the mist of the small hours. For a moment, the officers listened to the unholy choir, the incantation spreading across the estate like smoke in an empty room. Then, silently, the wheels turned, and with a quiet swish the car sped off, disappearing into the darkness.

Twenty kilometres west of Chartres lay the small village of Illiers-Combray.

Like hundreds of other villages in France, Illiers-Combray was little more than a collection of a few dozen two-storey stone houses, a handful of large, outlying farms, a one-pavilion railway station, hundreds of acres of fertile land, all neatly divided up into tidy rectangles, and finally, of course, the inevitable châteaux, a little way out of town, resplendent in their own grounds. Little had changed here over the past few centuries. The local church still sounded the time, and the fieldworkers organized their day according to the peal of the bells. Two bakers serviced the whole community, working day and night, as their fathers had done before them, fashioning a pantheon of cakes and breads from the local wheat. The petite madeleine was their speciality, and the one thing that made this tiny village distinctive. A single carpenter still made, and repaired, all the furniture in all the houses, using tools handed down from generation to generation.

Casual tourists passed through the village, and noticed little difference between its sleepy lanes and secluded avenues, and the hundreds of others that characterized the hidden villages of Eure-et-Loir. Casual tourists often chose not to stop in the village, preferring instead to rush on to Chartres, then onwards to Paris. And yet, despite the superficial similarities, Illiers-Combray was unlike any other village, not only in the province, but in the whole of France. Indeed, to many it was a place of pilgrimage, a spiritual home, to be visited and revisited over the course of a lifetime.

It was particularly unusual for foreigners to want to stay overnight in Illiers-Combray. So, when Imogen had finally managed to get through to the only hotel in the village, the Fleur de Lys, Madame Barthélemy, the proprietress, had been most disconcerted by the request for ten rooms.

'Mais c'est absolument impossible, madame,' she had said, straining to keep the indignation out of her voice, 'absolument impossible. We are not a tourist hotel. Illiers is not a touristique place, you understand, only very few people come here and usually, they are making their own arrangements for staying.'

'I do understand, Madame Barthélemy,' said Imogen, politely, her French becoming more fluent as the conversation gathered pace, 'but you see, we are going to make a film about Marcel Proust, and we are coming to Illiers to do some filming in the house of his aunt Léonie. All the childhood scenes of Proust's life will be filmed in Illiers. So, please understand, it is important the actors and the filming team can stay as close to the village as possible.'

'Absolument impossible,' repeated Madame Barthélemy. Then the phone had been put down on a table, and in the distance Imogen had heard a rapid conversation in French between Madame Barthélemy and a man, possibly her husband. A few moments later, the receiver was picked up again and Madame Barthélemy had come back onto the line.

'Perhaps we can help you and your team,' she said. 'Alors, there is a château a few miles out of the village. It is owned by a friend of ours, Monsieur Séchard. It is possible that he might be able to give to you some chambres. I will ask. Please, you telephone me demain matin, and I will let you know.'

That had been at the beginning of the week. Now, four days later, Imogen was speeding along the autoroute from Paris, just on the outskirts of Chartres. By her side, her researcher Axel was making a few hasty notes in his dog-eared copy of *A la Recherche du temps perdu*.

'How long do you expect the actual filming to last?' asked Axel, his head still buried in the book.

'Well, Paul's coming out on Friday to look at the locations. He'll want to finalize camera locations and positions this weekend. Then next week the actors come out and I reckon we can start filming in about ten days. I expect we'll go on for about a month all in all. Then I want to stay on to get some landscape shots. I wouldn't have thought we'll be back home for a couple of months altogether.'

Axel looked up as the fields rolled by. Imogen had taken a road off the autoroute, and was now following the signs to Illiers, through deserted country lanes and narrow single-track avenues. Dusk had fallen rapidly, leaving behind it only the memory of the distinctive metallic grey of the French twilight.

'What does Max think about that?' asked Axel.

Imogen smiled. 'Oh, he's used to it by now. I was away in Prague for over two months for Kafka. Anyway, he's coming out as soon as his Easter break begins. So, we'll see him before too long.'

'Will he bring Miranda?'

'Oh yes,' replied Imogen, firmly. 'Now,' she continued, peering out of the car at a collection of ancient wooden road signs, 'we're just coming into the village. Could you look up the Château de l'Avenir on the map? I think it should be a few miles south of the village.'

'Château de l'Avenir,' repeated Axel, reflectively, taking out the map from the glove compartment, 'strange name for a château. Is it a particularly historic one?'

'I'm not sure,' replied Imogen, bringing the car to a halt beneath a weak orange street lamp. 'But it is the only place we can all stay together. Let's hope it will be okay. You know how fussy crews and actors can be.'

'Here it is, right here,' said Axel, pointing to a small picture of a château on the map, 'I reckon if we turn left here, and continue out of the village, we should get to it in ten minutes or so.'

Imogen started up the car once more. Illiers-Combray was

unnervingly quiet, like a ghost town. Through some of the shutters on the houses Imogen could just make out faint yellow lights, but all the homes and the shops and the public buildings seemed sealed, locked up against the outside world. There was not a soul on any of the streets so, as Imogen pulled out of the corner, she was not as vigilant as she might otherwise have been.

'Look out!' shouted Axel, making Imogen jump. She crashed on the brakes, making the car stall awkwardly, half-way round the turn. There, in front of them, out of the faint orange darkness, a shadow walked casually across the street, seemingly impervious to the vehicle that had almost killed him.

'Gosh,' sighed Imogen. 'Glad one of us was awake. You all right?'

'I'm fine. Strange man,' said Axel. Starting up the car once more, Imogen noticed that the pedestrian had stopped on the other side of the road and had turned to look at the two English visitors. The car engine complained a few times. The more Imogen put her foot down, the more the car shook, but with no effect on the engine. She continued to twist the key in the ignition, keeping her eyes on the young Frenchman across the street. He remained motionless, apparently amused at the plight of the tourists. Something about his mocking posture disconcerted Imogen. Standing there, his hands plunged firmly in his pockets, and so obviously unaffected by the near miss of a few moments ago, the Frenchman began to assume a threatening, sinister air. Imogen was relieved Axel was with her. The more the car engine whirred and ground, the more the French youth enjoyed the spectacle.

'Come on,' begged Imogen of the car, 'come on.' Soon, the young man seemed to be laughing. Imogen could not hear him over the din of the car, but even in the darkness she could see his teeth shining as he roared with mirth. She looked over to Axel, who too was amazed. Suddenly, the engine fired and the car jumped forward. Keeping her foot down hard on the accelerator, Imogen steered the car off into the darkness, letting out a sigh of relief.

Within minutes, the lights of Illiers were left far behind and the car had plunged once more into the deep blackness of the French night. The lane they were following led Imogen and Axel through fields, through yards, and through waste ground that smelled of decomposing vegetation. Soon the beam of the headlights picked out a brick wall a few hundred yards ahead.

'Aha,' said Axel, pleased with his map-reading, 'that should be the boundary wall of the château.'

Driving along the tree-lined avenue, Imogen noticed that the manor house seemed suspiciously dark and silent.

'They are expecting us, aren't they?' asked Axel.

'I spoke with Monsieur Séchard yesterday afternoon. He said he'd have the rooms ready and the maid would leave a cold dinner out for us.'

'Bon,' said Axel, with gusto, pleased that their long journey was now at an end. 'Allons-y!'

As the car turned into the crescent in front of the main door, the wheels skidded on the gravel before coming to an abrupt halt. The headlamps beamed into a row of thick trees, the dust from the gravel still giving the stream of light a definite shape. Imogen walked over to the main door of the château while Axel retrieved the bags from the boot of the car. There did not appear to be any sort of doorbell, so after a few moments of searching vainly in the dark, Imogen decided to bang on the wooden door. The sound of her fist on the wood, coupled with the jangling of the door on its hinges, reverberated around the courtyard. A bird rustled in nearby foliage, retreating deeper into the safety of the leaves. There was no reply. Imogen banged the door once more. By this time, Axel had reached her with the bags and was searching the windows for any evidence of life. They were all shuttered.

'Perhaps they're asleep,' he suggested. 'It *is* getting late.'

'They knew we would be coming,' replied Imogen, turning once more to the door, determined this time to shake it with all her strength. Just as she pulled back her hand to hit the door, the gravel nearby crunched with the sound of approaching footsteps. Imogen and Axel turned, searching the darkness for the source of the noise. Gradually, as the regular crunching came closer and closer, Imogen noticed the tiny orange glow of a cigarette floating in mid-air, like a solitary firefly searching for its mates. Soon the shadows formed themselves into a human shape.

'Vous êtes?' asked a disgruntled voice, the firefly bobbing up and down with the sound of the words.

'We are from London,' explained Imogen, switching into French. 'I telephoned.'

'Ah, oui,' uttered the faceless shadow encouragingly. 'Madame Burton, n'est-ce pas?'

'We booked some rooms,' continued Imogen.

'Oui oui, bien sûr. Please, follow me. We can enter from the back.'

The firefly glowed brighter momentarily, then floated effortlessly and silently over to the wall next to the main door. Suddenly a faint yellow light bulb came on, high up the wall, throwing a sombre hue over everything. The firefly almost disappeared in the yellow, and the shadow suddenly turned into an old man, dressed in an ancient artist's smock and looking as if he had been disturbed in the middle of some important commission.

'Are you Monsieur Séchard?' asked Imogen, now that she had a face to relate to.

'Ah, oui,' grunted the old man, after a moment's hesitation. He crunched his way through the gravel, guiding Imogen and Axel round the back of the manor house. Here, a light shone from a kitchen window and a door was open, revealing a cosy wood-panelled interior. Séchard strolled in, pushing the door open wider, and headed straight for the chimney in the corner, on which sat a battered metal coffeepot, steam pouring out of its spout. He grabbed a nearby teacloth, opened the pot to inspect the contents, and hastily banged the lid closed once again.

'Perhaps you will like some café, when you are ready?' he asked, turning to Imogen.

'I think we would like to go to our rooms first and clean up. We would love to have the coffee later, if we may?'

Without a word, Séchard led his guests over to another door, then up steep, creaking wooden stairs, eroded by generations of climbing feet. Each step had its own peculiar sound. The stairs spiralled round, giving onto a long corridor, dimly lit, with a dozen or so rooms leading off. Still neither turning round nor speaking a word, Séchard continued on his way, strolling nonchalantly down the corridor, until he reached the final two rooms. He twisted the handle and pushed open the door, reaching inside to switch on the light. The forty-watt bulb that came on was, like all the others, barely up to the task of dispelling the gloom.

'Voilà,' declared the Frenchman, inviting Axel to enter the room. The researcher peered inside the bedroom. Despite the half-light, the room seemed luxuriously decorated.

'Excellent,' he said. 'Thank you very much, monsieur.'

'See you in the morning, Axel,' said Imogen. 'We'll talk through tomorrow's schedule at breakfast. And, monsieur, is there a telephone I could use?'

'There is one downstairs in the lobby. I can show you the way.'

'Fine. Let me just drop my bag, then I'll come down.'

In contrast to the rather shabby look of the corridor, Imogen's bedroom too was voluptuously decorated, a thick Oriental carpet on the wooden floor and rich curtains draped ceiling to floor over the sweeping windows. She put her case on the bed, and went out into the corridor once more. Séchard had already crossed to the far end of the corridor and was waiting patiently, examining some fascinating facet of the small stained-glass window. As Imogen hurried past the other rooms towards him, she noticed that one of the doors was slightly open, revealing a faint streak of light. Inside, an old woman moved quickly past the crack in the door. Reaching the Frenchman, Imogen heard the occupant of the room shut the door quietly then turn the key in the lock.

'Are there other guests in the château, monsieur?' asked Imogen, following the owner along yet another badly-lit stairway.

'Mais non,' answered Séchard, 'we do not normally have people to stay at this time, but Madame Barthélemy told me you were desperate and we must help you. Voilà. Here is the telephone, madame. I leave you now?'

'Yes, yes of course,' replied Imogen, 'thank you. I will find my own way back to my room.' Before she had finished speaking, Imogen saw Séchard disappear up the narrow staircase, his footsteps accompanying an eerie symphony of creaks as he mounted each step.

The telephone was clearly not used very often, for a thick cloud of dust rose into the air as Imogen picked up the receiver. The dial too was stiff, the oil having long ago dried to a thick paste. Miraculously, she got through first time.

'Hello, Max?'

'Hello, darling, where are you?'

'We're safely here in Illiers, at the château. I'm settled in to my room and I'm just about to crash out.'

'Was the journey all right?'

'Yes, no problems. I almost killed a Frenchman in the village, though, but he escaped. I can hear your watch chiming, Max.'

'Yes, it's getting late.'

'How's Miranda?'

'Oh fine, fine. She's asleep, all tucked up and safe. What's the telephone number there?'

'It's 02.58.94.66. But the phone's in the hall, so it's not very private. Listen, I must go, because we've got an early start tomorrow morning and I want to get a good night's sleep.'

'Okay, darling. Look after yourself. And don't worry about things here. All is well. I'll speak to you in a few days.'

'Be careful, and eat properly. And make sure you don't spoil Miranda. Okay Max, good night.'

'Good night darling, sleep well.'

The receivers went down simultaneously at each end, one on a phone covered in a cloud of dust, the other on a meticulously polished cream cradle. For a moment, both Imogen and Max looked pensively at their respective phones, trying to visualize the other. Suddenly a sharp chill caught Imogen, making her shiver. She whirled round swiftly, conscious of a hostile gaze at the back of her head. But there was no one there. When she thought of Max, there was a shadow in her mind where his face should have been. She returned slowly to her bedroom, obscurely wounded.

'Was that Imogen?'

'Yes. She always rings in wherever she is, regular as clockwork.'

'Do you miss her?'

'Of course,' said Max, turning from the phone impatiently. 'It gets quite lonely in this house.' He walked across the lounge and sat back in his sofa chair. Picking up his drink, he looked over to Anjali, sitting cosily on the settee, her bare feet tucked up underneath her. She had slim, fragile legs, conditioned perfectly by all the dancing, and Max felt his eyes drawn inevitably to the smooth line of her thighs, the shiny wool of her ski pants stretched tightly across the muscles. He let his eyes linger momentarily, then looked up to find Anjali staring him straight in the eyes. She must have seen him gazing at her body. Max tried to cover up his indiscretion by continuing the conversation nonchalantly.

'I want Imogen to do well, so I don't really mind her being away on this project. And I can always get out to meet her on location. It's Miranda I really worry about, though. I wonder what all this is doing to her.'

'Children can be very resilient. Anyway, it's probably making you a lot closer to her.'

'Oh yes, it's certainly doing that.'

Max heard his voice trail off once more. He found it difficult to concentrate this evening, and he was ashamed to be honest about the reason for his distraction. A heavy silence hung in the air, filling both Max and Anjali with trepidation. Max couldn't work out quite what was disturbing him tonight. He had often met up with Anjali on his own. Her dancing had haunted him and she had become a close friend since that first meeting in Oxford. He wasn't doing anything wrong. It wasn't as if Imogen would disapprove. So why had he held back from telling Imogen on the telephone that they were together? Just an oversight, thought Max, reassuring himself. He sipped his drink, a little nervously.

'Anyway,' continued Max, 'you were just about to tell me all about music and dance.'

'Yes,' said Anjali, searching her mind for the threads of the previous conversation, 'what I was trying to explain was that dance in Hindu philosophy symbolizes the frenetic movement of the cosmos, the perennial motion of the stars and the planets, the constant change of the seasons, of time, of energy. But at its heart is a stability. The faster the movement, the closer it moves towards stillness, until it is so frantic that it is perfectly at rest. That's what the Nataraja, the dance of Shiva, represents: destruction and creation, movement and stillness, action and peace. And it's not just Shiva. Think how many Hindu gods and goddesses are symbolized as dancing. Some devotees see dance as the highest form of prayer, when body and spirit are totally in harmony. The same with Indian music.

'There is a story of a famous master of music whose instruction to his pupils lasted a whole lifetime. The first thing he would get his student to do was to pluck a single string on the instrument and sound one note. Again and again, the student would listen to this single note, playing it day and night, learning how to differentiate its various harmonies as they changed over the course of a full twenty-four hours. For a whole season, the disciple would commit himself to this one note until it became a very part of his being, until he heard it in the world about him, in the birdsong, in the trees, in the wind. Soon, the single note became so much a part of the student's life that it was in his spirit: he could hear it inside his soul even when there was no external sound. At this point, the master musician permitted his pupil to progress onto another note. And so it went on, for a whole lifetime. By the end, the musician was so much a part of the music, the music so much a part of him, that he didn't really need to play an instrument to hear the harmony of the ragas. He could simply shut his eyes, meditate and hear the rhythms unfold within his soul.'

Max continued to stare into Anjali's face long after she had paused. She held his eyes, then smiled, breaking the spell. 'It's also true of dance,' she continued. 'During my training, I spend months on single movements, repeating them over and over again, until it's not a conscious decision. Once the flow begins, the dance erupts from within, its sequences emerging from the depths of the spirit. It has very little to do with the body, it isn't really physical at all. The satisfaction of it comes from the complete mastery one has over the sense of time.

'The musician hearing the perfect raga in his mind, the dancer captured by the rhythm of her soul, each is transcending time in a way that is impossible in one's normal existence. You see, the perfect note never changes, the perfect movement never alters: it might seem different at various times of the day or night – that's the importance of performing at different times – but the fundamental note or the primary movement is fixed. It exists in a sort of Platonic world of ideas and is therefore totally unaffected by mundane changes.'

Anjali paused, noticing the bafflement cross Max's face. 'Does this make any sense?' she asked. 'I know it's a difficult concept to grasp.'

'Oh yes,' mumbled Max, momentarily caught off-guard, 'I think I understand.' His eyes had been wandering absent-mindedly over Anjali's body and back to her calm face. All the time, the idea of the dance filled his mind. There was something about Anjali's dancing that had disturbed Max. He had tried, unsuccessfully, to pin down what it was. He felt that if he thought hard enough, searched long enough, unravelled the dance carefully enough, it would give him the answer to a question that had been troubling him for a long time. But what was the question? At the moment, Max couldn't even articulate the puzzle, let alone grasp its solution. What he did know was that it stretched back into his past, was a key that would unlock a door he had long ago given up trying to open. The harder Max tried to focus upon the conundrum, the more obscure it became. Finally, like a perfume dispersing in the wind, the enigma disappeared, lost once more in the labyrinth of the past.

He looked at Anjali pleadingly. Did she have the key to that locked door? She continued gently, as if reading Max's troubled mind.

'The West is locked into a linear view of time. Past, present and future, are all a part of straight continuum. One leads neatly into the next: that's why there's this incredible interest in history, and the desperate pursuit of fashion. It's all an attempt to slow down time, using the past to plot the future, marking the present in some memorable way. And it all makes sense when you see that most people here believe that their one life is all they're going to get on earth. So, they're desperately racing against the clock, and it's a race they're losing. Each second of each day, they're passing away, into the void. Nothing can recover that particular moment, nothing. No art, no science, no mysticism can bring back the minute that is past.

'It's like the musician who thinks that he is playing his instrument, that it is his effort that is creating the rhythm. Or like the dancer who tries to follow a series of movements that she has rehearsed and committed to memory. There is no real empathy there, no connection between the individual and the idea. It's always a struggle, and it's a struggle you're bound to lose.

Max, think of time as a note of music sounding within your spirit. Hear its perfection. Again and again it plays, a single note, flowing through every part of you. Feel it as a part of your spirit, just like the musician. Soon, it resonates with your soul, and then, instead of being locked in battle with time, you become a part of its rhythm. Past, present and future all merge into one: the note remains the same, totally immutable. Only your perception of it changes, as greater experience of the world leaves its mark upon you.'

'So, in fact, there is no time as we might define it,' said Max, hearing in the distance the faint echoes of another voice, 'no ticking away of the precious minutes. Just a harmony, to which we have to attune ourselves.'

'Exactly,' said Anjali, delighted that Max had made the breakthrough. He smiled. Anjali had focused and articulated so many of the disparate emotions and half-understood notions that had haunted him since he began to visit India and which had thrown his own world view into chaos. Now he felt as if, with her help, he might at last be able to replace those fragments with a coherent structure, a definite framework that could support his own perceptions. Max leaned over and refilled Anjali's drink. As he did so, he caught a breath of her perfume, musky and erotic, and glancing up, he met her dark, sensuous eyes. He sat back uncomfortably, disconcerted by the unfamiliar scent. The clear processes of thought set in train by Anjali's measured tones dissipated once again in lurid imaginings. Max had convinced himself that she was helping him to rearrange his disorganized thoughts. Perhaps he was wrong. Perhaps she was innocently adding to the chaos.

Bernard Parsivaux had been the caretaker of the Maison Proust for over fifty years. His parents had been in the service of the Proust family, and it seemed perfectly natural that Bernard should continue the tradition, even though the family had left long ago, and the house was now no more than a dusty museum.

'Par ici,' he beckoned, treading heavily on the wooden stairs, as if he were in his own home, 'I will take you to the chambre in which the petit Proust used to be sleeping.'

'This is where we'll shoot the magic lantern sequence,' said Imogen to Paul, her cameraman, and Axel, following close behind.

'They should have the original lantern still up there,' said Axel. 'That's what the Proust Society in Paris told me.' They were at the top of the stairs now and Monsieur Parsivaux had disappeared into the tiny bedroom on the left.

'Et voilà,' he said from inside. Imogen and the others entered the room. It had been preserved exactly as Proust had described it in *Swann's*

Way, with a few finishing touches put in here and there to make sure that reality lived up to the visions of the reader's imagination. In the centre of the room, enclosed in a glass case, was a shining brass magic lantern, still pointing towards the wall on which Proust's mother would project the magical world that so enchanted the young boy.

'Does this lantern still work?' asked Imogen.

'Mais non,' answered Bernard, with a chuckle, 'it is only for display.'

'And is this the original bed that Proust used to sleep on?' asked Axel.

'The very same, my friend. It is one of our best relics in this house.'

Imogen was walking around the bedroom, pointing out other artefacts to Paul on the mantelpiece and walls, calculating how these might be used in the filming.

'Thank you for showing us the house, monsieur,' she said, at last. 'Could we just spend some time here alone to make our arrangements for the filming?'

'Oui, oui, I will leave you the key. Please to give it to me when you depart, in the house opposite.'

Paul set about shifting some of the furniture about the room. 'I'll have to try to get the camera high up in this corner for a good top shot,' he said, 'and we'll certainly have to black out the windows. Now, let's see . . .' He got a light-meter out of a leather pouch strapped to his waist and took various readings all around the room. He seemed worried about the amount of natural light coming in through the window, and the restricted space.

'That window looks out over the back garden, doesn't it? We'll have to take out the frame and put the camera outside to get a full-frame shot of the bed.'

'I'm sure that'll be all right, if we put it back just as it was,' added Imogen.

'Presumably you want the scene with his mother reading to Proust shot on the bed itself?' inquired Paul, looking over to Imogen.

'Yes, I think that would work quite well.'

Paul jumped nimbly across the room, bouncing on his air-cushioned trainers. 'So, if we have the boy here and if we put the mother here,' he sat down near the head of the bed, shifting the pillow, 'then we could angle it so we get the whole lot in one frame. Axel, just sit there, where the boy's going to be.'

Axel walked over to the bed. His weight made the floorboards creak ominously. 'Right here?' he asked. As Paul nodded, Axel slumped onto the mattress. The bed groaned, then as Axel's extra weight settled, the searing noise of cracking wood cut across the room. The bed moved, then another more substantial crack pierced the silence. Axel was now looking up at Paul, still sitting near the pillows but suddenly higher than him. The foot of the bed had totally collapsed.

'Oh my God!' exclaimed Imogen. 'Are you okay?'

'Yeah,' gasped Axel, picking himself up off the floor, 'I'm all right. That's all we need.'

'I told you you shouldn't have had that chocolate mousse last night,' joked Paul, getting up off the bed. Axel pulled off the white linen cover from the bed and lifted up the mattress, exposing the wooden frame underneath. It was full of woodworm holes.

'Look at that,' exclaimed Paul, 'lucky we didn't both break our necks. This thing's rotted right through.'

'Well, look, we've got to get it repaired as soon as we can,' said Imogen. 'If the Proust Society finds out, we'll get it in the neck. I'll go off and see if I can find a carpenter in the village, and bring him here. We'll probably have to pay him a month's wages to keep his mouth shut. Just don't let the caretaker find out, otherwise we'll all get thrown out.'

'I think we should piece it back together and make it look decent before you go off,' advised Axel. 'Old Parsivaux might wander back any minute.'

'Axel and I'll do that,' said Paul. 'You just get off, Imogen, and see if there's a handyman around.'

As Imogen descended the staircase of the house, she heard Paul teasing Axel: 'I thought you were supposed to be losing weight . . . Wait till I tell the others in the bar at Riverside . . .' She was pleased to get out of the dusty atmosphere of the house and into the fresh air of the village street. Shutting the door behind her gently, she looked up and down the narrow avenue, wondering which way led to the market square. She had some vague recollection that she had seen a hardware shop a few streets away. Deciding to take the street to the left, Imogen wandered down a few hundred yards, reflecting upon the scenes they had to shoot the following morning. The rest of the crew were arriving that evening, along with the actors, and all the locations had now been recce'd. Imogen and Paul had walked the full length of Swann's way and the Guermantes way, had seen Tansonville, the house owned by Charles Swann, had discovered the château described by Proust as the Guermantes family seat. They had also, earlier that same day, chosen the stretches of path that were in full blossom with the hawthorn so loved by the young Marcel. The village itself had barely changed over the years and the same families still lived here that had inhabited the world of Marcel's youth. Each morning since they had arrived, Imogen and Axel had had petites madeleines for breakfast at the Château de l'Avenir, this being what Monsieur Séchard presumed they had come for. By the end of their stay in Illiers, they would be sick of the sight of the tiny cakes.

The streets were empty. A lone cyclist pedalled his ancient machine down the narrow lanes; another local inhabitant disappeared into the bakery, to emerge a few minutes later with a batch of baguettes under his arm. By now, Imogen recognized most of the villagers who worked in the shops and cafés: the arrival of a television producer from London had caused quite a stir in the quiet community, and a local journalist had driven down from Chartres the previous week to interview Imogen for the provincial paper. Her photograph in the journal had made Imogen a star and had broken the ice with many of the local tradespeople. That, and her fluent French, which they all commented upon and admired. Turning another corner, Imogen felt she must be getting close to the hardware store. There it was, half-way down the street, metal watering cans and a variety of heavier farming machinery sprawling onto the pavement.

The storekeeper was busy adding up figures behind the counter. He looked up at the young Englishwoman as she examined the hardware outside his shop. The door swung open, accompanied by the sharp tinkle of a bell.

'Bonjour,' said Imogen cheerily. The shopkeeper, a surly old man of sixty, grunted in reluctant acknowledgement of the greeting.

'Are you Monsieur Selz?' asked Imogen, having noticed the name of the proprietor nailed over the front door. Again the old man grunted. Undeterred by his unfriendliness, Imogen continued in her best French: 'I wonder if you can help us. We are making a film in the Maison Proust, and we have had a small accident. We need a carpenter who can come to the house for half an hour or so. Do you think you can help us, please?' The old man listened, then buried his head in his figures once more as if he had not heard or was not interested in Imogen's request.

'I know you must be terribly busy,' persisted Imogen, not betraying her impatience, 'but we would be very grateful and we would pay anything that was reasonable for the service.'

At the mention of money, Monsieur Selz looked up and grunted once more. He was thinking. Then, looking back down at his paperwork once more, he called out to the inside of the shop: 'Lamarck!' No answer. 'Lamarck!' repeated the old Frenchman. There was a frantic scurrying somewhere within the building, then the sound of footsteps hurrying towards the front of the shop. A few moments later a young man emerged, wearing a dirty leather apron, his hair wildly dishevelled, his arms and hands blackened by the tools he had been using. Imogen started as he came out into the shop. It was the man she had almost run down the first night they had driven into Illiers, who had found the whole incident terribly amusing. Imogen had not seen him since that first night. She tried to hide her surprise and consternation. Lamarck looked first at her, then towards Monsieur Selz. The old man was still immersed in his calculations.

'Take your tools and go with her,' he commanded, sharply. Lamarck acknowledged the order, and disappeared into the back once more. Further conversation with Monsieur Selz seemed superfluous, so Imogen waited quietly until Lamarck re-emerged. He had tidied himself up a little, and was carrying a cloth holdall overflowing with carpentry tools.

'Thank you, Monsieur Selz,' said Imogen, 'we won't be long.'

'Ah, madame,' Monsieur Selz suddenly stood up, leaving his

paperwork on the table, 'I would be grateful if you could pay me first.' He seemed to have found his voice now that the question of payment had arisen. 'You see,' he continued, most obsequiously, 'you see, Lamarck is a little simple, and I do not trust him to handle money.'

'I would prefer to return later with Lamarck, once the work is completed and pay you then, monsieur,' replied Imogen. Monsieur Selz shrugged his shoulders, whispered something under his breath and sat down to his calculations once more.

Walking out of the shop, Imogen took the lead and guided Lamarck up the street. He was a quiet boy, walking along intently, shy and afraid to speak as if he had been told never to address his betters.

'How long have you been working for monsieur?' asked Imogen, determined to break the ice. Lamarck did not reply. Perhaps he had not understood. 'Do you enjoy working as a carpenter?' persisted Imogen, gently. This time the young man looked up at her and seemed about to speak but then suddenly decided not to and remained silent.

'Don't be shy, Lamarck. I'm sorry I almost knocked you down that night. You probably don't even remember. I would like us to be friends.' Imogen was determined that he should come out of the shell in which Monsieur Selz, she felt sure, had enclosed him. They were hurrying along the street and were nearing the corner of the Maison Proust. All of a sudden Lamarck stopped and turned to Imogen, forcing her to stop as well. He stared at her, directly into her eyes, a penetrating gaze. Once again, he seemed to be making a monumental effort to speak. Imogen could see the pained movements of the young man's Adam's apple, but not a sound was emerging from his mouth. At last, with a gargantuan burst of energy, a long drawn-out moan sounded from Lamarck. He was dumb.

'Oh, I am so sorry, I did not know. Please forgive me. But you can understand what I am saying, n'est-ce pas?' Lamarck nodded excitedly and smiled. Underneath the grime and the awful shyness occasioned by his disability, the young man was striking, his blond hair falling casually about his brow.

'Well, I'll have to talk for both of us,' said Imogen, as the two of them continued along their way. 'Do you live in Illiers?' Lamarck nodded and waved his free hand over the rooftops, gesturing into the distance.

'You live out of the village? A long way out?' Lamarck shook his head.

'And do you like to work for Monsieur Selz?' The young man smiled and gestured with his hand as if to say it wasn't too bad. Soon they had reached the Maison Proust. Imogen knocked gently on the door, for fear of attracting the caretaker's attention across the street. She could hear footsteps descending the stairs inside. Paul opened the door, only a few inches at first, then, seeing it was Imogen, all the way.

'Great,' he said, 'I thought it might have been old Parsivaux. Is this the carpenter?'

'He's called Lamarck, and he's a man of few words, aren't you,

Lamarck?' He had not understood the exchanges in English but smiled nonetheless, knowing that the kind lady must have said something nice about him. Deprived of his ability to communicate, Lamarck had developed a much finer sense of people. He had come to like Imogen immensely in the space of a few short minutes.

'Very pleased to meet you, Lamarck,' said Paul, jovially, taking the young man's free hand and holding it warmly. Lamarck smiled. He had never been treated so kindly before. 'Come with me and I'll show you the damage.' Paul led the carpenter upstairs, leaving Imogen to wander around the large ground-floor living room, now turned into a museum of Proustian paraphernalia.

Dominating the room were two oil-paintings, portraits of Proust's mother and father. Imogen stared at the picture of the woman in her thirties, a lovely warm face, with shining bright eyes and an alabaster complexion. It was a kind face, and Imogen could well believe that Proust had loved no woman other than his mother. Perhaps that was the reason his affairs had all come to nothing, both in the *Recherche* and in his life. How strange to think of this woman still dominating the house, as she did, with the strength of her image. Lamarck had clearly begun work upstairs, for there was the reassuring sound of hammering and sawing coming from Marcel's bedroom. Imogen continued to explore the museum. They had every translation of the *Recherche*, even one in Mandarin Chinese, and also examples of the original manuscripts. Imogen peered at the great man's handwriting, almost illegible, as was the case with so many of her 'literary masters'. She could barely make head or tail of it. It was as if the actual mechanism of transferring words from the mind onto the page had been an irritating inconvenience and the author, impatient of his hand and fearful of approaching death, had paid little heed to calligraphy. Some of the names were just legible: Albertine, Guermantes, Swann and, of course, the frequent Marcel himself. As Imogen was scrutinizing the faded yellow paper, she suddenly heard the sound of shouting from upstairs. It was an unfamiliar voice, screaming in French.

'Allons-y! Get out at once! You madman! You imbecile! What do you think you are doing to our precious furniture!' There followed the sound of someone hurrying down the stairs, stumbling and falling in a rush to escape, and someone else in pursuit. Imogen left the room, just in time to find Lamarck reach the foot of the stairs with Monsieur Parsivaux hot on his heels. Seeing Imogen emerge from the front room, Lamarck stopped in his tracks and looked pleadingly into her eyes. The concierge too, catching sight of Imogen, pulled himself up short and caught his breath. Neither Paul nor Axel were anywhere to be seen.

'Madame!' shouted the caretaker, 'I leave you and your team for a few hours and what happens? I return to find that all the furniture has been moved in the Marcel bedroom and this idiot, this halfwit, is sawing through the bed that has been the treasure of this house for so many years!' Parsivaux cast another poisonous look in the direction of the young carpenter. Imogen took a deep breath, composed herself and walked over slowly to the caretaker.

'Monsieur Parsivaux,' she began calmly, 'let me explain. It is all my responsibility. This young man is not to blame. He is simply doing as I instructed. You see, we were making all the preparations for the filming, when we discovered that the bed of petit Marcel was all decayed with – how do you say in French – the insects that eat through the wood?'

'Vernis de bois,' said the concierge, coldly.

'Oui, vernis de bois. Anyway, the bed was all rotten. You really should have had it treated a long time ago, monsieur. Still, we all make mistakes.' A look of fear combined with guilt crossed the face of the old man. 'And I thought, it will be a great shame to see the bed collapse altogether. So I asked Lamarck here to come with his tools and to repair the bed as it is, in order to make it more strong. That way, it will last for another hundred years.'

Bernard Parsivaux seemed suspicious, reluctant to let go of the conspiracy theory he had already formulated and which had been the springboard of his anger. He knew people were trying to undermine his position as concierge of the Maison Proust. Lamarck had come to the house as a spy and had begun to dismantle it piece by piece. But still, for the time being, he would have to bite his tongue. If what Imogen had said were true, he himself would be in trouble for not spotting the woodworm. Just then, Paul and Axel returned through the front door, to find the confrontation just ending. Their smiles froze.

'Ah, Paul,' said Imogen, brightly, 'just in time, as always. I've explained to Monsieur Parsivaux the need to repair Marcel's bed, so if you and Axel would like to help Lamarck with his tools, I'm sure all you men can make a good job of it.' Unable to hide the fact that they had skived off at a crucial moment, Paul and Axel crossed the hallway sheepishly. Passing Lamarck, Paul put his arm affectionately around the shoulder of the young carpenter, whispered in his ear and guided him back up towards the bedroom. As they passed Imogen, she looked at Paul and smiled. 'Did you know that the French for woodworm is vernis de bois?' she asked.

The wipers of the Saab were struggling to keep the windscreen clear, even at their faster pace. The motorway was being dug up, once again, yet the traffic was still whizzing by at over seventy. Max heard the distant siren of an ambulance. He checked in his rear-view mirror and made out the familiar white van weaving in and out of the cars behind him, its blue and white lights flashing in the grey spray. Max indicated to the left and pulled over, just in time to see the ambulance speed past. He wondered what personal drama was contained inside the emergency vehicle, whose life it was that hung so precariously in the balance. He listened as the shrill siren elongated into the distance. A sign flashed by, its green and white colours standing out in the grey rain: Oxford – 35. Max eased off the accelerator. He would be too early at this rate, and he didn't really fancy sitting around in the car in some side street. He wondered how Imogen was getting on: she had phoned the previous evening, and all seemed well. The filming was coming along. Anyway, he'd soon be out in Illiers, come the Easter vacation. Max looked at the cars flashing by, throwing up dirty black spray onto the windscreen. It seemed odd to be travelling to Oxford alone on a Saturday afternoon, but then the past few weeks had been very dislocating in a number of ways.

Max was becoming increasingly worried by the relationship that was developing between Anjali and himself. He was looking forward to their meetings in a way he hadn't felt, if he were being honest, since he first met Imogen. But it was all so unreal. Anjali clearly valued Max's friendship, but there was surely nothing more in it than that. Apart from anything else, she was very loyal to her friends, and Imogen *was* one of her closest friends. Max knew he was being silly, childish, but it was the ease with which he fell into speculation about Anjali that worried him. He couldn't deny his own feelings to himself, try as he might.

There was something about the Indian dancer that captivated Max and it wasn't just her exquisite looks. He had no need to search beyond Imogen for that. It was Anjali's spirit that enthralled Max. She was so different, had such original values, held such unusual beliefs. It was all part of the interest in India that, ironically, Imogen had encouraged in Max. In Anjali, all that fascination with the East seemed to find focus in a person.

Max was bored with his Western traditions and Western values. He was restless and craved fresh insight. Anjali was not afraid to theorize in abstract terms, and yet retained the ability to combine the mystical with the practical. She had given new impetus to the process of transformation that Imogen had begun. And now, in Imogen's long absences, Max was beginning to realize how much he was coming to rely on Anjali for the inspiration he had taken so freely from Imogen. Max did not want his relationship with Anjali to end. But did he want it to go further? It was precisely this question which made Max reluctant to share this increasingly consuming part of his life with Imogen. It made the occasions they met Anjali together very tense. Max felt he could barely meet his wife's eyes, so heavy was the atmosphere of unspoken emotion. For her part, Anjali was very discreet. She was not insensitive to Max's desire to keep the full extent of their relationship private, and she too placed a high value upon the time they spent together. That much Max was sure of. But it was beginning to get more and more difficult. Max was finding it harder to conceal his feelings for Anjali and was increasingly afraid that his behaviour towards her would betray his innermost desires, to her and, perhaps, to Imogen.

As usual, Anjali's dancing was superb and brought vociferous calls from the audience for an encore. She had moved up now from the Holywell Music Rooms to the Playhouse and still managed to fill the house to overflowing. Watching her twist and turn on the stage in perfect harmony to the music, Max could hear her voice in his head. Each note, each movement becomes a part of your spirit, Max. The dancer no longer moves a muscle. The dance possesses her and carries her along with its eternal rhythm.

'So, think of life as a dance. We learn the movements, commit them to memory, and repeat them as time directs us into ever new situations. Soon, we forget what it is like to be still: we begin to think that performing the dance as best we can is, in fact, the point of our existence. And that's the mistake we fall into, frantically trying to keep up with our peers, mistaking movement for progress. We become victims of the flow of time, battling ever harder against the current, hoping through our efforts to overcome the relentless tide. Yet no amount of effort can turn the clock back one single second. Some even come to believe they might cheat death, hope to escape the inevitable. If only we accepted that time, like music, like dance, has a preordained pattern, exists as a perfect idea, in the mind of God if you like, and we are merely the vehicles through which that idea is realized. Stop fighting it, Max. Let me tell you a story. . .

In ancient Baghdad, during the time of the great caliphs, when Persia was the envy of the world, there lived a young man named Hieron. He was a handsome youth, much admired by all the women of the court, despite being only a servant. Soon, Hieron became the personal companion to the great Shah and accompanied him all over the world, from the courts of Hindustan to the palaces of ancient China. A close and affectionate bond grew up between the Shah and his servant until, one day, after many years of devoted service, Hieron was awarded his freedom. What was more, the Shah gave his loyal companion a thousand pieces of gold and a hundred more each year, to ensure that Hieron could enjoy his liberty.

For a time, all was well. It was the first time anyone in his family had lived as a free man. He lived frugally but well, always remembering that his new life was a gift. Unlike the rich noblemen, Hieron never employed servants, preferring instead to do all his own chores. And for years, despite many an invitation from the young and beautiful daughters of wealthy merchants, Hieron never gave his heart to anyone.

Then one day, in the market square, Hieron saw a woman who bewitched him. Within ten days they were married. A year later, Rustoma bore Hieron a son and a year after that, another boy, as handsome and as free as his father. Hieron had everything. And still, each day, he would remind himself that his life was a gift. He never took anything for granted and brought his sons up to cherish each minute of their freedom.

Years passed. Hieron and Rustoma were a popular couple and any jealousy harboured by neighbours was dispelled by their generosity and humility.

One day, Rustoma awoke before dawn, bathed, dressed and made herself ready to go off to the marketplace. A batch of the finest Chinese silk was to be delivered that morning and Rustoma was keen to secure the best specimen as a gift for Hieron and the boys. By the time she reached the square, it was full of people. Traders dressed in nomad robes, recently arrived from months-long journeys across the deserts; women in black purdah from head to toe, staring suspiciously from behind their pointed face masks; children in brightly-coloured pyjamas, running in and out of the gathered crowds. Noblemen jostled with slaves. Exotic animals from all parts of the globe filled the air with strange shrieks and screams. Rustoma was worried she might have missed the silk merchants so she rushed onwards, weaving in and out of the stalls, keeping her eyes peeled for the distinctive flags they flew above their carts. Straining to see over the heads of the people in the bazaar, Rustoma took her eyes off where she was going and crashed straight into a group of women gathered around a spice-dealer. There was much commotion as the women all turned upon her, each one wearing the distinctive black robe and black face mask, revealing only the eyes. For a moment, as they all turned in unison, Rustoma thought she had stumbled into some horrific nightmare. And there was one woman in particular who terrified her.

'Come come, my dear,' she said, helping Rustoma to find her feet, 'I never expected to find you here in this marketplace.'

Did she know this woman? Rustoma stared into her eyes and felt her blood turn cold. This was no nightmare. Beneath the black lace coverings she saw the unmistakable face of Death, bearing a welcoming smile.

Rustoma picked herself up and rushed on, trying frantically to lose herself in the crowd. If she disappeared quickly, she thought, Death might forget all about the chance encounter and pass on to someone else. A few minutes later, as she was deep in the mass of traders, Rustoma looked back to the spice stall where she had crashed into the strange women. And in the distance, she still saw Death, motionless amid the frantic comings and goings all around, her eyes fixed on Rustoma.

Rustoma forgot about the silks she had come to buy. She rushed home, locked the doors and retired to the deepest bedroom of all, slamming the bolts tightly shut. When Hieron and the boys asked her what was wrong, she told them Death was after her and they must not, at any cost, let in strange visitors. For days she hid inside the house, not daring to go out. She didn't sleep, didn't eat, didn't bathe, terrified that a moment's lapse in vigilance would prove fatal. On the fifth night, Hieron decided he had to talk sense into his wife. But she was terrified. The only solution was to send her away from Baghdad, away from the Death she so feared. Rustoma's sister lived in Basra, a few hundred miles to the south. She would be safe there, deep in the desert. So Hieron arranged for his wife to join a caravan of traders heading towards Basra and a few days later, under cover of darkness, Rustoma left Baghdad.

The house seemed very quiet without her. Hieron had forgotten how lonely the evenings and nights could become, and, more than for himself, he felt sorry for the boys, deprived of their mother. All night Hieron tossed and turned. In the end, he decided that it was cowardice for them to have given in like this. The following morning he would go down to the marketplace, find the old woman Death and resolve the matter with her. He would then be able to retrieve his wife from her enforced exile.

Dawn came with its fiery streaks, filling the sky with blood. The boys were still asleep as Hieron got himself ready and rode off to the market square. The closer he got to the marketplace, the more bloody the sky seemed to become. Hieron looked up into the clouds, searching for the sun, but it was nowhere to be seen, just a red glow filling the heavens from horizon to horizon. He rode into the square under the huge marble arch carved for the Shah's father in celebration of his victory over the Greeks. Everything was silent. There was none of the usual hustle and bustle, no traders engaged in fierce rounds of bargaining, no customers rushing from stall to stall, fearful of missing the sale of precious clothing and foods. The whole place was deserted. The stalls stood empty, their flags of identification flapping hopelessly in the morning breeze. Where usually thousands of enthusiastic buyers fought with each other for space, there was nothing but the distant rustle of sand, blown into geometric patterns by the wind. Somewhere in the distance a cat was wailing, like a human baby, bemoaning its isolation. Hieron looked about him at the emptiness. Where was everyone? He felt as if he had stumbled, unawares, into his wife's nightmare.

Wrapping his headscarf tightly around his face as protection against the increasing whirlwinds, Hieron cast one final look around the deserted marketplace. As he surveyed the panorama, he thought he saw a dark figure out of the corner of his eye, shrinking away into cover of the shadows. But by the time Hieron had turned his head, he could see nothing but the wind and the sand and torn silk flags carried off into the crimson sky.

Pulling his horse round by the reins, Hieron turned his back on the ghostly bazaar and galloped away, hoping to return home before the boys awoke. That day passed slowly. The blood-red sky did not lift for a minute, deepening in colour as day turned into night. Eating his evening meal with his sons, Hieron thought about Rustoma, safe with her sister, far away from the danger that terrified her. The hours dragged. It was a dark night, more black than Hieron had ever seen anywhere on his travels. The moon was nowhere to be found, concealed by thick clouds. Even inside the house, the darkness devoured the candlelight. In an attempt to bring the day to a close, Hieron put the boys to bed, bathed and then retired himself, blowing out the final candle by his bedside. Exhausted by the efforts of the day and by his loneliness, Hieron drifted off into a deep sleep. One by one each house in the city extinguished its lights. Gradually the silence and the darkness took over. At the deserted marketplace, the solitary cat continued to wail.

In the dead of night, a loud banging awoke Hieron. For a few moments he thought it was part of his dream. But coming round, he soon realized that someone was at his door desperate to get in. Perhaps it was Rustoma. Hieron jumped out of bed, lit his candle and walked tentatively through the house. The banging was getting louder, more impassioned. He unbolted the locks on the front door one by one, and felt the heavy wood loosen on its frame. Casting the final bolt aside, he pulled open the door. At first, he could see no one in the pitch-black night. A thick mist clung to the ground, spreading its vapours into every corner. As Hieron held up his candle, he just made out a figure, dressed from head to toe in dark, funereal clothes, standing motionless a few feet from the doorstep.

'Who's there?' demanded Hieron. The figure remained silent. 'Who are you?'

The stranger moved forward, parting the low-lying mist, and came into the faint light thrown by Hieron's candle. It was a woman, her face masked by her purdah, but through the narrow opening for her eyes, Hieron could see that it was the face of Death.

'What do you want with us?' asked Hieron. 'You have no business here.'

'So unwelcoming, my son?' answered Death, her soft voice like the voice of his mother, soothing Hieron's turbulent heart. 'I have had a busy day, here in Baghdad. I think you were looking for me.' The mist was beginning to spread slowly inside the open doorway.

'Leave us in peace,' said Hieron, 'you have no right to plague us in this way. My family has done no wrong.'

'Come, come, my boy,' continued Death in her honeyed tones, 'I did not mean to frighten you. I come as a friend. It is your wife I wish to see and I have journeyed far for this rendezvous.'

'Then it has been a wasted journey. Rustoma is no longer here. She has gone far away. Now leave us alone, let us live our lives and go about your business elsewhere.'

For a moment, Death looked Hieron in the eyes, captivating his gaze and hypnotizing him with her power. Then she cast her glance upwards, surveying the house.

'Yes,' she said, at length, 'yes, I can feel Rustoma is not here. No matter. I shall continue my harvest. I shall have a fruitful day tomorrow, for a whole city has been promised me.' With those words, Death moved back from Hieron's doorstep and, pulling her shawl tighter around her face, moved off into the dark mist. Hieron watched her as she disappeared into the night but, just as he was about to lose sight of the supernatural woman, he heard his own voice ask: 'Where does your journey take you now?'

The dark figure halted and turned, her eyes smiling. 'Didn't I say, my son?' said the old woman, tenderly. 'The morning shall see me in Basra. Look at the sky. The fires are already burning . . .'

Walking up the garden path, Max could just hear the high-pitched warble of the telephone in the study. He was too far away to catch it, he thought, and in any case it would definitely be Imogen at this late hour, and she was bound to call back soon. Miranda was away for the night, staying with a schoolfriend in Kew, so the sound of the unanswered phone seemed all the more to underline the emptiness of the house. Surprisingly, the caller persisted. Max unlocked the front door, with no great urgency, and still the phone rang. Imogen was obviously determined to speak to him. He crossed the hallway, opened the door to the study, walked over to the phone and picked up the receiver.

'Hello, Max?'

'Oh Dad, it's you. It's a bit late to be phoning, isn't it? Is everything all right?'

'It's your mother, Max.'

A fire burst through Max's body, exploding in his head. 'Oh my God.'

'She had a stroke early this morning.'

'This morning? Why didn't you. . . ?'

'I've been trying to get in touch with you all day. No one knew where you were. I even rang Imogen in France. She didn't know either.'

Max saw the whole wretched day flash before his eyes. 'Sorry, Dad, I've been seeing friends in Oxford.'

'It doesn't matter, Max, there's nothing you could have done anyway. We took her to Harefield Hospital first, but they didn't have the special equipment she needed, so they transferred her to St Augustine's.'

'What, just outside Oxford?'

'Yes.'

Max sighed. If only he'd known, he was only a few minutes away. 'Would they let me see her?'

'What, now?'

'Oh, no, I suppose not. Well, what about first thing? I'll come round and pick you up, then we can drive down together.'

'Is there any chance you could pop round now, Max? The house is terribly quiet without her. Bring your things.'

Imogen was finding it virtually impossible to concentrate that morning, her mind constantly returning to Max and his mother's health. Her stay in hospital was going to be longer than anyone had anticipated and Imogen wondered whether Max would be able to come out for Easter as planned. They were about a quarter of the way through the shoot and it was proving uphill all the way. The young actor playing Marcel undoubtedly looked the part in his French costume, but he was, in reality, a rascal. And it showed in his streetwise voice. The scenes they had shot in the Maison Proust would all have to be dubbed over. That was easy enough. But the scene by the riverbank was proving more problematic.

'Now listen carefully, Simon,' said Imogen patiently to the young actor, 'when you come over the bridge, you're facing a choice: do I turn left, towards the Guermantes château, or do I turn right, and head towards the house of Monsieur Swann? You cross the bridge, stop for a few moments on this side, weigh up the choice and decide to take the path towards Monsieur Swann.' Imogen turned to take up her position behind camera and pulled a face of exasperation at Paul. In the meantime, Simon had crossed back to the far side of the bridge, had stopped smirking, pulled on his cloth cap and was ready to set off along Swann's way.

The habitual small crowd of townspeople had gathered for the filming, like spectators watching a surgeon perform a public operation. Imogen didn't mind the fan club. It was their village, after all. Paul was always generous to them, letting them look through the eyepiece and explaining the moves to them. Lamarck was there in the afternoons, after finishing work. His dumbness set him apart from the others and he always kept his distance. But the crew were especially friendly to Lamarck and on one occasion Paul even let him bang the clapperboard.

'Action!' shouted Imogen. Axel looked down to the script and read the commentary that would accompany the scene. They had already recorded most of the voiceover before leaving England. As Axel watched the young Marcel and reread the commentary, he could hear the measured and dramatic tones in his mind.

'Memory: a fragment of pure life, preserved in its purity, which we can only know when it is so preserved, because in the moment when we live it, it is not present to our memory, but surrounded by sensations which suppress it. It is sometimes at the moment when we think everything is lost that the intimation arrives which may save us. One has knocked at all the doors which lead nowhere, and then one stumbles without knowing it on the only door through which one can enter, which one might have sought in vain for a hundred years, and it opens of its own accord.'

It was a successful day of filming. Simon gave a superb performance and even Imogen had to laugh on a few occasions.

'These mayflowers, miss,' he said as Paul lined up his camera angles for the avenue through the blossoms, 'what's so special about them?'

'It's all to do with memory, Simon,' explained Imogen. 'Marcel loves the smell because it reminds him of his childhood, the women he's loved and his parents. You see, in the end, memory is all you're left with.' Simon pulled down one of the more lush branches and breathed in the hawthorn blossom. 'I hope you'll have happy memories of this time,' said Imogen.

Simon lingered over the branch, then let it spring back up to its natural position. 'I don't know yet,' he said, 'the day's not over.'

The camera positions finalized, Simon turned again into Marcel and the illusion was complete. Once more, Axel turned to the commentary.

'I found the whole path throbbing with the fragrance of hawthorn blossom . . . And their scent swept over me as unctuous, as circumscribed in its range as though I had been standing before the Lady altar. But it was in vain I lingered beside the hawthorns, breathing in their invisible and unchanging odour, trying to fix it in my mind, which didn't know what to do with it, losing it, recapturing it, absorbing myself in the rhythm which disposed the flowers here and there with a youthful lightheartedness and at intervals, as unexpected as certain intervals in music, they went on, offering me the same charm in inexhaustible profusion, but without letting me delve any more deeply, like those melodies which one can play a hundred times in succession, without coming any nearer to their secret.'

It was a nightmare every time for Max. Once again, he drove into the car park of St Augustine's, his father by his side, and parked in the usual space. His nerves were beginning to show the strain. It wasn't easy making this long journey every day, and staying at home with his father and Miranda was an added strain. Still, things had been a bit easier now that Max was on his Easter vacation, though he was concerned about just how to break the news to his father that, despite his mother's illness, he was still intending to go to France to be with Imogen, at least for the final week of the vacation. He had thought about it quite hard and had decided that his mother was now well enough to be left for that time. Imogen had said it was up to him, but Max knew she wanted him out there, for his own good and for Miranda's sake. The young girl also needed to get away from the atmosphere of disease and depression.

Max's mother had been moved from the intensive care unit, which was a great relief. She still had a drip-feed in her arm, but at least she was able to sit up and talk, and read magazines. In the other place, she had been wired up like a machine and the people around her had behaved as if she were no more than a component of the electronics and computers that were keeping her alive. As Max and his father walked down the ward, some of the other patients, propped up against their crisp white pillows, greeted them with affectionate familiarity. There was a bond that had grown up between the visitors and the patients over the past weeks and Max felt as if some of the more constant faces had become like members of an extended family, thrown together by their individual misfortunes.

'Oh Max,' said his mother, 'you look so handsome tonight, just like your father used to be.'

'What do you mean, "used to be"?' asked his father teasingly. Max's mother smiled, and he noticed the youthful sparkle return momentarily to her eyes. Then it was gone again, submerged beneath the tension and the exhaustion of the past month. Max began to see in her face a faint image of his grandmother as she had been at the time of her last photograph, the much-loved print his parents still displayed on the mantelpiece at home.

'Sister Conrad says you've been mumbling in your sleep again, Mum, keeping the other patients awake at night.'

'They sleep all day anyway,' answered his mother.

'Have you been having bad dreams?' continued Max.

His mother turned away and took her husband by the hand. 'Now, look, my love, are you eating properly? Seems to me you're getting thinner every time I see you.'

'Oh stop fussing, Elizabeth. We're both doing fine. Want you back, though. House gets awfully quiet these days.'

'And how's my beautiful granddaughter? You didn't bring her today.'

'No, Mum,' said Max, 'she's gone to a birthday party at a friend's house. She'll spend the night there. She sent you this, though.' Max took out a hand-painted card and gave it to his mother. She smiled as she saw the painstakingly drawn wizard on it, a craggy old man wearing a long pointed hat and waving a magic wand out of the page. Underneath, Miranda had written, in her best handwriting, 'Time To Live'.

'And how's Imogen?' asked Max's mother, stretching sideways and placing the card carefully on top of the wooden cabinet by the side of her bed.

'I spoke to her just before we came here tonight.' Max thought this might be the best time to broach the subject of his going away. 'She asked after you, hoped you were well. Thing is, she's been really working hard and has got about another ten days to go. She wondered if you were well enough for me to go out to France for a few days?' Max felt his father stiffen, so he deliberately didn't look over to him, keeping his gaze firmly fixed on his mother.

'Oh for goodness sake, Max, you don't even have to ask. Of course I'm all right. I don't actually know why I'm still in here, to tell you the truth.' She looked over to her husband. 'Max, I'd love you to go. Will you take Miranda with you?'

'That was the general idea. She's just beginning to learn French at school.'

'When would you be going?' asked Max's father, trying desperately to keep the disappointment out of his voice.

'Well, I wanted to talk to you about that. I haven't got much holiday left, so quite soon, really.'

'As far as I'm concerned, Max,' said his mother, 'I'd rather you went straight away. Enjoy your time off. I know how hard it's been for you, with me being ill. The last thing you want to do is to spend your holiday in and out of hospital wards.' Max watched his mother take his hand and press it warmly. It felt damp, and Max could sense that there was not much strength left in it. He grasped it firmly, hoping to transfer some of his youth and energy into the sick limbs. He looked up at the drip above the bed. It was almost at an end and he could see that the nurses were agitating to put the patients to bed.

'Time you went, I think,' said his mother, sensing her son's restlessness. Max's father got up slowly, bent over the bed and kissed his wife. 'I'll be back soon, darling,' he said. 'Keep your spirits up.'

Max stepped back to let his father leave the bed, then stooped down to his mother's face. For a moment the smell of her skin transported him back to his childhood and visions of the past flashed by. Visions of a small boy, his leg grazed by a fall from his bike, and a strong young woman crouching down and dabbing the wound with a wet ball of cotton wool; visions of a slightly older boy, in tears after dropping his father's favourite china horse, looking up to her from where he knelt on the carpet and instead of the angry face he expected, seeing his mother, calm and collected, willing to help cover up the mistake; visions of a young man dressed in his best suit, standing arm in arm with an adoring, now older-looking woman, proud and upright in the new dress her son had bought her for his wedding. Max closed his eyes as he kissed his mother on the cheek.

'Please get better soon, Mum,' he whispered.

His mother looked at Max thoughtfully. Then, turning to her husband, now standing at the foot of the bed, she said, 'Could I have a few minutes alone with Max please, my dear?'

'Of course, of course. I'll wait outside, Max,' said his father. For a few moments Max and his mother watched the tall erect figure march off down the ward. As soon as he was gone, Max turned to his mother, wondering what it was she wanted to say that was such a secret.

'Sit down a minute, Max, please. I won't be long.' He helped his mother prop herself up a little higher on the pillow. 'Your father's very dependent on me, you know. He's never really learnt how to look after himself. It's as much as I could do to teach him how to make an omelette. Anyway Max, what I'm trying to say is, look after him, won't you? You and Imogen. Don't forget him. I'd like to know he will be well looked after.'

Max felt a rising sickness and the tears began to well up in his eyes. This was the sort of conversation he had always feared, always had nightmares about. Now that it was actually happening, he felt numbed and at a loss for words. 'I want you to look after him,' he said, at length. 'You've got a long life ahead of you yet. Why are you talking like this?'

His mother laughed. 'And Imogen. I'm so glad you found someone you're happy with. What you have with Imogen is very precious. Don't ever forget that.'

For a moment Max turned his eyes away. How easily his mother saw through him. He took her hand and squeezed it gently. He could tell that she was now exhausted and wanted her to get a good night's rest. 'I'll try to see you again before I go,' said Max.

Sister Conrad was standing by the bed, ready with a rainbow of tablets. Max kissed his mother again and walked off down the ward, past the rows of half-asleep patients. Just as he reached the door to the corridor, he remembered something he had forgotten to say to his mother. Max stopped and turned. Sister had now finished her rounds and the lights were being put out one by one, slowly covering the whole ward in darkness. Even as he turned, Max saw the light above his mother's bed being turned off. He just caught a glimpse of her face, still staring in his direction, before it disappeared into the darkness.

Max decided not to disturb her now. What he had to say could wait.

'Scuse me, oi, scuse me, are we goin' to get served or what?'

' 'Ang on mate, I'll be righ' over . . .'

Craig was fed up waiting at the bar for his drinks. It wasn't just the waiting that was getting to him, though. The fact was that he had told Ian and Pete that he was skint, and they still made him pay for a round. Fair enough, he thought. The problem was that, when it came to his turn, everyone ordered much more expensive drinks than he had had. Still, it was getting close to eleven, so they'd probably need a few stiff ones.

'C'mon, Craig, I'll be too old for that drink.'

'It's comin', it's comin'.' As the barman pulled the third pint, a sudden silence descended upon the bar. Craig turned to see what had happened. The door to the street was open and a group of Crusaders, dressed in their standard black outfits, was standing in regular formation around the entrance. No one dared speak. Only the intrusive electronic singsong of the computer games in the far corner broke the silence. After a few seconds, a tall, good-looking man stood up from one of the crowded tables. It was clear that the gang reported to him. 'What news?' he asked.

The captain of the expedition force pulled off his black balaclava. His hair crackled with the static, and for a moment a few fine strands stood on end. He flicked his forehead clear.

'Good news,' said the Crusader, 'the patch is clean.' Only a select few in the bar really knew what the cryptic message meant: Craig hadn't quite made it into that group yet, but he was well on his way. Anyway, what he did know was that the shooting party, as they were called, had been sent off on a hit earlier that evening and now they were all back, their mission accomplished.

Ever since that first evening, when he had gone to the Crusader meeting in the church hall, Craig had become more fascinated by the work they were embarked upon. And the fortnight course he'd been on had really made him think, sort himself out a bit. It made such good sense. So many of the country's problems could be traced back to the overcrowding caused by foreigners. They had no respect for the traditions of the country, no sense of its history, no desire to see its greatness continue. As Craig now saw it, they were actually over here to get revenge. Revenge for all those hundreds of years that the British had ruled their countries, in Asia, the Far East, in the West Indies, in Africa. But if it weren't for the British, those countries would still be in the Dark Ages, wouldn't they? People there still lived in mud huts and in villages with no water or electricity. And they had the nerve to come here, to this beautiful country, with its best systems of law and government, and now they were trying to undermine them, bit by bit. It was revenge, no doubt about it. Streets being renamed after their own countrymen, their own places of worship into which they wouldn't even allow a white person, their own shops and restaurants. Sometimes, Craig couldn't work out why they'd come here at all. All they did was go on about how great it was back home, and they spent most of the time trying to make parts of Britain look, and smell, like where they came from. Well, it was obvious what they were up to. Slowly, but surely, they were beginning to erode the system, nibbling away at it from inside. They wanted all the good things, though, didn't they? The social. It made Craig sick. Anytime he went down the dole office, they were always there, with their hundreds of babies, and their funny clothes, stinking of strange spices, getting right up your nose. And it was true what the Crusaders said. They were bleeding this country dry. They knew how to play the system, that was how they did it. Single black women, getting themselves pregnant to get council flats. It was disgusting. Craig's old uncle had been waiting years for a flat in Plaistow, but he wasn't one of them, was he? And the people in charge now were all foreign as well. No wonder they looked after their own.

Something had to be done. It couldn't go on like this. They were taking over. The worst thing was when you saw one of them with an English girlfriend. Traitors. Had they no honour, no pride in their nation, their culture, their superiority, these white girls? And what about the weird kids they produced, half-castes, mongrels? That was something the Crusaders could deal with. Someone had to. Otherwise the whole place would be overrun, the whole – what was it the General had called it at that meeting? – the whole 'infrastructure' would begin to break down. Thank God Craig had woken up when he had. It was incredible how blind he had been to what was going on all around him. If only he had known about it sooner. Anyway, better late than never. He was happy now, felt for the first time in years that he had a purpose for getting up in the mornings, a direction in his life. And his Mum and Dad were pleased. The black suited him and he was looking forward to the time when he would go out on his first shooting party. It was so good to feel part of something like this, something that was actually benefiting society. All his life, Craig had just drifted along, not knowing where the hell he was going or where he would end up. But this had sorted him out. He looked over to the private table in the corner of the pub, round which were seated the local Brigadier, the officers of the shooting party and their guests. Craig felt proud to be mixing with such people. He had really moved up now, and one day he would be at that table, drinking and chatting like old mates with the likes of, well, like the man there tonight. Who was it? The Brigadier had told them earlier. One of those minister blokes, someone pretty important. If only Craig's Mum could see him now.

The following morning, the empty glasses and the overflowing ashtrays of the saloon bar still gave off their hedonistic stench, filling the air with staleness. There was an unnatural silence now, as the computer games machine lay disconnected and cold in its filthy corner. Suddenly a small metallic crash filled the room, followed by a dull thud. The morning's *East End Gazette* had arrived. As it fell to the floor, the paper unfolded to reveal the front page. Under a photograph of a row of burnt-out houses, a huge headline read: 'Brick Row Razed To The Ground'. Then, in smaller letters underneath, the suggestion: 'Blacks Blame Crusaders'.

By the time Max and Miranda arrived in Illiers-Combray, most of the filming had been completed. Imogen came to life once they were with her and the whole crew were charmed by the simple but perfect French that Miranda would practise at every opportunity. Most days, Max would go out with the crew and watch the filming, leaving Miranda to play at the château. He loved to watch Imogen at work, relishing the opportunity to observe her when she was completely unconscious of his gaze. Lamarck was always there, spending each afternoon as a casual helper on the set.

The scenes to be shot today included the dramatic tasting of the madeleine, a seminal experience in the development of the young Marcel. Imogen had set the whole scene up in the garden of the Maison Proust and Simon was already dressed and seated by the garden table, ready for the tasting. Axel had bought a bag full of the tiny cakes, and water had been boiled for the mint tea. All was set. While Imogen concentrated on getting the shots right, Axel fixed his attention on the script, recalling once more the eloquent tones of the commentary that would accompany this sequence.

'In all my desires, concentrated around a single dream, I might have recognized as their first cause an idea, an idea for which I would have laid down my life. And at the central point of which, as in my reveries during the afternoons when I used to read in the Combray garden, was the idea of perfection.

'Is it because we relive our past years, not in their continuous sequence, day by day, but in a morning or afternoon, suffused with the shade of some isolated and enclosed setting, immovable, arrested, lost, remote from all the rest, and thus the changes gradually wrought not only in the world outside, but in our dreams and our evolving character, are eliminated, that if we relive another memory, taken from a different year, we find between the two, thanks to vast stretches of oblivion, the distance that there would be between two separate universes, whose substance is not the same.'

'Cut!' Imogen's voice broke the spell that had entranced the whole company. She looked over to Paul. He was unhappy with the take and suggested that they shoot the sequence once more. While they waited for the reset, Simon wandered over to Imogen and Max, casually munching a madeleine. 'Miss,' he said, 'have you ever wondered what would happen if we could, say, taste this madeleine thing now and see all those future times when we'd eat the same thing? Like Proust, but only in reverse. I mean, Proust eats the cake when he's old and thinks back to the time when he was a boy. Well, I could eat this now and think forward to the time that I'm going to be eating the same cake, when I'm sixty.'

Imogen looked at Simon in surprise. 'Yes, but you don't know that you will be eating the same cake when you're old, do you?'

'I do if I decide now that I'm definitely going to make it happen. If I promise myself that I must remember to make it happen.'

Imogen caught Max's eye. He had been listening to the exchange with interest. Max thought back to all the promises he had made, both to himself and to others. The promise to Imogen at Khajuraho, the promise to Jonas Schindler, the promise to his mother. What were these but attempts to project the present into the future?

Paul indicated that he was ready. The camera began rolling again, and Axel found his place in the script once more.

'I understood clearly that what my sensations had reawakened in me had no connection with what I had frequently tried to recall to myself with the help of an undifferentiated memory. The truth surely was that the being within me which had enjoyed these impressions had enjoyed them because they had in them something that was common to a day long past, and to the present. For in some way, they were extra-temporal, and this being made its appearance only when it was likely to find itself in the one and only medium in which it could exist, and enjoy the essence of things. That is to say, outside time.

'And only this being had the power to perform that task which had always defeated the efforts of my memory and my intellect, the power to make me rediscover the days that were long past, the time that was lost.'

Max drove Imogen back through the darkening fields to the château. Simon's words that afternoon had chimed oddly with Max's thoughts and he was very quiet. When he spoke to Imogen, his voice sounded strained. He was reluctant to give her too clear a view into his own mind. 'Wasn't it interesting what Simon said about making sure certain things happen in the future because you make a pledge with yourself?'

'Yes,' replied Imogen wryly, 'he managed to say something intelligent for once. I wonder if any of this really means anything to him?'

'I was wondering that too. Suppose the tasting of the madeleine became a significant event in his life, perhaps as significant as it was in Proust's? That would be a real comment on the nature of art and its transcendence of time . . .' Max trailed off. Imogen looked at him curiously as he drove through the narrow lanes. She had not realized that he had been getting quite so immersed in the filming. He kept his eyes firmly fixed on the road ahead, concentrating on his thoughts and embarrassed to look towards Imogen. He was thinking back to a late-night conversation he had had a few weeks ago with Anjali.

Imogen decided to change the subject. 'What's the latest on your mother?'

'I rang earlier this afternoon. She'd been sleeping but Sister Conrad insisted on waking her up. Said it would do her good to talk to me. Apparently, her dreamtalk has become much more regular and louder. The other patients are beginning to complain, so they might have to move her into her own room soon.'

'What exactly is this talk of hers? Do you know?'

'Not really. It was the night sister who first reported it. It used to be just whispers, no more than dream conversations I expect, but recently it seems to have got more dramatic and louder. Just before I left, the nurses said that she'd been ranting most of the night.' Imogen looked across the open fields on either side of the avenue. In the distance, a lone farmer was busy putting up a large scarecrow, its long black coat flapping wildly in the wind.

'And has anyone been able to work out what it is she's actually saying or are they just incoherent noises?' she asked.

'It's a mishmash of words and phrases. Her brain's probably just running through sounds, like a cassette recorder on fast-forward.' The Château de l'Avenir had come into view, dramatically framed by a collection of dark grey clouds hanging directly overhead. 'Is there much more filming still to do?' asked Max, easing the car through the narrow gateway at the bottom of the drive.

'Just another couple of days and we're through. It's been a good shoot, all things considered. But I'll be glad to get it all in the can. Max,' Imogen paused, taking a few seconds to consider her words, 'Max, do you think we should really be staying on, with your Mum so ill? Wouldn't it be better to get back and be near to her? It might cheer her up a bit.'

Imogen's suggestion struck a nerve. Max had convinced himself that all was well, mainly because he didn't want to let Imogen down. He had wanted to spend a few days at least with her, away from the troubles back home. And now she was being restless. 'I don't think there's much we can do by rushing back,' he said. 'Her condition's stable and the hospital's really looking after her. Dad goes over every day. Perhaps we won't stay on too long, but I would like a bit of a rest.'

As the car came to a halt, skidding the last few feet on the gravel, Max saw Miranda come running out of the side door of the château. Imogen got out, and in the same movement bent down and picked up Miranda, holding her close to her face. Max locked the car, and watched mother and daughter hugging each other. The sight filled him with a warm affection and for a moment he forgot about his own mother, far away, who was even then rehearsing in her mind an irresistible vision of the future.

That night, watching Imogen get Miranda ready for bed, Max felt a deep, relaxed satisfaction. The little girl had missed her mother, though she was far too sensitive to say so to Max, but now, reunited, she could barely contain her excitement, making up for all the lost time. Miranda took ages to brush her teeth and her hair, chattering all the while to her mother in serious, confidential tones. There was so much to be said. Eventually, she jumped energetically into her bed, betraying no signs of tiredness. Max sighed inwardly. The bedtime story Imogen read to Miranda seemed to go on for ever. She had bought some new books in Chartres and was tonight reading out the tale of a family of rats who lived beneath the Opéra in Paris and who had over the years become great aficionados of Mozart. Max loved to hear Imogen's French and could just about understand the language of the children's fable. Gradually, the little girl's eyelids began to grow heavy, despite her best efforts to prolong the time with her mother. At last, they closed, and remained closed.

Imogen sat motionless for a few moments, listening to Miranda's regular breathing. Then she tucked her into the small bed beside her own and moved languidly over to Max. He shifted, making room for her. Despite his apparent affection, Max felt perplexed. Here was his wife, her body warm and open for him, smiling at him, her smooth brow free of any shadows. When Imogen looked at him with her frank passion, Max knew that it was only him she saw. But his eyes, when he returned her gaze, were veiled and guarded. He wondered if she could see, buried in their depths, not her own reflection but that of another figure, graceful and exotic, willing, waiting. Max leaned over and grasped Imogen's arm. He pulled her to him, brushing aside her nightshirt, and impatiently surveyed the expanse of delicate white flesh. Imogen resisted momentarily, a little fearful.

'Miranda,' she whispered. Max rose, keeping hold of her wrist possessively, and eased Imogen towards the bathroom. She took his cue and tiptoed softly into the adjoining room, closing the door behind them. Max's face was hard and flushed, and his silence disconcerted Imogen. She glanced around her, nervously. The bathroom was vast and a thick Oriental rug covered the floor, its patterns intricate and still fresh. She could feel Max's eagerness. She pulled off her nightshirt, letting it fall to the ground as Max stepped forward and kissed her, caressing her breasts. Despite all the years of lovemaking, Imogen still sensed a nervousness in Max's touch, a reticence that excited her. She pressed her body closer to his, encouragingly. For a moment, they stood in the chill of the bathroom, their limbs intertwined. Max looked up past Imogen, and his eyes met his own. In a distant mirror, high on the far wall, Max could see an image of two lovers. In the half-light, the reflection of Imogen's body seemed unfamiliar, smaller, and the mottling of the mirror had transformed her shining red hair to a glossy black. Max fixed on the view for a moment, then with an effort eradicated the errant thought from his mind. He urged Imogen down onto the rug. She lay back, dragging his mouth down onto hers, feeling all the power of Max's pent-up passion against her. He drew away from her, burying his head between her breasts, sliding his hands underneath her to feel the supple muscles of her back.

Imogen was troubled. Max's questing fingers felt harsh to her and she missed the deep, soft blue of his eyes staring directly into her own. He was moving his head lower, flicking her stomach with his tongue. Gently, she pushed him onto his back. His eyes were closed tightly as he lay back on the ornate rug, his face framed by two elaborate dragons, orange and gold, breathing fire. Imogen wondered why he was not observing her as he always did. She began to caress his body slowly, rubbing her fingers through the light covering of hair on his chest. She paused, glancing at his distorted face, then pressed her lips against his once more. Max moaned and abruptly drew his head away from her. For a moment, he stared straight up at Imogen, puzzled. She gazed back into his eyes, searching, but Max looked away, down to where her breasts touched his chest. Then, unexpectedly, he strained up to kiss her again, his mouth bruising her lips. As his tongue probed her mouth, she felt his hand reaching down eagerly, to guide himself into her. At first she refused, but then relented. Imogen heard him gasp deeply, then felt his grip on her tighten as he began to thrust. The magical creatures on the rug began to rock back and forth. She braced herself hard against Max, his motion furious and inhuman beneath her. Her body shook with each powerful movement, but she held herself firm, instinctively allowing his urgent desire free rein.

Imogen clasped Max closely to her as she felt him gush inside her. Again and again the warmth filled her, as it had done so many times before. Like the fierce dragons either side of him, Max's face contorted in violent pleasure. Then slowly he relaxed, his passion ebbing away. He looked up at the exquisite, flushed face staring down at him. The trusting, loyal gaze was one he recognized immediately. Imogen, the Imogen he loved and cherished, was still here. All Max had to do was open his eyes. Imogen smiled.

'Hello Max,' she said.

It was one of those dreary wet days in Oxford. The stone walls of the colleges had started to turn dark brown as the rainwater seeped through, and the cobblestones on Merton Street had become treacherous. Walking down the cramped lane between University College and Merton, Max had already seen two bicycles skid, making their riders twist and turn rapidly, like circus clowns. He had been wandering about in a daze all day, and had by now forgotten what exactly he had come to Merton Street to do. He still had his subfusc on and he had a vague recollection that there might still be another paper of his Finals later on in the afternoon. But he had no idea what the exam was on, and he certainly hadn't prepared for it. Anyhow, it was all too late now.

The clouds continued to mass over the Oxford landscape, moving slowly across the tops of Magdalen Tower and Christ Church cathedral. Max had wandered into Christ Church meadow, which seemed unusually quiet for this time in the afternoon, even in view of the weather. There were usually runners and rowers about, come rain or shine: the Americans in particular loved to show off in anything the English climate could throw at them. But today there was no one. A distant clock struck the hour, followed closely by another chiming from a different direction, then another and another. For three or four minutes the chiming continued. Max looked at his watch instinctively, but it was gone. Still staring at his empty wrist, trying to recall where he had left it, Max wandered on a few paces. Suddenly he felt someone behind him, watching him carefully as he edged along the meadow. He turned but there was no one there, only the autumnal leaves, blown here and there by the rising wind. Max continued along his walk, listening intently to the sound of rain beating softly against the high walls bordering the college garden. A few paces further on, he fancied that he heard the wind form the sound of his own name: 'Max,' whispered the leaves, swirling along the dusty ground, 'Max.' Wrapping his gown about him securely, Max turned the corner towards the Memorial Gardens, braving the full force of the wind and the rain as it rushed at him along the main avenue of the meadow.

The sky was now a dark, uniform charcoal. Max hurried along the pathway, finally reaching the great wooden side door of Christ Church. He decided to take shelter for a few moments inside the lodge, but the door was locked. 'Max,' whispered the wind, more loudly this time, 'Max.' He rushed on, trying to escape the reproach in the voices of the leaves.

'Max,' said his mother, 'remember to look after your father.' Max bent down over his mother's hospital bed, and, being careful not to disturb the opaque tubes leading into her arms, he put his face close to hers. Closer and closer he moved his lips, reaching out to the skin whose fragrance was so evocative for him. He closed his eyes, transported by the familiar aroma. As his lips touched her skin, Max believed for a moment that he was a young boy once again, that his mother's skin was not dry and full of folds and wrinkles, but smooth and supple as it used to be.

Opening his eyes, Max found himself looking straight into two dark, dilated pupils. He pulled back and saw a face begin to form before him. It was Anjali. No, he said, no.

'Max,' she whispered, 'remember that time is not an enemy that we have to fight. Time is a friend. Learn its special language, and don't be afraid.' Max felt guilty that he had been so close to her, to Imogen's friend. What was he doing here? Where was he? He looked about him and saw that he was in his own room at Oxford. Dusk was falling and the orange light of the electric bar heater filled the room with its mellow glow. On the stairs outside, Max could hear the shuffling of feet as the other students went off to hall. A distant bell was sounding, calling the diners to their meal. Max lay back in his bed and felt once more the warmth of the body next to him. Its touch was electric, and he felt himself stiffen. But all the time the thought of Imogen filled his turbulent mind. Max closed his eyes, lulled into a shallow sleep.

'Max,' whispered a gentle voice, 'are you all right? Can I get you anything?' Max opened his eyes and saw the examination paper come into focus on the table in front of him. He looked to his side, where one of his own tutors from college, an invigilator at the examination, was bending over him in concern. As usual, Max was alone in the hall, the other students having completed their scripts long ago. The wind that had blown about him all day was rushing in and out of the marble pillars of the Examination Schools, bringing in the damp leaves and throwing the scripts the other students had left behind into disarray. For a few minutes, Max just watched the leaves and the papers blowing about the hall. Some of them floated around his table and came to rest on the floor by his feet. Max looked at the scripts. Instead of the writing he expected to see, he found himself staring at a series of drawings, pencil sketches made up of violent strokes, some so deep that the paper had been torn. They were drawings of a woman's face. It was a face Max recognized. It was Imogen.

'Max,' whispered a familiar voice close to his ear, 'we should have listened to the boy. It was his gift to us. It was all he had to give.' Max looked up from the sketches to see a tall figure, silhouetted against a distant window. The sun was streaming in now, its rays picking out diagonal columns of dust thrown up by the wind. Staring at the outline by the window, Max's eyes began to water. Gradually, a teardrop rolled down his cheek, winding its way into his mouth.

It was the salt taste that woke Max up.

'Fragments of existence, withdrawn from time . . . The contemplation, though it was of eternity, had been fugitive. And yet, I was vaguely aware that the pleasure which this contemplation had, at rare intervals, given me in my life was the only genuine and truthful pleasure I had known. I remembered, with pleasure, because it showed me that already in those days I had been the same, and this type of experience sprang from a fundamental trait in my character, that already at Combray I used to fix before my mind for its attention, some image which had compelled me to look at it. Because I had the feeling that perhaps beneath these symbols, there lay something of a quite different kind, which I must try to discover. No doubt, the process of decipherment was difficult, but only by accomplishing it could one arrive at whatever truth there was to read . . . The task was to interpret the given sensations, the signs of so many laws and ideas, by trying to draw forth from the shadows what I had merely felt, by trying to convert it to its spiritual equivalent. And this method, which seemed to me the sole method, what was it but the creation of a work of art?'

Axel turned over the final page of the script. The camera continued to roll for a few seconds longer, then, on Imogen's command, Paul cut for the last time. 'Now,' he said, 'shall we do it all again properly, with film in the camera?' Imogen laughed and gave her cameraman a peck on the cheek as she walked past.

'Thanks Paul, everyone! That's great. Well, I do believe it's a wrap!' Instantly, a loud cheer went up from the rest of the crew, followed by spontaneous applause. Max walked up to Imogen, put his arm around her shoulder and gave her a warm kiss. 'Well done, darling. You can relax for a bit now.' Someone had had the foresight to bring along a few bottles of champagne and the sound of corks popping made the whole crew turn, just in time to see the make-up assistant being showered with froth. It was the beginning of an evening of celebration and festivity. An end-of-shoot dinner had been arranged at the Fleur de Lys and Monsieur Séchard had been thoughtful enough to offer that he and his wife look after Miranda for the evening.

But Max and Imogen were destined to take no part in the revelry. Dusk was falling now and most of the townsfolk had retreated to their beds. They had tired of the retakes and had dispersed, one by one, bored with watching Marcel get through a whole packet of madeleines. Only Lamarck remained, persistent to the last. Something about his patience on this last day disturbed Imogen. He seemed to have lost interest in the filming some hours previously yet he had hung on, as if desperate to see the day through to its end. Then, as Paul and Colin were packing away their lenses and tripods with much hilarity, Lamarck came over to her and tentatively put his hand on her shoulder. As Imogen swung round, startled, the young carpenter pulled back, afraid that he had done the wrong thing.

'Oh Lamarck, it's you,' said Imogen. The Frenchman smiled broadly, then suddenly his smile dropped away and his face became serious. Imogen was embarrassed by his childish display but was far too sensitive, even at the end of an exhausting shoot, to betray her impatience. She really was looking forward to the evening celebrations but she could see that Lamarck was making a monumental effort to coax his larynx into speech.

'What is it, Lamarck, what's the matter?' Hearing Imogen's concern, Paul stopped his loading and came over to them. 'Ça va?' he asked kindly. Lamarck looked at Paul as if at a complete stranger whose presence he deeply resented. 'Steady on, old chap, only trying to see if I could help . . .'

The others had by now stowed away the gear and were ready to go. Colin sounded the horn a few times, disturbing the stillness of the dusk. Just out of her line of vision, Imogen could sense Max fidgeting. 'It's all right, Paul, you go on. Max and I will be right behind you.' As they all walked out of the garden of the Maison Proust, Max gazed suspiciously at Lamarck. The young woodworker stared back at him flatly.

'Now Lamarck,' said Imogen, unlocking the passenger door of her car, 'you just sit there in the back, Max will sit in the front and we'll be off.' Lamarck found her voice gentle and soothing. Now that Paul was gone, the carpenter visibly relaxed. He even managed to smile at Max. Dusk had turned into night and the darkness was becoming impenetrable. Setting off, Imogen just concentrated on sticking to the tail-lights of Paul's car as it insinuated itself through the narrow lanes between the fields.

'What a long day,' she said at length, eager to break the silence. She looked over to Max, who glanced at Lamarck and was taken aback to find the Frenchman staring directly at his wife, as if scrutinizing every movement. He sighed, already fearing for their plans that evening. Imogen too saw Lamarck in the mirror. Her stomach sank and she instinctively pressed harder on the accelerator. Paul's tail-lights closed in on their car, and she eased her foot off. Slowly, the red lights moved away. Up ahead, in the distance, a small cottage came into view, its ground-floor lights shining weakly over a freshly-ploughed field. Imogen was relieved that they would soon be back at their château. She had decided to ask Monsieur Séchard the whereabouts of Lamarck's home and Colin or Axel could drive him the rest of the way. The road continued to meander, like a river, turning back upon itself, then twisting sharply. As a result, the cars were crawling along, feeling their way fearfully, like mice in a labyrinth. As the farmhouse approached, Imogen felt Lamarck begin to agitate. He fidgeted and shifted in his seat and then, holding both legs firmly together with his arms, the young woodworker lowered his head onto his knees as if keen to avoid the shadowy field. Glancing out of the window, Imogen thought she could just see the outline of the scarecrow they had seen the farmer putting up earlier that week. The closer the cars came to the field, the more agitated Lamarck became. Imogen snatched brief glances at their distressed companion in the mirror. At one point, it appeared as if Lamarck were letting out a long, silent scream.

Max, twisting round in his seat, could only stare at Lamarck silently, aghast, feeling the uncontrolled fever of nightmare invading the car. The farmhouse was now a few hundred yards away. Negotiating more of the road's serpentine turns, the cars swished past the cottage. Lamarck was covering his face in fear, holding his head down to his knees. Imogen glanced over quickly as the building floated by. All the windows and the front door were closed but not shuttered. Through the glass, Imogen could make out rooms full of antique farming tools. A moment later, the building was no more than a shadow, receding rapidly in the rear-view mirror.

Another fifteen minutes along the winding avenues, driven in silence, the Château de l'Avenir came into view, its forecourt lit by small white spotlights under the eaves. Imogen looked over to Max, pleased that the journey was almost at an end. In the darkness, as the lights played a dance of shadows inside the car, Max noticed that Lamarck's face was shining, covered in tears. The drive past the isolated field had clearly been traumatic for him, but what deep associations did the pasture and the farmhouse hold for him? And why was he now regarding Max with such terror? Imogen opened her door, flooding the inside of the car with light. She looked at Lamarck, and smiled cheerfully. 'Viens, Lamarck, cheer up. Life's not that bad. Don't be sad.' Just then, Monsieur Séchard opened the front door of the château and came rushing out, his feet crunching heavily on the gravel of the forecourt.

'Madame, Madame Imogen, where have you been? We have all been very very worried. Is Lamarck with you?'

'Yes, monsieur, he is here. Is there a problem?' Séchard turned towards the entrance to the château as Axel came out, accompanied by an elderly woman. As she slowly came into view, Imogen noticed that the old lady was leaning heavily on an ornately carved walking-stick and was immediately reminded of the glimpse she had had earlier, through the windows, of the dimly-lit antiques inside the cottage.

'Imogen,' said Axel, 'this is Madame Sarnet. She's Lamarck's mother.'

'Madame,' responded Imogen. 'Enchantée. I hope you have not been too worried about your son. He has spent all day with us, learning how to make films, n'est-ce pas, Lamarck?'

'Monsieur Séchard was worried,' said the dignified old woman, her elocution perfect, tinged with an aristocracy that Imogen found most intriguing. 'As for me, I have not been worried at all, madame. I knew my son would be with you. He has spoken of nothing else ever since you arrived.'

Imogen wondered if Madame Sarnet were using a sort of family shorthand. 'Spoken, madame?' she asked the old lady, 'I must say, Lamarck maintains a resolute silence with us.'

Madame Sarnet looked directly at Imogen. Then she shrugged, and dismissed the inquiry with a casual French splutter. Axel edged closer to Imogen. 'Madame Sarnet was wondering if you wouldn't mind running her and Lamarck back home? They live about ten minutes from here.'

Max looked at Imogen with a barely perceptible shrug of the shoulders. He had given up on the evening anyway. Reading Max's expression, Axel said, 'I'll do it if you like.'

Madame Sarnet clearly understood the exchange, for she was quick to interject. 'If you really wouldn't mind, madame, I would prefer if you and your husband could take us home.'

Imogen turned to the old lady and smiled. 'Of course, I was forgetting my manners. It will be no problem.'

Driving out of the château grounds, the car was plunged once more into pitch-black night. There was a definite chill coming over the surrounding fields, and Imogen shivered.

'Ah, ma petite,' said Madame Sarnet affectionately, 'you will get cold.'

Imogen wound up her window and put on the heater. For a few moments, they drove in silence, looking at the thick foliage of the trees as they floated past, lit up momentarily by the headlights, then plunging once more into darkness as the vehicle passed.

'Thank you for looking after Lamarck for me,' said Madame Sarnet, after a pause. 'I hope he was no trouble?'

'Not at all. He is welcome at any time. Are we going in the right direction, madame?'

'Oui. I will tell you where to turn.' Another few lingering seconds of silence, then Madame Sarnet spoke again. 'Madame Imogen, might I ask a question of you? I hope you do not think I am interfering. Are you, how shall we say, are you a spiritual person?'

'I'm not sure what you mean, madame.'

'Please turn left here. I mean, are you a believer?'

'I suppose I can say I am. I do believe in God, I think.' She found it incredible that she was having this conversation driving through the deep darkness of the French countryside, with a woman she had barely met ten minutes earlier. She wondered what Max must be thinking, trapped in the back with Lamarck.

'Good. You see, I feel I must be honest with you. You have been very good to Lamarck. My son has come to life since you have been in Illiers. To tell the truth, I think he is secretly in love with you.'

'Oh, madame . . .'

'I mean it. He's a good son and a good man. And excuse me, Monsieur Max, he would never harm anyone. But life has not been kind to him. Just to the right here, please.' Imogen turned into a single-track avenue which seemed to lead nowhere. A few hundred yards up this road, she noticed a small cottage, dark and almost invisible in the night.

'Voilà,' said Madame Sarnet, 'on est arrivé.' As Imogen pulled up outside the house, Madame Sarnet looked at her with a penetrating gaze. 'Please,' said the elegant old woman, 'I know you are tired, but do come into the house for a few minutes, both of you.'

'It is very late, madame. Perhaps we can come some other time?'

'I would not insist unless it were important.' Imogen could tell that Madame Sarnet was adamant. She looked back to Lamarck. He too seemed to be urging them to come in, his large eyes still shimmering with tears. Imogen turned off the ignition and swung open her door. At the same time, Lamarck got out of his side and helped his mother to walk up the short path to the house.

A thick mist had floated in from the surrounding fields and was clinging closely to the ground, covering everything in a milky cloud. Walking up to the front door, Imogen heard the faint tinkle of Chinese bells. The breeze was blowing directly into the porch and a set of tiny golden tuning bars was shaking with the disturbance. Imogen turned back to Max who had stopped by the gate and seemed engrossed in his own thoughts, staring at the mist as it wound itself around his ankles. He raised his hand to his face, then seemed to shake himself and moved on to follow her.

The front door gave directly onto the sitting-room and Imogen was intrigued to find it furnished with just the same sort of dark wooden antiques she had glimpsed inside the farmhouse. On the wall there hung mysterious implements which Imogen assumed must be farming tools of the past. Some looked brutal, framed by their own long shadows, the dark wood devouring what faint yellow light was thrown by the now customary, hopelessly weak light-bulb. Outside, the Chinese bells continued with their simple, high-pitched symphony.

As Madame Sarnet settled into her chair, Imogen saw her face clearly for the first time. The old woman was handsome, her features refined and still retaining their youthful sharpness. Like her son, Madame Sarnet was slim and tall, and held herself with dignity, despite the efforts of age to bend her. In her close-fitting black dress, with her hair tightly wrapped, armed with a ferocious cane, the old lady looked like a strict governess from some Victorian novel. It was clear to Imogen that at some point the Sarnet family had been well-to-do, but that circumstances had overtaken them and reduced them to their present humble condition. Now she stared at Max without embarrassment. For an uncomfortable minute, Max felt as if he were being assessed, and was reluctant to stare back at the old woman. Yet there was something so magnetic about her eyes, so dark and piercing, set like two sparkling jewels within a faded, wrinkled face. As if satisfied, she smiled briefly and motioned to Max to sit down. Then she whispered to Lamarck and, giving Imogen a final look, the young man disappeared, rushing off to his room upstairs. Madame Sarnet waited for the footsteps on the wooden staircase and floor to recede, then continued.

'Madame Imogen, I would like to tell you a little about Lamarck and myself and about our life in the village. It is important if you are to understand. When Lamarck was a young child, he had the same powers of speech as all his friends. I can still hear his laughter floating in from the fields. He had many friends but there was something detached about the way he behaved, something that gave the impression that he saw and felt and knew more than any of us around him.

'One night, I awoke to find my son gone from his bed. Jacques and I searched for him everywhere. At last we found him by the river that used to flow at the end of our field in our old house, the farmhouse not far from here. He was sitting on the bank, just staring into the water. As we came closer, we saw that he was crying. Jacques asked him what was wrong but he just kept crying. The sight of his father just seemed to make it worse. We carried him home in our arms, the poor child. I stayed by his bedside all the rest of the night but he wouldn't say anything, not to me, not to Jacques, nothing. For days, the boy would not speak. We thought he was being petulant. In fact I got rather angry with him. Not a word.

'Then about a week later, Jacques was working in the fields when he stepped back onto a land-mine. After the war, many of the mines were left uncleared. All the workers knew the dangers and we are all usually very careful, even now, so many years later. But that day, well, I don't know. Anyway, he was gone, and Lamarck and I were left all alone.

'Lamarck has never spoken a word since that night we found him by the river. Not a sound. He's become a bit of an outcast in the village. If it wasn't for the kindness of Monsieur Selz, I don't know what we would do.'

'Why are people afraid of him?' asked Imogen. 'He's one of the most gentle young men I've met.'

'The people of Illiers are simple folk. This community has been here for many centuries. We are still a highly superstitious people. Witches were being burnt here just a few decades ago, it's true. When Jacques died, word got round that Lamarck had foreseen the death and that was why he refused to speak. A rumour like that spreads like wildfire in a place like Illiers. What could I do? I was the boy's mother. I had to stand by him. As time passed, people, well, they never really accepted Lamarck but they came to tolerate him. He could not speak but I knew he still had a voice. So I said to him, "Lamarck, you must learn to speak with your hands." And he began to draw. I was so pleased when I saw his first sketches. It was the boy's skill with his hands, and his eye for detail that enabled me to go to Monsieur Selz and persuade him to take Lamarck on.' Madame Sarnet paused as if overcoming some inner restraint. 'The reason I have told you all this, Madame Imogen, is because there is something I would like you to see. On the table next to you, you will find some papers. They are drawings that Lamarck has made.'

Imogen leaned over and picked up a handful of ragged white papers, soft and thick, like blotting paper. She glanced at the first sheet, and her heart jumped with surprise. It was a pencil portrait of her, accurate in every detail, a half-profile executed with compelling precision. She gasped audibly. Imogen hastily passed on to the next sheet, handing the first to Max. This too was a portrait of her, from a different angle, highlighting another facet of her face and personality. Lamarck must have been watching her every mood, her every expression and committing the images to memory. The third picture was equally well observed, and the fourth. Before her, Imogen had an uncanny selection of her moods and emotions. Anger, frustration, impatience, excitement and affection. This last seemed to have been the most carefully executed as if Lamarck had been particularly drawn to the image. Imogen began to feel uncomfortably exposed. She wasn't quite sure if she liked the idea of her image being appropriated in this way. Max, for his part, was leafing through the sketches with mounting pleasure and a sense of wonder.

'Don't be frightened, ma petite,' said Madame Sarnet reassuringly, 'he means no harm. I told you, you have transformed his life since you came.' Madame Sarnet stopped, leant down to the side of her chair and picked up another selection of drawings. She offered them to Imogen. For a moment, Imogen heard the gentle tinkling of the Chinese bells outside. Many of the drawings in the new batch were unfinished, simple sketches of Imogen, the features of her face only half etched in. But the final three pictures were the most finely observed of all. Imogen looked them over slowly. Madame Sarnet stared unblinkingly at Max, sitting tense in her chair, observing every nuance of his reaction.

The first showed a strange, alien landscape, somewhere in an isolated desert. It was evening, for an enormous sun hung low in the sky. Two huge towers framed the whole page, reminiscent of the Moghul turrets of the ancient desert forts of Rajasthan. The perspective of the sketch was from a third, higher turret, as if the reader were himself standing within one of the exotic towers. As Imogen looked closer at the drawing, her eye was drawn to the centre of the sheet and to the figure of a man, standing tall, casting a long shadow in the dim half-light. He carried in his arms the limp body of a young woman. The detail in the sketch was obsessive. Peering at the face of the man, Imogen could make out, amid the shadows, a definite scar running the full length of his left cheek. And there was no mistaking the identity of the man's painful burden. Tilting the paper towards the dim light, Imogen saw the woman's face and the familiar features so well observed in the other sketches.

She turned the page, handing it to Max. Preoccupied, she did not notice his expression. But Madame Sarnet did. A waxy pallor crept over his face. The hand that held the sheet of paper shook.

The second drawing startled Imogen and it took her a few seconds to compose her thoughts. For there, unmistakably, was a sketch of a young woman, sitting at work at the desk of Imogen's own study back home. Once more, the perspective of the picture was that of an observer within the tableau, this time as if the reader were standing just inside the door of the study, coming in from the hall. How on earth could the young Frenchman have picked up the details of their home back in England? Could he have overheard Imogen describing her house to one of the team? Or maybe he had sensed something within her own memories? Perhaps, deprived of the normal channels of communication, Lamarck had developed a refined sixth sense? The description of the room was extraordinarily precise. At the far end sat Imogen herself, paused at her typewriter, her body twisted towards the door as if welcoming the new arrival.

Madame Sarnet kept her eyes fixed on Max who, swept by repeated waves of nausea, was fighting to keep his composure.

Imogen passed on to the third and final sketch. The page was covered in wide sweeps of pencil, depicting thick, lush foliage, enormous trees, their leaves forming a cathedral of arches and canopies. The vegetation looked tropical, totally unlike the ordered and well-cultivated greenery of the French countryside. Almost the whole sheet was covered in these visions of rare palms and lush, faraway forests. And there in the centre of the picture was Imogen once more, almost merging into the vegetation all around her. The closer she looked, the more Imogen became aware of another figure that Lamarck had drawn by her side in the forest but which he had subsequently decided to remove, incorporating it into the lines of the nearby trees and leaves. But the original shape was still apparent, despite the effort to erase it. Perhaps it was her imagination, but Imogen felt she recognized the second figure. Taking the drawing from her, Max seemed almost reluctant to look at it. When he did so, he breathed deeply, relieved, and put it aside impatiently. For a few moments, they both stared at the sheets, now all spread out at his feet.

Max turned back to the drawing of the ghost city. Holding the paper up to his face, he peered closely at the face of the Englishman, trying desperately to pick out the features. The scar was evident. He compared the drawing with his own visions of almost a decade ago. Suddenly Max felt a pang of jealousy. Who was Lamarck to expose his precious secret to Imogen? At last he found the voice to ask: 'Madame, who is this man?'

Madame Sarnet replied, 'I do not know, Monsieur Max. All I can tell you is that Lamarck seems to know him well.'

Silence descended upon the room. Max felt so close to unravelling the mystery that had plagued him all these years, and so frustrated that the answer was held by a young man who could not or would not communicate it to him. He looked over to Imogen. Her face seemed naked, as if the layers of skin had been peeled away. Max had the impression of a hand reaching out and grasping at nothing in the darkness. He looked away, shielding his mind from hers. 'Madame Sarnet,' he heard Imogen say softly, 'what is the significance of these pictures?'

The breeze was blowing stronger now, carrying into the room the distant, persistent chimes of the Chinese bells. Madame Sarnet looked at Imogen.

'Madame Imogen, I have no special powers, nothing you do not possess yourself. But over the years, I think I have found a way of understanding the language we all hear, deciphering the signals that our own mind sends to us. Look at poor Lamarck. He feels so much, has so much to say yet no way of saying it. At least, that's the way it might seem. But Lamarck has already learnt what most of us never see. He knows that words can never communicate the truth. These drawings are his gift to you. You must be the best judge of their meaning.'

'But madame,' interrupted Max, his voice forced and anxious, 'could you please ask Lamarck to explain his vision to us?'

Madame Sarnet smiled compassionately at Max. 'You do not need Lamarck to tell you, Monsieur Max. You yourself must find the key to what is hidden. The true seeing is within.'

The sun had been streaming in all afternoon and the room had become terribly warm. As the hours wore on, Thomas Burton had gradually taken off his mackintosh, then his jacket, his hand-knitted sweater and now, finally, he was driven to loosen his tie. He had been keeping a patient and silent vigil by the bedside of his wife, and occasionally, as she slept, he could feel her hand twitch, as if responding to some urgent action in her dreams. They had moved Elizabeth into a single room after her nighttime rantings became too disruptive for the other patients. Thomas was pleased that his wife was now away from the depressing claustrophobia of the open ward.

Elizabeth had got better recently, and had regained the use of her limbs. But the disturbed nights had weakened her and delayed her recovery, so the drips were still attached and the bed was covered by an overhead canopy of tubes and metal stands, all positioned to service the frail human body lying underneath. Listening to her deep, rhythmic breathing, Thomas looked at his wife's wrist, at the clear plastic band of her identity bracelet. There was something extraordinarily pathetic about seeing the stark plastic label against warm, pink human flesh. As he looked closely at the two wrinkled hands, his own and his wife's, he thought back to the time when they had first courted and to the day of their wedding, when he had held her hand so shyly in his own, when their skin had been smooth. All those years: where had they gone? Were they concealed within the crevices and folds of the flesh he saw before him?

Elizabeth was resting peacefully now. She had settled into a strange pattern of waking and sleeping. At night, in her deep slumbers, she regularly declaimed all through the dark hours, as if having vehement conversations and raging arguments with some unseen opponent. By day, despite her condition, she would sit up, active and alert, waiting with eager anticipation for the arrival of her husband. As soon as he was there, after ten minutes or so of animated conversation, Elizabeth would fall into a heavy childlike sleep. On one or two occasions Thomas had tried to get up and leave, but the moment he moved she would wake up and pull him back into place. Then she would drift off once more into a profound slumber. All his life with Elizabeth, Thomas had loved to watch her sleep. She seemed so innocent, so trusting, so secure. It made him feel protective and powerful. He thought, in the end, that all his efforts as a husband and a father could be judged by the peacefulness of her sleep. Her spirit had become a measure of the stability of the family. Which was why it worried Thomas that Elizabeth seemed so turbulent at night.

The door leading into the room opened quietly. Sister Conrad brought in some tea for the Burtons, carefully handing Thomas his cup. Noticing Elizabeth sound asleep, she decided to have the other cup herself and take advantage of the few moments alone with Mr Burton to talk to him about his wife.

'Perhaps she'll not be so disturbed at home,' said the nurse. 'It might be the strange surroundings, you know, they have an odd effect on people.'

'Could be,' said Thomas, sipping his tea with one hand, while still clutching his wife's fingers with the other. 'I'd like to get her back to the house soon, anyway. My son and his wife will be back any day now.'

'Is that Max and Imogen you're talking about?' asked Sister Conrad.

'Yes,' replied Thomas Burton, surprised that she had recalled the names so easily.

'I thought so. It's about the only two things the nurses have picked up amidst the mumble-jumble.'

'Has anyone any idea what it is she's saying?'

'Not really. To tell the truth, some of the younger night nurses have been quite spooked by it. I haven't heard it myself yet.'

Thomas finished off his tea and stared for a moment at the familiar face, breathing evenly, on the starched white pillowcase. The nurse looked for a moment at the anxious figure sitting hunched over the bed, his hand softly grasping the woman he had loved all his life. The vision of the ageing couple made her words seem intrusive.

'I'll be going now, Mr Burton,' she said. 'You're welcome to stay as long as you like. Just call me or the duty nurse if you want something.'

Thomas nodded. 'I'll just stay a bit longer,' he said.

As the sun lost its heat, the shadows of the Venetian blind began to fade on the shining, scrubbed floor. Through the open door, Thomas heard a distant television come on, just in time for the early evening news. The familiar opening music floated across the ward, failing to interest or even to wake the majority of the potential audience. Most of them had heard enough news to last them a lifetime. As the final strains of the opening theme died away, a woman's voice, its elocution crystal clear, announced the headlines. Despite his own preoccupation, Thomas could not help but listen. He could just pick up the high notes, every third word or so, and if he strained his neck, he could see the screen, its myriad colours flickering.

The first item was about some riots in London. Thomas didn't really bother to listen. They had been going on for weeks now, these street fights between white and black youths. There was always trouble nowadays, racial trouble. The whites burning down the shops and houses of Asian families; the Asian youths retaliating. They had the same anger and passion as the thugs who were out for them. Thomas recalled the Paki-bashing when Max was at school. The Asian kids then were pretty meek. Their parents always told them never to fight back. It wasn't their country, after all, they would be told. Not now. Now things were very different. Thomas felt it was all getting out of control.

Only last week a whole family of Bangladeshis in Tower Hamlets had been burnt alive as they slept, father, mother and three young children. Apparently, local community leaders had been warning about just such an attack but the police said there was nothing they could do. Afterwards, the whole community had gone on a peaceful demonstration, ending with a silent vigil outside the home of the victims. They knew who had done it. The front wall, despite its blackening by fire, still carried the distinctive hammer and arrow symbol, painted with an aerosol can. A few days later, two white youths had been found stabbed through the neck, in their car, just outside Mile End underground station. The local press tried to make out it was a vicious, unprovoked attack on two innocent white kids, but everyone knew that the victims were Crusaders. Even the police.

Out of the corner of his eye, Thomas could see scenes of street fighting caught by a running cameraman, the pictures jogging wildly. Police on horseback tried in vain to control the mob. The screen was full of fires raging, and fire-engines and police cars racing wildly through crowds of young people. What a mess it was. The shots were changing frantically on the distant screen, and for a moment Thomas was struck by the unreal contrast between the turbulence on the television and the quiet, oblivious serenity of the hospital ward, the patients lying in neat rows, either asleep or at best regarding the events of the world outside with silent contempt. He turned his back on the television and tried to cut out the noise and the kaleidoscope of changing colours.

'Glad we're away from all this,' he whispered gently to his wife.

It was another tempestuous night for Max's mother. At first, soon after her husband had left, she seemed to have fallen into a deep contented sleep, silent and peaceful. But a few hours into the night, the whisperings began. Sister Conrad was on duty that night and was at last given the opportunity to hear what had so fascinated the other nurses. She stood beside Mrs Burton's bed, listening intently to the dreamtalk. The nurse could hear that her patient was talking in complete sentences, as if making a speech. And the intonation was quite forceful. It was as if the distraught woman was trying to warn someone of something. Sister Conrad knew exactly what to do. Trying to wake the patient was never a good idea: the disorientation could be extremely distressing and with those whose physique had been weakened by a stroke, the shock of coming round suddenly could prove fatal. So the sister sat quietly by Elizabeth Burton's bed, holding her head and her hand, soothing her as she tossed and turned in her restless dreams.

The names came through clearly, every so often: Max and Imogen. And it was obvious that the old woman was trying desperately to communicate a message. Her eyeballs were moving frantically beneath the tightly closed eyelids, as if she were participating in some violent action, and the contortions of her face indicated panic. Sister Conrad noticed the perspiration break out on Elizabeth Burton's forehead and her hand become hot and damp.

The volume of the ranting rose, then retreated again to a whisper. Sister Conrad recognized a number of the words as being similar to the names of some of the pills and injections the doctors prescribed. Could her patient's addled brain just be running through the sounds she had heard in the ward all around her? It didn't seem so. There was clearly a definite pattern to the words, a strict order, and a formality. As the nurse listened more attentively, she realized that some of the phrases were Latin. But what did they mean? And how could Mrs Burton talk so fluently in a long-dead language? Just as the whispers began to be recognizable, the sounds suddenly changed and Sister Conrad found herself listening to a completely different language. Now, the sentences were far less structured. It sounded Arabian or Eastern, but not the way they spoke now.

The nurse watched the sleeping face carefully as it contorted into all sorts of funny shapes in order to form the awkward words. Then, just as she was about to put out the nightlight above the bed, Sister Conrad noticed a silver pool form itself in the corner of her patient's eye and elongate into a thin streak crawling along her cheek.

'Oh dear,' said the nurse quietly to herself, 'no need for that, Mrs Burton.' Just then, Max's mother opened her eyes wide and looked straight at the ward sister.

The nurse gasped and stepped back, startled. 'Oh my goodness, Mrs Burton, you frightened me.'

By the bedside, the machines monitoring Elizabeth's heart and breathing began to fluctuate erratically, adding their own electronic warnings to the chaotic symphony in the room. The sister pushed the emergency button. The raving continued unabated. Within minutes, the doctor arrived. The nurse was exhausted, and pleased to hand over charge of her patient into more capable hands. The bleary-eyed young graduate, his hair still ruffled from his own disturbed sleep, injected Elizabeth Burton with a strong sedative. For a few more minutes, the patient struggled and the monitors continued their frantic warnings. Then, gradually, she quietened down, retreating into a silent but still fitful sleep for a few hours. Beside her, the electronic sentinels resumed their vigilance, settling back into their regular rhythms.

As dawn broke, Elizabeth's harrowing dreams were replaced by more serene visions: happier memories of her son, when he was a little boy, running up and down the newly carpeted stairs, hiding in the warm understairs cupboard, hugging the central-heating boiler for its warmth, filling the house with his soft, unbroken voice.

The stormy weather had passed at last and for the first time in days Max was able to leave the château after dinner and go for a quiet walk across the fields. He reflected on his stay in Illiers-Combray, not at all what he had expected. The re-emergence of the Englishman through Lamarck's drawings had let loose within Max a whole range of emotions that had lain buried for years.

Walking across the newly ploughed ground, soft after days of rain,

Max felt the smell of the damp earth flow through him, and bring with it a deep serenity he had not felt for years. He let his memories flow freely and he felt his spirit begin to unwind, finding the most appropriate places for the host of recollections that had been swimming unhoused in his mind. The past few years had been pandemonium: not just Imogen's job, though her constant absences had a lot to do with it. His own growing concerns about his family, the sense of time running out. And then the friendship with Anjali, which had come so close, so dangerously close to indiscretion. All these had thrown Max into inner chaos. But now he felt as if he had turned a dangerous corner in his life. The road before him was in shadow but it was straight. He thought of Anjali, but with equanimity now, the turmoil of his waking dreams all passed. He wished only for the solitude he had always craved, to allow his soul stillness.

He must have walked for miles, for the next time he turned round, Max could barely see the château beneath the rapidly darkening sky. A few faint flickers of a crimson sun still touched the clouds and, looking up for a few moments, Max saw Venus clearly, shining brightly in the leaden sky. He had always tried, whenever he could, to pick out the planet in the night sky. It gave him a warm sense of continuity, a feeling that there were certain things in life that were constant and able to resist the incursions of time. He thought back to the evening at Khajuraho, all those years ago, when Imogen had made him promise to bring her back to India all her life, and indeed to return even if it was by himself, alone. What a thought! Max had come to see Imogen as invincible, so in control, so self-possessed.

Max passed the scarecrow that he and Imogen had seen the farmer putting up some days earlier. Its long black tail-coat was flapping in the evening breeze and the rain had made the straw of its body damp, dark and heavy. As a result, the scarecrow had begun to lean over precariously and its hat had settled into a rakish angle over its brow. The local crows had become accustomed to all these sorts of devices: the very day the scarecrow had gone up, they had flown down and picked off its eyes, nose and mouth. And now, as Max approached, a single magpie flew up screaming from beneath the ragged trousers, angry at being disturbed. Passing the scarecrow, Max decided to straighten it and give it back some of its dignity. He pulled the body up to its full height, a foot or so taller than him, and pushed the central pole deeper into the sodden ground. The scarecrow stood erect, with a military precision. Then Max straightened its hat and, looking on the ground about him, picked up a few large stones and pushed them into the damp straw, giving the guard back his eyes, nose and mouth. Max stared at his handiwork for a moment, pleased at the resurrection.

The scarecrow smiled back foolishly, pieces of straw flying off in the wind.

Max walked on, heading towards a distant avenue of trees. He thought about Miranda, and how much like Imogen she was becoming. On one occasion, Mrs Fielding had shown Max some photographs of Imogen as a girl of five or six. Miranda was almost a carbon copy of that young girl and she was developing the same mannerisms and idiosyncrasies as her mother. Perhaps they would take her out to India on their next trip, the following autumn. Max had resisted taking Miranda along up till now, ostensibly for the sake of her health and because it would have changed the nature of the vacation altogether. In truth, he had come to value the Indian trips as one of the few periods when he could be with Imogen on her own, and he was not prepared as yet to share that privilege with anyone, not even his own child. He knew it was selfish. His own mother and father would never have done that to him. He had always accompanied them on their outings and holidays, and his mother often used to tell him what an added pleasure it had been for them both.

Max was now at the edge of the scarecrow's field. He looked back over the land he had crossed and could just make out the distant silhouette, still standing to attention, still an attractive plaything for the crows and magpies. Max turned back and looked towards the lush common on the other side of the stile, bordered by the blossoming hawthorn. He began to climb the fragile wooden platform and swung his leg over the top beam. Pulling his other leg across he jumped down, onto the deep, wet grass.

'Hello Max,' said a woman's voice he recognized instantly. Max looked about him but could see no one in the long shadows. He walked on, thinking he must have heard it inside his head. He had gone about twenty yards into the common when he heard the same familiar voice again: 'Max. Don't rush on.' The whisper was behind him and just as he thought of turning, the voice said: 'No, Max. Don't turn around. Just stop for a moment. Do as your mother says.'

His heart was pounding audibly now and Max felt his temples throbbing painfully. He knew instantly what had happened.

I wasn't there, thought Max. After all these years, after all the efforts to be a good son, I wasn't there. He bent his head towards the ground, the tears rolling off his face. There was so much I still had to say to you. So many feelings I kept to myself. For what? For fear of embarrassment. Max felt his spirit torn apart as he heard the words in his head.

He raised his head and began to turn and face the voice. As he did so, he felt his whole body filled with a deep and penetrating sweetness, an intoxicating warmth. Compassion and forgiveness hung in the air like a delicate perfume. Max smiled, looking around him at the over-arching sky, the hawthorn blossom, the fecund earth. A sudden gust shook the petals from the branches above his head. They were moist with the recent rain and as they swirled about him, Max felt the touch of a gentle hand sweep across his face and wipe away his tears.

For several years now, the chime on Max's watch had seized up. He had been meaning to go to Jonas Schindler and have it repaired, but somehow he never got round to it.

The *Literary Masters* series had been a great success for Rex Fischer, for Riverside and for Imogen. The Proust film in particular was hailed as a masterpiece and carried off a string of awards that year. Imogen had been made Rex's deputy Head of Arts at Riverside, which brought a certain stability back into her family life. Now, she only made the occasional programme herself, spending much of her time running the team from London and being taken out to expensive lunches by rich co-producers. The more Rex became an elder statesman of the arts, the more he delegated to Imogen. It would only be a matter of time before she became head of the department.

The massive benefits that accompanied her position enabled Imogen and Max to send Miranda to the best preparatory school in London: St Julian's, just off the river at Barnes, and conveniently close to their Richmond home. She was going to be a formidable beauty and already showed evidence of quite an intellect. The other parents were all most complimentary, and a little envious, but Miranda was a popular girl, and they were popular parents. Whatever her other commitments, Imogen always made time to attend school functions and had arranged for many famous actors and actresses to come to the school to give talks and open fêtes. More than anything else, she was quite a role model for the girls. They loved to see her and most of them wanted to grow up to be like her, glamorous and powerful, successful in the media. They were always reading articles about her in the papers, or hearing her on radio. It seemed that every few months, Imogen Burton was collecting another award for outstanding contribution to the arts.

Life was very different for Max since his mother died. He was now spending a lot more time with his father. He and Imogen had offered him the opportunity to sell the house in Burnham and for all of them to buy a large house together, but he turned down the offer, preferring instead to live on his own in the house that held so many memories for him. Max was disappointed that his dad was so obstinate, but a part of him was pleased that his childhood home was not sold off. Most weekends, he, Imogen and Miranda would drive over and spend time with his father. He dearly wished he had done the same when his mother had been alive but he had never thought, had never realized just how final death is, that it never gives you a second chance. Max was determined not to make the same mistake again. He knew it pleased his father to have a youngster in the house again, particularly such an endearing one as Miranda. And it was a special pleasure when Imogen brought with her his favourite forties' and fifties' Hollywood videos. She had found a special film library that stocked them, and on pretext of research she would get Thomas whatever obscure black-and-white film he fancied.

Anjali was now quite a star, a leading member of the Shanti Dance Company of New Delhi. After Oxford, she had decided to return to her own country and pursue her dancing professionally. She and Imogen, and Max, still kept in regular contact and whenever Anjali came to London to perform, usually three or four times a year, she would meet up with them. On those occasions, she would always say that it was Imogen who had given her the first real break, and Max who had guided her personally. He knew he owed much more to her than she to him, but it was good to feel that they were still close companions after all these years. Looking back, Max would always sense a pang of shame and guilt that he had ever considered Anjali as anything other than a platonic friend. Still, there was no doubting her loveliness. Even now, he sometimes dreamt about her.

Miranda loved her Indian aunty and when Max and Imogen went to India, Miranda would stay with Anjali in Delhi. Like her mother, Miranda was developing a close bond with India, and would often come back from her excursions determined to live and work out there. She held long, serious conversations with her mother on the subject, as Imogen brushed her hair at night. And it was the first question she would ask whenever Anjali came to stay in Stearns Mews.

'Do you think I should marry someone Indian?' said Miranda, shifting up closer to Anjali on the settee, while Max and Imogen fussed about in the kitchen, putting the final touches to the dinner party they had organized.

'Oh, you're far too young to think about getting married, Miranda. You have to go to the big school first.'

'I suppose so. But wouldn't it be exciting to meet some Indian prince, the son of a maharaja perhaps, down on his luck and living as a pauper, who could tell you all about life and show you things you could only dream about? He might be a dacoit, but only a good one, robbing the most wealthy people and giving to the poor. Oh well,' sighed Miranda, 'we'll see . . .'

Anjali put her arm around the child and kissed her silken auburn hair. 'I'm sure we can arrange a dacoit-prince for you, darling. I'll find one just as soon as I go back.' Miranda looked innocently at Anjali, and moved her head closer to her chest, snuggling up like a cat in the soft folds of the sari. With her long, feminine fingers Anjali stroked the child's head, smoothing her hair and thinking about her own plans for the future. She knew that her parents wanted her to get married, and there had been scores of offers, some quite attractive. But Anjali just wasn't ready for all that. Perhaps she would never get married. Yet she so much wanted a daughter like Miranda, someone she could teach to dance, and pass on her expertise. Anjali felt the child breathing deeply. She knew she was denying the truth to herself but was far too ashamed to admit it. Still, life is full of things that might have been.

'When are you dancing next?' asked Miranda.

'Diwali, in ten days' time. That's really the purpose of this trip. The Dance Company's been invited by the Ramakrishna Society to perform at the celebrations out at their manor house in Hatchmere Heath. You will come, won't you?'

'Of course. Mummy and Daddy have been talking about it for months. I know it's in their diaries. I've never been to Diwali at the Ramakrishna Society – someone told me they celebrate it really traditionally.'

'It's quite an occasion. There'll be a big firework display, and the whole house is being lit up with candles and oil-lamps. You'll love it, but you'll have to take the next day off school. The celebrations go on all night.'

'I'll let Daddy sort all that out with Miss Sutherland. She's our headmistress. Can I bring my best friend Emily?'

Anjali laughed. 'I'm so glad you've got your mother's affection for India, you know.'

'Oh, and my Daddy's,' retorted Miranda, suddenly shifting and looking up at Anjali. 'He loves India too, you know. It's just he's a lot more shy than Mummy. He doesn't like people to see his feelings. But I know Mummy and Daddy feel the same about everything.' The girl held Anjali's stare, searching for agreement. Deep down Anjali knew why Max was so reticent, but it would be impossible to explain it to his daughter. She looked at the girl, and Miranda smiled knowingly, the same breathtaking smile with which Anjali had so often seen Imogen claim Max.

It had been years since Max and Imogen had been to a Diwali festival. The Ramakrishna Society had grown considerably in the past few years, both in Britain and in the West generally, replacing with a more authentic and credible version of Hinduism the earlier cult-like communes that most people associated with Eastern mysticism. Donations, some huge from multi-millionaires and others modest from everyday pilgrims, had enabled the society to grow and maintain its spiritual ethics. Here at Hatchmere Heath, some fifty miles northwest of London, the manor house had become a focus for Ramakrishna activities and most weekends thousands of followers from all over Britain came to share their faith. It was testimony to the credibility of the society that the pilgrims were predominantly Asian, most third- and fourth-generation Indian Hindus. Along with these, many non-Asians would also come, some out of curiosity, others to join in and follow the faith that provided an alternative to the orthodoxies of the established churches.

A third group of pilgrims was also attracted to Hatchmere Heath, more secular in their motives.

The village around the manor house had been a quiet, sleepy community, mostly made up of commuters working in the City. At first, they were pleased to see the manor house being used and brought back to life after so many years of decrepitude, even if the new owners were a little unorthodox in their habits and appearance. The saffron-clad young men and women who lived at the house had gone out of their way to be friendly to the locals and had largely succeeded, organizing evening and weekend activities for the children and running their own little farm. But recently, all that had changed. As the fame of the centre spread and as it became a regular place of weekend pilgrimage, the villagers found themselves submerged each Saturday and Sunday by hordes of invading outsiders. For most of the local inhabitants, the weekend was the only time they were at home in the day, with the family, and now the seclusion and peace they had sought out of London, and paid such exorbitant property prices for, had been destroyed by this weekly carnival. Cars descended upon the village like a nestful of wasps homing in upon a pot of jam. Once in Hatchmere Heath, the visitors would leave their vehicles all over the neatly trimmed village green. Later, as they left, the place looked like a deserted fairground, with litter scattered everywhere and the turf of the lawns dug up by tyre treads.

Feelings on both sides had run high. The local, then the national, press had made it a cause célèbre, using the tension within the communities as a microcosm for the wider racial conflicts now manifest once more in British society. But in Hatchmere Heath at least, a compromise had been reached. Peace and goodwill had won out. The number of pilgrims on any one day was limited, and a car park built for them a few miles outside the village. From there, they were transported into the manor house by buses, quietly and neatly, causing the minimum of disturbance and distress to the locals. Emotions cooled, and an atmosphere of mutual respect had grown up once more.

For some others, however, not from the immediate vicinity, the conflict could not have come at a better time. They regretted the defusion of the tension.

Diwali, of course, was an exception. It was the most important annual festival for Hindus and it took place on a weekday, continuing all night. Unlike the weekend, where numbers could be regulated between the two days, there was no way of limiting the people coming to the evening celebrations, nor of expecting them to leave early. Organizing Diwali was a major logistical exercise in Hatchmere Heath. Extra police were recruited into the area and those locals who lived closest to the manor house, and who did not wish to attend the festivities, were offered the opportunity to spend the night at a luxury hotel in nearby Wheeler's Bar at the Society's expense. Most of them took up the offer.

The out-of-town car parks were already jam-packed by five in the afternoon, and Chief Inspector Christie had had all his men working flat out to cordon off vast areas of outlying farmland for use as overflow parking. He had specifically asked for the special force with him this evening to be a multiracial one. The last thing he wanted to do was to make the Hindus feel outnumbered, and he figured that a liberal sprinkling of brown and black officers would enhance the spirit of carnival. So far, the strategy seemed to have been successful. Despite the hectic comings and goings, everyone was in good spirits, and the operation was flowing smoothly. All being well, once the actual celebrations began at nightfall and the pilgrims were safely inside the manor grounds, his officers could take a brief rest, in time to be relieved by the night squad coming up from the Met. In addition to the police forces, the local fire brigades were on alert. They called it Operation Krishna, and they had all been told about the special emphasis on lighting candles and fireworks, and the large numbers of children attending, factors which made the Festival of Lights into a powder keg. Half a dozen fire officers had already recce'd the manor house and advised on escape routes. These had duly been cleared, and notices pinned up in English and in Hindi. But, as usual with Indian gatherings, within an hour of people arriving, and despite the very best efforts of the Society's sanayassins, all the emergency exits had become cluttered with bags and prams and pushchairs and coats. Hindu optimism overcame all fear of disaster. The local fire chief was not a Hindu: when he saw what had happened, he calmly ordered all obstructions to be cleared and dumped outside in a big skip. A half hour later, the exits were blocked once more.

It took Max, Imogen and the girls, Miranda and her friend Emily, over an hour to get from their parking space to the manor house. The Burtons were not particularly bothered, but for Emily it was a new experience, and there were times when the young girl was close to panic and tears.

'Just hold my Mummy's hand,' advised Miranda, 'and whatever you do, don't let go.'

With that instruction, Miranda herself grasped Max's hand firmly, and all of them pushed their way through the hordes. Caught in the typhoon of people rushing hither and thither, there were times when Emily thought she might be swept away forever. She need not have worried. Somehow they all reached the manor house and, once inside, found their way to the special rooms on the first floor reserved for Anjali and her group of dancers. The family fell into the room, closing the door on the turmoil outside.

Inside, all was calm and ordered. A group of dainty young Indian women, their lithe bodies clad in close-fitting silk trousers and tight blouses, were busy putting on their elaborate Eastern make-up. On the floor, piles of shining silk lay all unfolded, spread out along the carpet, ready to be wrapped around the slim dancers. Max wondered if his presence might be undesirable but Anjali, in turquoise, came over excitedly and welcomed them all. 'You made it!' she said.

'Just about,' replied Imogen, 'how are things going up here?'

'Oh, as well as can be expected. We've been here most of the day, practising and getting our costumes ready. It's obviously going to be quite a night.'

One of the younger dancers, having caught Miranda's curious eye, had come over and taken the young girls off to show them the make-up and costumes. Max turned towards Anjali and bent down for a chaste kiss on the cheek. 'Hello, Anjali,' he said, careful not to hold her gaze for too long. 'I'll leave Imogen and the girls with you and see what's going on downstairs.'

'Okay,' said Anjali, 'make sure you get some decent seats. You know what people are like.'

'And don't get lost,' added Imogen. 'It'll take till next Diwali to find you.' Max smiled, took one last look at the room full of exquisite dancers and backed out of the door. He was carried off almost instantly by the river of people outside.

As night fell, the oil-lamps placed all along the outline of the manor house were lit and the fireworks began to go off. Chief Inspector Christie had just closed off the final car-parking enclosure, and was now driving to the house to make his final checks. He planned to look in on the festivities himself. He was quite partial to Indian food, and the general secretary of the Ramakrishna Society had invited the Chief Inspector and his men to share in the prashad later. Accelerating away from the car parks, Christie was satisfied with the way things had turned out. There had been no bother, and the locals had been very good-humoured about the whole thing. He hoped the departure would be as smooth.

As the Chief Inspector's car cruised along the narrow country avenue towards the back entrance of the manor house, forty miles away from Hatchmere Heath other cars were also making haste. Travelling in well-orchestrated formation on all three carriageways of the motorway, twelve Espace vans were searing through the darkness towards the remote village.

Outside, in the grounds of the manor house, the firework display was coming to an end. The children had been enthralled for over an hour, watching the colourful rockets and Catherine wheels light up the night sky. Each family had been handed packets of sparklers, and as the display reached its climax, all the children joined together to light the tiny sticks, waving them in the air, their excited, innocent faces lit up by the diamond flames. Miranda and Emily had attached themselves to a larger group of children, and they were all having a marvellous time, free of parental supervision. Nonetheless, Miranda didn't want to miss Anjali's dancing and she kept a regular eye on her watch and on Emily, for whom she felt maturely responsible. Emily had made friends with a young Indian girl, who soon took her off around the temple to explain to her all the various deities, the statues dressed in the finest costumes specially sewn for Diwali. The two of them had promised to be back in time for the dancing, and Miranda had spoken quite firmly with the Indian girl, experimenting with a few words of Hindi that she had picked up from Anjali, and which she now used in order to show she meant business.

Chief Inspector Christie, satisfied that all was under control, dismissed most of his men, keeping only the core of the squad on duty at the manor house. The general secretary, Swami Anand, had attached himself to the police officer and was insisting that he partake of the prashad before the classical dancing programme began. The Chief Inspector accepted readily, following the Swami to the hall set aside for dining. Walking through the various rooms and hallways of the manor house, Christie was struck by the display of colourful paintings and marble statues, decked out in the most luxurious silks. He knew a little about the Hindu religion, but he certainly could not put a name to any more than a couple of the moortis he saw. The devotees had obviously been working for weeks in preparation for Diwali, for everything had been freshly cleaned and painted. Flower garlands were everywhere, draped around pillars, around statues, hanging from paintings, pinned along the banisters. All the ceilings were canopied with multicoloured streamers, and pungent joss sticks, held by brass containers, gave off their distinctive Indian aroma. In most rooms, groups of women crouched on the floor, singing bhajans, accompanied by the sound of temple bells and tablas. Visitors and sanayassins mixed freely, the saffron-clad devotees, their heads shaven, their foreheads marked with crimson powder, conversing easily with teenagers wearing the latest designer clothes. Families gathered in corners to eat from plastic plates overflowing with channas and halwa, women forcing huge mouthfuls down the throats of their children. Every now and then, the Chief Inspector was pleased to see a white face mingling with the crowd. As he passed on towards the main reception, he noticed across the hallway an attractive Englishwoman he recognized from the television. Catching Imogen's eye, Chief Inspector Christie nodded a respectful acknowledgement.

Following the Swami onwards, Christie finally reached the dining area. As he passed the crowds waiting outside, in their version of a queue, he noticed the abysmal obstruction to the emergency exit outside the hall. He was just about to say something to the waiting pilgrims when he saw the fire chief further down the hall, getting people to clear away the next exit down. Christie caught his eye with a mutual look of exasperation and anger. 'Keep up the good work,' he said, patting the fire chief gently on the shoulder as he passed.

'Thanks, Jim,' replied the harried officer, continuing to direct the reluctant women to clear up the mess. 'No rest for the wicked.'

Sitting the police officer down in a quiet corner, Swami Anand rushed off to get prashad for him and typically, the plate came overflowing with food. Using his plastic fork judiciously and bending his head forwards, away from his newly cleaned uniform, Christie managed to take in a few mouthfuls of the chickpeas and potatoes. While he was still grappling with his food, he heard an uncharacteristic silence descend upon the crowd, quickly followed by the opening strains of Indian classical music. There was a general rush in the dining-hall to finish off. As the room emptied, Chief Inspector Christie sat back, his plate now down to a reasonable size, and enjoyed the rest of his holy food.

Out of the village, the twelve Espace vans pulled off the motorway and carried on swiftly in single file down a series of quiet, dark country lanes. The leading driver obviously knew the way, for a few minutes later he turned off onto some waste ground, on the outskirts of Hatchmere Heath, and came to a halt, skidding on the dusty surface. One by one, the vans fanned out on either side of the leading Espace, each one coming to a halt around the perimeter of the wasteland. Then, as if in the same movement, the rear doors of the vans opened and from each vehicle a handful of fit young men jumped down heavily onto the ground and ran towards the central Espace, forming themselves into a precise circle around the vehicle.

Max had managed to hold four seats right at the front, and he was getting annoyed that, despite the efforts he had made, none of the others was anywhere to be seen. He was constantly fighting off usurpers to the seats, claiming they were occupied, but if Imogen and Miranda and Emily didn't turn up soon, he would have to let them go. Max craned his neck around to the back of the hall, looking out for the familiar faces. Seeing no one, he sighed and turned back, just in time to see them all rush in from the side door and take their seats.

'Thank goodness you're here,' he whispered, 'I was about to give up. Where have you been?'

'We've been eating prashad,' said Imogen, 'have you had any yet?'

'I had a few mouthfuls earlier.' Then, turning to the girls, Max said, 'Are you having a good time, you two?'

'It's brilliant, Mr Burton,' said Emily, 'absolutely brilliant!'

'Has Anjali been on yet?' asked Imogen.

'No, no, it's only just started. I expect she'll come on in a few minutes,' answered Max. The dancers on the stage were some of the younger girls they had seen getting ready. Now fully made-up and in costume, the dancers looked a lot older, their elaborate headdresses making them seem taller and more exotic. Even a cursory glance showed that Anjali had choreographed the pieces: her distinctive style and the inimitable flow of her movements was everywhere to be seen. In the corner, a small group of musicians sat on the floor, playing their tablas and sitars with all the enthusiasm they could muster. As the music rose to a climax, the young dancers finished off their repertoire, bowed and shuffled off, taking dainty little steps and barely able to contain their smiles and giggles. There was a momentary pause in the music, then it began again, this time the melody much more complex, the rhythms far more involved. The stage was clear as the music continued to build. Then, just as it hit the high notes, Anjali floated onto the stage, her feet moving effortlessly from side to side, her body gliding as if on air. Her costume was spectacular: it had been specially made by the girls at the Ramakrishna Society, and was an exact copy of the one they had put on the moorti of Radha, the consort to Lord Krishna. Reaching the centre of the stage, Anjali suddenly burst into free movement. Again and again, her perfect little body spun itself into all sorts of intricate shapes, keeping ahead of the music and counting its beats with synchronized gestures. The more Anjali challenged the music with her dance, the more the musicians increased their tempo, trying to outstrip her. And so the harmony continued, faster and faster until, with precise timing, both the dance and the music paused, caught its breath, then took off again, aspiring to ever greater heights.

Now that Max understood something about the philosophy behind Indian classical dance and music, he was much better able to appreciate its complex series of moves. All the time, he kept his eyes fixed on Anjali's face, the face he had so often seen in his dreams, held by its serenity and perfect control. However frantic the movements, the face remained impassive, stoic, untouched by the turbulence of the dance and the music. Again and again, Max fancied that Anjali caught his eye momentarily and that her smile was a smile of regretful understanding, specially directed towards him.

As the performance reached its climax, so Max felt his heart racing to keep to the rhythm. He pressed Imogen's hand in his own, reminding himself of the choice he had made.

Wiping his hands on the sodden towel by the side of the sink, Chief Inspector Christie straightened his jacket, adjusted his tie, and made for the hall to catch the last few minutes of the dancing. Looking at his watch, Christie decided to leave it another hour before calling his main squad back. He figured it would be about that long before people began to leave, and by then the relief squads from the Met would be here. His boys had worked hard enough to get everyone safely in. It was only fair the Met got them out.

Just as he was leaving the makeshift bathroom, he saw one of his junior officers rushing frantically towards him, panic all over his face. 'Sir! Sir!' hissed the officer, trying desperately to keep his voice down.

'What is it, Marsh? What's the problem?'

The young officer came to a halt a few inches from his superior, and whispered something urgently into his ear. Chief Inspector Christie went red and it took him a few moments to gather his composure. He dispatched his officer with immediate orders, put on his hat, and strode quickly into the hall full of celebrants.

Miranda had been fidgeting all evening, looking about her at the other people watching the dancing, keeping an eye on what was happening outside in the corridor, occasionally taking in a bit of the dancing. And so it was she who first saw the Chief Inspector hurry in, moving people out of his way as he made for the stage. Soon the commotion had caught everyone's attention, even the dancers', and the performance began to subside as people turned their eyes to the sombre-looking police chief.

Reaching the podium, Christie apologized to the young dancers, beckoned to the musicians to stop, and raised his arms for silence. A deep hush descended on the gathered crowd.

'Ladies and gentlemen,' he began, his voice straining with urgency, 'I am afraid I have to call the festivities to an end.' A murmur of disbelief went around the hall, people looking at each other in confusion and perplexity. 'There has been some trouble in the village. Some youths have set fire to cars parked in the enclosures. My men are there now and I can assure you we're doing our best to sort it out. But I would like to recommend that we bring things to a close.'

A general panic gripped the pilgrims. Instantly everyone got up from the seats they had occupied and, gathering their belongings, began to make for the exits.

'Ladies and gentlemen,' shouted Christie, his commanding voice stopping the flustered visitors in their tracks, 'I would suggest that you follow the advice of my officers before you go outside.' His warning fell on deaf ears. After a moment's pause, the crowd continued to move, shifting like an enormous pool of water towards the doorway. One of the senior-looking priests joined the Chief Inspector on the podium, and added his advice in Hindi.

Half-way through his speech, a young Indian man came running into the hall from outside the front entrance and screamed at the top of his voice: 'It's Crusaders! They've burnt all our cars with petrol bombs! Now they're on their way here!'

Hearing the warning, Christie jumped off the stage and turned on his radio. Immediately, a frantic, high-pitched voice came over the airwaves, the words incomprehensible over the static and interference, but the panic quite clear. Everyone turned towards the Chief, drawn by the desperate electronic voice of the radio. Christie decided it was best to turn it off, otherwise there would be a full-scale riot here.

Out in the corridors, he saw the consoling sight of a dozen of his men, obviously looking for him. Making his way towards them, Christie yelled: 'Over here! What's going on?'

The senior officer turned towards the Chief, and pushed through the crowd. 'It's bad news sir. We're outnumbered. There must be almost a hundred of them out there. They've burnt all the cars, now they're on their way to the manor house.'

'Have you called the back-up squads?' asked Christie.

'Of course, sir. They're on their way now . . .'

'And what about the Met? Any sign of them?'

'No, sir.'

'Well, get on the radio and find out where they are. Now, what we've got to do is to keep these people calm. Peters, you and Gupta take four men and keep everyone in the main hall. Harker, you come with me.' As soon as he was alone with the young recruit, Christie lowered his voice. 'Now listen, Frank,' he said, 'who the hell is out there?'

'It *is* Crusaders, sir.'

Christie put both hands up to his face and covered it in exasperation. Rubbing his skin, he lowered his hands, revealing anger mingled with terror. 'We're going to need all the help we can get, then. Go into this room, on your own, and call up the station on the mayday frequency. Tell them to get every squad over here that they can. I'll help the others out here.'

Harker disappeared into the side room, a makeshift store cupboard, and from there, amidst a collection of half-broken marble statues and torn paintings of Hindu gods and goddesses, he sent out his distress call.

At the front of the hall, Anjali had rushed out from the side of the stage and was talking rapidly to Max and Imogen. It was clear they must get out. Max knew that staying here was not the best option. If they could leave by the back, over the fields, they might get away from the chaos.

'I'll tell my dancers to get ready,' said Anjali.

'Hurry!' ordered Max. 'We're sitting ducks here.' Anjali rushed off and began to explain the plan to her girls. Max looked at Imogen. It was the first time he had seen real terror on her face and, for a passing moment, the vision recalled to his mind one of the images he had seen in his dreams.

'Just do as I say, and we'll be all right,' he said. Then, bending down to Miranda and Emily, Max pulled them towards him, kissed them both, and explained to them what they were planning to do. 'Whatever happens, stay together,' he said, 'don't run off on your own, okay?' Outside the hall, a window smashed, and the glass fell on a group of screaming pilgrims. Max looked back to the girls. They both nodded, their eyes wide with fear. 'Right,' said Max looking up at Imogen, 'let's find Anjali and get out of here.'

Groups of celebrants had already had the same idea, and were pouring out of the back of the manor house, running across the dark fields towards the distant main road. As he looked out from the back, Max could see flashing blue lights in the distance, and for a moment he wondered if it might be better to stay put and just wait for the emergency services to arrive. Another window smashed and he heard an aggressive chanting out at the front of the house. They had no choice. As soon as Anjali had come back with her group, Max smashed open a door and directed the girls through. Finally he too left, casting one final glance back at the mayhem in the hall.

Outside, all seemed quiet. There was a full-scale attack going on at the front, and he could hear the deep, ominous crackling of a fire beginning to take hold, but the back seemed untouched. The door Max had smashed led out onto the tarmac of a small car park. Beyond that, a few sheds, then the fields and the road, lit up with its distinctive orange streetlamps. There was a stream of families pouring out into the field already and Max was worried that the thugs round the front might soon realize that people were escaping, and transfer their efforts to the back.

'Quickly!' he whispered, 'And keep together!' The girls began to run across the tarmac, the dancers' silk costumes flying up behind them in the chill night air. Suddenly, as they were half-way across the car park, the tarmac was lit up as a convoy of police cars and vans screeched round the side of the manor house, circled the car park and skidded to a halt, their sirens wailing, blue lights flashing. Police officers clad in riot gear poured out of the vans, to be met by Christie, running out of a side door, directing as he came.

His squads despatched, the Chief noticed the strange party of fugitives caught in the lights of his vehicles, wondering what to do. He ran over and grabbed Max by the shoulders. Shouting above the din, Christie said: 'Get the girls into one of the vans! Stay in the back, and keep your heads down. Collins will get you out.'

Anjali and Imogen heard the Chief's command and sprang instantly towards the open door of the white police van. It still had a lot of gear in it and there wasn't enough room for all of them. Try as he might, Max could not fit in.

'Take the car!' screamed Christie. 'Cogan! Get these people out of here!' Max slammed the door of the police van shut, then made towards Cogan and the waiting police car. As he got in he looked over to the van, pleased that the girls were safe. Just then, he noticed a slim figure running away from it, towards the car. The van sped off. Max opened his door and, as the courtesy light came on, he saw Imogen, out of breath. 'I'm coming with you,' she said.

'Get in!' shouted Max. As Imogen jumped into the back, her door still open, the car sped away, sirens shrieking, lights flashing. The door slammed shut as they went round a corner, cutting out the outside noise.

The front of the manor house looked like a war zone. The roof was on fire, and the squad of riot police was bravely defending all the entrances to the temple. The mob attacking the shrine looked barbaric, working with military precision in their black uniforms. Each assailant carried handfuls of bottles filled with petrol and trailing long white rags as fuses, some already aflame.

Cogan was a proficient driver. 'Get down, and stay down!' he screamed to his passengers. Putting his foot hard on the accelerator, he sped through the crowd, using the momentum of the car as a ram. Bodies thumped on the metalwork and, looking up, Max could see the unreal characters in black, jumping or being pushed violently aside by the car.

'Out of the way, you bastards!' roared Cogan, careering his car around. Max raised his head to see if they were clear yet. 'Get down!' shouted Cogan as the car jumped and bumped over uneven ground. Seconds later, the vehicle was running smoothly, and Cogan seemed to have calmed down. Max looked up. They were out of the village and on some narrow lane, bounded by hedgerows. He sat back properly on his seat, and looked back to Imogen. 'It's okay, darling,' he said, 'we're out.'

She straightened up, and searched the dark lane in front for any sign of the police van.

'Did you see the van get away all right?' she asked.

'I'll check on the radio,' said Cogan, turning up the control at the centre of the dashboard. 'Hello alpha niner, come in alpha niner. This is omega. Please report status. Over.'

The radio crackled with static, then suddenly a voice came over clearly. 'This is alpha niner. Receiving you clearly omega. We're okay. How about you? Over.'

Max turned to Imogen, and smiled.

'Omega to alpha niner. All well here. What a night, Bob. Remind me not to get all dressed up for these parties in future. So, this is what those Hindus mean by a festival of lights . . . !'

Imogen felt her tense limbs relax as she heard the electronic voice of reassurance. The car slowed now to a reasonable speed, the carnage left far behind.

'Are the girls safe?' asked Cogan over the radio.

'All safe and sound,' came the reply, 'I'm going to call in at the station, Tony, then I think I might volunteer to drive the dancers home.'

'We'll meet up there, then,' replied Cogan, 'over and out.' As Cogan slotted the radio back onto its cradle on the dashboard, he settled into his seat and let out a deep sigh of relief. For a few more minutes the car cruised smoothly along the quiet country lane.

'What's that up ahead?' asked Max, squinting as he peered into the distant darkness. He thought he had seen a tiny flame flicker in the road. There it was again. Cogan flicked a switch and beamed his headlights. Instantly, out of the night, the lights picked out a distant band of young men dressed in black, blocking the road a hundred metres ahead. As the car sped along, its headlights fluctuated up and down in time with the suspension of the vehicle. Every now and then there shone in the hands of the waiting gang, picked out by the headlights, glass bottles filled with petrol, long white rags hanging from their necks. One of the fuses had been lit already and the flame was having difficulty catching in the night breeze. Max heard the engine rev up, as Cogan pushed his foot down once more. He seemed determined to crash through the human barrier. The needle on the rev counter in the car spun round, then eased back slightly, then spun round again, as the car moved up automatically through the gears. The gang of youths appeared to rush towards the car at eighty miles an hour.

'Keep your heads down!' said Cogan, and both Max and Imogen bent down once more. Any moment, they expected a dull thud as the car thrust its way through the line. Suddenly, there was the sound of glass crashing on metal, followed by a whoosh of fire.

'Jesus!' screamed Cogan, slamming on the brakes. The car swung round, pushing Max and Imogen against the side doors with its momentum. The screech and the sideways movement almost made

Imogen pass out. They felt the trailing side of the car lift off the road and, for a moment, Max expected the car to go into a tumble. He put his hands firmly over his head. The police car came to a halt. Max looked up to find himself staring straight into a wall of flames, rising up over the bonnet of the car like some sort of fantastic magical screen. He looked out of the rear of the car. They had done a complete spin round and the gang of Crusaders was now behind them, walking as one body, slowly and deliberately towards the vehicle.

'Stay down, Imogen!' said Max, desperately.

Cogan rammed the gear lever straight up into drive and pushed his foot down, hoping to speed off and use the wind to fan down the flames. But just as the car moved, the flames fell back onto the windscreen, blocking all visibility. Instantly, Cogan wound down the side window and tried to crane his neck to see ahead, around the edge of the flames. The heat was too much. For a few seconds the car continued its forward motion, then slowed. 'Damn!'

'What's the matter?' asked Max.

'We're boxed in,' replied Cogan, 'there's a bloody Espace up ahead, blocking the road.'

Max twisted his neck back to see the slow, certain advance of the youths coming up the lane. He heard more crashing glass as another petrol bomb landed a few feet from the car, spreading its fire like a vapour across the ground. Cogan had picked up the radio and was desperately trying to raise help. 'This is omega, omega, omega. Mayday, mayday, mayday. I'm trapped. Have civilians in my charge. Omega, omega, omega, mayday, mayday, mayday.'

Max looked out of the window at the hedgerows on the side. There was no possibility of making a run for it.

'Okay,' said Cogan, calmly, 'if that's the way it's going to be . . .'

Max looked over to him, in time to see him pull the gear stick into reverse. Cogan twisted his body so that he was three-quarters turned towards the rear and, looking out of the back window, he reversed the car at full speed towards the approaching gang. Max heard a deep scream and a thud as the car burst through the ranks, sweeping aside the thugs in the middle. Momentarily, the straight path of the car was diverted by the impact but Cogan kept control and continued to speed off in reverse. One of the side windows shattered as a bottle smashed into it, throwing fluid flames all across the side and roof of the car. Max looked forward, over the bonnet. The backward speed of the vehicle was fanning down the flames at the front and he could make out a disgruntled band of thugs, fast disappearing into the distance, some staring at the receding vehicle, others bent over their injured companions. On their far side, the fire of the second petrol bomb continued to burn, giving the black Crusaders a hellish backdrop. Cogan let out a nervous laugh. 'You bastards!' he screamed, 'You bastards!'

*

It was the first shooting party that Craig Hoskins had been invited to attend. Everyone in his squad knew he wasn't quite ready for it yet, but the assault on Hatchmere Heath was the biggest operation to date and the Brigadier had given clearance for all recruits who had been on the fortnight's induction course to participate. So the previous weekend Craig had gone down to the Crusade camp outside Guildford, for a dry run on the assault. By Sunday night, all the recruits had a clear idea of what was expected of them and just how they fitted into the operation. Craig was given the job of driving one of the Espace vans which would take the Crusaders to and from the target. This suited him down to the ground, though his mum was a bit disappointed that he wasn't one of the front-line troops. Apparently, Cath's son down the road had been chosen to be second-in-command of one of the lead units, and Craig's mum was a bit put out when she had to admit that *her* boy was just going to be driving. Still, as she told her friends down the Sundial, we all have to start somewhere. Anyway, it would give Craig a chance to use that black balaclava she had knitted for him.

Craig had been waiting patiently in the van for over half an hour. He had dropped off his unit at the waste ground outside the village, then picked up the Outfielders and brought them here, to Bollo Lane, one of the main avenues out of the village. They weren't expecting anyone here, but their job was to make sure that if anyone *did* come down the lane, either to or from the manor house, they didn't go any further.

So, having brought his unit here, Craig had dropped them off and parked out of sight in a cramped layby, designed to let vehicles pass each other along the single-track road. For Craig it had been a quiet expedition. Quiet, but a bit uncomfortable.

The stink of the petrol was beginning to make his eyes sting. The boys had spilt quite a lot in the back when they filled up their bottles, and the vapours were hanging heavily in the warm air inside the vehicle. Craig looked out over the dark, empty common opposite, rubbing his neck vigorously with his hand. He still hadn't got used to the uniform yet, and the black polo-neck he had been given was made of really rough wool. Despite washing it again and again all the past week, it still itched like mad. It had been irritating Craig all night, making him more and more angry and impatient. Still, they'd soon be on their way home, he thought. Then a few drinks down the pub – Harry would open up for them – and back to bed.

Craig wound down his driver's window to let some of the petrol fumes out. It was then that he knew something was up. In the distance, he could just hear the skid and screech of a car, followed by the glassy explosion of a petrol bomb. Try as he might, he couldn't see anything from where he was and he had to resist the temptation to get out of the van to have a look. That was a punishable offence for a driver on a shooting party, leaving his vehicle. So Craig had to rely on the distant sounds, like listening to an action drama on radio. He heard the car revving up, the Crusaders shouting, and the rapid screeching and skidding of the desperate, trapped vehicle. The last thing he caught was the high-pitched speeding of the car, as if it were travelling at top speed in first gear, followed by the scream of one of the boys, then the car continue its speeding, the noise getting closer and closer.

Craig's mind was racing. What was he to do? He decided to take a look, but without leaving the van. As the vehicle noise grew louder and louder, Craig turned on his own engine, pushed the gear stick into first, and pulled out into the narrow lane. The Espace lurched diagonally across the track.

The Brigadier would think Craig Hoskins had timed his operation perfectly.

Cogan was still shouting, letting out all his anger in triumph and relief, when he saw the black Espace pull out of the layby. He swerved immediately but it was too late. The police car smashed into the van at top speed. Its rear crumpled like an aluminium tin can which, emptied of its contents, becomes a trophy for an aggressive youth to show off his strength.

Imogen, still crouching in the back, was the nearest to the impact. She felt the explosion of metal and glass pass right through her, followed by a profound stillness and silence.

She straightened up, tentatively at first, sensing with relief that her body seemed still to be in one piece. Imogen looked out of the back of the car, through the jagged hole left by the shattered glass of the rear windscreen. For a brief moment, she saw the silhouette of a man still sitting at the wheel of the van they had rammed. Almost instantaneously, a ball of fire grew, silently, behind the shadowy figure, rising up from the darkness of the Espace. It devoured him like a monster engulfing its prey. Then suddenly the fireball burst forth as the van exploded, throwing glass, metal and flames in all directions, lighting up the night sky with white heat.

Max dreamt that he was in his own bed at home, dreaming. Imogen was by his side: he could feel the warmth of her body. In his dream within a dream, Max saw once more the Indian boy, twisting and turning in agony as the flames grew up around his sodden legs, rising relentlessly until they covered his whole wretched body. Still the boy kept turning, waving his arms about, his legs running here and there within the circle of spectators, like some sort of hideous animated firework. Max looked closer at the young man's face. The skin across the nose and mouth had begun to burn and melt, exposing bright white patches of skull. But the eyes still had life in them and they were looking directly at Max, reproachfully, as if to say: 'So, my friend, you too share in the guilt.'

Max forced himself to wake up. He had often dreamt of the Indian boy sacrificing himself and always the dreams ended with the same reproach. He looked at the thin crevice in the curtains opposite the bed. It was already sunny outside and the sparrows had begun to twitter, demanding the breakfast Imogen always put out for them last thing at night. She must have forgotten, hence the impatient racket. Max looked over to where she slept, so peacefully, so innocently. She had turned her back to him in the night, and was now curled up in an embryonic position. Max edged over to her to give her a gentle morning kiss. He pulled her hair softly to one side and instantly jumped back in horror.

The body next to him was that of the Indian boy, motionless and dead, his face stripped of its skin, his skull charred and pitted with holes.

Max felt the blood rush to his head and the throbbing pounded within his brain. He thought he was going to burst, so violent was the thumping. Suddenly he opened his eyes and the light seared through him.

Max could hear the soft electronic buzz of the cardiogram, its ever-vigilant tone keeping time to the rhythm of his heart. He tried to move his head but, despite his wrenching effort, found that he was frozen. A few feet directly above him, Max could see an intricate network of tubes and wires, criss-crossing in a sort of knitted canopy, each one carrying some vital fluid into or out of his body. He closed his eyes again, felt them water, then opened them. He half expected to find himself safely tucked up in bed at home, but the fluorescent tubes were still there, shielded behind a case made of hundreds of tiny prisms. He felt someone press the palm of his right hand. Mustering all his energy, Max managed to turn his head a few inches. Pain shot through his left cheek. His father was sitting patiently by the side of the bed. 'Thank God, Max,' he whispered, 'thank God.'

He could see that his father was crying, but clearly excited. 'Can you hear me, son? Can you hear me, Max?'

Max gave a hint of a smile. As the skin on his face moved, stretching across his lips, Max felt again a sharp stab pass across his cheek, from his ear to the corner of his mouth. The whole of that side of his face felt wet and sticky.

'Don't say anything, Max. Just relax. Thank God you've woken up. It's been ten days. I thought . . . I thought you were gone.'

Max closed his eyes once more, listening to the regular beat of the cardiogram. He could imagine the green wave patterns forming across the circular screen, a tiny bright ball rising and falling in tune with his heart.

A sudden panic gripped Max and he felt the adrenalin surge through him. The beat of the machine quickened momentarily. His eyes still closed, Max whispered: 'Imogen?'

Intersection

The trip to India was an agony for Max.

Each step of the way was so full of memories, so full of lingering associations. The moment he left home, Max was overwhelmed by a jumble of recollections and emotions that detached him from the present and its practicalities. He thought back to the childlike excitement on Imogen's face as they would lock the front door before leaving on their trips. Max, neurotic as always, had a peculiar ritual he would insist on enacting before he left the house. All the doors and windows had to be double-locked and Imogen had to confirm that they were secured. Later, on the plane, or even weeks into the vacation, Max would occasionally turn to her and ask: 'Did I lock the front door properly?' and patiently she would reply, 'Yes, darling, I saw you do it.'

How he missed her consoling presence, her patient understanding of his obsessions.

Max watched the slim young woman, elegant in her pastel suit, walk briskly from the check-in desk over to the first-class lounge. She smiled as she caught his eye and, tidying up the neat wallet of papers she was carrying, she held them up to Max. 'Here you are Daddy, all checked in. I've got you a seat by the window.'

Miranda was terribly efficient. She had her mother's ability to charm anyone, persuade them to do anything she wanted. Max stared into her eyes and saw the Imogen who had taken him to India for the first time, all those years ago. Miranda was just finishing at Oxford herself, and was assured a brilliant First in Oriental Studies. Her command of the Indian languages was formidable, and the Foreign Office had already offered her a place on their graduate intake. Max was proud of her, and jealously afraid of the coming years that would take her away from him. Still, he knew one couldn't fight the march of time.

'All the luggage has gone through and they'll be calling you in any time.' Miranda could see that her father was miles away. 'Would you like some coffee before you go?' she asked. Max smiled and put away his tickets and passport. He wondered even at this stage whether he was doing the right thing in going back. For twelve years Max had shunned the idea of returning to India, the very thought of it being far too painful to contemplate. Year after year, he had made some excuse to himself why it was impossible or inconvenient to go. Yet, all the time, the guilt of not keeping his promise to Imogen would haunt him. Finally, battling against himself, Max had overcome his fear. He had given his word to Imogen. So now, over a decade after her death, Max was at last ready to tread again the path through the subcontinent that he and Imogen knew so well.

Linking her arm through his, Miranda guided Max through the first-class lounge and towards the empty sofa by the observation window. The tarmac outside was full of activity, planes of all colours and shapes moving about, lining up, taking off, like huge insects marshalled in a strict order.

Miranda sat down next to her father, followed closely by a smart attendant, dressed in an immaculately pressed blue suit, carrying a silver tray of elegant china cups and cafetière. Pressing down the plunger of the coffee-maker, Miranda looked at her father, staring at the planes outside the window. 'I think that's your one, over there,' she said.

Max turned towards her, a puzzled look on his face.

'Your plane,' explained Miranda. Max smiled and pressed his daughter's hand. She understood. 'Don't be too sad,' she said. 'I know Mummy wouldn't have wanted that.'

'I know,' replied Max. Then, looking back towards the departing planes, he said, 'It's not fair on her, or on you. Poor Miranda. I'm sorry, darling. Forgive me. I'll be okay.'

Miranda flashed her radiant smile towards Max. The vision cut through him, but he maintained his self-control for her sake.

'I've got you a going-away present,' announced Miranda.

'Oh no, Miranda. You shouldn't have . . .'

'Wait till you see it, Daddy. I wanted to make your first trip to India on your own special.' Opening the clasp on her handbag, Miranda pulled out a small leather box and handed it to her father.

Max took it cautiously. 'Shall I open it now?'

'Close your eyes,' demanded Miranda. Max obeyed. He felt his daughter's soft hands grab his wrist, manipulate the strap of his ten-year-old Piaget, and remove the watch.

'Keep them shut,' ordered Miranda. As he waited patiently, in the darkness, Max heard the attendant announce the boarding of the flight. A few seconds later, he felt Miranda's hands replace the watch, tighten up the strap once again and straighten the dial round his wrist. 'You can look now,' she said.

Max opened his eyes and looked at his wrist. There, instead of the watch he had grown used to over the past decade, he saw his grandmother's watch, the heirloom he had put away so long ago, its gold sparkling, its white dial freshly cleaned, and its ticking strong and persistent.

'Miranda. How on earth. . . ?'

'I took it to Schindler's. Remember, you used to tell me all about how you got it serviced there, and how old Mr Schindler had taken a real fancy to it? Well, I thought it was a shame to let it just lie around in a safe, so I decided to get it repaired.'

'And you actually found the old man himself?'

'Not quite,' replied Miranda, sipping her coffee. 'Jonas Schindler died some time ago.' She paused, seeing the expression of defeat cross her father's face. 'But his son's taken over now. And the business is thriving. Apparently, the fashion for antique watches has really revived the trade. And young Jonas Schindler has even had the shop done up in the original Victorian style. He told me the Americans love it!'

Max laughed. Like Imogen, Miranda had an infinite capacity for talking and chattering, as if silence were a fate to be avoided at all costs, a waste of precious time that could be filled with words. 'Look,' she continued, tapping her father's wrist, 'Schindler's even reset the decade counter. It's at the beginning again.'

A thought crossed Max's mind, a recollection of Jonas Schindler warning him not to take the antique watch out of England, particularly into hot climes. But it would break the spell for Miranda if Max were to bring up such a mundane practicality. He decided to take the risk.

The flight attendant came over to Max, and reminded him that the plane was ready for boarding.

'You should go,' said Miranda, finishing her coffee. 'Now, Daddy, you have a good time, won't you?'

'I will, darling. And you be careful. Look after yourself, and good luck with your revision.'

Miranda groaned, pulling a face. Then, leaning over, she kissed her father on both cheeks, first the right, then the left, feeling the long scar rub against her skin.

Sinking back into his deep, cushioned chair, feeling the pull of the jet engines as the plane took off, Max thought back to the promise he had made to Imogen during their honeymoon. He recalled that unreal day in Khajuraho, so long ago. How absurd the pact had seemed to him then, absurd the very notion of ever being separated from the woman he loved, absurd the prospect of ever travelling alone to the sights he and Imogen so cherished. At the time, Max had thought of the future as a logical, safe continuum from the present, in the same way the present had flowed on naturally from the past. Life had seemed so simple then, a journey from here to there, taking so much time, involving so much effort, pain and pleasure. Max had plotted his route, planned how to negotiate the obstacles. And for a time all had gone well. Too well. The debts had begun to mount up. Now he understood the import of his superstitions and fears.

When Fate intervenes, thought Max, it does so with a vengeance. It was the injustice of it that had most affected him. What had Imogen ever done to deserve such an unfortunate death? Where was the logic of it? For years Max had searched for an explanation, a justification. He felt that if he could find even some tenuous cause and effect to the absurd twist of destiny, he might be able to come to terms with it. He found it virtually impossible to function in a world that seemed so arbitrary, so capricious, so illogical. Had those centuries of great minds all been wrong, those philosophers of existence misguided, when they so eloquently overturned the medieval view of a universe turning on the wheel of Fortune? Had it all just been clever words, fine language, intricate arguments, signifying nothing?

There were times when, in his desperate search for an answer, Max would blame himself. Perhaps it all came back to him, perhaps he was being punished for his misdemeanours and sins. That he could think of nothing so heinous as to have warranted such retribution was immaterial. It was more consoling for him to believe that he had committed some terrible aberration than to concede that life was no more than a game of pure chance.

As before, Max made directly for Fatehpur Sikri once he arrived in India. He took solace in habit and ritual, and his itinerary was the same as it had been on the trips with Imogen. The city in the wilderness never failed to grip him, its seclusion and grandeur activating a profound sense of kinship with past generations. Here, on the edge of the Rajasthani plains, man was truly in combat with nature. The sun, the dry plains, the ever-watchful vultures, circling patiently, confident in the knowledge that time would deliver them their prey. To construct a city here, in defiance of the inimical environment, was surely the greatest act of faith, optimism and loyalty. And it was these very qualities, still evident in continuing adversity, which had always bound Imogen and Max to India and its people.

'Mister Max! Mister Max! Over here, sahib! I am here!'

Max looked up from the small wooden table he had been using to write his letter to Miranda. Through the inevitable crowd he could see a thin man, in his early thirties, rushing towards him. His olive skin was glistening in the heat, and his black hair looked as if it had been slicked back with a whole bottle of Vaseline: it was receding from his forehead, and the man's brow shone like a polished chestnut in the midday sun. Max straightened his panama hat and stood up, ready to greet his old friend.

'Raju,' said Max, grabbing him by the hands as he gasped to a halt by the table, 'my dear, dear Raju. You didn't forget . . .'

'Forget, sahib? Not Raju. I knew this was your time of coming, sahib. I have your letter with me even now.' Raju stopped suddenly, recalling the rest of the contents of the letter. 'Sahib,' he continued solemnly, 'we all very sorry to hear of madam's tragedy, very very sorry.'

Max acknowledged the condolences. 'It was a long time ago now, Raju. Life must go on.' Even Raju could hear the insincerity in Max's assurance. But he thought it best to fall in with Max's display of optimism and courage.

'Anyway, knowing you coming, I say to my wife and children, I must take time off business to look after Mister Max. He my most special client. I his special guide. I always his guide.' Max smiled, recalling something half-heard in a dream. Raju immediately bared his teeth in a startlingly broad grin.

'Is your family well, Raju?'

'Oh, very well, sahib. My son, he always get top marks in school. I am hoping he will go to college. And daughters, they growing up fast. They helping their mother and grandmother in business, in hotel. Raju very happy. Always very many foreigners at hotel, always wanting good guide for ancient city of Fatehpur Sikri.'

Something about the Indian's intonation of the phrase 'ancient city of Fatehpur Sikri' triggered off another distant recollection within Max. They had been almost the very first words Raju had spoken to him when, as a little boy, desperate to earn a few rupees and keen to please his English client, he had attached himself to Max.

'You've done very well for yourself, my friend,' said Max, 'very, very well.'

They walked side by side, more as close friends now than client and guide, Raju in his best short-sleeved sports shirt, Max wearing the new cream cotton suit Miranda had picked out for him at Aquascutum. Whilst he had been taking his mid-morning tea at the café, Max had been swamped by an army of tiny boys insisting on polishing his black brogues, despite the fact that they hardly had a speck on them as yet. In the end he had had to relent, so now everyone who passed Max on the walk to the ancient city gate had their eyes instantly drawn to the dazzling shine of his shoes. Approaching a café selling a kaleidoscope of Indian sweetmeats, Raju patted Max on the shoulder and, throwing a knowing glance towards the shop, dived in to buy a selection of burfis and halwa for his guest. Max continued to walk on, unable to stop outside the shop because of the sheer volume of visitors climbing the long, sinuous path to the city. A few hundred yards along, past the beggars and the entertainers with their dancing monkeys in colourful silk jackets and dusty performing bears, Max came to a tree set back slightly from the path. He took advantage of the shade and stopped, staring up towards the entrance to Fatehpur Sikri.

The city had not changed at all in the years Max and Imogen had been coming here. Even with the new tourist hotel, built a few miles out along the road to Agra, and even with the increased flow of indigenous travellers taking advantage of their new-found prosperity, the atmosphere of Fatehpur Sikri was unalloyed. Tourist pollution had touched it, but had not infected it. Other dark-skinned boys had taken Raju's place and were busy even now pestering huge, crimson-faced Americans who were trying desperately to ignore their tiny demonic tormentors. Max looked up towards the ornate towers and turrets, high above the city walls. He had often seen these pillars, and their empty chambers, haunting his dreams. The vultures used them as a resting-place, a vantage point from which to survey their empire. There was still no sign of Raju.

Max thought back to the first time he had come to the ghost city, the time he had first met Raju. It was as if they had grown up together, he and his guide, crossed the years each in his own way. Nearby, an old woman was beginning to fan a fire, ready to roast corncobs for the lunchtime rush. The smell of woodsmoke brought his early memories back with renewed vigour. Max saw the young man, just out of university, just married, invincible and immortal, setting off on his voyage of discovery within the walled city. Through the swirls of smoke, and the haze of the heat, he could still make out, as if it were substantial before him now, the slim European figure, a little Indian boy by his side, arguing half-heartedly about a fee for his service. The embarrassed young traveller, unused to Indian persistence, looked about him coyly, wondering what to do. Max knew what he was thinking. If only Imogen were here.

'Sorry, sahib, burfi was being made fresh.' Raju's arrival broke the spell. Max turned to his friend, beads of perspiration on his brow from waiting so long inside the sweet shop.

'Not to worry,' said Max, reassuringly. 'We have time.'

Max could easily have flown to Delhi, but he felt that that would not have been in the spirit of the pledge. Now that he was here, the last thing he wanted to do was to use his money to buy himself out of confrontation with real life. This, after all, was the panacea he so desperately needed for his mournful introspection.

The presence of the well-dressed Englishman, obviously wealthy, aboard an ordinary Indian bus left the other passengers manifestly perplexed. Why would anyone choose to travel this way? Their puzzlement had silenced the travellers so, instead of the usual conversations held at full volume, the bus was conspicuously silent. It was as if the locals were on their best behaviour in the presence of a VIP. Max tried to break the ice by talking affectionately to the little girl next to him but she just smiled shyly and buried her tiny face in her shoulder, hiding from the eccentric foreigner. Soon, as the morning drew on, the child fell asleep, and in her dreams tilted her head gently onto Max's arm, finding there a safe resting-place. Imogen used to travel so well in these sorts of circumstances. Max recalled how she too, unlike him, could sleep easily on long journeys and how he used to watch *her* as she slept, safe in the knowledge that he was there.

'Namaste, sahib. Samosas for you?'

Guru had been selling samosas at the rest-station for over thirty years. His mother had taught him how to make the thin, crispy pastry, and how to measure by eye the exact amount of potato and peas for each one. When she died, Guru asked his own young son to help out with the stall, and so, for the past five years, the oil-can had had a new, smaller occupant. The routine was fairly mindless and Guru would use the time to play mental games in order to keep his brain alive. He could now predict quite accurately, from the shape and colours of the luggage strapped to the top of the buses as they pulled in, the exact origins of the passengers: which province, which city, which town. Each had its own distinctive clues and from these Guru could ascertain how much custom a particular bus was likely to bring in and what price he should fix for his samosas. As people came and went, in their hundreds of thousands, year in, year out, Guru also became quite proficient at recognizing the more regular visitors. He had an uncanny ability to pick out people he had served before, faces that had passed his way. Some he came to know quite well, and he could even chart the outward signs of their particular family histories: families with new arrivals, families with recent departures, couples on honeymoon, couples whose marriages were happy, couples whose marriages were unhappy. As the years passed, Guru could quite accurately relate the stories of numerous travellers, to whom he himself was no more than a casual samosa-seller.

But it was different with the Englishman. Guru recalled the very first time he had served the handsome young man, and the lasting impression the foreigner had left upon him. And since then, every time the Englishman had come this way, Guru had been pleased to serve him and his exquisite English wife. Every few years or so, they would return, and although they were obviously rich, and getting richer every time, the intrepid travellers still stuck to this humble mode of transport. This impressed Guru, and he would often tell his children about the greatness of the English and their humility, exemplifying it with the story of the wealthy young couple who had been buying his samosas ever since he was a boy. His own English wasn't very good, but Guru had picked up enough to be able to converse with the tourists who passed through. The first time the Englishman had spoken to him more than just asking for samosas, Guru had been too shy to answer properly. He had stuttered and stumbled, making a mess of the samosas he had been frying. But as the years went on, and Guru became a man, he welcomed the conversation as a privilege, and would make a great effort to polish up his English for such exchanges. He particularly looked forward to the rare occasions that the charming memsahib talked to him. Her interest in his family and his business gave him a lift for months, made him feel that his service and his life were valuable.

Then, some time ago now, the English couple had stopped coming to the rest-station. Guru had assumed they had finally decided that bus travel was too inconvenient for them, and that train or plane was better. He was sorry not to see them again, and he missed their presence.

So it was with great surprise, mixed with an overpowering excitement, that Guru saw Max arrive at the refreshment stop once again. When the samosa-seller saw the Englishman get off the bus all alone, he had assumed that the memsahib must be inside, perhaps sleeping. Immediately, as was his old habit, Guru put four extra-large samosas into the frying pan, watching them begin to bubble as the pastry slowly turned brown. But the closer Max came to the stall, the more apparent it became to Guru that there was something terribly wrong. His walk, his demeanour, his bearing were transformed. The Englishman looked defeated. And he carried an unfamiliar wound on his cheek. When the traveller spoke, his voice was unrecognizable, its energy and optimism gone, as well as the hope that had so touched Guru since the first time he heard it. The awful truth became clear when the Englishman asked for just two samosas instead of the customary four. Guru was saddened and plucked up enough courage to ask after the memsahib: was she perhaps unable to come this time? When Max told him the truth, Guru felt a sharp sense of loss, as if a close relative had died. He looked at the Englishman, communicating his sorrow silently. The traveller spent a long time at the stall, longer than he used to when his wife was with him, standing silently. Yet even now, the Englishman would look around him searchingly, as if he expected his companion to reappear at any moment. Watching Max, Guru found himself expecting the memsahib too.

Now that he was on his own, Guru expected the Englishman would soon stop his visits to the humble samosa stall. Perhaps he would stop coming to India altogether. The Indian looked once more at Max. Not even he could guess at the force that drew the traveller to his country and, in particular, to his remote station.

'Is rest family all right?' asked Guru, helping Max to the chutneys and relish for the samosas.

'All well,' replied Max. 'How about your family, Guru?'

'Healthy and happy, sahib. All we ask.'

Max knew that it was useless trying to offer any money for the snacks. Guru had never accepted payment from him or Imogen. But it was possible to give the young boy something. Max took out a hundred-rupee note and handed it to the little child sitting on the oil-can. 'That's for you, and for your brothers and sisters, little rajah,' said Max.

Guru acknowledged the gesture and gave a little salute to the foreigner. The bus had started revving up, and the passengers were rushing back. 'See you soon, sahib,' said Guru, hopefully. He was always unsure of seeing people again, and had become used to a life full of transient friendships.

'In a few years, my friend,' replied Max. He wiped his greasy hands on the paper that the samosas had been wrapped in, and threw it into the cardboard box Guru used as a bin.

'You promise, sahib?' asked Guru, laughing.

'Yes,' replied Max thoughtfully, 'I promise.'

India had settled down a lot since Max and Imogen first came. It retained its heady atmosphere of anarchy just held in check, and there was still a lot of unrest and turmoil. But Max had come to recognize this as part of the nation that India was and would always be. The caste war lingered on, a chronic illness that never came to a head or showed any sign of disappearing. Perhaps the people liked the drama in their midst? It certainly brought vigour to their lives, gave them a sense of significance beyond their own private struggles.

Max looked about him at the fine features of the faces on the bus. Intelligence shone from their eyes, intelligence and energy. They were a restless people, the Indians, but potentially a great people, if their innate shrewdness had not been so perverted by years of poverty and hardship. Perhaps that would change. Over the past decades, a lot of people who had earlier emigrated to the West had returned, bringing back with them both the wealth and the values that they had accumulated in the years abroad. Slowly but surely, India was beginning to acquire a new method in its madness. And it still had its perennial power to draw the youth from affluent, developed countries. The trains and buses and planes were as full as ever of young white teenagers, endlessly seeking experience and enlightenment away from the cosy lives of their parents. Ironically, India had changed, but the youngsters still looked exactly the same as they had done two decades ago, still the same standard uniform, the same hungry look on their faces, the same avid desire to befriend the locals in ramshackle cafés and dhabbas. What happened to these immature explorers when they finally grew up? Most of them probably went back into the safe cocoons of lifestyles not dissimilar to the ones their parents led, the ones they now so vehemently shunned. But for some, it *was* different. Some did remain faithful to the country and to the experience. People like Charles, for instance.

'I never thought you'd spend your whole life here, in Varanasi, Charles,' said Max, sipping his milky coffee out of a glass at a small teahouse in the ancient city. 'Still, I suppose you've got half the country owing you a favour.'

Charles laughed. 'Well, it is strange how life works out.' He looked for a moment at Max, saw the look of disappointment cross his face and rushed on, realizing that he had touched a nerve. 'When the time came for me to go back, I just couldn't do it. And it wasn't just fear of change, fear of returning to the rat race. I would have been well set up. Dad wanted me to go into the family business and I'm sure it would have worked out. Even as we speak, my brother is probably lounging back in his garden somewhere in Surrey, watching his wife and children and dog grow older . . . No Max, it just wasn't for me.

'I don't know if I ever told you. I even got as far as the airport in New Delhi. I'd given away everything I had before heading back. The Indians so rarely get the chance to own foreign things, I decided to donate all my possessions to the servants who used to clean my lodgings. Anyway, so there I was, just my ticket and passport in hand, and the clothes I stood in. And you know, I honestly felt as if I was about to plunge back into a horrendous prison-house. It felt so good to be free. No possessions, no ties, no commitments. When they announced the flight, I decided to cut and run. So I made the decision there and then. And I've not looked back since.'

Max looked across at Charles's gaunt, refined features. His skin had become permanently burnt, and the Indian diet had taken its toll on the healthy young body Max recalled accompanying them on their first tour around Varanasi. But he was clearly happy, and content with his life, for which the physical degeneration seemed a small price to pay.

'So how did you get involved in the mission?' asked Max.

Charles sipped a new glass of scalding tea which had been put before him automatically. 'It was Prabhu's idea, actually. I was in a real mess, just drifting around, doing nothing in particular, no use to anyone. I'd made my decision at the airport, but I didn't know what I wanted, just what I didn't want, that is, what England had to offer. So, I went to Prabhu. He's running his own ashram now, you know. He's looking forward to seeing you again . . .'

Max recalled the handsome young priest wrapped in saffron robes, and his affection for Charles.

'Anyway, I spent weeks at the ashram, and Prabhu and I talked a lot about what I should do. I definitely wanted to stay in Varanasi. It was about this time that the Ramakrishna Society had teamed up with the Society of Saints Cosmos and Damian to open a centre for lepers here. Thousands of them come every year to the holy city, but no one wants to put them up or feed them or look after them. Usually they end up living on the streets, outcasts, begging for food. The intention was to change all that. And I happened to be in the right place at the right time. The benefactors asked me to run it. Yes, Max, the Jesuits have finally caught up with me.'

Max laughed. 'It's obviously been a success. I admire your courage.'

'*My* courage, Max?' said Charles incredulously. 'Don't admire my courage. Every day, I see people for whom every single movement is a struggle. Yet they go on, finding some way to be useful. That's courage. They come from all over India, the pilgrims. Even now, after all these years, I never cease to be amazed by people's capacity for hope and their resilience. Believe me, Max, the body might be crippled, but the spirit is intact. And that, for me, sums up what India is all about.'

Max understood only too well the significance of Charles' words for himself. He averted his gaze. There was a long pause as the two men finished off their drinks.

As in Max's recollections, the café was buzzing with activity, the pilgrims resting after their excursions into the narrow alleyways of the ancient city. Max noticed the same garish souvenirs he had seen years before, clutched so excitedly in the hands of eager devotees. The religious paraphernalia looked the same, so did its new owners, so did their children, and so did their desperation to acquire as much of it as possible before it all ran out. That it never actually did run out was immaterial. In India, everyone was brought up to be on the safe side, to get things while the going was good. Even if the objects of desire never disappeared, one's own ability to acquire them might, hence the frantic storing up of treasures.

Charles looked at Max as he surveyed the dhabba. His aloneness was almost a physical quality.

'How long is it now, Max?'

'Twelve years,' he replied, without hesitation, as if he had been expecting the question.

'Have you been able to come to terms with it?' continued Charles.

'Not really, no.' Max paused, smiling at a young boy who had strolled over to their table to show off his colourful moortis of Rama and Sita. 'You never really get over it. You just get used to it, and you learn how to carry on with it. It's always there.'

'You've changed a lot since you lost Imogen.'

Max turned back to face Charles, meeting his eyes momentarily. The smile on Max's lips was not reflected in his eyes. There was so much he wanted to say, so much he wanted to share. But who could he trust to understand? In the back of his mind, Max felt the stirrings of a memory, a faint recollection that there was someone he *could* rely upon, entrust with his most private sentiments. As the thought crystallized, Max realized with disappointment that the confidante was gone.

How he had relied upon Imogen to be his constant companion. All the time they were together, the world thought he was the point of stability amid the turbulence of their lives. For a long time, Max even believed it himself. But now that Imogen was gone, it was clear to him that he had needed her reliance upon him just as much as she had needed his strength. Without it, Max felt redundant. His life lacked all direction. Miranda was so self-sufficient, she never made him feel indispensable, the way Imogen had done. That was understandable. After all, she had had to get through most of her childhood and teenage years without her mother, and it was clear to Max that she had done her best not to be a burden on him. She was harder than her mother. Imogen's death had taught Miranda that nothing lasts and that, in the end, those we love are hostages to fortune. Perhaps it was for this reason that Miranda had made herself so self-reliant. If she needed Max more, he might not now feel so superfluous.

'Everything's changed since Imogen went, Charles, everything, not just me. I suppose I could relax a bit when she was around, you know, take comfort in the knowledge that I had an ally, someone to help in the struggle. Now, well, you're on your own really. Oh, it's good to have friends, of course, don't get me wrong. And I'm very lucky that Imogen left me with a lot of very dear friends, people who have been a great support. But it's like losing a part of yourself, suddenly gone, and your mind can't quite comprehend it. It can't accept that the companion you expected to spend all your life with is no longer there, and it also can't accept its new perception of you, as a single person once again. I still can't make a decision without thinking: I'll just ask Imogen first. And of course, I can't ask her. Every experience I have, every mood, every taste and sensation is now only half felt. A part of me is always comparing the experience to what it might have been had Imogen been there as well.'

'But you must have got used to living without her quite a bit when she was so busy in her job,' interjected Charles.

How difficult it was to explain the difference. Max paused, gazing at the stream of passing pilgrims, rushing into the labyrinth of streets and temples. 'Physical absence is very different from death,' he said, keeping his eyes fixed on the milling crowds. 'Even when she was away, there was always the possibility of sharing the memory with her, a few days, at worst a few weeks, later. And that prospect of sharing radically alters your own perception of an event or a person. So often, I would go to a function or meet a new person in Imogen's absence, and become aware during the occasion of already turning it into a narrative for her. People would talk to me at parties and I only half heard what they were saying. Their mannerisms and their way of telling the story would fascinate me more, for it was so much more important to the narrative I would relate to Imogen. I would seek out the details that I knew would interest or amuse her, search for the idiosyncrasies that Imogen would notice and register. And the experience I had had alone would not be completed until I had shared it with her, got her perspective on it.'

'Did it ever worry you, this extraordinary bond?' asked Charles. 'Did you never think: "whatever happened to my individuality?" '

'Individuality?' Max could barely contain his contempt for the word. 'What's so great about individuality? The world is full of people pursuing individuality. It's unity that is important, it's the bond that is so vital. Otherwise, what are we all doing here? What is all this about?' Max looked about him at the families in the teahouse, and the pilgrims rushing past. 'The thing that holds all these people together is their belief that united, we can meet life and fate on more equal terms than we could do alone. You must know that, Charles, from your work at the leper mission. They need you, you need them. All along, we search out companions who will agree to share that struggle with us, consent to work out a joint strategy.'

Max trailed off. It seemed futile to go on. Words were inadequate to express the need for solidarity in the face of an inimical and absurd universe. Charles was fiddling with his glass, and Max realized that the nakedness of his emotion must be embarrassing him. And you are unmarried, thought Max. How presumptuous of me to think you could understand. He wished he had kept quiet. After all, Imogen had been friends with Charles before she had ever met Max. They had shared secrets, had laughed together. It was not only Max who suffered in her absence.

Charles gestured to the waiter and brought his shifting, uncertain gaze to rest on Max's damaged face. 'It's good that you've come back to India, Max,' he said. 'India will heal the wounds.'

That evening, Max went to the Vishwanath temple alone. He knew now how to talk his way in, and he was obviously so personable, so official-looking that few temple attendants would have had the nerve to challenge him. As usual, Max's shoes had been polished at least half a dozen times that day by persistent boot-boys. The brogues were spotless, and their shine caught the orange lights of the candles as Max handed them over to Pundit Sharma. Max remembered the old man from his previous visits to the temple, and the old man certainly remembered him. Pundit Sharma had become quite an expert on footwear in the many decades he had been attending shoes at the temple. He could tell a lot about the visitors from the way they were shod, and there was something very special about the Englishman, something that had stuck in the pundit's memory over the years. In fact, he could still recall the very first time that the young traveller had come to the Vishwanath temple, so innocent and awkward, just on the edge of adulthood. Since then, the old man had noticed the Englishman and his wife return every few years to the temple, and each time Pundit Sharma was pleased to see them together.

People often complained about the Westerners' lax morality, but this couple were a perfect example of a true Hindu union, and the pundit felt sure they were attracted to the ancient shrine because of a deep spiritual affinity. He was convinced that Max and Imogen had been Hindus in a past incarnation and were drawn inexorably to the site of their earlier union.

In all the years he had seen them, the pundit had spoken barely a handful of words to the English couple. But this time, his joy at meeting Max again after so long overcame his reticence. For years, the pundit had thought something terrible had happened to his friends. He would often think of the couple as he saw other foreigners visiting the temple, and in his imagination, grim disasters took shape in order to explain their sudden absence and breaking of the routine. So now, when he saw Max emerge from the dark crowd massing around the heavy doors of the entrance, he stopped his ritual handing out and taking in of shoes and stared at the vision from the past. In the half-light Pundit Sharma could not see the ravages that time had wrought upon the Englishman's face, but it soon became apparent that the visitor was alone. Taking his shoes, the pundit grappled with the dilemma of speaking with the foreigner. At last, just as Max was turning away, he found his voice.

'Much time not here, sahib,' he said, over the hustle and bustle of the shoe table. Even the few seconds of interruption in the pundit's slick routine was beginning to cause a bottleneck further back. Max was surprised to be addressed by the Indian, whom he had come to regard as a perennially silent operator.

'Yes,' replied Max, twisting back, unable to turn round fully, 'it has been a long time, too long.'

'Memsahib?' asked the old man, fearful of the reply.

Max had been dreading the inquiry. He could get out of it easily by lying. That might be kinder. 'Memsahib, I am afraid, is no longer with us. She passed away twelve years ago, in an accident.'

Pundit Sharma continued to smile, not fully understanding Max's English. Then, slowly, the import of the words sank in and a sorrowful look spread across the old man's face. Still holding Max's shining brogues in his hands, the pundit bent his head down, and silently, in a solemn gesture of despair, touched his brow with the shoes. Max felt the Indian's agony, and his heart cried out to the man who had been till then a stranger. When the shoe attendant looked back up, raising his head slowly, Max noticed a sparkle of candle-flames in his eyes.

'Sorry, sahib,' said the old man, his voice heavy and halting, 'very sorry.'

All that was familiar in the temple struck a long-forgotten chord in Max, like a ceremonial bell tolling intermittently, mocking his impotence in the face of the passing years. At each praying-station, Max paused and stared challengingly at the ornate sculptures, the moortis all dressed up in their festive costumes. He was reminded inevitably of the last time he had seen such decorations, and the flames that burned in front of the tiny gods and goddesses recalled to his mind other more terrible and unholy fires. He stared at the seated figure of Lord Shiva, his eyes half closed in the characteristic narcotic dream, a three-pronged trishul in his hand, a cobra wrapped around his neck. After losing Imogen, Max had drifted towards at first religious indifference, then apathy, and finally an angry, aggressive atheism. He had never really been a strong believer, but he had had a faith, of sorts. Now, that was gone, and he resented the suggestion that there was a great, universally powerful and benevolent God, who occasionally made mistakes, but who ultimately made things come out all right.

Things had not come out all right for Max. And he had, for a time, inclined seriously towards the belief that if there were indeed a universal presence, then it might be a force for evil, not good.

He continued to look long and hard at the dreaming eyes of the Shiva. Perhaps it was this very inconsistency in the universal pattern that Hindus had tried to symbolize in their notion of a creator and a destroyer. Further along, in the same temple chamber, Max saw Lord Shiva dancing joyfully within a circle of fire. The Nataraja had always been his favourite symbol of Hindu mysticism, with its juxtaposition of the energetic dance and the lashing flames, the perfect symmetry of the circle of existence, and the slim, lithe figure of the god at the centre, within the fire, but untouched by it. Hypnotized by the sculpture, Max saw it begin to lose focus as his eyes became fixed, and his thoughts started to crystallize. The same love that had so energized Max now tormented him, like an intolerable shirt of flame. The more he gazed at the dancing figure, the more the god stared back at him, mockingly. Love. How unfamiliar the name sounded to him now.

Dawn over the riverside ghats at Varanasi. Time held no sway over the perennial rhythms that had been enacted here for thousands of years. Walking down the slippery steps towards the waiting boat, Max looked out over the fast-flowing brown waters, the surface almost completely concealed by a field of thin, sunburnt bodies, each one ducking into the river and emerging a few seconds later, eyes tightly closed, rubbing the water vigorously from their faces. The sight of the ritual bathing refreshed Max.

The whole journey to India was a pilgrimage, an expiation for him. By travelling the routes that he and Imogen had shared together, Max was able, momentarily at least, to restore some of his faith in the stability of the universe. As Anjali used to say to Max, time was not an enemy here, more an ally. There wasn't the constant sense of people desperately trying to outrun time. The days seemed longer: sunrise to sunset was a substantial period, and one felt as if the hours were under control. And then, India changed very little over the years, unlike the frantic West, which seemed to pride itself on reform. Buildings remained untouched, just as firm or as ramshackle as they had been decades earlier. People stayed put, often seeing out their lives in the villages where they had been born; foods tasted the same; even the days maintained a recognizable, familiar pattern, opening and closing in the way they had done for centuries, impervious to the superficial scratchings of civilization.

India was a safe place. It gave you time to think, time to take stock, time to catch your breath. And Max recalled how each time he and Imogen had returned to India, their relationship had been restored to its pristine freshness.When he thought of her in India, she was always his new bride, eager and willing, untouched by life. Under the constant Indian sky, they made love with the passion of their first encounter and, each morning, Max awoke to the ecstatic lifting of the spirit he had felt when he had first looked at her peaceful sleeping face on the pillow next to his own.

The ferryman who offered to take Max across the river seemed centuries old. His body was little more than a conglomeration of sinewy limbs, and his head was barely covered by a stubble of grey hair. Standing precariously on his rocking boat, he wiped his hands on a small towel hanging from his waist, and held out his delicate, bony fingers to the Englishman. Max was reluctant to get into the rickety boat, but the ferryman's encouragement, and his amusement when he saw Max's reticence, were too strong to resist and Max stepped in. The timbers creaked and sagged beneath the weight of a healthy English body. The ferryman, pleased with his catch, pushed off from the teeming shore. As the boat rocked violently on the uneven waters, Max looked back at the receding temples and the human figures peppered over the shifting waters. He then turned and gazed out towards the shore they were approaching, slowly, wave by wave.

The two banks were totally disparate in appearance and in atmosphere. The shore he had left, so full of life and energy, with people welcoming the arrival of a new day, playing and laughing, praising the universe for its eternal gifts; the shore he approached, so secluded and quiet, reserved mostly for the funeral pyres, many still smouldering, wisps of dark smoke from the previous day's holocausts rising into the dawn air. Here and there Max saw a few isolated individuals, reluctant to accept the departure of loved ones.

Max stared back at the wake the boat was leaving behind. He had heard much about the therapeutic powers of the Ganges. If the river really could heal, then why couldn't it heal his broken spirit? Max looked up at the sky, its morning red turning fast to a warm yellow. Where did he belong now, he wondered, on which of the two shores? With the living, or with the dead?

Max descended from the boat at the makeshift pier he remembered from the time he had first come here. Somehow, it had managed to hang on doggedly, refusing to tumble over. It creaked unpromisingly as Max stepped onto the rotting timbers, pulling himself along by the rope guides on either side. Jumping off onto the dusty ground, he felt the pier sway behind him. Max turned in time to see the ferryman push off from the station, and begin his return journey, back to the distant, bustling shore.

The customary coachloads of tourists had not yet arrived at Sarnath by the time Max got there. The sun was high in the sky, and was beginning to beat down upon him ferociously. Max pulled his panama forward to give his face more cover, and as he did so he caught sight of his own shadow, slim and elongated, on the dusty path ahead. The dark shape betrayed no age. It looked just as it had done all those years ago, when he first saw it cast by the same sun on the same ground. As he stared at it, Max thought about the complex process of ageing that he had undergone. What did it really mean, after all? He still felt the same as he had done all those decades ago, still was susceptible to the same fears and the same aspirations. All that had changed was his ability to process those sentiments, sift out the irrational fears and hopes from the real ones. More than that, it was all a question of disguise. He behaved as an older person might be expected to behave: gave his thoughts and feelings more consideration, talked in a more mature fashion, learned to keep his own counsel. All the things, in fact, that society expected an adult to do. Yet, in reality, deep within himself, Max could still detect the spirit of youth and ebullience, now subdued by the chastisement he felt life had inflicted upon him. The narrow pathway twisted and turned, and Max's shadow disappeared, first to the side, then behind him.

The avenue leading to the Buddha mound had recently been tidied up and developed into a beauty spot. The undergrowth Max remembered, and which had left him with so many painful lacerations, was gone, replaced by expertly tended roses and carnations, their orange and red colours so striking in the sun. It was still possible to walk along the central pathway between the two embankments, and the promenade now provided an excellent view of the Sarnath temple at its end, framed artistically by the twin lines of juvenile palm trees. Beneath one of the palms, about half way down the avenue, Max noticed a familiar figure. A sadhu, clad in bright saffron, his hair tied up in a tight knot on his head, was deep in meditation, in the traditional lotus position. As Max walked closer to the devotee, he began to see once more the grey ash patterns painted on the sanayassin's forehead, the sacred insignia marked out on each arm. The sight of the contemplative figure calmed Max's own turbulent spirit, and he decided to rest beneath the shade of a nearby tree, opposite the sadhu, and perhaps emulate in his own way the meditations of the holy man.

The grass was dry and dusty, and Max was unwilling to dirty his fresh suit. So he stood for a few moments beneath the branches of a young palm tree, looking out towards the figure on the opposite embankment. The free flow of the spirit was the secret of real meditation, the refusal to allow the mind to hang on to any single thought. One must rather let it wander at will, and find its own resting-place. Max began to breathe deeply, as if about to go to sleep, the rhythm serving to calm his frantic thoughts. Inevitably, freed of the need to take account of external reality, his mind began to tread again the familiar track.

He thought about Imogen, and the life they had anticipated together. Somehow, even after all these years, Max still couldn't believe all that had taken place. He couldn't accept that he had become caught up in something so . . . so unreal. Who could ever possibly have imagined that a dramatic death could visit one's own life in such a way? In his heightened state of consciousness, his recollections took on the threatening and numinous quality of a nightmare. Surely those things had not happened to him? Max must have read about them, must only have imagined that they had touched him. He must put them back where they belonged, where they were safe, within the phantasmagoria of a narrative. Max stared at the quiet sanayassin, jealous of his submissive faith. It was all true, of course. It *had* happened and it was up to Max to find a way of absorbing the devastating unreality. But when fantasy manifest itself so cruelly in one's own life, it was impossible to keep a grasp, a perspective that meant anything. The irrationality was disconcerting and shocking. How was it possible to plan anything, to look forward to anything, when life could be so full of arbitrary fates? It made a nonsense of it all. Max thought back to the dreams he and Imogen had shared together, never considering for one moment that the progress towards their realization might be so horribly interrupted.

Max glanced up briefly at the incandescent sun, then back to the unmoving figure of the sadhu. The cicadas and busy insects ceased their timeless whir for a moment, and it seemed to him that the very blades of grass were still. Max recalled the mysterious Englishman he had seen on the honeymoon to India. He knew now, of course, the trick that time had played upon him.

All along, Max had been mystified by the appearance of the stranger. His literary training had given him a taste for enigmas. But he had been accustomed to deciphering codes in language, not action. He should have remembered that messages – the most important messages – come in symbols. They demand an effort of interpretation. He had been a poor reader of his own life. He had failed to see in the melancholy figure of the Englishman the distorted reflection of his own future. Failed, or refused? Max thought back to his desperate efforts to break the stranger's silence. Why, indeed, should the Englishman ever have spoken to the young man? Instead of trying to resolve the mystery with his mind, Max should have listened instead to the message of his heart. The stirrings within him had been a recognition, an acknowledgement that it was up to him, the observer, the spectator on his own life, to unravel the artistry of the creation.

The work of art was complete, had always been complete. But like the reclining statue of Vishnu, Max had only seen it in fragments.

Thinking back, Max could see the young man, all those years past, fixed to the spot not far from here, seeing the meditative holy man, then noticing soon after the presence of the stranger. Try as he might, Max could not dispel from his mind the feeling that he had been used as a plaything, that he had been toyed with, that all through his life time had spoken to him in riddles and dreams, knowing full well that he would be unable to decode the mystery. If only he had not been so caught up in the hectic process of living, Max might have been able to take stock of life, perhaps even see through the clouds that had floated past him. It was here, at Sarnath, that the young man had first tried to break through the barriers: Max could see himself, his body youthful and lithe, his face so smooth and untouched, rushing across the thorny undergrowth, determined to catch the fleeting visitor before he disappeared.

Yes, my friend, thought Max, you were right to feel I had a message to give you. I too wanted to speak across the years, guide you through the labyrinth. If only I could have warned you, advised you to keep something of yourself back. But time had sealed my lips, and all I could do was watch silently, a onlooker to the images of my own life.

I was there when you were at the peaks of your happiness. I was there when your spirit was open. You had eyes to see. But your soul did not understand. Your soul was too young, too trusting. And those were the times when you were most vulnerable, the times when you forgot the fact of your mortality.

Max had been reluctant to make the journey to Khajuraho, knowing as he did that it would be the most painful part of the trip. He had been trying to find a way of avoiding it, yet another part of him felt compelled to return to the remote town in the plains of Madhya Pradesh, with its ornate temples and clustering erotic sculptures. He knew there were ghosts there he must put to rest, and it would be an inadequate fulfilment of his promise not to revisit the place. But the prospect of going back was unbearable. Max couldn't predict what his reaction would be once there, and he was unwilling to put himself to the test.

So, instead, he made his way directly to Trivandrum, and to the balmy warmth of the deep, lush forests of Kerala.

The huge palm tree in the middle of the reception of the Maya Continental Hotel had been cut down five years earlier, and was now replaced by an elaborate fountain, all gold and marble, gushing cool water into a large round pool. Cutting through the waters, a variety of fish swam lazily, disgruntled by their imprisonment. Max asked after the tree, and was shown a photograph of it being demolished: apparently, its rampant foliage could no longer be contained within the building, and despite every effort on the part of the hoteliers to save the ancient palm, there had been no choice but to cut it down. And what an operation it had been. For weeks, an army of men worked day and night to lop off the enormous leaves, then finally, the tree having been reduced to its central trunk, a special saw had been flown in from Cochin in order to finish off the job. Bit by bit, the tree had been removed, until the ground where it had stood was bare. A powerful acid had been poured into the soil to stop further growth, a concrete foundation laid, then covered with the marble base of the pool.

'It was exciting few weeks, sir,' said the young assistant manager. The previous incumbent, whom Max remembered, had now been promoted to director of the hotel, and it was clear that one of his first directives to the younger recruits was that they must listen to the BBC. For Max could still detect the strains of the World Service in the language of his attendant. But now, without Imogen, the formal intonations no longer seemed funny.

'Most exciting few weeks in the history of our hotel. The tree was an ancient soul, sir, and was very reluctant to leave his home. After all, he had been here far longer than any of us. But he was beginning to destroy the building. He was beginning to take over. We could not contain him any more. So we had to chop him down.'

The young man could see Max's disappointment. He was not prepared for the Englishman's distress at seeing the photograph of the recumbent trunk, cut into various parts, like a huge Swiss roll.

'But the tree has not completely been taken from his home, sir. You see, the wood of these trees is very precious, and we asked some local carvers to make up furniture for the hotel from the body of our old friend. Look around you: chairs and tables, and some of the beds in the rooms, they are made from the wood of that ancient tree.'

Max took a look at the couch nearby, its back dark and richly-carved, chiselled out with the utmost care. The chairs in the lobby, the tables, a sofa, they were indeed all made from the same luxurious wood, polished up and shining, moulded into various intricate patterns. 'So the spirit lives on,' said Max, handing back the photograph.

'Oh yes, sir, most certainly. The spirit lives on.' The Indian made the characteristic circular motion with his head, signifying agreement and consolation at once.

As Max walked back across the lobby, following the porter's thin body struggling with his luggage, he paused for a moment to gaze into the pool. The fish moved indolently, exotic creatures, some trailing huge whiskers flowing back past their tails. The water gushing from the fountain was clear, tumbling down over a miniature mountain of marble. But the water in the pool was murky, and Max was intrigued to find out the source of the dirt. He saw tiny pieces of soil floating in the streams, gradually disintegrating with the force of the gush. He stared at the line of dirt, and traced it back towards a hairline crack in the bottom of the pool's marble floor. As he focused on the crevice, Max could see, through the distortions of the water, a frail green shoot rising up through the crack, letting in some of the soil of the ground beneath the pool. He smiled to himself. The spirit of the tree had not been extinguished. Within a few generations, its trunk would break through the artificial and garish imposition over it. In time, it would reassert its birthright.

Early next morning Max walked out into the cool of the dawn, in time to see the dark hues of the trees turn gradually lighter as the first rays of the sun broke through the omnipresent canopies of foliage. The bells of the Padmanabhaswamy temple were already sounding the morning celebrations, and Max was eager to witness the first prayers of the day, before the crowds gathered. Turning into the avenue that led to the temple, he saw the familiar flocks of large fruit bats, hanging upside down from the high branches of the taller palm trees and the carved terraces of the temple gopuram. Silhouetted against the crimson dawn, the creatures seemed archaic, a reminder of darkness, their prehistoric faces twitching and writhing as if in agony at the coming of day.

Max rushed on. He had put on a simple white shirt and, just before entering the temple, he unfolded the neatly pressed square of white cloth he carried with him, and wrapped the cotton around his waist and legs, tucking the top into the waistband of his trousers. It wasn't perfect, but it would do: it was as close to a dhoti as he could reasonably achieve without expert help.

The interior of the Padmanabhaswamy temple was cool and breezy. The flames still burned from the thousands of tiny oil-lamps and candles kept alight all night, and in the outer courtyards numerous temple attendants were washing the stone floors with buckets of clear, cool water. They stopped momentarily as they saw the Englishman walk in awkwardly, then bent down once more, diligent in their labours. Max wound his way around the labyrinth of corridors housing the hundreds of sculptures of gods and goddesses, until finally he turned the corner into the inner courtyard where the statue of Vishnu reclined. Max looked at his watch. He was still a little early for his rendezvous.

While he waited, Max decided to peer in through the three windows that gave onto the divine statue within the chamber. He walked over to the first window and looked in. The flowers of the previous day had been cleared away, and the statue was clear of all offerings. Once more, Max marvelled at the enormity of the feet, and the fine sculpting of the calf muscles. The marble, recently polished, shone with a renewed intensity, and Max had to close his eyes slightly to cope with the unexpected glare. He climbed down from the first window, and continued on to the second. From here, he could see the midriff of the god, again shining with the recent polish. The clean lines picking out the abdominal muscles had become a little worn with age and constant cleaning. Max tried, as he always did, to see down the length of the sculpture but his gaze reached only the waist at one end and the chest at the other. Finally, he moved on to the third and final window, and looked in at the head. The face was familiar, its expression so gentle and welcoming, so protective. Max regretted not having been back here for so long. As he gazed at the sculpture, he began to see the features of the head change and melt into more familiar ones. He saw Imogen before him, smiling, her lips curved in perfect contentment. The statue's features shifted, and he found himself gazing at the clear, regular lines of Anjali's face. Then it was as if fire sprang from the god's eyes, and Max saw Miranda shining brightly in all her unsullied youthfulness, glowing with his own early optimism. An image of perfection, the god spoke to each pilgrim in different echoes of the divine harmony.

Max heard someone say his name softly. At first, he thought he had imagined it, and continued to stare fixedly at the sculpture. But there it was again, the whispered name, carried along on the morning breeze. Max turned and saw a priest framed in the doorway leading to the inner court.

'Still trying to see more than your fair share?' asked the pundit, beginning to walk towards Max out of the shadows. Max stepped down from the window and let his eyes adjust back to the faint lights of the temple.

'I hope I haven't kept you waiting,' said Prabhu, holding up with his left hand the spare material of his priestly robes. Max rushed to his old friend, and they greeted each other affectionately after the too-long absence.

The prayers over, Prabhu and Max decided to stay within the temple, strolling along its winding corridors and courtyards.

'It's amazing how you've hardly aged at all,' said Max. 'The last time we met was over ten years ago, yet you seem, well, you seem just the same.'

'We lead a quiet life out at the ashram. Most of our time is spent in meditation and contemplation. We try to concentrate on God and on the positive aspects of our existence on earth. That's my secret, I suppose. It's the spirit that is young: the body just reflects the inner truth.'

Max wondered what his outward appearance gave away about the truth of his inner turmoil. They walked on in silence, passing the watchful ranks of gods and goddesses. Max looked down at Prabhu's bare feet as they walked over the shining stones of the temple floor. 'I wish I had your self-discipline,' said Max. 'I feel my life is just slipping away now. Ever since Imogen died, there doesn't seem to be any point anymore.'

He expected Prabhu to be shocked at his pessimism, chastise him for his defeatist attitude. Instead, Prabhu said, 'I know, Max. I know what Imogen meant to you.'

Max looked up at Prabhu and caught his eyes, so full of empathy and shared suffering. 'I don't know where I go from here, Prabhu.'

The priest considered his friend's sorrow and his predicament. There were many who came to the ashram, their hearts broken, their spirits bruised by life. 'Only you can decide which way to go now, Max. The question is: which way do you want to go? If life really has come to an end for you, if you see no further point in pursuing the existence you have, then perhaps you must make a decision of renunciation. Perhaps that is the most positive thing you can do, to make sense of the loss.'

Max felt attracted to the idea of a radical change, a total departure from the lifestyle in which he was so cruelly trapped, all alone. 'But that would be like running away, wouldn't it?' he asked, fearful of the answer.

'Yes,' replied Prabhu, 'it would. But there is nothing wrong in running away from a life or a situation that is destroying you. Escaping from that decay might be the most courageous thing to do. Look, at the moment you're just going through with life, serving your time. That's not what life is about. Not for anyone, especially not for a man like you, Max. Suppose the situation had been reversed and it was Imogen who had survived you? Is this what you would have wanted of her in your absence, this living death?'

Max stopped by one of the row of statues and felt the smooth stone with his hands, letting his fingers run over the finely sculpted face. The features seemed vibrant, almost alive. Suddenly, Max pulled his hand away, certain that he had felt a faint pulse throbbing gently beneath the cold forehead of the god. Prabhu observed his friend's surprise, and smiled.

'Imogen was always so much stronger than me,' said Max, recalling the priest's question, 'so much more resilient. She could have handled this much better. You know, that's the worst thing: why me? Why did I have to survive? Imogen and I always did things together.'

The crowds of daily visitors were beginning to arrive now, and the kitchens got ready to serve the prashad. Prabhu waited patiently for Max to complete his reflections before moving on, but he was lost amongst the recollections of the fateful night of Diwali, twelve years back.

'You know, she was already in the other police van, already safe with the others . . . And she decided to leave that safety and come with me. She wanted to be with me, Prabhu.' Max looked pleadingly into the eyes of the holy man, as if he could provide some answer. 'She wouldn't let me risk the journey on my own. She even left Miranda, to come to me. And I took her straight to her death.'

Prabhu began to understand something of his friend's guilt and his sense of responsibility. 'Come on, Max, that's not fair on yourself, nor on Imogen. How could anyone possibly have known? You're feeling guilty because you think it should have been you. Do you think it's a solution to the guilt to stop living, in the way that you have? Is that the price you've put upon your survival? Are you trying to do what Fate refused to do? Max, believe me, what happened has a purpose behind it, a reason.'

Max looked away, refusing to accept such determinism.

'I know, it sounds ludicrous, and you can't see it yet,' continued Prabhu, 'but it does. What's the quotation? "There's providence in the fall of a sparrow . . ." One day, you might be able to understand. Just because you cannot accept it yet doesn't mean the whole thing was arbitrary or illogical. And what's more, the fact that you survived also has a reason behind it, a purpose.'

His contempt abating, Max looked attentively at Prabhu. What *was* the reason for his survival? For years, Max had put it down to Fate taking its ultimate revenge: punishing him for the happiness he and Imogen had enjoyed so unreservedly, the joy they had stolen from time. But could it be that the natural order was not so perverse? Could it be that Max had crystallized his resentment and projected it onto providence because he was unwilling to accept the burden and responsibility of life alone? He looked back at Prabhu. The priest saw the set hardness of Max's face soften and, maintaining his stoic expression, he said: 'Stop fighting, Max. Let go of your anger. Accept your destiny.'

That night Max wandered off into the town, passing through the busy streets, stopping here and there to gaze at the shining silver utensils hanging from shopfronts, the multicoloured saris and silks flowing out onto tables along the pavement, and staring with amusement at the selections of photographs in gilt frames venerating political and show-business personalities. A few more recent characters had been added to the pantheon. He gradually moved on past the stall-holders selling exotic fruits and nuts, across shanty areas full of little children playing with scrawny animals, then eventually over the bridge, out into the bush beyond the noise and the lights and the people.

Max could feel the sea breeze even here, mingled with the sticky, damp smell of the palms oozing gum under cover of darkness. The warm air soothed him, filling his head with its numbing scent. Soon, the road had meandered deep into the forest, and all signs of the town, now left far behind, were gone. An occasional cyclist wobbled by, staring curiously at the perverse foreigner walking off into the bush.

The proximity of the trees calmed Max. Their benevolence and stoicism were impressed on his frenetic spirit, and he drew a consoling reassurance from the serenity of the foliage. If the cosmic order were indeed as inconsequential as it seemed, then here at least was one method of combatting its unpredictability: an unhurried, persistent peacefulness, unaffected by the fluctuations of fortune. The deeper he penetrated into the forest of the night, the more Max relaxed into the security offered by the bush, its womb-like softness, and the comfort of its protective anonymity. Little creatures scurried past, disturbing the dry leaves on the ground, and Max was aware that his progress was being observed carefully by thousands of curious eyes, fearful at this encroachment on their territory.

Here was one solution to the inexorable march of time. Here time, if not arrested, was at least subdued into a secondary player by the sheer longevity of the trees. Nothing seemed to touch them. Their towering strength and exuberance stood as a challenge to age, a reminder that the spirit of life does survive the forces of change. Max stopped and stared up at the canopies of dark leaves swaying gently, high above his head. He took a deep breath, inhaling once more the sweet ambrosia of the plants. Was this, perhaps, the paradisiac state of detachment for which man yearned so relentlessly, this the highest stage of evolution, when, at last, the spirit is freed from the shackles of love, possessiveness and egotism?

The fertile chaos of the bush consoled Max, reminding him that life survives strongest where it survives at will. He could feel the liberty around him, the freedom of the spirit. Here, there were no constraints, no barriers constructed in order to control the power of the life force. All was peace and harmony. If storms blew, the trees bent together. If branches fell, they returned to the soil, decomposing into the very ground from which the tree derived its energy. If ancient trees collapsed, their leaves and pods sank into the soft earth, creating life out of death. There was no mourning, no sorrow. Death was just another step along the path to timelessness.

Max felt a dramatic surge of optimism, an enthusiasm in his spirit he had not experienced for over a decade. The tiny muscles of his face lifted, energized by new hope.

All around him, Max suddenly became aware of a cacophony of sound, millions of creatures all celebrating life and their role in the eternal cycle of the forest. He stood very still, letting the sounds and the smells of the bush pass through him. The symphony became louder and louder until it deafened Max, and his head swam, intoxicated by the abandoned assault on his senses.

He closed his eyes, and instead of seeing the familiar visions of his memory and imagination, Max saw a new imagery, a landscape such as he had never beheld in dreams or in reality. He fancied he could see the sap rushing through each individual vein and capillary of the trees around him. The leaves were transparent, and within each fold he beheld a familiar face, images of those people in his life he had loved, smiling and laughing, disdainful of his own melancholy. All about him this pandemonium of glee burst forth, from each leaf, each branch, each tree-trunk.

Max felt a familiar presence by his side. He turned and found himself gazing straight into Imogen's wide, sparkling eyes, her face lit up by the happiness of the soulmates all about her. Max felt his lips begin to form a word, but it was too late. She was gone.

Suddenly the explosion of laughter stopped, its echoes dying away into the darkness of the forest. Gradually, the natural sounds of the bush reasserted their presence, step by step assuming their natural volume. Hearing the hissing of silence in his ears, Max came round from his visions and became aware of himself, standing motionless, surrounded on all sides by thick green foliage.

Hints and guesses, out of time. In the velvet darkness of the south Indian forest, the visions of a tongue-tied young Frenchman took shape before Max. Not cruel but benign. Lamarck had resolved the enigma long before him, yet how dismissively Max had cast aside the third sketch, impatient at the unfamiliarity of the imagery. The consolation had always been available, he thought.

Max must keep his promise. And now, with renewed optimism, he felt he could face the return to Khajuraho.

So Max wrote to Stan Dyer and warned him that he would be arriving at the end of the week, before flying back to London. The prospect of meeting up once more with the energetic Australian invigorated him and he began to feel that India had, indeed, performed its secret therapy.

As the bus pulled into the small bus station, Max saw once more the familiar multicoloured neon lights flashing high above the tourist hotels. The Tempel Garden had long since disappeared, to be replaced by the Hanuman Hotel. The plumbing had never worked properly in all the years Max and Imogen had been coming to Khajuraho, but this time Max would be spared the horror of days of inadequate bathing and dusty bedrooms, complemented by the usual ingratiating service. Stan was waiting at the bus station to meet his old friend, and insisted that Max stay with him.

'You look great, Max,' he said, loading the luggage into the boot of the cream Ambassador. Stan had been shocked to see the transformation in Max's whole demeanour, but felt compelled to say something positive. Max had obviously taken things very badly. As they settled into the back of the car, Stan looked over to Max, trying hard but failing to stop his eyes from focusing on the visible signs of his friend's distress. Max, sensing Stan's unease, continued to look straight ahead, deliberately avoiding his eyes. The driver finished arranging the luggage, jumped in, and the car rattled off, clearing people as it bounced along through rutted streets and over potholes.

'It's been too long, Stan,' said Max, looking at the hanging yellow lightbulbs outside the rows of shops along the main street. 'How's the centre doing?'

'Oh, it's surviving. We've got so many people wanting to come in, we have to restrict numbers now. But we do get a government grant. A few years ago, the local authority decided we were good types. The disabled are always at the bottom of the pile here, so I think we're a useful ad for their policy of equal opportunity. Jeez, I couldn't believe it: after years of struggling and fighting for everything, even a decent water supply, suddenly we were being showered with gifts. Everyone wanted to write about us. People offered their services to us free of charge. We're inundated with donations, every day. I just hope we stay in favour. It's done wonders for the centre and for the youngsters. Lots of them now go on to decent jobs. It's been a slow process but the barriers are beginning to break down, in a small way at least.'

The car reached the outskirts of town and turned onto the open road.

Max looked back at the lights receding behind them, the neon making Khajuraho look like some sort of sordid fairground constructed in the dark, hostile wilderness, an overflowing of youthful spirit on the very edge of civilization. With the lights the noise receded too, and soon the car was in almost complete darkness, heading towards the village of Suratpur.

'So things have worked out for you,' said Max at length. 'I'm really glad. I always thought you'd come through, Stan.'

'Yeah, I suppose you could say things have worked out good for me. It's bloody hard work, you know. Most important thing is, I enjoy it. Expect I'll still be here when your grandchildren are coming out.'

Max looked out across the plains on either side of the car. In the distance, a few lonely fires burned. For a moment, Max fancied he saw some darker shadows among the distant silhouettes. Was this perhaps their temple, the shrine that Max and Imogen had made their own all those years back? The more he peered, the more impossible it became to discern the shapes before the night rapidly devoured them.

'I'm glad you decided to return, Max. It's good to see you again. Is Miranda well?'

'Growing up far too fast,' said Max, wondering for an instant what she might be doing right now, back in Oxford. Revising, he hoped.

'She's a good girl. You're very lucky.'

'I was always surprised, you know,' continued Max, 'that you never got married, Stan. I expect you were spoilt for choice.'

Stan laughed. 'No no. I never met the right person, I suppose. And I'm far too involved with my centre and my children. I mean, think about it, sport. Who'd want to come out here and do this?'

'Oh, I can think of a few women who'd make the break. Imogen would have done.'

Stan turned his head suddenly towards Max, not really understanding what his friend had said. He could just make out the dark outline of the profile.

'She was a very special woman,' said the Australian. 'There aren't many like her around.'

Max smiled. The night air was cool, and its sharp chill was refreshing, streaming in from the driver's open window. He knew Stan had always liked Imogen. And he had suspected for some time that the Australian's refusal to settle down with any one of his many girlfriends, each a different nationality it seemed, had something to do with his affection for Imogen. Over the years, Max imagined she had come to represent for Stan the ideal he wanted in a wife, and he was an uncompromising man. He respected Max, and he admired Imogen. His energetic involvement in the work of his centre was, in some ways, a sublimation of his personal desires and ambitions.

The following morning Max was taken on a tour around the school by a young boy who had had both legs shattered in a scooter accident when he was a baby. Dinesh, captain of his third-year class, was obviously a very popular boy, judging by the number of people who greeted him along the many different corridors of the centre. The metal limbs he had been given were the latest design: Stan had managed to secure an advantageous deal with a Sydney-based medical company, so the children in his centre got the most up-to-date technology, a small compensation for the price nature had exacted from each one of them. As Max looked around he saw young girls and boys, their eyes full of youthful hope, struggling to come to terms with their physical limitations: blind children, learning to use Braille word-processors; children with arms and legs missing, experimenting with complex mechanical limbs, treating the whole thing as if it were another school activity; deaf children, conversing happily with each other at speed, lip-reading and using advanced sign language.

The sight of the pupils made Max feel ashamed. Here he was, his health intact, so privileged and so lucky, destroying himself. In one of the junior classes, a little blind girl came up to Max, grabbed his jacket with her tiny fist and, tugging it, asked: 'Are you our dear director's friend from England?'

'Yes,' answered Max, bending down and gently stroking the young child's long black hair with his hand, 'my name's Max Burton.'

'My name's Prema,' said the little girl. Then, after a moment's reflection, she looked up once again, and said, 'Can you see, Max Burton?'

Max was shocked and saddened by the inquiry. It took him a few moments to compose his answer. 'Yes,' he said, 'yes, I can see.' Then, as an afterthought, he added, 'But not as clearly as you.'

The child smiled, wondering why the Englishman had such a sad voice.

'They're lovely children,' said Max as Stan joined him on the verandah leading off from his office. 'You're quite a hero.'

'Not me, Max. You wouldn't imagine what they have had to put up with, these children. Some of them have been just dumped by their families. There are some Hindus who still believe that disability is the result of past sins, punishment for the misdemeanours of previous lives. They don't see why they should harbour such "evil" souls in their families, so they dump them. And what's more, they don't see anything wrong in that. Just like returning a defective machine. So these poor children begin their lives with both disability and rejection. We just try to repair some of the damage, but who really knows what's going on inside those tiny heads.'

'Imogen would have loved to have done something like this, you know, done some good. I suppose I stopped her.'

'Oh come on, Max, of course you didn't stop her. She made her choices like everyone else. If she had really wanted to do it, I knew Imogen, believe me, she would have done it.'

'She really wanted to do it, Stan. She just ran out of time.'

Stan nodded, acknowledging Max's observations. 'And what about you, Max? What are you going to do with the time you've still got?'

'What do you mean?'

'Just what I say, mate. Imogen *did* run out of time. Do you know when your time will run out? Tomorrow, perhaps? Next week? Next year? Or not for thirty years, maybe?' Max looked at Stan as if he rather resented the implication that he was wasting away his life. Then he realized that it was the truth of it that he resented.

'It's been twelve years now, Max. That's more than a lifetime for some of these kids at the school. You have to give yourself a chance. Let Imogen go.'

'How can I? She's everything I've got.'

'No one's going to take that away from you. Look, you and Imogen had something most of us only dream about. It gave both of you life and energy and hope. For years, your love fulfilled all its promise to you. The love isn't lost just because Imogen's no longer with you. That love existed beyond you and beyond her. You still have a commitment to that . . . if you really believed in it in the first place.'

'Of course I believed in it. I gave everything for it.'

'Then give a bit now,' said Stan firmly, 'give up some of your anger and your resentment. What happened wasn't done to get back at you. You're not in battle with Fate, you know. Take a leaf out of these children's book. Accept what happened, and see it as part of the balance of the universe.'

There was that word again, 'balance', the word Max had grown to hate. He looked around the courtyard, at the stream of children moving slowly out of the classrooms into the sunshine. In the distance, he saw Prema. Her friend, who could obviously see, whispered to the girl that the Englishman was watching. Prema turned towards the verandah and waved. Max waved back, was seen by the blind girl's companion, and the message was passed on. Prema smiled.

Stan had noticed the brief interchange, and also Max's tenderness, something he remembered seeing when Max and Imogen had been together. A few seconds went by in silence. Then Stan said, 'We could use a man like you, Max.'

Max laughed. 'I'm no hero, Stan. Anyway, I'm too tied in with my life back home.'

'Think about it. A man of your skills, and energy. You said Imogen would have liked to have done something like this. She ran out of time. But you haven't. You could do what she wanted, fulfil her aspiration.'

Max looked at Stan, still smiling. 'You're serious, aren't you?' he asked.

'Jeez, you bloody Pom. Of course I'm serious.'

'Well, it's not quite that easy for me,' said Max, hesitating. He still could not believe that the Australian was quite in earnest.

'You think about it,' said Stan. 'As far as I'm concerned, the offer is open for you any time. Now, Max, do you want my driver to take you over to the temples this afternoon?'

Max looked out at the playground full of children, playing their games in the ingenious ways they had each developed according to their abilities, helping one another as best they could. He took in a deep breath, held it for a moment while he reflected, then sighed.

'I'd like to go to the temples alone. Could I take the car myself?'

'Sure, sure. I'll ask Khan to get it ready.' Stan walked over to the door of his office, but before leaving the room turned and said, 'Remember. Time to come, not time past.'

It was mid-afternoon by the time Max had parked the car in a safe, shady place, bribed a local youngster to look after it, and wandered down the long dusty path to the derelict temples he remembered so well. The undergrowth had really taken over now. The state-run Historic Monuments Renovation Programme had never taken off, the administrator having run off with the funds. According to latest reports, he had set up a hotel in Jaipur with the money. But Max was glad the temples had not been tampered with. There was a certain authenticity to the dereliction, and more than anything else, it kept the hordes of visitors away. The temples that were part of the tourist track were so horribly compromised that little of the original atmosphere was left, and many were no more than haunts for middle-aged voyeurs.

Stepping over the broken stones and bricks of some outer wall, Max picked his way carefully through the thorns and the creepers, searching out the alcove under which he and Imogen had made love that afternoon. The sculptures were looking more decayed than when he last saw them, and many of the pathways were now totally overgrown. Still Max knew he must be near, for he could see the empty plains beyond the temple complex and he recalled that their temple was one of the last before the wilderness began. A brightly-coloured lizard scurried across the pathway, disappearing into the shade of a nearby rock. Max looked around at the sculptures, with their broken noses and cracked torsos.

Many duos were now incomplete, one lover still engaged in some impossibly acrobatic act, unaware that his partner had disappeared. On the ground, sculptures lay in pieces, reeds and grass growing out from between bulbous breasts or long, slim legs. What a waste it all seemed. Max explored the empty alcoves, trying to imagine the original beauty and glory of the temples. As he trod further along the narrow stone avenues, he began to see familiar shapes, sculptures that triggered off distant memories. He stopped and surveyed the courtyard he had entered. This was the inner sanctum he and Imogen had found on their honeymoon.

Max walked further along, and out of the temple walls, to the far side of the shrine. There was the alcove, with its lovers still intact. Sheltered on this side of the building, the figures had been protected from the elements and from the vandals. And there too was the tree Max remembered, the final outpost of life before hundreds of miles of hard, infertile plains. For a moment, he remained motionless, the sun beating down on him. A light breeze was beginning to blow, and dust and sand flew up into his face, making him turn away. He rubbed his eyes. The wind also disturbed a family of dogs who had been sleeping nearby, in the shade of the wall, unaware of the recently arrived visitor. The mother looked up indolently, decided that Max was no threat, then settled down again, nestling five puppies in the curve of her black body.

Max walked over to the tree, pulling his panama tight over his brow to keep the sun off his face. The wind was beginning to blow again, and Max's jacket flapped uncontrollably for a moment. Buttoning it up with one hand, he held his hat with the other, shielding his face from the flying dust. The breeze passed and the swirling dust calmed down. From his vantage point beneath the tree, Max could see the side of the temple, almost untouched, and the alcove housing the lovers forever imprinted on his memory. The patch of grass still grew beneath the erotic chamber, now a lush tangle of creepers and roots, probably the home of a hundred minute creatures.

It was here that Imogen had transported Max with her energy and enthusiasm, here that he had lost himself in her, here that their affair had become so all-consuming for him. Looking back over the course of their time together, Max could now identify a number of events, or days, or hours, which had been turning-points in his sense of himself and his perception of Imogen. By the time they found themselves here, in the shade of the temple, Max and Imogen had made love often. They were familiar with each other's bodies, and the initial excitement of discovery and experimentation was beginning to be replaced by the deeper satisfaction of mutual fulfilment and altruism. And since then, as well, he and Imogen had made love countless times, each time a new sensation for Max, each time an unsullied pleasure, untainted by habit. Yet, of all the times they had been together, in all the exotic locations they had visited, whenever he thought of their passion Max still recalled this afternoon, here on the dry, dusty ground, beneath the erotic sculptures, baking in the heat of the Madhya Pradesh plains. He could remember each movement, each sensation, all the vigour of youth. He thought back to Imogen's hunger, her voracious desire to take and to give, her unwillingness to compromise her passions. And he recalled his own abandon, the absolute impunity with which he had released himself that day.

Standing beneath the tree, Max fancied he could hear the energetic groans of the lovers, their whispered intimations, the unspoken dialogue of their bodies. He saw Imogen's graceful outline once more, rising up above the reclining youth. She was absorbed in her pleasure, and for a moment Max felt guilty to be staring at her efforts, so vivid was the recollection. Her slim back arched with a sensual rhythm, and her hair stuck to her back as her skin became damp. Even from this distance, Max could smell the secret aroma of her skin. He closed his eyes, and heard his own lips form her name.

For a moment, Imogen stopped in her passionate activity and turned round, twisting her body as she sat above her young lover, eager to see who had spoken her name. Her eyes met the Englishman's. For a few lingering seconds they held each other's stare, then Imogen smiled in recognition, turned back to her husband of three weeks, and continued their lovemaking with renewed vigour.

So, thought Max, Imogen did see the stranger.

But, unlike himself, she, with her ability to see beyond mere externals, had recognized him. Max's heart contracted with pain as he thought of his needlessly protected secret. If they had talked of the Englishman, what then? Max had lain all those years beside Imogen and he had never guessed what was in her heart. Infidelity of the spirit, he reflected, brings far more pain than a spasm of physical betrayal.

It was a stormy night. The breeze Max had felt at the derelict temple had continued to develop all afternoon, changing into a full-scale desert wind by the evening. The electricity supply to Suratpur had been cut, so Stan and Max had spent most of the evening sitting in the living-room, eating and chatting by candlelight. It was Max's final night in India. In the morning, he would be setting off, back to Delhi, then straight onto a flight bound for London. He had decided, for the time being at least, to pass on Stan Dyer's offer of a change of career, but he did agree to give it serious consideration, in a few years perhaps, when Miranda was well settled.

As Max's watch struck twelve, the familiar but long-unheard chimes filled the warm air. Max decided to call it a day. He retired to his bedroom, high above the school.

The wind whistled around the turrets of the building all night, keeping Max awake. A tiny oil-lamp was alight on the mantelpiece to the side of the bed, and its flickerings cast grotesque shadows on the ceiling and walls. He watched the figures dance and tumble across the room. Gradually his eyes began to close, slowly at first, and the dancing shadows became a part of his dreams.

Max was back at the temple in the plains of Madhya Pradesh. But it was not derelict. Looking about him, he found himself outside the walls, gazing at a resplendent building, newly completed, the marble of its walls sparkling with oil. The desert landscape, the temple building, everything was suffused with a deep blue light. Max turned and looked up, to see the huge disc of a low-lying sun, burning with a cold heat, spreading its violet rays across the over-arching sky like a thick vapour. He watched the sun throw off gigantic shafts of blue flame, the fire rising and falling all over the dark sphere. Still hypnotized, Max felt someone approach him where he stood. Instinctively, he recalled the long-dead masters of his youth. He continued to gaze at the unfamiliar star.

'Beautiful, isn't it?' said the stranger.

Max remained silent, enthralled by the sight. The stranger joined him in his silent vigil, his face hidden by the dark silken folds of his cowl. Soon, Max felt the soft hand of the newcomer on his shoulder. He knew it was time to move on.

They entered the temple, passing through the massive gateway into the outer courtyards. There was no one to be seen. Max surveyed the square, marvelling at its recently completed fountains and its freshly laid marble. One fountain was gushing blue water, its pool overflowing and the viscous liquid spreading slowly, like thick oil, across the alabaster floors. Max watched the water creep over the ground, reach his feet, and form a thin channel between him and the stranger by his side. He looked up at the dark figure.

'Be patient,' said the stranger, 'you have time.'

Max looked around him, surveying the alcoves all around the outer court of the temple. He saw the sculptures, their features sharp and newly chiselled. The temple was deserted and a gentle breeze was passing through it, coming off the plains beyond, carrying with it the coolness of the nighttime desert.

'Look closely at the figures, Max,' said a new voice by his side. He saw that the stranger had disappeared to be replaced by an old man, his face wizened with age, his skeletal hands reaching up to touch the stonework of the sculptures.

'For centuries I, Srivastava, royal sculptor to the Prince of Madhya Pradesh, have travelled the labyrinths of my dreams to discover the source of my inspiration.' The craftsman was a long way from his hometown of Alleppey by the sea, in Kerala. He stared reflectively at his handiwork. 'Look carefully, Max. See if you can help an old man to solve the enigma.'

Max moved closer to the alcove, and reached out to touch the figures housed in the chamber. Slowly, his fingers moved closer and closer to the crafted stonework. In the chiselled faces, he saw himself and Imogen once again, as they had been that unforgettable afternoon, enraptured, abandoned, their bodies moist and youthful.

And he heard Anjali's voice. 'Time past, present and future, all are one, an eternal present.'

Max started. So, what Stan had said was true after all. The love he and Imogen had: it existed independently of them. Srivastava had seen this already, long ago, in his dreams. As Max touched the erotic shapes, the sculptures collapsed suddenly, crumbling into dust. He pulled back, and turned once again to the sculptor.

'I have the answer,' Max heard himself say.

But Srivastava was gone, replaced once more by the dark stranger in his silken gown.

'Come,' he said. 'Time to move on.'

Instinctively, Max knew his way around the temple. As he walked across the warm marble floors, he saw the stranger's gown trailing its soft folds along the perfectly sculpted stones. Max moved smoothly across the even ground, heading towards another doorway, leading deeper into the shrine. The stranger fell behind, allowing Max to follow his own impulse. Just as he reached the threshold, Max turned to look at his companion, eager that they should both step through together. But the stranger was gone, and the courtyard was derelict once more.

Max strode through into the chamber, and found himself dazzled by a bright white light. He held his hand up to his face to shade his eyes, and when he lowered it, Max felt his heart jump at the sight in front of him.

His father was sitting by the side of a bed, holding a hand that stretched out from beneath a thin white sheet. Max could see that there was someone beneath the cover. The pale flesh was clearly visible through the cotton, but the sheet covered the whole person, from head to toe, like a shroud. He walked over to the head of the bed, and reached out to pull back the sheet.

'No!' said his father firmly. 'No, Max. It's too late.'

Max let his hand drop. He peered through the fabric once more, trying desperately to discern the face beneath the gossamer cloth.

'I searched and searched for you, Max. She called out for you night after night, but you didn't hear her.'

Max felt his breathing quicken, and tears well inside his eyes. 'And now it's too late,' he said.

He saw his father stroking the lifeless hand softly, as if trying to rub some warmth into it, his eyes fixed on the figure within the shroud.

The dark stranger reappeared, standing a few feet behind Max. There was no need for him to speak this time. Max knew. He turned, left the chamber, and stepped back into the deep blue of the alien landscape.

The courtyard was returned to its pristine condition, the fountain still overflowing, the marble floors covered with the oily liquid. Another door came into view, and Max felt himself inexorably drawn towards it. Once more, the stranger followed silently. Standing outside the door, Max hesitated for a moment, wondering whether he should go through. The stranger waited patiently, motionless, by his side. At last, Max crossed the threshold.

He was back in the Rajasthani desert, and in the distance, Max could make out the familiar ghost city he had seen so many times in his dreams. The sky was saffron, and the deserted city shone in the orange light as if on fire. Once more, the little guide was by Max's side, looking out across the plain.

'Always my guide?' said Max to the little boy.

'Always, sahib . . .'

The two of them began the long trek to the walled metropolis. Max stared up at the sky, and was surprised to see that no vultures circled overhead. His eyes began to sting the longer they focused on the bright light. As he looked back down, he saw that he and Raju had now attained the outer walls of the city, and were standing beneath its dizzying towers. There was not a sound anywhere, not a whisper: even the sands were motionless, as if frozen in time. For a moment, Max contemplated the stillness and the silence. It brought a peace to his spirit he had long since forgotten. Then, softly, in the distance, he heard the faint sounds of an ancient Indian melody, the tabla begin its insistent rhythm, joined surreptitiously by a harmonious sitar. Max recognized the music.

'This way, sahib,' said the little Indian boy by his side. 'They're waiting.'

Max walked through the great wooden door leading to the interior of the ancient city, and found himself in the midst of a busy courtyard, full of people hustling and bustling, yet making not a sound. They were in some sort of thriving marketplace, stalls overflowing with silks, multicoloured fruits piled high on wooden tables, monkeys and bears, all playing and amusing the crowds. People moved hurriedly, as if there were a limitation on their time. Yet all was silent. It was like watching a film with the volume turned off. In his ears, Max still heard the faint tones of the distant melody, rising and falling. More instruments had now joined in the rhythm, and the symphony was building, slowly, to a climax.

Familiar faces passed in the crowd. Max felt he knew these people, but he did not know from where, or from when. And they knew him. As they passed, a number of them acknowledged his presence, rushing on with their compelling tasks.

Raju walked on, cutting a safe path through the thronging mass, and relying on Max to follow. By the time they had reached the opposite end of the courtyard, the music was more definite and distinct, clearly coming from within one of the palace chambers. Raju directed Max to a door, ornate with wooden carvings of gods and goddesses dancing within circles of fire. He stepped onto the threshold, but before passing through, felt an urge to cast one more backward glance at the busy courtyard. He turned his head, expecting to see the frantic activity he and Raju had just witnessed. But the marketplace was now empty. There was not a single person in sight, and the stalls were deserted, their golden silks falling carelessly and unwanted onto the ground, the fruits decaying as if they had been left to rot in the desert sun for weeks. Max looked all around the courtyard, hoping to catch some glimpse of a straggler, even one of the amusement creatures, as an assurance that he had not simply imagined the scene. But there was no one. He looked back at the stall full of rotting fruit.

Suddenly the sound of hooves approached. Max cast his eyes towards the great door leading into the courtyard, the door he and Raju had entered minutes past. Closer and closer came the horseman. Then, momentarily, Max saw the silhouette of a rider rise up out of the golden light of the desert beyond the gateway. The horse reared back as the rider came to a halt. Max stared at the gaunt, otherworldly figure, his face shrouded in black cloth. He too seemed to be searching for something or someone. Faintly, like an echo falling away, Max heard the horseman cry: 'Rustoma!'

Max left the threshold he had almost crossed, and made as if to return towards the mysterious horseman. The rider surveyed the scene of devastation, moving his eyes slowly around the courtyard. Then, suddenly, the horse's head twisted back, the animal turned, and the horseman was gone.

Max walked through the door, into the palace. He was now in the room from where the music emanated, but all was dark inside the chamber. Patiently, he waited for his eyes to adjust from the glare outside. Raju had gone now. As Max's eyes began to focus, he could pick out shapes in the darkness. The music continued, its intricate harmonies rising in a crescendo. Just as it reached its peak, a shaft of bright light burst from the ceiling, filling one corner of the huge chamber. Max shielded his eyes from the brightness and the heat. As he lowered his hand, he saw that the light had picked out a distant group of classical Indian dancers, moving rapidly to the harmony of the music. He walked closer, trying to pick out familiar figures. As the girls twisted and turned, their golden costumes flying with each revolution of their slim bodies, Max saw the dancer at the head of the group. The light gave her a dramatic outline, and as she turned and turned, he could barely catch a glimpse of her face. All around her head, a simple garland of tiny carnations decorated her jet-black hair.

For a moment, Max watched the dance, reminded of the cosmic Nataraja as Anjali kept time to the music, her body revolving, faster and faster, until it seemed to Max that she was absolutely still, frozen in the centre of her movement.

He formed her name with his lips. As he heard the long-cherished syllables inside his head, the vision vanished, plunging the chamber back into darkness.

Max waited, listening to the final echoes of the music die away. Suddenly, another sound took the place of the harmony. It was the chiming of his watch. He grasped his left wrist, to feel for the familiar shape, but the watch was no longer there. The chime sounded, again and again. Another shaft of light burst into the chamber, filling a different corner of the room. This time, the image was that of an old man, in a cramped room, surrounded by hundreds of clocks and watches, bent in absolute concentration over his table. Max could see that the workman was engaged in some delicate task requiring all his attention. The watch continued to chime. Jonas Schindler looked up, gazing out into the darkness, peering towards the place where Max stood. Could he see him, wondered Max? He moved a step closer, only to find that the image of the watchmaker, the whole tableau, his room and his collection of timepieces, also moved back, exactly the same distance as Max had moved forward.

Annoyed at being disturbed, Jonas Schindler bent his head down again and continued with his labours, fading slowly as the chimes died away.

Once more in the darkness, Max wondered which image would rise up next. He felt a soft breeze on his face, and heard a set of Chinese bells, disturbed by the movement of the air. A third shaft of light filled the room, shooting into another of its corners. There, sitting in their small living-room, Max saw Madame Sarnet and Lamarck, busy in animated conversation. The sound of the Chinese bells filled the room. He could see the movements of Lamarck's lips. His mother held on her lap a single sheet of paper. As he talked, Max could see that Lamarck, having regained the power of speech, was explaining the drawing to his mother. What was on the paper? Max tried to see, but was too far away to discern anything more than a few dark pencil marks. He noticed Madame Sarnet take stock of the explanation, and look carefully at the picture. Then the old woman put her hand softly around Lamarck's neck, pulled him towards her, and kissed him on the forehead. The tinkling of the bells began to fade and the image subsided.

Max felt a tiny hand take hold of his own. Without looking down, he knew it was Raju. It was time to go.

Stepping back through the palace doorway, Max found himself not in the derelict marketplace he had left outside, but in the deep blue courtyard of the Khajuraho temple. The dark stranger was waiting for him. Without a word, the two of them moved on, passing along more corridors, meandering through the heart of the temple. Max knew they were heading towards the centre, but had no idea of the route. Yet his spirit seemed to know the way, for as before it was he who led, and the stranger who followed. Deeper and deeper they penetrated into the shrine, passing courtyards full of erotic sculptures. Eventually, they came to another entrance like the ones they had left far behind, another door into the past. This time, there was no hesitation. Max stepped through, leaving the stranger behind.

Another rainy Sunday in Oxford. A young man stood by the window of his room in Merton Street, watching the water roll down the panes of glass. In the distance the college bell tolled, calling the students to dinner. Where was Imogen? He had been waiting for over an hour, and still there was no sign of her. It wasn't like her to be so late. He knew there would be a perfectly good explanation when she arrived. But that didn't stop him from being angry. He paced about the room, the orange glow of the electric fire casting jagged, elongated shadows across the dark walls. The college bell continued to toll, and he could hear the shuffling of feet as the other students in the house hurried down the stairs. He picked up a letter he had received that morning from his mother, and read it through for the hundredth time.

It was time he made up his mind about Imogen. His parents had fallen in love with her, and he knew they were keen to see him make the relationship permanent. And he knew that Imogen too was eager for a decision. Yet, somehow, despite his euphoria whenever they were together, he was holding back from the commitment. It felt too much like another step into adulthood and he wanted to prolong the youthful freedom of the affair as long as possible.

Max watched the young man wandering about his darkened Oxford room, the rain now beginning to beat harder upon the windowpanes. The college bell continued to toll, and the students persisted in their shuffling on the stairs outside. Even now, after all these years, Max could sense the young man's anger and impatience, and frustration.

Be patient, Max. Be patient. She won't let you down.

A knock sounded. Max stepped aside, letting the young man rush to the door.

He pulled open the door, expecting to see Imogen standing there, perhaps drenched from coming through the rain. But there was no one there, and he found himself looking at a stream of people rushing down the stairs, desperate to beat the tolling bell. On and on they rushed, interminably. Where were they all coming from?

He waited on the threshold of his bedroom, watching the passing throng. As his eyes focused on some of the rapidly moving faces, he realized that these were not the other student residents of the house. They were all strangers, some from foreign lands, yet they all seemed to know the young man who had opened his door upon their frenzied rushing.

Max stepped behind the young man standing on the threshold, and placed his hands gently on the shoulders of the confused student. Slowly, the two minds merged, and Max began to recognize the strangers gushing past.

They were people he had met throughout his life. There, running past, was the pundit at the temple at Varanasi, the shoe attendant, his years now overcome by the alacrity of youth. Close behind him, the Eastons, uncharacteristically quiet, moving in pace with the crowd. A few seconds later, a young Indian boy passed. Max felt a pang upon seeing the face, and the boy hesitated for a moment, slowing down to gaze momentarily into Max's eyes. The burns were gone. So, time has healed your wounds, thought Max. The boy smiled before hurrying on.

The bell continued to toll. There, Max noticed the familiar face of Cogan, their fates joined forever. And Charles, shuffling past, no time to stop. Then figures to which Max could put no names, all dressed in black, their hair closely cropped. Rex Fischer was there, accompanied by his producer, Stephen, still desperate for attention. Then, the dancers of Anjali's company, followed closely by streams and streams of young boys, pupils whom Max had taught at St John's. And still the procession continued. The little actor Simon who, in another incarnation, had become Marcel Proust. Sister Conrad, still in her uniform, hurrying to tend to more patients.

Max looked up the narrow staircase, wondering when the flow of faces would come to an end. Yet still they came, no time to stop, each one mindful of the tolling bell.

Lamarck rushed by, holding his mother by the hand. The samosa-seller Guru, his face still full of sorrow at the news about his memsahib. Prabhu was there, his robes flowing behind him, his face serene and happy, testimony to a peaceful life of contemplation. The sound of feet grew louder and louder, and still the crowd came. Monsieur Selz, his eyes fixed in front of him, counting his profits. Monsieur and Madame Séchard, carrying in their arms a little girl. Max turned his head to catch a longer glimpse of the young child. Was that Miranda?

More children came streaming down the stairs, little Indian children, laughing and talking excitedly. Max recognized the faces. They were the pupils of Stan Dyer's centre at Suratpur, but they were all fit and healthy. The lame boys and girls could walk, the blind children could see, and the deaf could hear. Max looked affectionately at the youngsters. Following close behind came Stan himself, his hand held tightly by the little blind girl, Prema, who had befriended Max at the school.

As she stepped onto the landing outside Max's doorway, Prema stopped. Suddenly the din ended as the shuffling feet came to a halt. All Max could hear now was the college bell, still tolling.

The Indian girl let go of Stan's hand, and walked over to Max where he stood in the frame of the door. As Prema came closer, Stan stepped forward to stop her from crossing the threshold. She edged back, looking straight into Max's face. He noticed that her bright eyes sparkled with all the optimism and expectations of childhood. The girl put out her arm and touched the door-handle gently, pulling it towards her. Max stepped back, seeing the vision outside disappear as the door slotted into its frame. The shuffling of feet started again, its sound muffled now behind the closed door.

The rain continued to beat down, and the darkness drew in. Max knew that Imogen would be here any minute. He stared out of the window, down the street, eagerly searching for the familiar figure, but the lane was deserted.

Max settled back into the sofa by his bed. The constant tolling of the bell, the noise of the passers-by outside the door, the lashing of the rain on the windows and the warmth of the electric heater lulled him into a deep sleep.

Max watched the young man, exhausted by his visions, close his eyes and his face relax into a peaceful repose.

It was hours later when Max awoke. As he came round, he listened out for the sounds to which he had fallen asleep. But all was now silent. The bell had stopped, and the frantic procession on the stairs had come to an end. The rain too had eased. Another knock sounded. Imogen. It must be. Max rushed up and grabbed hold of the handle. For a moment he hesitated, then pulled open the door.

The dark stranger was waiting patiently, as before, his tall figure silhouetted against the deep azure skyscape. The blue sun continued to burn overhead, throwing up its huge shafts of cold fire into the sky. It seemed to have moved closer, for the sphere was beginning to dominate the whole firmament. Reluctantly, Max stepped back into the temple grounds, and the door closed behind him.

The journey continued. More corridors, more statues, more marble pathways, winding their way ever deeper into the heart of the shrine. The route was familiar. Max felt himself carried along relentlessly, past images of ecstasy and devotion. Another doorway appeared, at the end of a long corridor. As they walked towards it, he felt the stranger holding back, reluctant to keep pace. Max turned, a few feet from the entrance.

'Imogen?'

The stranger looked up, and for the first time, as his long silken cowl rose, Max saw his eyes, shining brightly in the blue haze. Always my guide, thought Max.

'Remember,' said the stranger, placing his hand on Max's shoulder, his deep voice resounding within the chamber of the narrow corridor, 'remember, Max, time is not your enemy.'

Max knew what the stranger meant. He turned back to the doorway, and eagerly crossed the threshold.

Max was in their study at home, standing by the door through which he had just entered. The typewriter keys were pounding furiously as a young woman worked impatiently at the machine on the table by the bay window. He did not want to disturb her. He waited silently, trying to calm his breathing, watching the girl's head and back, her arms twitching as her hands moved over the typewriter keys. Suddenly she became aware of someone watching her. She stopped her typing, but remained where she was, looking out across the garden. The rain had stopped now and the sun was struggling to break through the massed clouds. The silence hung in the air. At last Max whispered, 'Imogen.'

The young woman turned, twisting her body round slowly. Max saw each degree of the turn as if it lasted an hour. By the time the familiar profile was in his sight, he could not resist the urge to rush forward and hold her in his arms.

'No Max,' said Imogen, 'not yet.'

Max stared at her face, now turned completely towards him. The vision sent a tremor through his body.

'At last,' gasped Max, 'I've found you, at last.'

Imogen laughed, filling the room and Max's spirit with her happiness. 'Oh Max, you took it so hard. Surely you knew it couldn't last forever?'

He frowned, perplexed by Imogen's casualness. 'I know,' he said hesitantly, 'I just wanted, well, a little longer.'

Imogen smiled, making Max feel warm and safe. She turned back, looking out through the bay window at the garden. Max saw once more the elegant neck, the shining hair, so full of life, and vigour, and beauty. He wanted to touch her, as he used to do, but was terrified he might lose the precious encounter.

'I kept my promise, Imogen,' he said.

Imogen continued to stare out of the window. 'I know.'

A few more moments passed in silence.

'Imogen.'

She turned. Max noticed the smile in her eyes, the contentment that filled her face. 'Why did you leave me behind, Imogen?'

Imogen could see the distress and the disappointment on her lover's face. 'Oh Max, poor Max. You always thought of yourself as a guardian, an older soul, given the task of guiding me through my early years.' Max smiled. How well she had understood him. 'But what you didn't see, Max, what you couldn't understand was that you were the young spirit, and I your guide.'

'So why did you leave me?'

'None of us can choose the time of our arrival or our departure. We were lucky. We spent a few moments together, shared some of our love and our wisdom. But attachment would have destroyed both of us in the end.'

'So you left me all alone, without direction, without meaning, my life in pieces?'

'Your life has always had a very definite direction, Max. You know it has. All through time, people have helped you, given you hints about your destination. You saw and heard, but your heart did not understand.'

Imogen held out her hand, then recalled, and drew it back. She continued, 'You've always been so close to the truth. All that we had, all that we did, all that we felt together, it's not gone. It's not past. I may not be with you as I used to be, but that doesn't mean I've abandoned you.

'You still see time as a journey. You resent the past for promising you a future you never had. You're still on the edges of the wheel, spinning round desperately, confusing movement for progress. All you're doing is treading the same old paths, the same old patterns, getting nowhere.'

'Then tell me what I should do. If time's not a journey, then what is it? Give me something, Imogen, something to hold on to.'

'There is in all motion, Max, a still point, unmoved by the turbulence around it. Look at the dancer as she turns and turns, creating stillness out of motion. All that you've seen in the temple, all the doors you've crossed to get to me, all lead to the same truth. Past, present and future: they're not different points along a straight line. The line twists and turns, like the dancer. Occasionally, it turns back upon itself, and that too is part of the dance. Nothing breaks the flow. The dance continues, faster and faster, until it reaches the still point.'

'But it was time that took you away from me,' said Max, 'time that brought our happiness to an end. That was a definite event, that had a past before it and a future after it.'

'And that past still exists,' replied Imogen, 'as substantial as the moments you recall. It's you who have moved on.'

'I had no choice. I moved on because I had to. Give me the option and I would stop time.'

'When, Max? When would you stop it?'

'The afternoon at the temple at Khajuraho, perhaps . . . one of the mornings we spent together in Oxford . . . I don't know, Imogen. Stop it at the moment we were most happy.'

'Dear Max,' said Imogen, shaking her head, the smile still lighting up her face, 'dear, young Max. All those moments, those perfect moments together, they were perfect only because they were transient. You want the stillness of the dancer who has stopped dancing, not the perfect stillness that comes from eternal motion. Your sort of stillness leads to decay, to dereliction and disintegration. Look about you. Look at the souls who have chosen to stop the dance. What do they aspire to, or look back on? They cannot grow, cannot change, cannot learn. Moments cannot be preserved in the way you want, Max. If they are, time itself begins to fester.'

Max felt a chord of understanding sound within him. Tears formed in his eyes and, as he bowed his head, he saw the drops fall through the air onto the ground.

'Will we be together again, some day, Imogen?' he asked.

Silently, Imogen rose from her chair and walked over to him. He felt her warm hands hold his head gently, and pull it up. The touch electrified Max, sending a profound calmness through his soul. He felt his tears abate and his spirits lift. Through the watery haze before his eyes, Max could make out Imogen's tranquil face, close to his own. He gazed deep into her eyes, held by their serenity.

'Feel the stillness, Max. The truth is, we were never apart.'

As Imogen's face approached his own, Max closed his eyes in anticipation of the kiss. He felt her soft lips brush his own, as light as the touch of a dragonfly's wings, and the incarnation was complete.

Stan Dyer leant back onto the hot metal of the cream Ambassador, taking the weight off his feet. Khan, his driver, had fallen asleep inside the vehicle. Stan was becoming concerned about the time left before Max's flight to Delhi, so he strolled a little way along the road to see if his friend was in sight. All he could make out were the ruins of the derelict temple in the distant haze. Stan looked once more at his watch. Max had better return soon, otherwise it would be too late.

Max had asked Stan to take a short detour to pass by the deserted temple on the outskirts of Khajuraho. They still had time, so Max was keen to spend a final few moments at the shrine that had been, on two occasions, such an important turning point for him. Since the morning, he had felt a strong compulsion to visit the ruins once more, to check something that had troubled him all these years.

Having left the others a few hundred yards from the ancient temple, Max made the final part of the journey on foot, rushing energetically over the creepers and undergrowth. This time he found his way easily, like a local, and headed straight for the sculptures on the far side of the temple wall.

Once there, Max trod down the deep undergrowth at the foot of the erotic statues and, disregarding the dirt coming off on his shoes and trousers, he eagerly stepped up to the foot of the alcove. The creepers had grown right up the broken wall, covering the ancient bricks with their dry, dirty green. He tore aside the leaves and the thorns, searching for the wall beneath. The plants gave easily, dried out by the unrelenting sun. One by one, the creepers came off. At last, the wall was exposed, the brickwork dark from the bush that had been growing on it.

Max stepped back. There, unmistakable, in the stones, crawling with all the hidden life of the plains, was the carved message whose meaning had now become so clear to him: VIDHI.

Deep in his soul, Max felt something shift, and fall into place. So many centuries of Western civilization, so many generations of philosophy, and he had finally learnt wisdom through the dreams of a long-dead sculptor.

Rushing back across the dusty pathway, Max waved to Stan, who in turn woke up Khan. The Indian jumped up, caught unawares, and immediately turned on the ignition.

'Come on, Max!' shouted Stan, 'I know you want an excuse to stay . . .'

Max jumped in and sat back into the deep leather seat as the car went through the gears, bumped up and down, rocked from side to side, then finally settled into a strong cruise along the road.

'Did you find what you were looking for?' asked Stan.

Max nodded. After a few moments, having caught his breath, he turned to his friend and said, 'There's something I'd like you to do for me, Stan.'

'Sure,' said the Australian.

Max took out a slim leather box from his pocket, and handed it to his companion. 'I'd like you to give this to Prema.'

Stan opened the case carefully, and saw the antique watch inside, ticking away, its three dials busy in their respective movements.

'You'll have to have the strap altered for her,' said Max. He paused for a moment, and looked out over the passing plains. 'I know she won't be able to see the dials,' he continued, 'but she will be able to listen to the chime.'